When We Kiss

By Darcy Burke

CONTEMPORARY ROMANCE

Ribbon Ridge

Where the Heart Is (a prequel novella)
Only In My Dreams
Yours to Hold
When Love Happens
The Idea of You
When We Kiss

Coming Soon:
You're Still the One

HISTORICAL ROMANCE

Secrets and Scandals

Her Wicked Ways
His Wicked Heart
To Seduce a Scoundrel
To Love a Thief (a novella)
Never Love a Scoundrel
Scoundrel Ever After

Regency Treasure Hunters

The de Valery Code
Romancing the Earl
Raiders of the Lost Heart
The Legacy of an Extraordinary Gentleman

The Untouchables

The Forbidden Duke
The Duke of Daring
The Duke of Deception
The Duke of Desire

When We Kiss

RIBBON RIDGE BOOK FIVE

DARCY BURKE

AVONIMPULSE
An Imprint of HarperCollinsPublishers

When We Kiss

Excerpt from *Dirty Deeds* copyright © 2015 by Megan Erickson.
Excerpt from *Montana Hearts: Sweet Talkin' Cowboy* copyright © 2015 by Darlene Panzera.

EPub Edition JANUARY 2016 ISBN: 9780062443380
Print Edition ISBN: 9780062443403

Avon, Avon Impulse, and the Avon Impulse logo are trademarks of HarperCollins Publishers.

AM 10 9 8 7 6 5 4 3 2

For Dominique
Your light will always shine.

Chapter One

April
Ribbon Ridge, Oregon

AUBREY TALLINGER FINISHED drying her hands and set the towel down. Lifting her head, she caught her reflection in the mirror. Her hazel eyes stared back at her and seemed to ask what she was doing dawdling in the bathroom when a perfectly lovely wedding reception was going on.

Isn't it obvious? I'm avoiding Liam.

She was proud of herself tonight. She'd done a good job of ignoring the one person who always seemed to command her attention: Liam Archer. It helped to have a date along. A date she should get back to.

She took a deep breath and opened the door. Liam stood on the other side of the threshold.

He grabbed her hand and dragged her to the left through a doorway. He let go of her to close the door, then stood in front of it, his blue-gray eyes narrowed. "Who's the loser?"

Aubrey registered that they were in a sitting room attached to his parents' bedroom. She wanted to turn and look at the sun setting over the garden through the back windows but couldn't tear her eyes from Liam. Dressed in a crisp black suit with a natty striped tie, he was the sexiest best man she'd ever seen. His dark wavy hair was perfectly styled, and as usual, she had an almost irrepressible urge to mess it up.

She tensed as she forced herself to present a cool demeanor. "I introduced you to him at the church."

"Yes, Stuart the Accountant. But why did you bring him in the first place?"

She cocked her head and gave him a sarcastic stare. "Was I supposed to wait for you to ask me? You don't take me on *dates*, Liam. You never have." The dinner he'd surprised her with at her house when he'd been home for the long Thanksgiving weekend didn't count. Dates were *public*.

He frowned, and she was shocked when he didn't fire a snappy comeback. "I might've, actually."

Ha! She'd believe that when she saw it. "Too late. I told you on New Year's that our little…*thing* was done."

"It wasn't a *thing*."

"No, I think you're right. It was a series of convenient hook-ups, and they are no longer convenient to me."

She called them hook-ups, but they'd been more than that. Every time they were together, she'd felt as though they'd connected on some sort of intimate level that went beyond just sex. But that was stupid. While she'd come to know him at least a little bit, they hadn't spent enough day-to-day time together to allow anything meaningful to spark. Except for Labor Day weekend. They'd spent the better part of four days in each other's company, and it had been bliss. They'd laughed, they'd danced, they'd talked. And yes, they'd had a lot of sex. The physical aspect of their connection was so far the most powerful.

He prowled toward her, like a jungle cat on the hunt. She had no intention of being his prey. Nor did she want to run. She stiffened her spine and crossed her arms over her chest. Meager protection when she knew just how dangerous his weapons of mass seduction could be.

"Come on, they were a little more than hook-ups. We *planned* to hang out over Labor Day."

That was true, but they'd both been going to the Dave Matthews Band concerts up in central Washington anyway. It wasn't like they'd formulated and executed the trip together.

He stopped in front of her, his lips curving up. "And you have to admit it was pretty great."

Incredible. Right up to the point when she'd suggested they see each other again soon. He'd said, "Sure, I always call you up when I'm in town."

Like she was a convenience. And there was that word again. She didn't want to be anyone's hook-up girl. She'd quashed her burgeoning feelings, but it had maybe been too late. She'd already been crazily infatuated with him. So much so that when she'd seen him at Thanksgiving, she'd allowed herself to be the convenience she didn't want to be.

But no more.

She gave him an arch look. "So it was a great weekend. You still can't argue it was more than a hook-up. I walked away from that without knowing when—or if—I'd see you again."

He frowned at her. "That's absurd. You're our attorney. Of course you'd see me again."

Was he being purposely obnoxious?

He put his hands on his hips. "I suppose you're going to tell me Thanksgiving was just a hook-up, too? I brought you dinner."

After they'd flirted all day at a winery event they'd just happened to meet at. She'd accepted his sister Tori's invitation to attend without realizing Liam would be there. Wait, had he known? "Did you know I would be at the winery that day?"

He arched a brow. "Who do you think suggested we invite you?"

Damn it. She didn't want to know that. "Now you tell me," she muttered.

He flashed her a grin. "Am I wearing you down?"

She thought of what had happened next, after yet another spectacular night together. She tightened her arms across her chest. "No. Do you remember what we did after that night?" She watched his expression go from thoughtful to confused to blank. "That's right. Absolutely nothing. You went back to Denver without a word."

He winced. "Hey, I tried to see you at Christmas, but you weren't here."

Because she'd gone out of town with her aunt and uncle—the better to avoid Liam. With every hook-up, she'd fallen a little more under the spell of their attraction while he'd seemed impervious. She hadn't wanted to lose her heart. She still didn't.

"And I actually did try to ask you out for New Year's, but you wouldn't return my texts. When you did text me back—*after* the new year, I might add—you said you didn't want to see me anymore."

Oh, she'd wanted to see him, but she couldn't. Not on the terms he'd expected. He couldn't even *call* her. She was willing to bet her house that asking her out wouldn't have involved actually going *out*. "I lost interest."

"You're lying."

She pretended to stifle a yawn. "Admit it, the sex wasn't *that* great." If she'd been Pinocchio, her nose would've stretched to Hawaii.

His gaze dipped over her body appreciatively. "Well, now I have to call bullshit," he said softly. "I think your pants are definitely on fire."

"Knock it off."

He inched closer. "What? Can I help it if we set off enough sparks to start a conflagration? It's been like that since the start. You remember that, right?"

How could she forget? That first time had been nothing short of explosive. He'd come to see her after she'd read the details of Alex Archer's trust to his family. As Alex's identical twin brother, Liam perhaps felt his suicide the most keenly. He was definitely the most pissed off, and he'd directed that anger at her.

Fourteen months ago, he'd stalked into her office, his eyes blazing. She'd been weary and overwhelmed by trying to rein in her own crippling grief while she'd visited the Archers just days after Alex's death. Alone in her office, she'd wanted—no, needed—to open the emotional floodgates.

"What the hell kind of attorney are you?" Liam had thundered. "What sort of hourly rate do you charge to help a guy off himself? Do you have a special package for that?"

His words had socked her in the gut. Hard. Tears had risen fast and bitter, and her breath had gone immediately shallow.

"Get out," she'd rasped.

He'd advanced on her until only her desk had separated them. "Why didn't you tell any of us? Why would you let my family—my parents, for fuck's sake—why would you let them go through this?"

She'd wiped her hand over her eyes and gladly welcomed fury to replace her agonizing sadness. "You think I knew what he was doing?" She'd glared at him, glad to have someone to unleash her own frustration on. "You think I somehow helped him? He told me he was preparing for the worst-case scenario, that his lung issues would likely send him to an early grave. I had no idea he intended to kill himself!"

He'd sneered at her, his face so familiar because it was the image of Alex—the man she'd come to know and like so much over the past year. "You're a fool then."

"Screw you," she'd spat. "And get out of my office."

He'd yelled something else at her, something she didn't remember because at that moment she'd realized he was crying. She'd never seen tears of anger. She'd reached out to touch his face, and everything had changed. He pulled her against him and kissed her. Moments later, they'd cleared her desktop and had torn at each other's clothes.

"You're overthinking," he said, drawing her back to the here and now. She was back in his parents' sitting room instead of her dim office.

"I'm trying to forget." As if she ever could. His scent, his taste, his touch—everything about him was seared into every part of her.

"You always overthink," he whispered, moving closer until he was just in front of her.

"Don't." She refused to look at him. If she did, she'd be ruined. She'd succumb to Liam's magnetism or whatever the hell it was that seemed to be her own personal kryptonite.

Then he touched her, his fingertips grazing along the edge of her jaw. "I can't help it. I don't want to walk away. It's too bad you brought that other guy."

She looked at him then. His dark lashes drooped over his slate-blue eyes, and it was like he was a tractor beam on the goddamn Death Star.

She steeled herself against him. "Why, because it interferes with your sexual agenda? Tell me, Liam, would you really have asked me to be your date tonight?"

He pressed his lips together, and she already knew the answer.

"Great. Good talk. I brought Stuart just so I could hopefully avoid these little moments with you. They make me feel so pathetic. Thanks for that." She gave him a brittle smile, dropped her arms, and tried to step around him.

But his arm snaked around her and brought her hard against his chest. "I don't want you to feel pathetic. I can't ask you to be my date at my brother's wedding."

She simultaneously wanted to push up against him to feel his heat and knee him in the nuts. "Why, because I'm the woman who helped your brother kill himself? No one thinks that anymore, if they ever did past the first few weeks when grief controlled all of our lives. No, Liam, the hang-up is all *you*." She pulled back, but he held her fast.

"Please don't go. I miss being with you. We have fun together, don't we?" He splayed his hands across her back and buried his nose in the hair at her temple. "God, you smell so amazing. Like Aubrey. Delicious, fabulous, gorgeous Aubrey."

Every resolve she had was stretched to the limit. She didn't know how much more she could take. The desire to put her arms around him, to kiss him, to fold her body into his was nearly painful.

Man, this was sick.

His hand skimmed up her back and cupped the side of her neck, tilting her face toward his. "Tell me you don't miss me, too." He kissed the flesh next to her eye, then her cheek, then her jawline. "Tell me."

"I don't miss you." Naturally, because she was weak and probably halfway in love with this jerk, her voice broke at the very end of that lie.

"You really suck at lying." His lips found hers in a searing kiss.

She wrapped her arms around his shoulders and closed her eyes, seeing him in her mind and ripping every spectacular piece of clothing from his athletic, rugged body. She knew him so well—the rippled muscles of his chest, the hard curve of his ass, the deep moan he let out when she took him in her mouth…

Damn, she should not be doing this!

But he knew just how to kiss her. His tongue was hot and precise, spearing past her lips and ramping her lust to ridiculous heights. She curled her hands behind his neck and pressed on his flesh, opening her mouth to his exploration and launching her own invasion. This was heaven. This was bliss. This was Liam.

He bent her backward and held her tight, his finger-tips digging into her back and ass. Flush against his groin, she felt the hard ridge of his cock. Overcome, she thrust her hands into his thick hair and threaded it through her eager fingers as she'd longed to do since he'd grabbed her from the bathroom.

They could be up against the door or over on the couch in less than a minute. Wild, crazed, mind-blowing sex…and back at the reception in under ten minutes. They'd done it before—last summer at Derek and Chloe's wedding. They'd ducked into the small office at the back of the Ridgeview cottage and screwed each other hard and fast. She could still smell the scent of lavender and grass wafting through the open window. In fact, she couldn't smell lavender or grass now and not think of Liam. Maybe she'd never be able to attend another wedding reception without thinking of him either.

No. He was not going to own her. She had a life, and he wasn't going to be part of it. They wanted very different things. Hell, she *knew* what she wanted. He only knew what he wanted *right now*. And that wasn't enough.

She ripped her mouth from his and shoved at his chest. On trembling legs, she stumbled backward, one hand wiping her wet lips, the other smoothing the skirt of her dress down over her thighs because it had started to hike up. Apparently even her clothing was on board with another Liam Archer hook-up.

No!

"Liam, I'm leaving. I brought a date. Stuart is nice. Respectable. He doesn't deserve me kissing *you*."

Liam's face was flushed, his gorgeous hair mussed. "He doesn't deserve to be kissing you."

She gritted her teeth. "That's not what I said. We aren't to that…stage." How laughable. She and Liam hadn't paid any attention to such nonsense. They'd gone pedal to the metal since day one. It was time to slam on the brakes. *Again.* "It's none of your business."

She took a deep breath to calm her racing pulse and pressed her hands against her cheeks, hoping she didn't look as worked up as Liam did. She likely did, but it was warm in the main rooms where the reception was going on, and she could blame it on the heat.

"When you get bored with him, call me," Liam said as she walked past him.

She was surprised he was letting her go so easily, but she heard the arrogance in his tone and caught the smug set of his mouth. She paused at the door and turned. He'd also pivoted.

Pulling her lips into a saccharine smile she hoped gave him a toothache, she said, "Even if I *do* get bored, I will *not* call you. We're done. And next time you try something like that, I will use every bit of kickboxing I've ever learned and beat you into the floor."

She opened the door and shut it loudly behind herself. Feeling moderately better but still frustratingly and inconveniently aroused, she started along the hallway back toward the reception.

And ran straight into Liam's mother, Emily Archer.

She smiled. "Aubrey, I don't suppose you've seen Liam, have you?"

Caught red-handed. She forced a tight smile. "No, I haven't. I was just using the restroom." She wanted to make it clear she hadn't been in the sitting room with Liam, just in case Emily found him in there. "Sorry."

"It's all right. It's time to make the toasts, and since he's the best man, we need him."

Aubrey was still a bit surprised that Evan had chosen Liam for the role, especially when he had several other candidates, from his brother Kyle to his adoptive brother, Derek, to his sister's fiancée, Dylan, to his brother-in-law, Sean. Any of them would have been a far more obvious choice. Since their brother's suicide, Liam was the lone holdout to supporting Alex's legacy.

Alex had left his six siblings and adoptive brother a monastery for them to renovate and operate as a premier hotel and restaurant, the crown jewel in their family's chain of popular brewpubs. One by one, they'd each accepted the role Alex had set out for them. Everyone except Liam. His younger brother, Hayden, didn't count. He'd initially taken a major part in the project until his lifelong dream of making wine in France had come to fruition last year.

Hayden had a very good reason for leaving, while Liam had nothing but selfish arrogance keeping him away.

Aubrey wanted to get out of the hallway before Liam emerged from the sitting room. She'd had quite enough of him for one day.

Yes, keep telling yourself that. Keep reminding yourself that he hasn't shown the slightest interest in anything more permanent than getting together for sex and a good time. Sure, you laugh together and share some things in common, but every moment you spent with him was temporary. Fleeting. Do whatever you have to in order to keep him from settling into your heart.

LIAM STOOD NEAR the massive fireplace in his parents' great room and watched Aubrey laugh with her date. Stuart the Accountant was tall, broad-shouldered, and bearded. Truth be told, he looked more like a lumberjack than an accountant. And he was completely entranced by Aubrey. But who wouldn't be? She was stunning.

Her brows were perfectly crafted to draw attention to her sultry hazel eyes, and she wore just enough makeup to accentuate the elegant line of her cheekbones and the suppleness of her lips. Her red hair was twisted up, baring her long and graceful neck. She wore a dark green fitted dress and black heels. She was sleek and sexy, but he knew that as great as she looked dressed, she looked even better undressed.

Scowling, he turned away and strode into the kitchen to refill his beer at the tap. He found his brother Kyle and his brother-in-law, Sean, doing the same.

"Hey," Kyle said. "Need a refill? Sean's doing duty."

Liam walked around the bar to where Kyle was standing opposite Sean, who was behind the tap. "Beer me." He slid his empty pint glass emblazoned with both the Archer logo and Evan's and Alaina's names and the date of their marriage across the bar to Sean. Guests would take home a pint glass and a growler of special-edition beer Dad had just managed to brew in time. This had been a relatively quickie wedding, since Alaina was pregnant.

"Hard to believe so many of us are married or getting married." Kyle shook his head with a bemused smile.

"Including you," Liam said. "I can't believe you're monogomizing, let alone getting married."

"Monogomizing?" Sean asked, his British accent giving the made-up word gravitas. He handed Liam his refilled glass.

Liam took the beer and brought it to his mouth. "What else would you call it?" He sipped the IPA. "Before Maggie, Kyle didn't do girlfriends."

Sean sipped his beer. "You don't really either, from what I can tell."

"Oh, Liam does girlfriends—for three to six months maybe," Kyle said. "But damn, brother, seems like you've had a drought the past year or so. Unless you've been keeping someone secret."

Liam nearly choked on his next drink of beer. Aubrey might be a secret, but he couldn't call her a girlfriend. And if she was to be believed about their *thing* being over, she wasn't even a secret anymore. She wasn't anything except the attorney administering their brother's trust and handling this stupid zoning appeal for the property.

And why hadn't she been one of his girlfriends? She met every single one of his requirements and then some.

Duh, because she lived in Ribbon Ridge, and he lived in Denver. It was hard to have a relationship, even the casual ones he preferred, long-distance. A voice deep in his head said it was the *and then some* that was the problem. Aubrey was unlike any woman he'd ever known. Aside from being crazy attracted to her, he liked spending time with her. And that wasn't good for a guy who preferred to keep things unfettered. He liked to be in total control, and sharing your life with someone meant sharing control. *Pass.*

Kyle pulled a stool out from the bar and sat down. "Looking back, it seems like you went dormant after Alex died. You never talk about him, about what happened. You okay?"

He flashed Kyle a smug smile. "King of the world, man." Liam knew Kyle was genuinely asking about him, but he didn't want to go there right now. If he ever did. Instead, he defaulted to flipping him shit, which was their norm. They'd been particularly competitive in their youth, with sports and girls and popularity. Kyle had struggled academically, washing out of college in the first year and then going on to culinary school, where he'd found his niche. He'd become a rock-star chef until his gambling addiction had completely derailed him and driven him to Florida for several years.

Liam had felt like he'd won, but that was stupid. And looking at Kyle now, it seemed that he was the winner—happily engaged with a five-star restaurant set to open. Provided Aubrey could make this zoning problem go away.

Damn, Alex's entire project—his dream—hung in the balance because of some asshole who didn't want a commercial property adjoining his acreage. An acreage on which Liam was pretty sure sat an empty shed, a creek, and not much else. "Who's behind the appeal again? I forgot."

If he'd ever known. He'd kept himself out of pretty much everything to do with The Alex—they'd even named the hotel after their brother, a decision Liam had also had nothing to do with. Just what they needed, another reminder of the brother who'd cut a hole in each of them by selfishly ending his life.

"Russ Parker," Kyle said. "Do you know the story there?"

Holy fuck. Liam would've remembered that name. And yes, he goddamn well knew the story, but he sure as hell wouldn't say so to Kyle or anyone else in his meddling family. Wait…If Kyle knew the story, he would've called Liam months ago and yelled at him to fix it. So whatever story Kyle was referencing couldn't be what Liam knew…

"What?" Liam asked cautiously.

"Parker used to date Mom in college. She dumped him to go out with Dad. He's hated Dad ever since."

Son of a bitch. Not many things rendered Liam speechless, but for a moment he simply couldn't form words. This was a total clusterfuck. If he'd known about that, he never would've started up with Whitney Parker a couple of years ago. Had she known?

When Liam had heard her father's name a minute ago, he'd assumed *she* was the reason behind the appeal. She'd been pissed when he'd ended things with her eighteen months or so ago. But she'd run her course. Although she'd been a long-distance hook-up, Liam had still grown bored by the six-month mark, prompting him to stop seeing her when he came to town.

He suddenly realized their *thing* had been similar to what he'd done with Aubrey last year. Except with Whitney, she'd done all the initiating, while with Aubrey, it had been more mutual. The other exception was that Liam had tired of Whitney, but he still couldn't get enough of Aubrey. And it wasn't just her body, because Whitney could've fulfilled that need at any time. With Aubrey it had been something more, something he couldn't define and didn't want to.

Hell, there was no point thinking about that right now. Or ever really. A vision of her laughing with her lame-ass date rose in his mind, and he shoved it all away. He looked from Kyle to Sean, who'd secretly married their sister Tori in Vegas on the eve of their brother's suicide, much to Tori's absolute devastation. She'd spent most of last year pushing everyone away, including her secret husband, but they'd found their way back to each other last fall. They had settled into Ribbon Ridge like an old married couple—her with a burgeoning architecture firm and Sean with his production company, which he co-owned with Evan's new wife, the spectacularly famous actress Alaina Pierce.

"What, no response?" Kyle asked, narrowing his eyes. "What's up with you, Liam?"

"Nothing." He pulled himself back to the conversation about Parker. "That's effed up. Glad to know our business matters are someone else's revenge trip."

Kyle paused in lifting his glass to drink. " 'Our' business matters? You just mean Archer business, since *you* don't really have anything to do with them, right?"

Liam got the dig, and he deserved it. Immediately following Alex's suicide, he hadn't been the only one who'd refused to come home, but the others who had—Kyle and Evan—had both returned since then and had done so in spades. Kyle had exceeded everyone's expectations, taking over for Hayden as COO at Archer when Hayden had accepted the wine-making internship in France and jumping into The Alex project like he'd been there from the start. He'd even found a top-notch landscape architect and groundskeeper in his fiancée, Maggie. Meanwhile, Evan had taken over Alex's old job at Archer as creative director, plus he was managing the creative aspects for The Alex. Everyone had a hand in the family business. Everyone but Liam.

Not that he cared—he had his own real-estate development company in Denver. He'd taken over the true family business that their forefathers had started when they'd founded Ribbon Ridge. The Archers owned half the town, and Liam had inherited his great-grandfather's head for development and business. So Dad had repeatedly told him. Liam could've easily stepped into that role at Archer, freeing Dad up to focus more on his true love: crafting beer. But Liam hadn't wanted a hand-me-down. He'd wanted to build something from nothing. And he'd wanted to do it nice and far away from Ribbon Ridge.

More accurately, he'd wanted to do it nice and far away from his family.

Oh, come on, asshole, you can at least be honest with yourself—you wanted to be far away from Alex.

He gulped down half his beer. "Nope, none of it has anything to do with me. You're right about that," he said at last.

"Why is that?" Sean asked, leaning on the counter and looking at Liam. "How come you're the only one who stays away?"

Because I was a constant reminder to my twin of what he could never be.

But now that twin was gone. Why *couldn't* he come home? Ugh, too much shit to think about when all he wanted was a really good buzz. And since jumping out of an airplane wasn't going to happen at eight o'clock on a Saturday night, he'd have to settle for more beer. Or maybe something stronger. Hell, maybe he should blow out of here altogether.

Yes, run upstairs and change his clothes, then sneak out the back to the garage, where he kept a bike for when he was in town. A nice night ride—the weather was perfect—would give him enough of a buzz to release some of his pent-up frustration. Or pent-up lust, more like it. Wind whipping through his hair, bike beneath him devouring the road at sixty miles an hour. Sounded like heaven.

As close to heaven as he was going to get tonight, since Aubrey seemed intent on dogging him. *Fine.* He didn't need her. He didn't need anybody. Hadn't he established that over the past six years?

Kyle clapped him on the shoulder. "Dude, are you even here tonight?"

"For a little while longer." Liam drank the rest of his beer and set it back down. "Another one, Sean." Not if he wanted to ride. "On second thought, never mind." He looked at Sean and answered his question. "I don't come back here permanently because, let's face it, no one really wants me to. I don't fit here anymore, and that's fine by me. I come back four, five times a year. I think everyone sees me just enough to remember why they prefer I live somewhere else." He slid Kyle a glance. "Right, bro?"

"Nailed it." The snarky response was expected and made Liam grin, but there was something behind Kyle's eyes that made him uncomfortable. Something that Liam hoped Kyle would keep to his damn self.

"See you guys later," Liam said, turning from the counter and intending to steal up the back stairs to his childhood bedroom, where he stayed when he was in Ribbon Ridge.

"Hey," Kyle called after him. "If you're leaving, don't forget about the wedding brunch tomorrow morning. Eleven o'clock."

He paused on his way out of the kitchen and looked over his shoulder at his younger-by-a-few-minutes brother. With his surfer blond hair and blue-green eyes, he took more after Mom, while Liam took more after Dad. But they shared the trademark Archer nose and square chin.

"Why do you assume I'll be gone all night?" The fact that Kyle had reminded him of an event that was taking place *here*, where Liam was staying and therefore sleeping, inferred he didn't think Liam would be home.

Kyle laughed. "Dude, you hook up with someone every time you come back to town. You disappear overnight all the time. No worries—go do your thing."

Yes, he did do that. There'd been a long line of women before Aubrey, but the thought of finding someone else who wasn't her gave him a bad taste in his mouth.

He jogged upstairs and changed into jeans, a long-sleeved shirt, and the riding boots he kept here. He shrugged into his leather jacket and zipped it up to his chin before snagging his helmet and gloves from the closet.

Another quick trek down the back stairs and he was soon outside, weaving his way through the cars parked between the garages. It was a good thing he didn't want to take a car; he wouldn't have been able to get one out. His bike was in the last garage, parked with a handful of ATVs they used from time to time on his parents' property. That sounded fun, too—maybe someone would want to go for a ride tomorrow.

Right now, though, he was going for a ride. Hopefully the speed and the brisk night wind would be enough to drive Aubrey Tallinger from his mind. That's all he could hope for, since he was pretty sure his body would never be able to forget her.

Chapter Two

LIAM RODE NEARLY to the beach and back, taking back roads he'd traveled hundreds of times. Though it was only April, it was warm, and the promise of summer was in the air.

He was exhausted, and it was going on eleven o'clock, but he wasn't ready to head home just yet in case people were still milling around the house at the reception. He didn't want to see his family, and he sure as hell didn't want to see Aubrey or her date.

He pulled into Ruckus, Ribbon Ridge's answer to a dive bar. On the western edge of town, it was the only alternative to The Arch and Vine, the Archers' flagship pub at the center of Ribbon Ridge. No way in hell was he going there, even though he knew none of his family would be there. One of the employees would still tell someone who would tell someone else, and soon every Archer would know Liam had shown up.

Even going to Ruckus, there was still a chance they'd find out he'd chosen to hang out at a dive bar over his own brother's dwindling wedding reception. Ribbon Ridge was, after all, a small town, and its inhabitants pretty much knew everyone else. Or at least they knew someone who knew someone. It was two degrees of separation instead of six.

He parked his bike and went into the windowless building. It was moderately crowded, but then it was Saturday night. There'd be a lot of nonlocals passing through town on their way home from the casino, which was on the way to the coast.

He beelined for the bar and set his helmet down. He recognized the bartender and nodded. "Hey, Brian, shot of Patrón."

"You got it." He poured and slid it over to Liam. "Lime or salt or anything?"

Liam shook his head just before tossing it back. The tequila slid down his throat and gave him the perfect mix of heat and hell yeah. "One more. Then a beer—whatever IPA you have on tap." He preferred Archer beers to everything else, but you could only get them at an Archer brewpub or his parents' house. Okay, and at his place in Denver, since he regularly had kegs shipped to his condo and his office. It was the one piece of Ribbon Ridge he couldn't live without.

Really? *Beer* was the thing he couldn't live without? Shit, he was lame.

Brian refilled the shot glass with the tequila, then went to the tap at the other end of the bar.

"Drinking alone?" A honeyed, feminine voice came from his right. A voice he recognized. A voice he had a bone to pick with.

He turned his head and took in the curly blonde hair and razor-sharp brown eyes of Whitney Parker. "Not drinking with you, that's for sure."

She sat down on the stool beside his, not appearing to care that he'd basically told her to get lost. "Ouch." When Brian deposited Liam's beer, she flashed the bartender a smile. "I'll have what he's having—the shot and the beer. And put it on his tab."

Liam had to respect her gall. One thing about Whitney Parker—she had a mind and drive of her own, and screw anyone who got in her way. It was how she'd grown a women's fitness-wear company from a college project into a massive success that would likely go public in the next two years. She was exactly the kind of woman Liam ought to go for on paper: gorgeous, confident, wicked smart, and a larger-than-life personality. Too bad she was also batshit crazy.

And it sounded like her apple hadn't fallen far from her father's tree, given his revenge plot against Dad.

Liam turned his head to look at her. "I heard your dad is trying to screw us over. That hotel was my brother's dying wish. Trying to block it is a real dick move."

She turned toward the bar. "Yeah, well, I don't have anything to do with that."

"Are you sure? Because as soon as I heard about it, I was certain you did. Aren't you still pissed that I didn't want to see you anymore?"

Brian dropped off her drinks and, to his credit, tried to pretend like he hadn't heard what Liam had said. Not that Liam cared.

She threw back her tequila shot and slammed the empty glass on the bar before giving him a blazing glare. "Classic. You think I'm waiting around for you like some lovelorn puppy? Get over yourself."

Wait, she'd texted him not too long ago to ask if he'd be in town for Evan's wedding and, if so, suggested they hook up. Yep, crazy. "Okay, whatever you say. I still think you had something to do with the zoning appeal. What does your father care if we run a commercial business up there?"

"He owns the property at the bottom of the hill. He doesn't want a bunch of traffic going up the road."

Liam turned his stool toward her. "There's nothing on that property. He doesn't live there."

She sipped her beer. "Not yet, but he's considering building. He wants a retirement home. Or I might build something new there."

"Uh-uh, not buying it. I know you finished your mega mansion between here and McMinnville just last year." He'd been to the house while it was being built, and she'd regaled him with design plans. It was her dream house, and she was rightfully proud to be building it with her own money before she was even thirty. She looked at it like a goddamned trophy. "The amount of time and money you spent on that place? No way you're moving. Your dad's just being a prick because my mom dumped him a thousand years ago and married my dad, and you're probably egging him on."

She rolled her black-lined eyes. "You Archers are such arrogant jerks. It wouldn't matter who was trying to rezone that property. My dad would still be fighting it."

Liam laughed. "Bullshit. But whatever. We'll have our day in court and kick your asses."

"You can hope so, but our attorney is one of the best land-use lawyers in the state. While yours is…What's her name? Audrey Culpepper? Fulbright? Tarryton?" She shook her head. "I don't remember. Audrey never-heard-of-her. Good luck with that."

Liam wished he'd paid more attention to this entire situation. He'd dealt with a ton of zoning issues in Colorado, and granted the law was a bit different between states, but he had experience. Damn it, he should've gotten involved. Maybe it wasn't too late. "Who's your dad's attorney?"

"Frank Sutherlin," she said smugly.

Shit. He was one of the best land-use attorneys in Oregon—in the top five for sure. And expensive as hell. Meanwhile, they had Aubrey, who'd only been practicing for about three years, and while land use was one of her firm's areas of expertise, she didn't have the decades of experience Sutherlin did.

Liam took a long drink of beer and scrutinized Whitney. He hadn't seen her in almost a year—he'd run into her last summer, probably when he'd been home for Derek's wedding. That was the event that had garnered them an expensive fine from the county for supposedly having a commercial event at The Alex before it had been officially rezoned from agricultural. "You're the one who reported Derek's wedding to the county. We had to pay five thousand bucks for that bullshit."

She shrugged. "Not my problem. And no, I didn't report anything." She took another drink of her beer and turned toward him. "Why do you think so poorly of me? I thought we had a lot of fun together." She dropped her arm and situated it just so that her breast pushed up against the V-neck of her shirt.

He glanced at her impressive cleavage. "Very subtle, Parker. Still not interested."

"I don't know why. I don't make any demands. You come to town, we screw, you go back to Denver, it's all good. I don't even care who you fuck when you get home, do I?"

It's true that she'd never asked, never even seemed to care what he did when he wasn't in Ribbon Ridge. She *had* asked him to increase the frequency of his visits, which she'd thought he'd done. In actuality, he'd come home to earn his skydiving certification. He could've done the same in Denver, but he had a friend with a skydiving and flying business out in McMinnville, and they shared an intense love for all things extreme.

He set his beer on the bar. "Nice pitch, but I'm still not buying. I'll pay for your drinks, however, because I'm that kind of guy."

"A real gentleman." Her voice dripped with sarcasm.

Liam turned his stool and looked down the bar toward Brian, who was chatting with a server. It took him a moment to make eye contact, but he immediately knew Liam wanted his tab.

Liam glanced over at Whitney as he picked up his beer and downed half of what was left. "What would it take to get your dad to drop his opposition to the zoning change?"

Whitney pursed her lips, then blew air through them. "Gee, I don't know. I'd have to ask him. But I'm sure if his daughter was happy, he might be persuaded. I wonder what you could do to make me happy…" She tapped a manicured nail against her pink-glossed lip and slid him a seductive stare.

"Oh, for Christ's sake, you're as subtle as a goddamned two-by-four." His phone buzzed in his pocket, and he pulled it out to see a picture of Evan and Alaina with a text that read: *Thanks for everything, bro. You were a great best man.*

And now Liam felt like shit for leaving before the reception had ended. His eye landed on the background of the picture. There in the corner was Aubrey, her hand on her date's shirt, smiling as she looked up at him. They weren't kissing, but that was precisely the kind of look you exchanged right before you did. Well, if you were normal. If you were fucked up like Liam, smiling wasn't always part of the recipe for great sex.

Suddenly he didn't want to go home and see that. He wanted another shot of tequila.

Brian slapped the bill in front of him, but Liam shook his head, setting his phone on the bar. "Change of plans." He nudged the empty shot glass back toward him. "Double, please."

"Oooh, now we're talking," Whitney cooed beside him. "Another for me, too, but just a single. One of us has to drive."

Liam cast her a glare. "You are not driving me home. Why are you even still here?"

She batted her eyelashes at him and lowered her voice to the seductive growl he'd known so well. "Because deep down, you know you want me."

He snorted and waited for his tequila, downing it as soon as it came. A warm buzz started behind his eyes and took the edge off his frustration regarding Aubrey. Why was he so worked up? In his experience, she was way past her expiration date. It was time for him to move on to the next thing. He glanced over at Whitney and was instantly turned off. She wasn't only a step backward— and he didn't do that—she just wasn't Aubrey.

Apparently Aubrey didn't have an expiration date.

Damn and double damn. He slammed the rest of his beer.

"I'm so driving you home," Whitney said.

He narrowed his eyes at her but said nothing.

"I didn't say I'd take you back to my place and screw you six ways from Sunday, but I could totally do that, too." She gave him a saucy grin. "Just say the word."

"The word is *no*." He shook his head at her, perversely enjoying turning her down again and again. He didn't believe for one minute that she wasn't involved with their zoning trouble or that she was over him. "You were fun for a while, but that was a long time ago."

She shrugged, trying to give off an air of nonchalance, but he saw the fire burning in her eyes. She wanted him, and she was pulling out all the stops to get him. He wouldn't put it past her to roofie his drink. Shit, he'd turned his back on his beer when he'd asked for the damn check!

He looked at his empty pint glass. Too late now. Whatever damage might've been in his beer was done. He felt okay, just buzzed. And getting drunker by the minute actually. He picked up his phone to text Kyle to come pick him up, but that damn picture of Aubrey and her date taunted him.

Her words from earlier weaseled their way into his brain and dug their hooks into him.

Even if I do get bored, I will not call you. We're done.

He dropped his phone back down and waved for another shot. Brian poured a double without asking—good man.

Liam sipped this one. He willed the alcohol to burn all thoughts of Aubrey from his mind. He couldn't believe she was done. No, he couldn't believe he *wasn't*. Why couldn't he just accept Whitney's offer? She was beautiful, willing, and he knew exactly what sort of hot time he'd be getting.

But she was also nuts and probably fucking his family over. Worse, she was ruining Alex's legacy with all this zoning crap.

He threw the rest of the tequila back and pulled out his wallet. Time to get away from Toxic Tilly. He fished out a fifty and dropped it on the bar, then caught Brian's attention and gave him a nod.

He picked up his phone, turned, and slid off his chair. Whitney's hand caught his bicep.

"Whoa, there," she said. "You don't want to go face-first into the floor. This place is filthy."

He shook her off and tossed her a glare. "You thought I was falling?"

Her hand grazed his back. "I'm happy to catch you."

He flinched and moved away from her, striding toward the door with purpose despite the slight tunneling of his vision. Yeah, he was kind of fucked up right now.

He pushed open the door and stepped outside. The temperature had dropped, but it was still warm. Warm-ish. Okay, that breeze was a little chilly.

"Forget something?" Whitney's voice drew him to turn around. She held his helmet in her dark red manicured hands.

"Gimme that." He snatched it away from her and wove toward his bike.

"You aren't going to ride, are you?" She caught up to him and touched his arm. "Hey, Liam. I'm serious now. I'll drive you home."

He scowled at her. "I'll call my brother."

"And wait for him to come get you? It's getting cold." She shook her heads. *Heads? Dude, pull your head out of your drunk ass right now before you do something stupid.*

She pointed toward her BMW. "Come on, I'm right there. And I promise I won't take you to my house and jump your bones, although I think you'd probably come willingly in your state."

"Not a chance in hell." He wasn't that drunk. God, he hoped he wasn't that drunk.

She grabbed his hand and dragged him toward her car. "Not taking no for an answer on this."

He tried to pull away, but his reflexes were set to slow motion, and Whitney worked out like a banshee. She opened the passenger door and shoved him down into the seat. He pulled his feet in just before she slammed the door. Vicious bitch.

She climbed into the driver's seat.

"You could've taken my feet off," he drawled.

She laughed. "Sure." She fired up the engine and pulled out of the lot, going west toward the road that led to his parents' house.

"I seriously need you to talk to your dad." God, he wished he didn't sound so messed up. "He needs to drop the zoning appeal."

"My dad will do whatever he's going to do, no matter what I say."

"Come on, Whitney, you can do better than that, can't you?"

She turned up the road toward his parents' and slid him a narrow-eyed glance. "Why should I? You haven't exactly been nice to me."

"What do you mean? I didn't treat you like shit. We had a casual thing, and it ran its course."

"I didn't think it was that casual." Her voice had gone quiet. Serious. Scary as hell. "I was in love with you, Liam."

Oh fuck. Whatever. "How is that my fault? I didn't promise you anything."

"Maybe not in so many words, but how many times did you tell me that we'd be perfect for each other if you were the marrying kind? That if you wanted to settle down and come back home, I ticked everything off your list?"

Shit, had he said those things? He didn't remember. But then he *was* drunk as hell right now.

"Well, I'm *not* the marrying kind, and I'm pretty damned sure I said that, too." That was practically tattooed on his fucking forehead.

She pulled into the drive and through the gate, which was still open from the wedding reception, he guessed.

Wedding reception.

Dammit. Would everyone still be here? How the hell was he going to explain Whitney Fucking Parker driving him home?

She drove past the fountain in front of the house and through the porte cochere to the back door. How the hell did she know to drop him off here? "Have you been here before?" he asked.

"Duh. A couple of summers ago—it was September, actually—I came up here, and we went skinny-dipping in the pool. You don't remember?"

Vaguely. "Not really. Must not have been that great."

"Wow, you've turned into a real asshole since your brother died, you know that?" She threw the car into park, and he opened the door and practically fell out in his haste to get away.

But again, he was moving like his feet were encased in lead, and she was around the car and helping him stand before he had his bearings.

She stood in front of him and rested her hands on his shoulders with a sigh. "Really. You always were an arrogant prick, but that's one of the things I liked best about you. Since Alex died, though, you've taken it to a whole new level. I think if you work through your grief, you'd see that there's someone here who really cares about you. Someone who loves you." She stood on her toes and pressed her lips to his.

Liam heard the door to the house and used the helmet he still held between them to push her away.

"Liam?" Kyle came toward him. "Are you okay?"

"He's fine, just drunk." Whitney turned and linked her arm through Liam's. "Hi, I'm—"

"Leaving!" Liam interjected. Thank God he possessed enough wits to keep her from spilling her name. That's just what he needed—his entire family knowing he had a past with the crazy Parker family who was trying to screw them.

He took his arm from hers. "Thanks for the ride. Remember what I said."

She looked him in the eye, and the edge of malice in her gaze was sharp enough to cut through Liam's drunken stupor. "Remember what *I* said. We could be great together, and your problems could…maybe go away."

Was she really blackmailing him? No, he had to be beyond fucked up.

She looked past him at Kyle and smiled. "Good night!"

Liam didn't bother watching her drive away before he turned and walked toward the house.

Kyle followed him. "Who was she?"

"Just some girl at Ruckus who offered to give me a ride home."

"Some girl who kissed you. Uh-huh." The sarcasm in his tone would've riled Liam, but he was too wasted and suddenly too tired.

He walked into the back hallway and went straight for the stairs. "I'm going to bed."

"Alone, instead of with that hot blonde?" Kyle sounded shocked. "Weird. I don't know what's up with you, bro, but there's something. If I didn't know better, I'd say you were hung up on someone."

Maybe.

Probably.

Fuck.

Chapter Three

AUBREY WAS A little surprised that Evan and Alaina had invited her to their wedding breakfast on Sunday morning but wouldn't have dreamed of declining. She'd grown close to many of the Archers since Alex died, and of course she'd been quite close with him before that.

She was able to think of him now without the searing pain in her chest. It had eased into a dull ache, a bittersweet memory that would forever tug at her heart.

His death had been shocking to everyone, and no one more than her. For nearly a year, he'd enlisted her professional assistance to first purchase the abandoned monastery just outside Ribbon Ridge and then set up a trust for his siblings to renovate it in the event of his death. She never imagined he was contemplating suicide. He'd always been upbeat and charming, a more mellow version of his twin brother, Liam.

She hadn't met any of the other Archers until after Alex killed himself. It had been a rude introduction to the family with whom he'd expected her to work so closely. She'd been pissed at him for a long time. Pissed and sad.

She knocked on the front door, and Emily answered. The matriarch of the family, Emily was petite and blonde, a combination of pixie and firecracker. She'd been devastated by her son's suicide, which had only contributed to Aubrey's anger at Alex. He had two loving parents, and he'd completely crushed them. What Aubrey wouldn't have given for caring, supportive parents like Rob and Emily.

"Good morning, Aubrey!" Emily embraced her in a quick hug. "You're alone? Where's your date from last night?"

Aubrey didn't realize her invitation was plus one, but she wouldn't have brought him anyway. They'd only been on a few dates, and this seemed like an intimate event for close friends and family.

Aubrey smiled at Emily. "It's just me."

That ought to make Liam happy. He'd spent the rest of the wedding reception—after their kiss—scowling at her before disappearing for the night. She'd wondered where he'd gone but decided she was better off not knowing.

Emily moved across the entryway and looked at Aubrey over her shoulder. "You know you can come in the back door—you're practically family." She'd invited Aubrey to do that several times now, but for some reason, Aubrey couldn't bring herself to make that leap.

She blamed her ongoing *thing* with Liam. Or maybe the fact that she still felt like an outsider and probably always would. She wasn't an Archer, she wasn't ever going to be an Archer, and at some point she might actually like to close the book on one of the saddest, most challenging chapters of her life. She was ready to move on, at least in terms of her love life.

She followed Emily into the great room. The reception decorations were still up, and the gifts had been assembled into a pile in front of the windows. Alaina came forward to meet her. "Thanks for coming, Aubrey."

Aubrey wasn't sure she'd ever get used to the world's most famous actress hugging her, but who was she to complain? Alaina was just as real and friendly as the Archers—she fit right in with them. That she'd captured the heart of Evan, who had Asperger's syndrome, warmed Aubrey's heart. Alex had worried about him and hoped he'd find someone.

She could only imagine what Alex would say if he could be here now: *Holy shit, Alaina Pierce? Well done, Evan!*

"How are you today, feeling like an old married woman?" Aubrey asked as she pulled back from the hug.

Alaina chuckled. "Old married *pregnant* woman, for sure. I'll be really happy when this morning sickness is done. Although whomever called it 'morning' sickness was a moron, because I deal with this nausea all day sometimes. Bleh." She made a face, but nothing she did could detract from her radiant beauty.

"It should pass soon, right?"

"I hope so. The end of this first trimester can't come fast enough!"

Evan came over and put his arm around his wife's waist. "Hey, Aubrey." He looked somewhere past Aubrey's head, which she was used to. He rarely made eye contact.

"Hi, Evan. When are you headed out on your South Pacific honeymoon?"

"Tomorrow. Did you hear we're taking a private jet courtesy of a friend of Alaina's?"

Aubrey smiled at his excitement. Who wouldn't want to travel via private jet for such a long trip? "I heard that. Sounds amazing. Let me know if you need a flight attendant."

"Will do." He pressed a kiss to Alaina's temple, and she smiled up at him.

Their wedding might've been of the shotgun variety given Alaina's pregnancy, but their love was palpable. Aubrey was certain they would've ended up together anyway. She glanced around at the other Archer couples.

Sara, the youngest of the sextuplets, stood with her fiancé, Dylan Westcott. Aubrey had come to know Dylan very well, since he was the contractor for the monastery renovation project. They'd worked together on any number of issues, especially the zoning problems they were currently facing.

Kyle, a world-class chef and once the black sheep of the family, was talking to his dad, Rob, while his fiancée, Maggie, a former therapist and now the groundskeeper and landscape architect for The Alex, was over with Tori and her husband, Sean. Tori was an architect who'd designed the entire renovation, as per Alex's wishes, and had moved back to Ribbon Ridge as a result. She'd started her own architecture firm while Sean, a producer, ran a production company with Alaina.

Finally, standing by the fireplace were Derek Sumner, the not-really-adopted adoptive brother the Archers had taken in when he was orphaned at seventeen, and his wife, Chloe, who was the art director for the Archer brewpubs. Derek was the most business-minded of the family and the chief financial officer of Archer Enterprises. Aubrey fully expected him to be the one to take over for Rob Archer when he retired.

Actually, that wasn't true. Liam was equally as business-minded. He ran a real-estate empire in Denver that should've put him squarely in the role of his father's heir apparent, since Archer Enterprises was primarily a real-estate development company. The brewpub part of it was a relatively new division started by Rob, for whom brewing beer wasn't just a job, it was a passion.

As if summoned by her thoughts, Liam strolled in from the kitchen. His dark wavy hair was damp, suggesting he'd just come from the shower. That was *not* a vision she needed in her brain right now. Or ever, really.

Could she excise him from her mind so easily? Just because she'd ended things didn't mean she wouldn't think of him, especially when he was in town. However, doing so was dangerous. If she thought too long or too hard, she might find herself going right back to that well.

And she didn't need that kind of turmoil.

His gaze found hers, and she had her answer. No, she couldn't get rid of him that simply, even after terminating their *thing* months ago. Not when he looked so impossibly gorgeous and a simple look turned her knees to jelly.

She turned away from him and came face-to-face with Alaina's assistant and best friend, Crystal Donovan. "Hi!" Crystal was friendly and hilarious. She possessed the Southern twang that sometimes crept into Alaina's speech now and again. "How are you this morning?" She lowered her voice. "I'm a skosh hung over, I'm afraid, and I tried to be so good."

Aubrey smiled. "I was very good. I drank lots of water." Otherwise she would've been in the same boat. She'd learned long ago that the Archers knew how to throw a good party—Archer beer, the best wines from the area, and if Kyle started mixing cocktails…forget it.

"Smart girl. Note to self for next time." She inclined her head toward Liam, who'd gone to talk with his dad and Kyle. "What's the story with McHottiepants over there?"

Aubrey shrugged. "He lives in Denver. Owns his own company. He's a millionaire in his own right, even without his trust fund." Every one of the Archer kids—except Derek—had inherited a trust fund at the age of twenty-five. The funds didn't quite make each of them millionaires, but it was pretty close. Several of them had probably closed the gap, and she knew Liam definitely had.

Crystal's eyebrows shot up. "Interesting. Although, I don't much care about the money."

No, Aubrey didn't imagine she would. As Alaina's assistant, she was likely a millionaire, too. Meanwhile,

Aubrey was a modest attorney in a small town—a country lawyer, really, like her uncle who owned the firm at which she worked.

"I wouldn't be interested in him for any other reason, either, if I were you," Aubrey said. "He's a total player. I think his longest relationship was six months, and there are differing reports as to whether it was monogamous."

Crystal nodded. "Gotcha." She sighed. "Too bad. Damn, my radar must be broken. I can usually spot one of those a mile away. You learn that really fast in LA."

"I'm sure."

Kyle whistled to get everyone's attention. "Good morning! We thought we'd start with the brunch. It's being laid out in the dining room. Be sure to pick up a mimosa or a Bloody Mary at the bar in the kitchen. Little hair of the dog will do you all some good." He winked at the room at large.

People began to file toward the dining room. Aubrey cut into the kitchen—she loved Kyle's mimosas. When she turned from the bar, drink in hand, Liam stepped toward her.

"Morning," he said, flashing her a quick glance.

That's it? After last night's hard sell, he wasn't going to try again? They were alone in the kitchen, and he'd never missed an opportunity to flirt or touch or somehow flip her switch. Hell, just being in the same room with him was usually enough to get her going.

"Did you really take no for an answer finally?" She hadn't meant to say it, but the words had tumbled from her mouth before she could stop them.

His head snapped up, and his steel blue eyes were cool. "Isn't that what you want?"

"Well, yes, but that didn't stop you from pursuing me last night."

He cracked a smile. It was small and brief but completely disarming. Damn, she hated being vulnerable to his stupid charm. "I'm trying to be a stand-up guy. Besides, you were right—we've run our course. I've never been one to hang around too long."

Wasn't that the truth? "Speaking of which, when are you headed back home?"

"Tomorrow probably." His brow furrowed briefly, and this time she bit her tongue before asking what was wrong. His business wasn't hers. "I don't know yet. You going in for breakfast? I'm starved."

"Yeah."

He gestured for her to precede him. She half expected him to touch the small of her back as she walked by, but he didn't. Disappointment surged in her chest, and she immediately chastised herself. This is what she wanted. This is what she'd demanded.

Nevertheless, that didn't make letting Liam go any easier. Damn, she was beginning to hate this family and the way they made her feel. Or at least the way two of them had made her feel. The two who looked identical and who she'd thought were worlds apart. Turned out they were each as manipulative and soul-crushing as the other.

After filling her plate at the buffet in the dining room, she ate breakfast with Tori and Sara in the great room.

As usual, the conversation included a bit about work and more specifically the ongoing zoning appeal.

"Has Sutherlin turned in his brief yet?" Tori asked.

After months of stalling tactics, they'd finally entered the phase where the complainant—Parker—filed his brief. "Not yet, but it's due this week."

Tori sipped her mimosa. "The oral argument will be soon then, right?"

"After I submit my response, the Land Use Board of Appeals will set the court date."

Tori blew out a breath as she slathered mascarpone on a scone. "I can't wait. This has been so frustrating."

Emily came up to them where they were perched on a couch. "Aubrey, can I speak with you for a minute?" Her gaze flicked to Aubrey's plate. "Or when you're done."

Despite the half scone and few bites of frittata left, Aubrey was actually stuffed. "I'm done." She stood with her plate and followed Emily into the kitchen.

Emily turned and took the plate, setting it on the counter. "Let's step into my office." Literally. A small, circular office led off the kitchen and was used by a variety of people, though it was primarily Emily's home base.

Aubrey couldn't imagine what Emily wanted to talk to her about, let alone privately. Alarm bells pealed in her brain. She really hoped this wasn't about a legal matter. Aubrey didn't think she could handle another Archer problem, especially if it was something like divorce. For several months after Alex's death, Emily and Rob had gone through a very rough patch, and the *D* word had been quietly discussed by several of the Archer siblings.

Emily had even gone to France with Hayden for a few months, and that had seemed to give her and her husband the space they'd needed to deal with their grief. In fact, they'd appeared quite like their old selves recently—they'd even seemed romantic.

"Is everything all right?" Aubrey asked.

"Yes. Well, I think so. I'm hoping you can help me with something. I'd ask one of my children, but I don't think they'd be able to help. I wanted to ask you about Liam."

Aubrey's insides cinched up like a pair of hiking boots. "Uhhh, why me?"

Emily tipped her head to the side. "You seem friendly. Whenever Liam comes home, I see him chatting with you. I thought you'd become friends."

Friends. Aubrey bit her cheek to keep from laughing. She was his fuck buddy, not his friend. "We're not especially close, so I don't know that I can help you either, unfortunately. What did you want to know?"

Emily's brow creased, and Aubrey wanted to help her. This woman had been through so much, and she was so kind, so generous, so loving. "Do you know about Liam's hobbies?"

If she meant his thrill-seeking, adrenaline-junkie risk extravaganzas, then yes. "Like the heli-skiing?" He'd broken his wrist and dislocated his shoulder doing that back in February, the idiot. She'd been worried sick when she'd heard and had even texted him to ask how he was doing. No wonder he'd held out hope they were still hooking up, despite her declining to see him over the holidays. *Nice move, Aubrey.*

Emily nodded. "And the skydiving and the rock climbing and the extreme kayaking."

That was only the tip of the iceberg. Liam was always trying something new, always pushing the limits. That was another of the reasons she'd ended things. Worrying about his next exploit and whether he'd kill himself was not something she wanted to do. "I'm aware he does all of that, but I don't really know too much about it."

"He doesn't discuss it with you? I was hoping he might, or maybe you know someone he talks with. I'm worried about him. I have been for quite some time, but his accident in February really scared me. I've tried to impress upon him to take it easy, but he only seems to go even harder, especially since Alex died."

Aubrey had noticed that, too. She'd known all about his daredevil activities long before Alex's death, because Alex had shared them with her. Every time Liam jumped from a plane or navigated class V rapids or scaled a steep rock face, he sent the video footage to Alex, who ate it up. Alex couldn't do any of those things for himself, so Liam had done them for him. What had started out as a favor several years ago had turned into a full-blown way of life for both of them. Alex came up with the experience he wanted, and Liam went out and did it. It was both sick in that neither one of them seemed to care about the danger involved and beautiful in that it was something they shared. Aubrey didn't know if anyone else was aware of the situation, and she'd long ago decided she wasn't going to be the one to tell them.

Still, she wanted to help Emily if she could. "What can I do for you?"

"Maybe you could talk to him? I doubt you'll be able to talk him out of doing any of it—he won't even listen to me." She shook her head resignedly. "But maybe you could find out what he's planning. I'd like to know what he's up to. When he called to say he'd had an accident, my heart just dropped into my feet. I knew he was okay since it was his voice on the phone, but maybe someday it won't be. And I..." She swiped at her eye. "I don't know how I could go through that again."

In that moment Aubrey wanted to punch the living crap out of Liam. How could he put his mother—his entire family—through this after what they'd suffered with Alex? If there were two more selfish people on earth, she didn't know them. And one of them wasn't even on earth anymore, thanks to his selfishness.

Yes, she wanted to help Emily, *and* she wanted to smack some sense into Liam in the meantime. Furthermore, Alex had instructed Aubrey to deliver messages from him to his family members at various times that he'd outlined. The timing of Liam's was perhaps the trickiest. Alex had directed her to give Liam his message when he tried something truly foolhardy. She hadn't known how she was going to figure that out and more than once considered just giving him the damn thing to be done with it.

She smiled at Emily and touched her shoulder. "I'll see what I can do."

Emily relaxed and nodded. "Thank you. I really appreciate you doing this. I don't know if you'll be able to get much out of him, but I do think you have a better shot than his siblings. He's predisposed to be on defensive alert around them. With you, he seems more relaxed."

Did he? Somehow, in the course of maybe three or four events over the past fourteen months, Emily had sensed a relationship between them when Aubrey wasn't even sure one existed. But apparently it had. And it seemed to be far more conspicuous than she'd realized. A part of her wanted to seize on that and make it into something more than it had been, a series of mostly coincidental meetings that had sparked into sexual encounters. However, none of that amounted to anything. Liam was still a player and an adrenaline junkie. And her heart couldn't handle either of them.

LIAM WENT BACK for a second Bloody Mary while Evan and Alaina started in on their gifts. Kyle had nailed it when he'd said hair of the dog. The alcohol was just what he needed to power through his nasty hangover.

He had to make the cocktail himself, but he could pour just as well as Kyle. Okay, maybe not *quite* as well, but he'd never admit that out loud. He stirred the drink with a celery stick and speared a couple of olives to dunk.

"Liam." Aubrey's honeyed voice stirred his body to full attention. He'd done his best earlier to give her the aloof relationship she'd asked for, but damn it was hard.

"You want a Bloody Mary?" he asked.

She shook her head. "Mimosa."

"Those are easy. Kyle premixed them." He went to the fridge and pulled out a pitcher, which he poured into her empty glass. "Drink up. These won't be any good in a couple hours when the bubbly goes flat."

"Thanks." She took the drink and raised the glass in silent toast.

He went back to the other bar to grab his Bloody Mary.

She sampled her mimosa. "Earlier, when I asked when you were heading back to Denver, you seemed hesitant. Is there any chance you're planning to stay awhile? I'm due to get the opposing brief on the zoning appeal this week, and the oral argument will be in the next month or so, I think. It would be great to have you there."

He sipped his drink and narrowed his eyes at her. What kind of game was she playing? "You dumped me. Why would you want me around?"

"I didn't dump you—we weren't in anything formal." She studied him a moment. "Scratch that. I think I'd like to put 'dumped Liam Archer' on my résumé."

He laughed at that. "You mean your eHarmony profile? Or are you still on Tinder?"

Her gaze turned incredulous. "I have never been on Tinder. You must have me confused with one of your other hook-ups."

He raked her from the top of her ginger head to the toes of her ballet flats, which encased feet he knew to be extremely sexy. Who even knew feet could be sexy? But Aubrey's were. "Not a chance, sweetheart."

Her cheeks flushed a pale pink, and he inwardly smiled at having provoked her. "Whatever. I thought you might finally like to engage with this project. You're the only one who's completely turned away from Alex's legacy. I'd thought you two were closer than that."

He'd thought so, too, but when your identical twin could successfully hide from you the fact that he was plotting to kill himself, you didn't know shit. And that was both a sobering and horrifying realization.

He leaned closer, not bothering to hide his flash of temper—thinking of Alex often kindled that. "Don't talk to me about Alex. Ever. I thought we'd established that a long time ago."

She didn't appear to register his anger, or maybe she was trying to rile him on purpose. "Right, one of your pesky 'rules' for hooking up. My bad." Sarcasm oozed from her tone. "You'll do what you want—you always do—but I hope you'll consider coming for the zoning hearing at least. Maybe pretend you give a crap."

He exhaled, feeling suddenly weary. He did give a crap. He cared a lot, actually. Hadn't he just been thinking last night that he ought to do more? Especially with Whitney involved…He could use whatever connection they still had to maybe fix this entire messed-up situation.

Maybe.

"I'll think about it."

Her answering look was professionally bland, the trademark of a good lawyer who knew how to present a poker face. "Magnanimous of you." She leaned toward him. "Let me know what you decide."

"Decide what?" Tori came into the kitchen. "Oh good, you have the mimosas out." She refilled her glass from the pitcher Liam had set on the counter.

Kyle came in next and eyed Liam's drink. "Made your own Bloody Mary? I would've thrown it together for you."

"I can make a Bloody Mary."

Kyle grinned. "Not as good as mine." He moved behind the bar with the beer tap, where they also kept liquor. All the ingredients were already on the counter, and he went to work. "Admit it, I'm a better bartender. I'd better be, since I was a professional for a while."

"I'll admit nothing."

Kyle laughed. "You're such a prick."

Tori came over to the bar and stood near Aubrey. "What is Liam going to decide?"

Aubrey glanced at him. Would she tell them? Oh, the hell with it. "She asked me to come back for the zoning hearing," Liam said.

Tori pivoted toward him. "And?"

"I'm thinking about it."

"That's what he's deciding," Aubrey said.

Kyle stirred his drink. "I can tell you right now what his answer will be: no." He gave Liam a look that dared him to correct his assessment.

And just because Liam liked to be contrary—or as Kyle put it, liked to be a prick—he smiled. "I'm deciding yes, actually."

"You are?" The harmony of the question coming from his sister and his former lover rankled him even further. Damn, he was on edge today. He blamed the hangover.

"Don't sound so shocked."

Tori braced her hand on the counter. "Why not? That's about the last thing I expected to hear from you.

This project has held absolutely no interest for you. Less than no interest. You tried to give your portion away, if I remember correctly."

"But he couldn't," Aubrey said softly.

Kyle sipped his drink and set it on the counter with a clack. "Didn't stop him from trying. What gives? Why the sudden interest?"

Liam glared at his brother. "Why do you suspect something devious?"

"I never even thought the word *devious*."

"But you admit you're suspicious."

Kyle's voice climbed a bit. "Hell yes, I'm suspicious. You've made no secret about not wanting anything to do with this project. You've weighed in on *nothing*. And now you want to participate out of the blue." Kyle shook his head. "Makes no sense."

"You have to agree it doesn't," Tori said, her tone far more palatable than Kyle's.

Liam told himself to stop being a dick. He could do that, right? Did he always have to push them all away? Maybe for once he could just keep them at arm's length, instead of increasing the divide. "You're right—both of you."

Kyle glanced toward the back windows. "Holy shit, did I just hear the four horsemen of the apocalypse outside?"

Aubrey cracked a very brief but incredibly gorgeous smile. Maybe he should admit his fallibility more often. "Very funny. I've actually been thinking I should do…something. Aubrey came up with the perfect way for me to participate. I've been involved with dozens of zoning changes in Denver. I realize the laws are a bit different, but my experience will be helpful."

Tori exchanged looks with Aubrey. "Just remember that Aubrey's the attorney."

He just hoped she was good enough to take on Parker's bulldog. "I don't pretend to be a lawyer. This is Aubrey's game." To win or lose. Suddenly it seemed imperative that he was here—he wasn't going to let them lose. Not to Whitney Parker and her dad.

"So you'll come back for the hearing—that's when?" Kyle asked Aubrey.

"Likely next month." Her eyes briefly met Liam's, and they held a guarded look that he wanted to figure out. "But maybe you could make yourself available for consultation on the brief I have to file."

Wait, what? She wanted to consult him? He'd already said he wasn't a lawyer. Unless...she was *trying* to involve him. Wasn't that her job as assigned by Alex? Entice all of them to return to Ribbon Ridge, to rediscover their roots and embrace family and all that bullshit. It was such a crock. If Alex had really wanted them all to come home, he would've stuck around to be part of it. And that was one of many reasons Liam hadn't done it. After all he'd done for Alex, the least the bastard could do was be here when Liam finally came home. Except that would've ensured Liam never did. It was a damn Catch-22.

Liam took a drink of his Bloody Mary. "Sure. I'll hang out for a few days, will that work?"

"What about your precious real-estate empire?" Kyle asked.

"Boyd can manage things. It's not like I'm going to be on Mars."

Tori speared him with a piercing stare. "Of course not, but your job has always been your primary excuse for staying away. I'm with Kyle—this is suspicious. I'm also very glad, regardless of the reason. It'll be good to have you here, even if it's only temporary." She moved toward him and kissed his cheek. "Welcome home, Liam." Then she flashed him a smile and left the kitchen.

"I'm speechless," Kyle said. His lips twisted into a smile. "Savor it, because it doesn't happen very often." He followed Tori out.

Aubrey cleared her throat. "I want to be very clear. I have no interest in you beyond this business with your family. I've moved on."

Liam shrugged off his siblings' doubt. "I saw that last night. How's your lumberjack boyfriend?"

She crossed her arms but still held her glass. "Lumberjack?"

Liam shrugged. He noted she didn't question his use of *boyfriend* and tried to ignore the discomfort that caused—like an itch in the middle of his back that he couldn't reach. "He had a beard."

She rolled her eyes. "He's an accountant."

"I remember. I imagine he's pretty stiff."

She offered a half-smile. "In all the ways that count."

Her words left him ice cold. He cursed at himself, pissed that he'd somehow forgotten that despite the heat of their kiss last night, she'd sent him packing. He'd endeavor not to forget that again.

"I'm glad. You deserve someone who will treat you well."

She uncrossed her arms. "I do. Thanks." She turned, and he could've sworn he heard her whisper, "I'm sorry it couldn't have been you."

He was, too.

Chapter Four

AUBREY BLINKED AT her computer screen. Her eyes were tired. But she'd worked straight through lunch on this brief and was nearing the end—time for an afternoon snack break, at least.

She opened her desk drawer and rummaged around for a protein bar, then remembered she'd also brought an apple. And coffee. Yes, coffee would be required in order to power through to the end. She'd come in at seven this morning, but then that's usually how she started her workweek. She loved her job and for the most part was eager to jump back in after recharging over the weekend.

Before the coffee, however, she'd take a quick look at her e-mail, which she'd been ignoring while working on the brief. She launched the program as she took a bite of the golden delicious. Immediately a name jumped out at her.

The brief from Frank Sutherlin, the opposing attorney on the Archer land-use matter, had landed in her inbox two hours ago. Her clock for the response had officially started ticking.

She'd known it was coming, of course, but she'd half expected Sutherlin to ask for an extension. He'd certainly done enough to drag things out while they were agreeing to the record for the appeal. He'd ensured what should've taken a few weeks had taken months, which had delayed the Archers' opening of their project. The event space and the restaurant were ready, just sitting empty as they waited for the zoning variance to be resolved, and the hotel would be ready in six to eight weeks. She only hoped this would all be over by then—and that it would result in a win. If it didn't…She couldn't think about that. Not only would all of their hard work be for nothing, Alex's dream of his family owning and operating a five-star destination spot would go up in flames.

No pressure.

She skimmed the brief, the apple ignored in her hand. Unease mounted as she neared the end. Sutherlin knew how to argue, but then that's why he was one of the best in the state and commanded his five-hundred-dollar-an-hour fee.

Aubrey sat back in her chair and nibbled at the apple. She'd started her brief weeks ago but had waited to finish until she saw what Sutherlin put together. Now she had three weeks to file her response, and presumably the oral argument would happen a couple of weeks after that.

Her stomach in turmoil, she tossed what was left of the golden delicious into the trash. She needed a little pep talk.

Standing, she left her office. The building was small, a converted Victorian house with just four attorneys, including Aubrey and her uncle, who was the Tallinger in Tallinger and Associates. Uncle Dave, her father's younger brother, had given her a job the second she'd started law school. She'd interned here in the summers and started as a full-time associate immediately after graduating. His faith in and commitment to her were the constants in her life. She had no siblings, and her cousins—all on her mother's side—lived in California. Her parents also lived in California, in Carmel, where Aubrey had grown up. Right now her family consisted of Uncle Dave and Aunt Cyndi, and she wouldn't want it any other way.

She stopped in the kitchen at the back of the building and grabbed a cup of coffee before heading upstairs to Uncle Dave's office. He had the largest space, taking up the bay windows that looked out onto the street below. Just a block off Ribbon Ridge's main thoroughfare, they were close enough to walk to all the shops and businesses the town had to offer, including the Archers' flagship pub, The Arch and Vine. It was also only six blocks from Aubrey's house, resulting in a super easy commute on foot.

Uncle Dave's door was ajar, which meant he was working but interruptible. Aubrey tapped her knuckles against the wood before gently pushing it open. "Uncle Dave?"

He looked up from his computer screens—he had three—and turned his head to smile at her. "Come in." He took his glasses off and set them on the desk as he pivoted his chair to face her. "What's up?"

She sat in one of the chairs situated in front of the desk. Behind him, the wide windows framed a gorgeous spring day. The blossoms were nearly gone from the trees, whose green leaves were in various states of unfurling as they welcomed the warmer weather.

"Sutherlin's brief came in. I just forwarded it to you."

He glanced at his computer. "Yeah? What's in it?"

"Everything we expected, given his objections to the record."

Dave pursed his lips, then sighed as he sat back in his chair. "We've discussed how to argue it. Are you unsure?"

"Not about what to do." She struggled to find the right words. She was fighting the urge to hide her insecurity, something her parents had enforced. *Be sharp, be confident, be ruthless* was her father's motto. A successful entrepreneur, he peddled medical equipment. Rather, he had until he'd sold the company two years ago. He'd made a mint, and now he and Mom were professional amateur golfers and wine tasters. They came to the Ribbon Ridge area every July for the International Pinot Noir Celebration in nearby McMinnville. They golfed, they drank wine, they occasionally spent time with Aubrey. Last year she'd "accidentally" scheduled a trip out of town at the exact same time. Maybe she'd do the same this year, too.

But she wasn't talking to her critical parents, she was talking to Uncle Dave. She forced the tension from her shoulders. "I'm just having a moment of self-doubt. Sutherlin is a land-use rock star."

Dave sat forward and speared her with a compassionate, fatherly stare. "You are, too. Don't look at me like that. You know what I mean." He chuckled. "I know you worry that you're young, but you graduated third in your class for a reason. You could've taken a lot of different offers or clerked for a judge, but you chose to settle here at my rinky-dink firm in Ribbon Ridge. That doesn't make you a lesser lawyer. It makes you happy. Don't ever lose sight of what's truly important. I know that's hard, what with my brother's philosophy." He sighed. "Sometimes I wonder how we sprang from the same loins. But then, your grandparents wondered that, too."

Aubrey felt a pang of sadness—she still missed her grandparents, who'd died within a few months of each other two years ago. But that emotion was replaced with love and appreciation. Uncle Dave knew exactly how to cut right to the heart of what was bothering her. In this case, he reminded her that her father's expectations and demands didn't breed happiness. Following your heart did.

Her parents had been bitterly disappointed when she'd decided to move to Ribbon Ridge to practice law at Uncle Dave's firm. Dad had gone so far as to say he shouldn't have been surprised, since she didn't seem to want a serious career. Otherwise, she would've gone to Stanford Law instead of Lewis and Clark. Nitpicks like that had been the cornerstone of her life, along with harsh and often unfair punishments, like refusing to pick her up after every drama club meeting when she'd secretly joined that instead of the debate team during her freshman year in high school. They'd tried to control every aspect of her life. When she'd moved to Stanford for her undergrad, she'd finally pursued her own path. Despite that, it was sometimes hard to shake the self-doubt their habitual criticism had fostered.

Uncle Dave's unflinching support and encouragement had done a lot to minimize the effects of her parents' manipulation, and she loved him for it. But now wasn't the time to get sappy, so she focused on the humor in what he'd said. "Your firm is *not* rinky-dink."

He laughed more heartily. "It *is*, and that's just the way I like it. You're happy here, right?"

"Absolutely." She loved Ribbon Ridge. Carmel had the same sort of small-town feel, so she'd felt instantly at home. She missed the ocean a bit, but it wasn't all that far from Ribbon Ridge. She was saving up to buy a condo on the coast and planned to spend at least one weekend a month enjoying the peace of being near the sea. "There's nowhere else I'd rather be."

"Good, because when I retire in ten or so years, all of this will be yours."

It sounded daunting, but she knew a lot changed in a decade. By then she'd be thirty-eight, probably married, and hopefully with children. That was the one thing she saw in her future—motherhood. She longed to be the kind of mother she'd so desperately wanted: kind, loving, nurturing, someone who read to her and let her play softball instead of making her take piano lessons. She told herself she could be happy without children—her aunt and uncle were. They'd married eight years ago and had deemed themselves too old to start a family. But they also had each other. Right now, Aubrey didn't have anyone.

"Do you want any help with the response?" Uncle Dave asked, bringing the conversation back to why she'd come to his office in the first place.

"Not yet, but maybe." She sipped her coffee. "Thanks. I appreciate your pep talks."

"Really? I always worry they're corny or completely off base, since I have zero parental experience."

"That's not true. You've been more of a father to me the last decade than Dad."

He winced. "I know, and I'm sorry. He's an ass," he muttered.

Aubrey grinned. "I couldn't agree more. Are you going to copy what I did last year and plan a trip for when they're in town?"

Uncle Dave's amber eyes twinkled. "Cyndi's been thinking the same thing. How about we do something together? Maybe a trip to southern Oregon. We could take a rafting trip and hit the Shakespeare Festival in Ashland."

Aubrey loved the Shakespeare Festival, and she hadn't been rafting in years. "Sounds great. Tell Aunt Cyndi I'm in."

"We should probably schedule it so that we can at least have dinner with your folks," he said, turning back toward his computer and reaching for his glasses.

Aubrey rolled her eyes and stood. "Fine, be the voice of responsibility." She flashed him a smile. "Thanks, Uncle Dave."

She left his office, closing the door to its previously ajar position. Her mind went to Liam and his extreme sports and the fact that she'd told his mother she'd try to talk to him about them.

She could ask him for southern Oregon rafting recommendations as a way to start the conversation. They could do that, right? Have a conversation as friends?

As friends.

Ha. Had they ever really been friends? Sure, they'd laughed and had a good time together, but they hadn't been friends. Not like she'd been with Alex. He was the reason she knew why Liam jumped out of airplanes and rafted class V rapids, not because Liam had shared it with her.

She ought to tell Emily what she knew, but she couldn't. Alex had confided in her, and even though he was gone, she couldn't break his trust. Furthermore, she didn't want to involve herself in the situation that deeply. Liam had…issues, and he'd been clear about not wanting to open up about them to her. She was happy to help Emily and hopefully put her mind at ease, but she wasn't sure the latter would be possible.

On the other hand, maybe Liam was changing. His staying in Ribbon Ridge for a while and consulting with her on the zoning variance was a complete one-eighty from what he'd been saying since Alex's death. He hadn't wanted anything to do with the project, nor would he consider coming home. What had happened to change his mind?

Aubrey shouldn't care. If she was smart, she'd keep their interactions entirely professional—and she would. Along with asking him about his extreme sports.

Damn, what had she gotten herself into?

She went back to her desk and opened her protein bar. Before jumping back into her brief, she glanced at her phone and saw a text from Stuart: *Dinner tonight?*

Her mind flashed to Liam, and she gritted her teeth. He wasn't going to ruin a perfectly nice guy for her. Stuart was funny and smart and a pretty good candidate for that ten-year plan she'd been thinking about earlier.

She texted him back: *Sure. Just tell me when and where.*

As he texted the details, she blew out a breath and told herself she deserved a guy like Stuart, not a thrill-seeking playboy who maybe had a death wish. Her chest tightened. Did he?

That wasn't her problem. *Liam* wasn't her problem. The sooner she exorcised him from her system, the better.

ZOOMING THROUGH THE sky, head down, arms plastered to his sides, adrenaline pumping through him, Liam was on top of the world. Well, almost. He'd jumped out of the plane at thirteen thousand feet and was currently freefalling toward the earth. Did it get any better than this?

He hadn't jumped since last fall. He'd been busy with winter sports and then he'd broken his wrist and dislocated his shoulder in February. The shoulder still hurt now and again, but the hairline fracture in his wrist had healed very well.

Jumping after a long hiatus was almost like the first time. The surge of adrenaline as he stood at the edge of the plane, the whoosh of air as he launched himself into the sky, the noise rushing in his ears as he fell at 140 miles per hour, and the absolute blissful serenity that came over him just before he pulled the chute.

In fact, he was nearing the point where he'd need to do just that. As a certified skydiver, he could free-fall longer and faster than most, and he always pushed the limit. He checked his altitude, and when he hit 750 feet, he reached behind to the bottom of his pack and pulled out the drogue. He looked up and saw the pilot chute inflate. Slowly, the canopy released, and his speed gradually declined, taking him from super fast to gently drifting. He grabbed the toggles to steer toward his landing. He was home free.

Today, he could see all the way to Ribbon Ridge—a good twenty miles away—and the sight of his hometown made him feel…good. He'd skydived over McMinnville dozens of times, but this was the first time since Alex had died. Of all the places Liam had jumped, this had been Alex's favorite location. Which was why Liam had avoided it.

He pushed down the rising lump in his throat. He hadn't videotaped a jump—or anything else—since then. His GoPro sat unused at his high-rise condo in Denver. What was the point of recording anything? He'd only done it for Alex. He never watched the videos back, preferring to live in the moment, which Alex could never do.

It was odd to think that he owed his love of extreme sports to Alex. It had all started with a skydive during college. Alex had asked Liam if he'd jump out of an airplane and videotape it so that Alex could experience it "with" him. Liam had immediately agreed. He and Alex had always shared a bond—they were identical twins. Except they could never be completely the same. Liam had been born whole and healthy, while Alex had suffered the brunt of being the smallest and sickliest of six. Someone had to get the short end of the stick. And that had been Alex. The brother who looked exactly like Liam but who was a constant reminder of how Fate had chosen one of them over the other.

Liam closed his eyes briefly and floated for a moment. Up here he could forget that pain. Up here he could drift and just be. Down there he'd have to step back into reality.

He opened his eyes and saw the drop zone. He'd be there in just a moment. In years past, he'd feel a rush of excitement to download the video and send it to Alex. But not anymore.

The landing was easy, like stepping off a subway onto the platform. He longed for that rush of excitement he used to feel afterward, that inexplicable high that lasted for days.

But over the last fourteen months, the euphoria that came from his extreme hobbies had dwindled and become almost nonexistent. It was time to push the limits again. Time to find something new.

After repacking his chute, stowing his gear, and changing his clothes, Liam went in search of his friend Rylan Forbes. Rylan owned the skydiving outfit as well as a flight school, and one of his instructors had flown Liam up today. Three years Liam's senior, Rylan had taken Liam on his first jump seven years ago.

Liam walked into the hangar and found Rylan in his office.

Tall and broad-shouldered with dark wavy hair that he typically wore a bit on the long side, Rylan stood and greeted him with a wide smile. "Well, if it isn't my favorite asshole."

Liam grinned in return. "And my favorite prick." They embraced briefly.

"Dude, it's been a while." His brow gathered. "A long while. Where've you been?"

"Around. I dislocated my shoulder a few months ago. Heli-skiing."

Rylan's eyes widened briefly. "I hadn't heard. Be careful, man." He gestured for Liam to sit on a beat-up leather couch against the wall. Rylan folded his large frame back into his squeaky desk chair and turned it away from the desk to face the couch.

Liam dropped onto the couch and leaned back, stretching out his legs and crossing them at the ankles. "You know me."

"Why do you think I said to be careful?" Rylan asked wryly. "And keep in better touch. You suck at that. We used to hang when you were in town, at least a handful of times a year. Or have you been staying away?" He didn't say *since Alex died*, but the unspoken implication hung between them, as Rylan knew all about their extreme-sports situation.

Liam shrugged. Though Rylan was maybe his closest friend, there was still a wall Liam preferred to keep erected between himself and pretty much everyone else. "Somewhat. I've been here a bit, just busy."

He thought back to his visits over the past year— Derek's wedding, his annual trip at the end of summer to run Hood to Coast with the Archer team and to see the Dave Matthews Band, Thanksgiving, the holidays, and a quick weekend visit in February after the heli-skiing accident. Hooking up with Aubrey had been the highlight of each trip until New Year's, when she'd told him she didn't want to see him anymore. If she'd been any other woman, he would've moved on, but seeing her at Evan's wedding had reminded him that she wasn't like any other woman. And he wasn't sure why.

Maybe because she hadn't asked him to make a commitment, which is what practically every other woman had done. Instead, she'd been the one to drop him.

"Still hanging with Whitney Parker? She just finished a flying lesson with Dirk." Dirk was another of Rylan's instructors. Liam thought he had six or seven guys—both flight and skydiving instructors—working for him now.

Instinctively, Liam sat up and prepared to flee, in case she was stalking him. "God no. Too clingy." And now a bona fide enemy of the family. "In fact, I should probably get out of here before she finds me. Real quick, you still BASE jumping?"

Rylan nodded slowly. "Why, you finally ready to give it a go?"

"Definitely. I have enough experience."

"More than," Rylan agreed. "As it happens, I'm taking some guys to an FJC in Idaho in May. You want in?"

First jump course, or FJC, was BASE jump training. Liam had looked into several FJCs, including the one at Perrine Bridge in Idaho. "I do." The spike of adrenaline

Liam had missed following his jump jolted through him. "E-mail me the details."

"You got it." Rylan leaned forward and clapped him on the knee. "Now we have a party!" His smile faded into a grimace as his gaze trailed to his office door. "You're screwed. Parker's coming this way. Sorry, dude."

Bracing himself, Liam stood and left the office. He had to pass her to get to his bike. Maybe he could just wave in passing. Who was he kidding? She was barreling toward him like he was bait on a hook.

"Liam!" she called. "How fun to see you here. Jumping today?"

"Earlier, yeah. Rylan says you're taking flying lessons." He inwardly winced. In trying to be pleasant, he'd inadvertently invited conversation. Sometimes the lasting effect of his mother's lessons on how to be polite and gentlemanly was a pain in the ass.

She smiled warmly and moved closer. "I am. I thought you'd find that impressive. I was always disappointed that you never took me flying." She didn't visibly pout, but he heard it in her voice.

Was she doing this to try to woo him back? "Please tell me you aren't learning to fly planes to impress me, because that would be stupid, Whitney."

She laughed that high-pitched giggle that had maybe once been cute but now grated his nerves. "Of course not, silly. I'm a thrill seeker, you know that. It's one of the things we had in common, remember?"

He remembered. He also knew that he kept his sports life and his love life completely separate. Extreme sports were a constant he relied upon, whereas his love life was more of an extracurricular activity. Wow, put like that, he sounded *really* fucked up.

He ignored her question. "I need to get back to Ribbon Ridge."

"I'll walk with you."

Great.

She turned and fell into step beside him as he strode from the hangar. "So what's on tap next? I heard you dislocated your shoulder heli-skiing. Bummer. I wondered if you'd maybe try BASE jumping."

He flashed her a glance but said nothing.

"Maybe you're not ready, especially since you just recovered."

"I just jumped out of an airplane." He didn't bother suppressing his sarcasm.

She laughed, and his nerves frayed. "True. But then you're Iron Man, aren't you? Right down to the playboy mentality and the rich-boy arrogance." Her gaze flicked to his chest. "And I'm pretty sure you've got a battery-operated heart, if you have one at all."

Ouch. She had his number.

Except he hadn't been much of a playboy since Alex died. Or since he'd started hooking up with Aubrey, depending on how you looked at it. And for the first time, Liam was looking at it. Why hadn't he gone back to his revolving arm candy? Every six months or so he moved on to someone new. Someone who wasn't looking for forever, just a great, mutually satisfying time. Once in a while he wound up with someone like Whitney, but he'd been pretty careful to date women who understood his rules up front.

"Listen, Whitney, I know you're still interested in me, but I told you in the beginning that I wasn't a long-term guy. Then, when we parted ways, I made it clear that our fling was done. End of story."

She frowned. "That means we can't even be friends?" Something dawned in her eyes, something that turned her frown into a half-smile, something that gave him another uneasy feeling. "You have *no* women friends."

Sure he did. He thought of Tori and Sara, but they were his sisters. He could argue they were friends, but it wasn't the same, was it? Damn, he really *didn't* have any women friends. Nevertheless, he wasn't going to invite Whitney Parker to be the first. In fact, he was through trying to be polite. "Your dad is gunning for my family. He's trying to destroy my brother's legacy. You and I are not going to be friends." He quickened his pace toward his bike.

She caught up to him as he picked his helmet up. "Hey, that's not fair. That's my dad, not me."

He cocked his head to the side and stared at her. "You can't be serious. Anyway, even if it wasn't for that clusterfuck, I'm not interested in you romantically *or* as a friend."

She pursed her plump, probably collagen-enhanced lips. "Too bad. If you were, I'd talk to my dad and get him to stop his attack."

Her use of the word *attack* told him all he needed to know. The Parkers were on an offensive, and Liam didn't believe for one minute that she was blameless. "You know, my family thinks this is some jilted boyfriend revenge plot hatched by your dad, but I'm beginning to think you and he are both going after the people who dumped you. Pathetic."

She narrowed her eyes at him. "I wonder what your family would think if they knew you used to date me."

Date? "I wouldn't characterize it that way. Whenever I came to town, we got drunk and screwed. Try to at least be honest about that."

Her jaw hardened. "Whatever. I still think your family's reaction would be interesting."

Interesting was not the word he would use. They'd be pissed, not that Liam could've known that Whitney and her dad were crazies when he'd taken up with her. "What makes you think they don't know?"

"Because you're secretive, and you keep your women separate from your family. I'm not stupid, Liam." She took a deep breath. "I don't want to fight with you. If you don't want to date, fine. I'd be game for the drinking and sex, too. Anytime. And remember, I'd be happy to talk to my dad." She raked him with a lustful stare. "Think about it on your ride home." She turned and walked across the parking lot.

Gritting his teeth, Liam fastened his helmet and climbed onto his bike. All he had to do was sleep with Whitney Parker, and this entire zoning mess could potentially go away. He started up his bike and rode out of the lot onto the highway.

Maybe he should consider it. One night wouldn't do any harm, and it wasn't like he was seeing someone.

Hell, he hadn't even had sex since…shit *November*? With Aubrey.

No, he couldn't do it. He couldn't bone Whitney. Furthermore, he didn't have to. Aubrey was going to kick that high-powered attorney's ass. Even as he thought that, a voice in the back of his head said that Aubrey was relatively green compared to the Parkers' bulldog.

Shit, they'd better win. He couldn't imagine Alex's dream not coming to fruition. No, he wouldn't *let* that happen.

Chapter Five

AUBREY TRUDGED BACK to her house from the next door neighbors' and scowled at her car parked in the driveway. Her brand-new TV was trapped in the back because she couldn't lift it into the house by herself. Uncle Dave was out of town, Stuart was busy for the weekend, and her neighbors, whose door she'd just knocked on, weren't home.

The next name that popped into her head was bad news: Liam.

He was probably busy feeding his extreme-sports habit. Which she'd told Emily she'd talk to him about. She pulled her phone from her back pocket and pulled up his contact information. Before she could change her mind, she texted him and was surprised when his response came immediately.

Sure, I'll be there in about fifteen minutes.

He was coming here. To her house. Where they'd had sex on more than one occasion. *Smart move, Tallinger.*

Why hadn't she texted any of the other Archer men? Dylan would've come over in a heartbeat. As would've Derek. Or Sean. Or Kyle. But no, she'd texted Liam. So she could talk to him about his extreme sports.

Yeah, right.

Aubrey went inside to wait and further deride her foolish choice. A short while later, the sound of a motorcycle drew her to the front bay window. Liam parked his bike in the driveway and whipped off his helmet. His dark hair was tousled in an impossibly sexy way. No one's hair had a right to look that good without effort.

Aubrey crossed through the entryway and did a quick check of her own hair in the mirror in the dining room. A basic high ponytail was hard to screw up, but it was good to see she didn't look as anxious as she felt. What had she been thinking inviting Liam Archer to her house? Alone.

She heard his boots on the porch. Too late to do anything about her panic now, except swallow it. She pasted a smile on her face and opened the door. "Thanks for coming on such short notice."

He pulled his lightweight leather jacket off. "It's no problem. Glad I could help." He flashed her his trademark smile that never failed to melt her knees—as well as points north of them. "Where's this new TV?" he asked.

"It's, uh, in the back of my car."

He dropped his coat on the teak loveseat her aunt and uncle had bought her as a housewarming present two years ago. Aunt Cyndi had said the porch *needed* a loveseat and hadn't wanted Aubrey to have to wait until she could afford one.

Liam walked to the end of the porch. The sound of his footfalls prompted her to look down at his black motorcycle boots. Hot. She let her gaze slowly travel up his worn jeans. Sexy. And briefly linger on his ass. Sexier.

"Why didn't you have it delivered?" he asked as he went down the stairs to the driveway, jarring her from her embarrassing thoughts. She was supposed to be over this guy. Or at least trying to be.

He just made it so damn hard when he looked like that and when she knew how he could make her feel.

"I needed it right away—my TV died last night." Her voice trailed off as she realized she sounded like an addict.

He turned to look at her. "Important television event tonight?"

"Tomorrow, actually. *Game of Thrones* is on, and I'm not watching it on my laptop screen."

His answering laugh heated all of her darkest places. She followed him toward her car, then passed him to open the hatch.

"I didn't know you watched *Game of Thrones*," he said.

She looked at him over her shoulder. "There's a lot you don't know about me."

He stared at her a moment before dragging out the word *true* to twice its normal length. He stepped forward and tugged at the box. "This is going to be heavy. You sure you can manage it with me?"

He sounded legitimately concerned, so she didn't take offense. "I helped the guy at Costco get it in here. I figure I can help you into the house with it."

"I'm sure you can. One thing I do know about you is that you're a kickboxing machine, and you could probably thrash my ass in a sparring match."

"Damn straight."

He cracked a smile. "I'll pull the box out, and you grab the other end. I'll go backward into the house."

"Thanks."

He slid the box out of the car, and she picked up her side. They moved quickly, tilting the TV as they walked up the three steps to her porch. She'd left the front door open, and they brought the box fully vertical to cross over the threshold.

He paused in the entry. "I forgot to ask where we're going."

"To the right. Rather, your left."

He nodded. "Now I vaguely remember where your TV was installed. Did we even watch TV last time I was here?"

His recollection of the night he'd brought takeout during Thanksgiving weekend brought a flush to her cheeks and a rush of lava-hot desire to her core. She was better off not thinking about that.

He went to his left and backed through the small front sitting room into what she called the TV room.

"Go ahead and lean it here against the wall." Using her elbow, she indicated to the right of the television stand, where her old flat-screen still sat.

Together, they lowered the box to the floor.

"Should I not have mentioned the last time I was here?" he asked, reminding her again of that November night when he'd stripped her clothes off with agonizing slowness. Or the bath they'd taken after eating their dinner. Or the midnight snack that had resulted in ice cream being used in ways it most certainly wasn't intended. *Yeah, definitely stop thinking about that.*

"Maybe not." She wanted to ask how the memory affected him or if it even did. She couldn't tell. He was cool, collected, self-assured Liam. The total alpha who never let you see him sweat. Maybe he was a cyborg. She almost laughed. He was physically perfect enough to be a model for one, but he wasn't *quite* a machine. She recalled wearing him out pretty good, particularly with the icecream episode.

Really, Aubrey, knock it off. Think about something benign, something tame. Stuart popped into her head.

Stuart?

Their date earlier in the week had been fun. In the hang-out-with-your-buddy sort of way. The good-night kiss had been nice, but what was *nice* when you'd had earth-shattering? She forced herself to look away from Liam's lips.

Yep, Stuart was definitely tame, whereas Liam was wild and exciting and...*Stop it.*

"Do you have a box cutter or something I can use?" Again he pulled her away from her lurid thoughts.

"Yeah, sure." She went into the kitchen and found a sharp pair of scissors. "Will these do?" She handed them to him, careful not to actually touch him. She did not need physical contact along with the eye candy, thank you very much.

"Yep." He turned and opened the box. "It's so funny you ran out and bought a TV so you wouldn't miss *Game of Thrones*. We watch it at the house after our Sunday dinner—on the big screen in the theater. You should come over tomorrow night and watch it with us. Come for dinner first."

If this were any other guy, she might think he was asking her on a date, but it was Liam. No way was this a date. Still, it was…weird. "I'm not sure what to make of that invitation."

He looked up from pulling the inner packaging off the television. "What do you mean?"

"Liam, you've never invited me to anything."

His brow wrinkled, and his eyes narrowed. "The hell I haven't. You keep forgetting about the Gorge last Labor Day. And New Year's. I texted you."

Neither of those counted. "It's not the same. Your text said, 'I'd like to see you for New Year's'—that's not exactly inviting me to do something. And I was already going to the Gorge. Like you, I go to the concerts every year. We just decided to—" She'd been about to say "hook up," but she didn't want to say that. "Never mind."

He went back to his task. "This is just dinner and *Game of Thrones*. With my entire family."

Meaning it was as far from anything they'd ever done before as it could possibly be. That also meant it was safe. She wouldn't have to worry about being alone with him. Oh, who was she kidding? They hadn't been alone at the winery that day, and they'd flirted themselves into a sexually agitated state.

"I'll think about it. I sort of have my own thing here. I usually watch with my neighbors." If *usually* meant a couple times since she'd lived here, then sure.

"Kyle's cooking dinner, if that helps to sway you. I think he's doing gourmet pizzas."

Kyle was an amazing chef. She'd only sampled his food a handful of times, but it was enough to make her mouth water when she considered what sort of pizzas he'd craft. "You're making it really hard for me to say no, but then that's your specialty."

He looked up at her over his shoulder as he pulled the instructions from the box. He arched one dark, far too sexy eyebrow. "You've demonstrated your ability to give me a hard pass, so I'd argue with your assessment that it's my specialty."

If he only knew how difficult it was to stick to her guns.

"If Kyle's food doesn't persuade you, do it for The Alex. Everyone will want the latest on the zoning, and since you're working on the response brief, there are things to share, right?"

Damn it, he had a point. And he'd brought Alex into it, which only tugged at her guilt. Okay, he'd said *The* Alex, but in her mind they were the same thing, a man and the legacy that was all they had left of him.

"I'll think about it." More like try to think of a solid reason not to go.

"What are we doing with your old TV?" he asked.

"It's dead, according to my uncle." She'd called him last night and described the situation. "So I guess it has to go to the dump?"

Liam tried to turn it on, but it did nothing. "Ned Stark dead or Jon Snow dead? Maybe it can be resurrected."

She laughed at his joke. There were two kinds of dead on *Game of Thrones*—the Ned Stark kind, where there was no question as to whether the character could come back, and the Jon Snow sort, where there was every possibility and perhaps likelihood that death wasn't permanent. "I'm pretty sure it's Ned Stark dead."

"Too bad." He unplugged all of the cables and lifted it. "I can manage this on my own—where do you want me to put it for now?"

"The garage is fine. Here, bring it back through the kitchen to the mudroom, where there's a back door." She led him toward the back of the house, then opened the exterior door for him. "Watch the steps."

He went down first, and she followed to open the door to the side of the garage, which was a separate building at the end of her driveway.

"Just put it here." She indicated the floor.

He set it down, and they went back inside. "Give me a minute to read through these directions." He scanned the booklet that he'd pulled from the box. "You're setting this on the console table, right? No wall mount?"

She shook her head. "It came with something to sit on, didn't it?" She'd specifically looked at TVs that didn't have to be wall mounted.

"Yeah." He set the stand up on the top of the black console she'd bought with the old TV. "You ready to heft this up with me?"

"Sure."

They worked together to position the TV on its base.

"Now for the hard part," he said. "Hooking it up."

She heard "hooking up" at first and told herself to get her mind out of the gutter. "You sure you know what you're doing?"

He sent her a brief glance as he plugged in the TV. "Yep."

She didn't really doubt it. Liam Archer was the sort of person who was good at anything he set his mind to. He was incredibly driven and ambitious. As a result, he made success look easy. Alex had told her lots of things about their sibling dynamics. She knew that Liam and Kyle were competitive and that Liam and Tori were the phenoms, both of them taking their respective careers by storm, and much more. What Alex hadn't told her—what she'd figured out for herself—was that Liam's drive came directly from his need to live a life that was big enough for two people: him and his identical twin.

Just like his extreme sports. He did them for Alex, who'd spent most of his life dependent on oxygen. He'd never be able to jump out of a plane or go windsurfing. But Liam could. And by videotaping every excursion, he took Alex along for the ride. She'd wondered if he would stop when Alex had died, but if anything, he seemed to have stepped up his game, like he had with the heli-skiing.

As she watched him separate the cables, she wondered how the accident had affected him. "What happened when you got hurt a couple months ago?"

"I ended up on a dense trail, and I hit a tree well." He glanced at her. "That's where the snow around the tree is loose and usually covers a void. This was a pretty big void. I went ass over elbow and landed on my shoulder."

She winced. "That had to hurt like hell."

"It did."

"How'd you get off the mountain?"

"There was a guy behind me. He radioed for ski patrol. Took them a while to get to us, but I got down eventually." He didn't pause in his work as he told her the story. His retelling was rather emotionless.

She couldn't believe it hadn't affected him—pissed him off, at least. "That didn't scare the crap out of you?"

He looked up at her then. "You mean enough to not do it again?" His lips curved into a half-smile. "It was a new experience, that's for sure. And generally speaking, I like new experiences."

She crossed her arms and stared at him. "That's absurd. What is there to possibly like about dislocating your shoulder?"

He laughed. "Nothing. But sometimes it's good to remember that I'm fallible."

"What an obnoxiously arrogant thing to say."

He exhaled. "I know, right?"

His tone was weary, maybe even self-deprecating, which wasn't the Liam she knew. He was vigorous and cocksure, always one step ahead. Maybe the accident had rocked him more than he realized. Or maybe he did realize it. "Are you taking things a bit easier, then? Maybe just sticking to your motorcycle?" Like that wasn't dangerous enough.

He plugged in the last cable. "I had to take it easy while I healed, but I'm good now." He rotated his shoulder to demonstrate. "I powered through physical therapy like a champion."

"Of course you did," she muttered. He did everything like a champion, damn him.

He flicked her a curious glance but didn't say anything. At least not about her snarky comment. "I did a jump the other day, so I'd say I'm back to normal."

He'd been skydiving already? "Maybe you should take it easy for a while. As you so accurately put it, you aren't infallible."

"You worried about me?"

"As someone who cares about your family, yes. You should care about them, too. They worry."

His brow furrowed. "Did someone say something?"

Yikes. She was not going to throw his mom under the bus. "No. I'm just...I just care."

His features relaxed. "That's good to know." He turned the TV on and looked around. "Remote?"

She found it on the end table next to the couch and handed it to him.

He flicked through some channels. Naturally, he'd hooked it up perfectly.

"Were you a cable guy in a past life?"

He laughed. "I didn't actually hook up your cable, just connected the box to the TV. It's not that hard."

Easy for him to say. Aubrey was pretty good with electronics but admitted that she found computers easier to deal with than things like televisions or appliances. God forbid her dishwasher crapped out.

He turned the TV off. "I guess my work here is done." Did he sound disappointed?

She couldn't invite him to stay. She *wouldn't*. "Yep. Thanks again."

He handed her back the remote, and this time his fingers grazed her palm. Her entire body jolted with lust. "Why don't you come skydiving with me? You'd have a great time."

Wait, what? He was inviting her to do something else with him?

"Falling isn't really my thing." She suppressed a shudder. When she thought of him free-falling from ten thousand feet or however high up they went, she felt queasy.

"Okay, how about a ride on my bike instead? That's not high, and there's no falling."

"There is if you crash!" She smiled as she said this, realizing she sounded paranoid and doing it on purpose.

He laughed. "I won't. I'll take it easy with you on board. I would hate myself if you got hurt." His blue-gray gaze pierced into hers, and the pull to invite him to stay for dinner—hell, the night—was almost overwhelming.

"I'll think about it." She set the remote back on the table. "You're full of surprising invitations today." This was a thoughtful, considerate Liam—the man she'd spent Labor Day weekend with.

"Maybe I'm just looking for the right one to get you to say yes."

Damn, he was saying all the right things. Things that were weakening her resolve when it came to keeping him in the Friend Zone. Friends? She'd already decided they weren't friends, but today sure felt like it.

He broke the devastating eye contact and went to the porch, where he picked up his coat. The day was warm, but he shrugged it on because it was likely chillier as he rode his bike. That, and it provided protection, she supposed. Not that he would fall.

"I'll come tomorrow night. Will that satisfy you?" She hadn't meant the question to sound provocative, and maybe it only did to her ears.

His gaze did a slow perusal of her from head to toe. Nope, it had sounded provocative to him, too. "If you think that would satisfy me, you don't know me at all, sweetheart."

She rolled her eyes. "Knock it off. Flirting will get you nowhere." That was a bald-faced lie, but she wasn't going to succumb. She didn't want to be his Ribbon Ridge girl. She wanted more than that, and he wasn't the one who would give it to her.

He walked to the end of the porch, and she couldn't keep herself from appreciating the view again. He went down the stairs to the driveway and climbed onto his bike, picking up the helmet first. "You sure you don't want to come for a ride?"

She'd followed him to the end of the porch but stayed at the top of the stairs. She crossed her arms and leaned against the post. "I don't see a helmet."

He glanced at the small seat behind where he was perched. "You have a point. I'll have to rectify that."

"Don't, because then I won't have an excuse." And she needed an excuse.

His eyes sparkled as his lips curved into a seductive smile. "I'll remember that." He gave her a full-on toe-curling grin before putting his helmet on.

As she watched him go, she had the sense she was still in way over her head, despite her valiant efforts to swim to shore.

LIAM STEPPED INTO the kitchen from the back hall. He'd just showered after taking an afternoon bicycle ride with Dad. It was the one sport at which Dad could easily smoke any of his children, but then he'd been cycling since college. Liam credited his Dad's dedication to and love of the sport as having instilled a sense of athleticism and physical drive in his kids.

"There you are," Dad said as Liam walked toward the beer bar, where Dad was lording over the tap as usual. "Did I wear you out?"

"It'll take more than eighteen miles to wear me out. I run marathons, remember?"

"That's crap," Tori said, joining them. "When's the last time you ran an actual marathon?" Tori was the runner in the family, but Liam kept up pretty good.

"Just because I don't do as many races as you doesn't mean I can't. I'm busy doing other stuff."

She arched a brow at him as she raised her pint glass. "Like trying to kill yourself jumping out of airplanes?"

Liam thought of his conversation with Aubrey yesterday. He began to doubt Aubrey's response that no one had talked to her about his hobbies. But he didn't care. It wasn't any of their business. Consequently, he ignored

Tori's question—not that it was a legitimate question instead of a gibe. He looked at Dad behind the bar. "What's on tap?"

"My newest IPA. It's a red." He pulled a pint and handed it to Liam. "Let me know what you think."

Liam sampled the brew and clacked the glass down onto the granite counter. "So freaking good. When the hell are you going to bottle this?"

Dad shrugged. "You know that's never been my priority."

"Wait, that wasn't a flat no." Liam looked at Tori. "You heard that, right?"

She nodded. "I did. Dad, are you actually thinking about it?"

Dad gave them both his best fatherly stare. "No comment."

Tori grinned and looked between Dad and Liam. "First Liam comes home, and now Dad's considering bottling. I'm afraid to look outside for fear I might see the four riders of the apocalypse that Kyle glimpsed last weekend."

"Nope, just Aubrey," Derek said as he guided Aubrey toward the bar. "I found her outside loitering by the back door."

She smiled a bit tentatively. "I wasn't sure if I should come in that way. Your mom has invited me to, but…I don't know, it just feels weird to let myself in."

"It shouldn't. You ought to be a de facto Archer, like Derek here," Tori said.

Aubrey looked surprised and maybe a bit horrified. "Well, maybe not like Derek," she said. "He's actually a member of your family and has been for at least a decade, right?"

"That's about right," Derek said. "Someone has to bring some normalcy to this crazy group."

Tori snorted. "You bring as much crazy to the table as any of us."

"True." Derek laughed. "It's what makes me fit in."

Aubrey looked between them. "Another reason I can't join the club. I'm afraid I don't have any crazy to add. I'm just boring Aubrey."

"I wouldn't call you boring," Liam said softly. "I call BS. Everyone has crazy. You're just very good at hiding it." He looked at her intently, as if he could discern the secrets he was sure she had. Why did he suddenly want to know them? And everything else about her?

"Dish up!" Kyle called from the other side of the kitchen. "Show's on in thirty!"

Everyone headed over to the other bar, where several pizzas were laid out. Everyone except Dad, who looked at Aubrey. "Can I get you a beer? It's an IPA. Red, to be specific." He smiled. "Like your hair."

Like her hair. Liam loved her hair. When he'd first met her, it had been shorter, but he liked its current length. He imagined it splayed over his ivory sheets and started to sport wood. *Get a grip, Archer. Your dad is right there.*

"I love IPA, thanks," she said. She tugged her light raincoat off. "Can I hang this somewhere?"

Liam took it from her fingers. "I've got it." He went to the hallway where there were hooks, most of which were marked with one of the Archer kids' names. He hung it on his hook.

When he returned to the kitchen, Aubrey and Dad had joined the others, who were serving up the varieties of pizza. There was barbecued chicken, a pesto base with chicken, a meat-lovers, a veggie-lovers, and a couple of what Dylan was currently calling "foo-foo" recipes.

"Goat cheese is foo-foo?" Sara asked her fiancé. "I love goat cheese."

"And you are completely foo-foo. I wouldn't have you any other way." Dylan smiled down at her before giving her a fast kiss.

Being home had been eye-opening for Liam. He hadn't realized how pretty much everyone in the family was in love and had settled down. Only he and Hayden were single, and Hayden had a girlfriend in France, so really it was only Liam. It made him feel…strange.

He'd never wanted a long-term relationship. He didn't like the sense of having to be somewhere or do something with someone. He didn't want to have to plan his holidays or sports trips around someone else. Some—including his family—might say it sounded lonely, but he was happy. Or he had been until Alex had decided to pull the biggest dick move ever and off himself. Thinking of that still made Liam so angry. He ought to have progressed to another stage of grief, and he had on occasion, but mostly he was just mad.

He waited until everyone had their pizza and had sat at the table, leaving just him and Kyle, who usually served himself last.

"If Evan and Alaina were back from their honeymoon, we'd have to sit at the bar here," Kyle said as he tossed a couple of pieces onto his plate.

Liam looked at the nearly full table. There were two open chairs—one next to Maggie, which was presumably for Kyle, and one next to Aubrey. Had his family paired them off? He ought to find that annoying—he hated when they made assumptions about him—but he found it oddly nice. Which was stupid because they absolutely were *not* paired off. Still, had someone picked up on their fling? He hadn't thought so. Hell, for months after Alex's death, everyone had been pretty sure Liam despised Aubrey. He'd certainly been awful enough to her at the reading of the trust.

But all that had changed later that day when he'd gone to her office. Yeah, he'd been pissed all right. That hadn't stopped him from having the most spontaneous and, frankly, exciting sex of his entire life.

"Hey, I need to talk to you," Kyle said in a low voice. "That gal you were kissing last week. I know who she is." The low pitch of his blond brows and the tight set of his mouth told Liam exactly what he thought of it, too.

"I wasn't kissing her."

Kyle blinked at him. "I was there, dude."

"She kissed me. Big difference."

"So you don't have a thing with Whitney Parker? Because that would be…Dude, I don't even know how to characterize it. Bad form, for sure."

Liam could simply confirm that he didn't have a thing with Whitney—at least not currently—and that would be the end of the conversation. For now. What if Whitney decided to tell all? She'd already indicated she could be bought—rather, seduced—into complicity. He could see her blabbing their past fling just to be a pain in his ass.

He took a deep breath and hoped he didn't regret this. He couldn't believe he was going to fess up to Kyle, of all people. "We used to hook up. Before…before Alex died."

Kyle's eyes widened. "Seriously?"

Liam kept his voice low. He'd need to come clean with everyone, but not right now over dinner. And not with Aubrey sitting over there casting him intermittent glances that made him wonder what she was thinking. He turned his gaze from her, as if that simple movement could stave off temptation. It couldn't.

He looked at Kyle, who watched him intently. "Whenever I was in Ribbon Ridge, we got together. It wasn't serious. She got clingy, so I ended it."

"What were you doing with her last week, then?" Kyle asked.

Liam rolled his eyes. "She's still clingy, if you want to know. I went to Ruckus and had a few drinks. She drove me home."

Kyle picked up a piece of pizza. "And laid one on you."

"Like I said, clingy. It's not a big deal. Or a problem." Liam didn't like the look of uncertainty in Kyle's blue-green eyes. "I'll tell everyone, okay?"

Kyle swallowed. "You should. It's just good for everyone to be on the same page. You said she's clingy. Does that mean she's hung up? Like maybe her dad's not the only one who feels scorned?"

Liam picked up his plate and his beer. "How the hell should I know what's going on in her twisted head?" Why didn't he just say that he'd wondered the same thing? Because that would make it more true, and he didn't want to think that he was somehow responsible for this bullshit and the trouble it was causing everyone. In fact, the more he thought about it, the more pissed off he got.

Liam took his dinner and went to sit next to Aubrey.

She leaned over and whispered, "Everything all right?"

"Fine."

"Didn't look like it. You and Kyle aren't arguing again, are you? I thought you two were finally getting along."

He peered at her. "When did you become so involved in my family?"

Her eyes widened briefly before she turned her head to her plate. "Sorry."

Shit, he was a jerk. Kyle had riled him up. No, he couldn't blame it on Kyle. Whitney riled him up. Whitney and her dad and their fucked-up vendetta. "No, I'm sorry. Really, everything's fine."

She didn't look at him. "Sure."

He gritted his teeth and ate his pizza. He also polished off his beer and stood up to get another.

"Would you mind pulling a pitcher?" Dad asked as Liam went to the bar.

"Make that two," Derek called.

Liam nodded. As he pulled the tap and filled the pitchers, he couldn't shake the sense of irritation that his conversation with Kyle had wrought. He hated that

Whitney was trying to manipulate him. He refused to be managed.

When both pitchers were full he carried them back to the table, setting one at each end. "Hey, I need to tell you all something."

Kyle's head snapped up, and Liam gave him a subtle nod. Kyle nodded back, and his gaze was both approving and supportive. This brotherly...camaraderie between them was different. Liam had always felt it with Alex, but they'd been identical twins. Their bond was special. He hadn't thought he could share that with his other siblings, but maybe he was wrong.

"Listen, about the zoning problem with the Parkers..."

"You mean Russ Parker," Dad said darkly, his mouth hardening with anger.

"I mean Russ and his daughter, Whitney. She and I used to, uh, we used to see each other." He glanced at Aubrey to see her reaction, but she kept her head down. Damn it, he wanted her to look at him so he could tell her—nonverbally—that Whitney didn't mean anything.

He did? What did he care what Aubrey thought?

Because he'd just intimated that he and Whitney had dated, which is more than what he'd done with Aubrey. He supposed he should've just said they'd been fuck buddies, but he couldn't bring himself to articulate that in front of his parents.

He felt like the biggest ass. Why *hadn't* he dated Aubrey? Because she lived here in Ribbon Ridge, where he never planned to live again, and his home was in Denver. It wasn't like she could pick up and move. One, she wasn't licensed to practice law in Colorado, and two, that promised something he wasn't prepared to offer: permanence or at least longevity.

"When was this?" Mom asked.

"A couple of years ago. Before Alex died. I broke things off with her that Christmas." Why did it feel like his life had two distinct parts now? Before Alex's death and after. They had two very specific feelings. In the first, he'd been more carefree. Now he was burdened. No, that wasn't exactly true. He'd always felt burdened. Guilty.

Stop it, he told himself. He wasn't going down that path. Not today. Not ever again. Alex's death had at least relieved him of that weight.

"You think she's behind this?" Tori asked, sitting back in her chair.

Everyone was staring at him, he realized. Everyone but Aubrey. Why had he done this now? Why hadn't he thought to tell her first? Alone, when he could've explained things a little bit better. She deserved that.

"Not entirely, but I don't think she's blameless. She intimated that I could maybe make this problem go away if I get back with her." He tried to make it sound like what it was—a meaningless hook-up without saying that exactly. Damn it, this entire conversation was making him feel decidedly unpleasant. Dirty even.

"Yikes." Kyle took a drink of beer. "None of us want you to do that, bro."

There were answering nods and comments.

Dylan shook his head, grimacing. "She sounds like a piece of work."

Tori made a distasteful expression, her lips twisting. "I think I have a sports bra from her company. I'm tossing that in the garbage as soon as I get home."

"I might have one, too," Sara said. "Let's burn them."

"I'll light the fire," Liam said.

Aubrey glanced at him finally, but her eyes were clear. Absolutely devoid of emotion. Which likely meant she was pissed. Or hurt. Or both.

"Anyway, that's it." Liam sat down.

Conversation picked back up. Some people talked about the zoning, but Liam didn't join in. He tipped his head toward Aubrey. "I should've told you in private."

She shrugged, keeping her focus on her dinner. "Why? It's not really my business. I mean, not beyond the zoning, but the Parkers' reasons for appealing don't really matter."

"Can't you argue that their appeal is frivolous or something?"

"Maybe, but I doubt the board is going to care whether Russ and Whitney are scorned lovers." She picked up her beer. "Don't worry about it."

"I wasn't dating her," he said, wishing she'd turn her head to look at him.

She finally cocked her head, and he caught the fire in her eyes. "You were just hooking up, right? Like you did with me. No need to explain. That's your MO."

Yes, it was. And what had been his intent? *Don't worry, she didn't mean any more to me than you did, which is to say, you both meant nothing.*

"Actually, it wasn't like with you," Liam said. "I never once sought her out. When she heard I was in town, she called me."

She turned her head, and her gaze was incredulous. "Is that supposed to make me feel better?"

Chloe, maybe the biggest *Game of Thrones* fan in the room, jumped up from her chair. "Hey, it's time to watch the show!"

All heads turned to the clock on the wall, and nearly every chair moved back from the table in unison.

Sean reached for one of the pitchers. "Refill time."

Everyone collected their drinks and filtered downstairs.

Liam touched Aubrey's arm. "Hey, are you mad at me?"

She blinked. "Should I be?"

"I might be, if I were you."

She smiled, but it was deceptively serene. "Well, you're not me. There's a reason I broke things off with you, Liam. I'm a nice girl with simple dreams. You're a player seeking world domination. What you do doesn't affect me. I'm going down to watch the show." She turned and left the kitchen.

He followed but knew he'd have to watch the show again later, because he wasn't going to be able to focus while his mind was wrapped up with what she'd said. She *was* a nice girl, but he doubted her dreams were simple. She was far too intelligent, too fun-loving, too dynamic. But he really didn't know. He'd never bothered to ask what her dreams were. Now that he wanted to know, he doubted she would tell him.

Chapter Six

AUBREY SOMEHOW MANAGED to lose herself in the show. She'd been so angry at the start. And *that* made her mad. She didn't want to feel betrayed or jealous or anything else to do with Liam. That's why she'd broken things off—so she wouldn't feel those things.

Ugh. Get over it already, she told herself.

"I'm so glad you came tonight," Sara told her as they all stood up from the theater seats.

Aubrey had strategically positioned herself between Sara and Chloe so that she wouldn't have to sit by Liam. She wasn't sure where he'd sat or if he'd even come down to watch.

"I am, too," Aubrey said. "Thanks for having me."

Chloe touched her arm. "Come back next week. You can't beat watching it on that screen."

No, she couldn't. The television she'd bought was huge compared to what she'd had, but this was like watching it in a legitimate movie theater.

"Anyone want to hit the wine cellar?" Kyle asked the room at large.

"Yeah, stay," Chloe said to Aubrey.

"Thanks, but I need to get home. I have to get up early for work. I have a short trial this week, plus I need to work on the zoning brief." They'd talked about it briefly at the table while Liam and Kyle had been having their mysterious conversation. Aubrey thought she'd figured it out—they'd been talking about Whitney Parker, and that's why Liam had said something. He'd only spilled the beans because he'd had to. Kyle had likely found him out.

And that only made her angrier.

Sara exhaled. "That makes sense."

Tori, who'd been sitting in front of them, stood and turned to join the conversation. "What makes sense?"

"Aubrey's passing on the wine cellar because she has to get up early to work on the zoning brief," Sara explained.

"Yes she does!" Tori laughed. "No pressure."

Aubrey shook her head with a smile. "None at all."

"We should have a girls' night," Chloe suggested, looking between them. "Maggie," she called down to the other side of Sean.

Maggie stepped around Sean to stand beside Tori. "What's up?"

"We're planning a girls' night," Chloe said. "Sometime this week?"

Aubrey crossed her arms. "I don't know. I have a lot going on at work." She thought through her schedule. "Maybe Thursday?"

"I'm in," Maggie said, smiling.

"Me, too," Chloe said.

"Me, three," Sara chimed.

Tori nodded. "Sounds great. This will be fun." She grinned. "I've never seen you let your hair down, Aubrey. Do you even do that?"

"Sure." It had been a while. Aubrey's closest girlfriends were from college, and they didn't live nearby. One was in Vancouver, Washington, and the others lived in the bay area. They tried to get together at least once a year, but two of them were married now and one of the two had a baby, so it had become more difficult to schedule things. Even so, she and her Vancouver pal did the Dave Matthews Band thing every Labor Day.

That made her think of last year and how she'd ditched her friend in order to go off with Liam. Felicia hadn't minded, but Aubrey had still apologized profusely. To which Felicia had scoffed. She'd said it was clear Aubrey was smitten and that she deserved it. She'd practically shoved Aubrey out of their tent at the campground. Aubrey had wondered if Felicia had been hooking up with someone of her own. Those weekends were pretty wild and crazy.

"I definitely let my hair down. You'd be surprised."

Tori rubbed her hands together. "Oooh, sounds like a good story. I can't wait until Thursday."

Chloe smiled slyly. "A drinking game might be in order."

Everyone laughed.

"Too bad Alaina's still on her honeymoon," Maggie said. "I bet her stories would be epic!"

Aubrey nodded. "I'm sure. Okay, I'm outta here. See you guys Thursday." Chloe moved aside so she could get by.

On her way out of the theater, Aubrey made a point of thanking Emily and Rob for having her over.

"I'm just glad you finally used the back door," Emily said, giving her a brief hug. "You're welcome anytime, dear."

Aubrey thanked her again, then made her way upstairs. She was quite proud of herself for not looking for Liam. Then she nearly walked straight into him in the back hallway when she went to grab her jacket.

"There you are," he said, his face inscrutable.

"What, were you waiting for me?" She grabbed her coat and pulled it on. "I'm leaving. Good night."

She turned and left before he could stop her. But he just followed her.

"Yes, I was waiting for you. I don't believe that you don't care about me and Whitney. I really am sorry for how I told you."

She threw him a glare over her shoulder as she stalked to her car. "I told you it doesn't matter."

Before she could open the door, he pinned her against the car. Not with his body, but by standing close enough that she couldn't open the door without making physical contact with him. And that would be bad.

It had been drizzling earlier when she'd arrived, but it was dry now. It was also quite chilly. She zipped up her jacket and fished her keys from her pocket to unlock the door with the remote.

"It matters to me. I don't like thinking I've upset you."

"Are you sure you just don't hate the fact that I dumped you?"

He cracked a smile. "Maybe." He sobered almost instantly. "I wanted to ask you about what you said yesterday. You said I made it hard to say no. Were you...reluctant when we were together last year? If I forced you in any way or made you uncomfortable..." He ran his hand through his thick hair, tousling the dark waves. "Jesus, Aubrey—"

As crazy as he made her, she hated that he'd gotten the wrong idea. In fact, she preferred to look back on their time together with fondness and wanted him to do the same. "You didn't. I wanted everything that happened. And if I were interested in Mr. Right Now instead of finding Mr. Right, I'd probably invite you back to my place."

His eyes sparked, and her belly fired in response. "What's wrong with Mr. Right Now? I love living in the moment."

She'd loved living in the moment, too—with him. She'd never been with a more intoxicating person. He made her feel beautiful and alive and special. He was so full of vitality and confidence that when he shined his light on you, it made everything brighter. When they'd spent Labor Day weekend together, he'd done all of these little things for her—making sure she was hydrated because it was hot, arranging for her to get a shower in his friend's RV, scoring her first-ever spot on the rail so that the band had been literally in her face. But she had to think he made all of his women feel that way. That's why he was so damned alluring.

"I love living in the moment, too, but I'd rather do it with someone who can give me a lifetime of moments." A cold breeze rustled her hair and chilled her to the bone. She shivered.

He moved closer. "You're cold. Can I?" He started to put his arms around her.

She should say no. She should jump in her car and drive away as fast as she could. Instead, she just stood there, neither accepting nor declining his embrace.

He enfolded her in his arms. He wasn't wearing a coat, but he still felt warm. His chest was solid against hers as he rested his jaw alongside her hairline. "Why are you in such a hurry to find Mr. Right? We could have a good time."

They could. And she'd be broken by the end of it because he could be everything she wanted, even if he didn't realize it yet. He was successful, smart, kind in the ways that mattered, and he loved his family. In fact, he was defined by his family. All of the Archers were. They were fiercely competitive, loyal, and above all loving. How could she not want to be a part of that? A part of him?

She kept her head down and stared at a panel on the garage door several feet away. "I'm not in a hurry, but while I'm having a good time with someone like you, Mr. Right could be right in front of me."

"Like Stuart," he said softly, his breath warm against her skin.

No, not like Stuart. She'd bet he wasn't Mr. Right. But then, neither was Liam. She tipped her head up, and their gazes connected. The night was cold, but she didn't feel it just then. All she felt was the heat of his stare and the need in her soul. A need he couldn't fulfill.

He pulled away. "I get it. Stuart's a lucky guy."

No, Stuart was probably going to get his hopes dashed, but she didn't want to think about that right now.

"Good night, Liam." She climbed into her car and drove away. Though she didn't look, she knew he watched her go.

LIAM SPENT MOST of Monday closeted in his bedroom, focused on his real-estate business in Denver. He owned several commercial buildings and was in the process of buying another. Unfortunately, they'd discovered a problem with the structure, and Liam was weighing whether to go through with it. With its prime location, the space could be a huge moneymaker in the future, but if the mold they'd found beneath the floorboards of the former gym was toxic, it would be a money pit. For now, he'd put the deal on hold while they awaited the findings on the mold.

On Tuesday, he decided it was past time to visit the Archer Enterprises headquarters, where Dad, Derek, Evan, and even Kyle worked. That Kyle had come home a year ago and taken over as COO still stumped Liam. He hadn't thought Kyle had it in him to not just do the job but commit to it. Granted, it was temporary, but Kyle had acquitted himself well, and though he'd once been the outsider, the black sheep, Liam began to realize that role was now his.

Maybe he wasn't a black sheep exactly, but he was definitely an outsider. It was a role he'd cultivated and been quite content with. But now that he was home, he felt the distance in a way he never had—it was more than just mileage, like when he was in Denver and everyone was here. He was here now, and he still sensed the separation. They were all engaged to be married, all a part of something—of the family—in ways that he wasn't.

He parked his bike at the building and marveled at what his father had built. Well, his father and his father's father and his grandfather's father on down to the founding father of Ribbon Ridge. They'd all been real-estate tycoons in their own right. All but Dad, who was far happier brewing beer. He'd kept up the real-estate side of the business after his younger brother had up and left town, but he hadn't really grown it like Liam would've done.

Liam carried his helmet into the building with him. He hadn't been here in years. Since before Alex had died. There it was again, measuring everything in befores and afters.

He shook his head as he climbed the staircase up to the second floor, where the executive offices were located. It was lunchtime, so he wasn't surprised to see that Dad's secretary wasn't at her desk. The other admin desk was occupied by a young man who was probably right out of college.

"Hi, is anyone around?" Liam asked.

The guy cocked his head to the side. "Besides me, you mean?"

Liam chuckled. "Yeah, besides you. Sorry, I'm Liam Archer."

The kid's eyes widened, and he shot out of his chair. "Oh! Sorry, I didn't realize. I'm just a temp."

Liam knew they'd lost Derek and Kyle's former assistant last summer, but he hadn't realized they hadn't hired a permanent replacement. He tried not to think of the entire situation, because it made his blood boil. The woman had sold Alex the drugs he'd used to commit suicide and was now serving time for drug dealing. Kyle had found her out. It was yet another way in which Kyle had more than redeemed himself, while Liam stayed away.

Maybe his anger should be directed at himself as much as anyone else. Sure, why not? He'd lived with guilt and a varying degree of self-loathing his entire life. Why stop now?

"It's fine," Liam said. "I'm just going to wander around a bit." He glanced toward his dad's closed office door and Kyle's closed office door. The next door, Derek's, was open. Liam walked over to it and looked inside. Empty.

He continued along the corridor, passing a long conference room with glass walls and a spectacular view over the valley. He had to admit he missed the way Ribbon Ridge looked. Colorado was beautiful and suited his lifestyle, but so did Oregon, which was equally, if not more, breathtaking.

He passed the conference room and came to another closed office door. The name beside it read Evan Archer, Chief Creative Officer. That had been Alex's job. Evan had secretly obtained it last fall while posing as an independent contracting firm. He hadn't wanted to apply as himself for fear the family wouldn't accept him as a creative professional. Plus, he hadn't wanted to usurp Alex's position.

Liam understood that fear, and an irrational part of him wished Evan hadn't usurped it. This was Alex's job, Alex's *place*. But hadn't Alex surrendered any claims when he'd killed himself?

He absolutely had.

The familiar anger roiled in Liam's belly. He opened the door and stepped inside. The only thing that was the same was the view. Could Liam blame Evan for changing the furniture? No. Just like he couldn't blame him for taking the job, for *wanting* the job. From everything he'd seen and heard, he was great at it. Better even than Alex had been. A sharp pain, like regret, cut through Liam's anger.

He moved inside and noted the tidy, organized desk. There was one picture of a smiling Evan and Alaina. They stood together at a winery up in the hills, with the panorama of the valley behind them. Liam felt a surge of joy and pride for Evan that he'd found happiness and connection. He'd found his place.

"Hey, Liam." Dad's voice sliced into his thoughts, and Liam was grateful for the interruption. Being home had turned him into a maudlin son of a bitch. "Troy said you were here. What brings you by?"

Liam turned, his helmet tucked under his arm. "Just thought I should come in and check things out. You wanted me to, right?" Dad had urged him to stop in as soon as he'd announced he was hanging out in Ribbon Ridge for a while.

Dad nodded. "Of course. I'm glad you did. You get things sorted out back in Denver?"

He'd told Dad about the mold problem last night at dinner. "Not yet. I had to order some testing this morning. We'll see what happens." He felt strangely removed from the whole project, which was odd. He was usually right in the thick of everything. He loved his job, thrived on solving problems and closing major deals. Maybe it was just because he was so far away. Maybe he'd made a mistake in deciding to stay. He could still help with the zoning from Denver. In this day and age, just about everything could be done remotely.

"Is this weird?" Dad's quiet question startled him, but Liam knew exactly what he meant.

"The office looks different. But it looks good. It almost seems like things are the way they're supposed to be." His throat felt tight, and he wished he hadn't said that out loud.

"I know what you mean." Dad coughed. "The more things settle into a new rhythm, the more helpless I feel. Like what was the point if he wasn't going to be here? Why did he survive when you were all born, if he really wasn't meant to be?"

Liam stared at his dad. They didn't talk about this sort of thing. Raw feelings and true confessions weren't his forte. But he also couldn't walk away, not when he felt the same sense of unease, of frustration. "Because he *was* meant to be. *He's* the one who decided he wasn't."

"And yet you can't deny the wonderful things it's brought about. Sara came home and found Dylan, Kyle came home and, geez, completely turned his life around. I can't imagine where he'd be right now if Alex's death hadn't triggered him to make some changes." Dad walked over to the window and looked out, his back to Liam. "I do blame him for Tori. She was so messed up last year. Alex completely derailed her life." Dad turned. "Did he do the same to you? I don't know…I have no idea how you've coped with any of it. You haven't been here. You haven't said."

"I…I've managed." That was all Liam could say. The guilt, the anger…Those were things he couldn't share. And may never.

Dad put his hands in his pockets. "Did you know Alex called your sister the night before he did it? That was when she'd married Sean in Vegas."

Such shit timing for them. "Tori told me." What no one knew—and never would—was that Alex had called Liam, too. Only Liam had answered. That conversation was burned into his brain, and yet he'd kept himself from thinking of it for going on fourteen months now. He wasn't going to dredge it up.

Dad exhaled and looked at the floor. "She felt so guilty for missing the call. I can't imagine. Well, yes I can." He looked up, and there was torment in his gaze—a torment Liam knew only too well. "We all feel guilty. I know I do. But we can't. You were right to be angry with him. I was, too, for a long time. Sometimes I still am, but I'm learning to forgive. Have you?"

Forgive? That word hadn't even entered Liam's mind until this moment. "I'll be honest, Dad, I try not to think about it. What's the point?"

Dad frowned. "I did that, too. It drove a wedge between your mother and me. She was overwhelmed with grief, while I just pushed it away. You have to deal with it, son."

Liam transferred his helmet to his other arm and glanced at the ceiling. "I have. But you know me. I keep my eye on the prize."

Dad's frown only deepened. "Yes, I know. That's why I brought this up. You don't spend time on relationships. Not with women, not with your family. Yet, here you are, and I wondered if you might be ready for a change. Like your siblings."

Where was this going? "Do you have something specific you want to talk to me about?"

Dad pulled his hands from his pockets and took a couple of steps forward. "I do. I've always held out hope you might come back some day, that you might take over the real-estate portion of the business."

"I've never wanted it, not when you talked to me about it after college and not now." What he said was true, but Liam couldn't deny that for the first time, there was an appeal. Doing what he loved here in Ribbon Ridge. Taking this century-plus-old family business and turning it into something really phenomenal. He'd wanted to build something from nothing—that's why he'd said no after college. But he'd done that. Maybe it was time to shift his focus, take on a new challenge.

Dad sighed. "I know. I just hoped…The real estate has never been my passion. It's yours. If Alex's death gave me anything positive it was the desire to simplify my life and focus on the things that matter to me most."

Liam read between the lines. "You want to step back from Archer?"

"Maybe." Dad shrugged. "I'm mulling the bottling business—but don't say anything to anyone else yet. I don't want to do the day-to-day anymore. Derek can do it." He looked at Liam intently. "That won't bother you, will it?"

Liam shook his head. "Not at all. Derek's brilliant, and he'll do a great job."

"But he's not a real-estate guy," Dad said. "You could run that entire division. Kyle's going to leave as soon as the restaurant is ready to open. Plus, he's got this burgeoning career as a celebrity chef, it seems."

Liam had picked up on that. He'd won a competitive cooking show, and Sean was producing a series about Kyle's restaurant with Kyle starring. The other day, Kyle had mentioned guest hosting some other cooking show. He was ideally suited for all of that with his effortless charm and approachability. Everyone liked Kyle, and they liked his food even more.

"What about Hayden?" Liam asked. Interning at the winery in France had been a dream come true for him. His internship would be over in July, and he hadn't shared his future plans.

"I don't know what he's going to do, but I can't see him returning to Archer, even if he does come home. He was great at his job, but I'm not sure he was ever truly happy. I think he only stayed because no one else did—to be here for me."

Liam wanted to take issue with that. He wasn't going to feel guilty for pursuing his career and his goals because Hayden hadn't had the balls to go after his. Wait, is that how Liam really felt? That wasn't fair of him.

"Was that important to you?" Liam asked softly, hating this conversation. Dad had been right when he'd said that Liam didn't spend time on relationships. Too complicated and hard to manage. He preferred things he could control. "Did you need him to stay?"

"Need?" Dad shook his head. "No. But I wanted him to. I wanted all of you to stay. We're a family and the only Archers left in Ribbon Ridge. I'd hate to see us die out."

Liam laughed at that. "Uh, you had *seven* kids. I think you single-handedly saw to it that we wouldn't."

Dad joined in his laughter. "And there's already a grandkid on the way." His eyes widened briefly, and he whistled between his teeth. "I still can't get my head around that. And I can't believe it's Evan, of all people. My money was on Tori."

"I think everyone's money was on Tori. She was always the little mother, and she did get married first."

"Well, the only thing that would surprise me more than Evan becoming the first parent would be if you settled down," Dad said wryly.

"Ha, don't count on it."

Dad came forward and clapped him on the shoulder. "I know. So that's a no on coming back and overseeing real estate?"

Liam hated disappointing his dad, but he'd chosen to leave Ribbon Ridge, and he hadn't looked back. "That's a no."

Dad exhaled softly and nodded. He made to leave, but Liam stopped him. "Dad, thanks. You've always been supportive and understanding, and I appreciate it."

"Of course, son." Dad flashed him a smile, then left.

Liam looked around the office and was pleased to find the sense of discomfort had gone. This was Evan's place now. He walked out and closed the door behind him.

For some reason, Dad's offer resonated in Liam's brain. It was tempting, he had to admit, but he couldn't come back to Ribbon Ridge. He could maybe manage the division from Denver though, right? He'd been saving to buy a plane. He could fly himself back and forth.

Maybe Aubrey would fly with him, since she wouldn't jump. Wait, Aubrey? When had his brain transferred over to her? He realized she'd been there the whole time, just underneath the surface. He'd thought of her dozens of times yesterday, hating how Sunday night had gone. Then, outside, he'd nearly kissed her. He'd wanted to. If he could go back, he would.

Or not. She'd been justifiably mad at him.

He stalked out of the office building to his bike. His gaze fell on the seat behind his. Yes, he needed another helmet so she could ride with him. *But the helmet is no guarantee she'll do it.*

Still, he wanted to try. Whatever had happened between them, he liked her. He'd liked helping with her TV, and he'd liked having her over at the house. They could be friends, right? So he didn't typically have women friends. Maybe that was the change he was feeling. Maybe it was time he had a woman friend.

And he couldn't think of a better one than Aubrey.

Chapter Seven

AUBREY WAS GLAD she was so busy with work, because it meant she didn't have to lie when she'd invited Stuart over for a glass of wine at eight o'clock instead of for dinner due to having to work late. A glass of wine was a much better—and shorter—occasion over which to tell someone that you wanted to just be friends.

"Red or white?" she asked as Stuart sat on one of the stools at her kitchen island.

"Red, please." *So polite.*

She pulled a bottle of red from the small decorative rack on the wall and brought it to the island.

"Want me to open that?" he offered.

"Sure." She pulled a corkscrew from the drawer and slid the tool and the bottle toward him. Then she turned to grab a couple of glasses from the cabinet. As she pulled one off the shelf, it slipped from her fingers. She just managed to catch it before it hit the granite and splintered into a thousand shards.

Ugh, she was nervous. Why couldn't she like Stuart enough? He had a great job, a fantastic sense of humor, and respectable, normal hobbies like playing racquetball and hiking. And he looked great with a beard, which couldn't be said of all men. Liam looked freaking fantastic with three or four days of stubble. By the end of the concert weekend last Labor Day, he'd looked scrumptiously scruffy.

Scrumptiously scruffy?

She inwardly groaned as she headed back to the island with the glasses.

Stuart slid the bottle toward her. "I'll let you pour."

She splashed the garnet liquid into the glasses and summoned her courage. "We're friends, right?"

Stuart picked up his glass. "I think so."

She tapped her glass against his. "To friendship."

He drank, then his lips twisted into a frown. "Why don't I like the sound of where this is going?"

She exhaled and set her glass on the counter, then braced her hands against the edge. "I thought I should be clear with you—I don't see us as more than friends. You're a great guy, just not my great guy." She held her breath, waiting for his reaction.

He nodded slowly. "I'd say ouch, but I can't say I'm surprised. We've been on a half dozen dates and only kissed a few times. While they were nice kisses, they didn't set off any fireworks. At least for me," he added with an apologetic smile.

"I'll say ouch!" She laughed, feeling so much better about this than she had even thirty seconds ago. Nevertheless, that didn't make his take on their kisses go down any easier. Which was stupid, because she couldn't disagree. "See, you're a super great guy."

"Because I just insulted your kissing?"

"Hey, it takes two to make that work." The conversation had shifted to where they did feel like friends. Good friends. With no sexual expectation or weirdness. Like with Liam.

His eyes glinted with mirth. "True." He lifted his glass and took another drink. "Who's the lucky guy who *does* set off your fireworks?"

Damn, was she that transparent? "No one I want to be hung up on, unfortunately."

He winced. "That makes it tough. Do you want to talk about it?"

"Not especially." Instead, she steered the conversation to the hike he'd taken last weekend. When they finished their respective glasses of wine, Stuart stood up.

"I should take off. Thanks for inviting me over."

Aubrey walked around the island. "Thanks for coming. I hope everything's cool. Seems like it?"

He smiled down at her. "Definitely. Like I said, I wasn't surprised. Maybe a little disappointed, but I get it. I appreciate you being so great about it and not texting me or something."

"I meant it when I said I wanted to be friends."

"I'd like that, and I still think you're a great lawyer." They'd met at a young professionals mixer in McMinnville, where his accounting firm was located.

"That means you'll still toss me the occasional client?"

He laughed, but his answering look was earnest. "I think I have to. That last guy you sent me has been terrific."

"I'm so glad." Friends and professional allies then. She walked him to the door and gave him a hug. "Thanks."

He squeezed her tightly, then let her go. "I hope this guy's worth it."

"He's not. I just need to get him out of my system so I can really move on."

"Good luck with that. Took me a long time to get over my college girlfriend. Sometimes you just have to let time work its magic. It also helps if you live in different states." He winked at her.

Yes, that would help immensely. When Liam went back to Denver, maybe then she could get over him. She thought she'd been well on her way until he'd come home for Evan's wedding. That was the only reason she'd started dating Stuart this spring—she wouldn't have if she'd thought Liam would come between them as he had. She had a sudden urge to be the one to push Liam out of the plane next time he went skydiving.

She waved at Stuart as he drove away, then went back inside, locking the door behind her. Her gaze landed on the TV Liam had installed, then moved to the stairs on which Liam had stripped off half of her clothes one night last August—the day after Derek and Chloe's wedding.

Liam, Liam, Liam. Everywhere she looked.

With a groan, she headed back to the kitchen—and the wine. Just as she reached the island, there was a knock on the door. Instinctively, she glanced around looking for something Stuart might have left but didn't see anything.

Turning, she went back to the door and froze at the sight of Liam through the glass panes in the upper portion. He really was everywhere she looked.

Blinking hard, she hoped he was just a figment of her tired and overwrought imagination. Nope, he was really there. Taking a deep breath, she opened the door. "Liam, this is a surprise."

"I thought I'd stop in to ask if you wanted to go flying with me—not skydiving, since I'm pretty sure I know your stance on that."

She shuddered. The idea of flinging herself out of a plane on purpose was the stuff of nightmares. Flying, however, she could get behind. But flying with Liam? Hadn't she just had a conversation about getting over this guy?

She crossed her arms. "I don't know. I'm pretty busy with the appeal, and when that's done you'll be gone."

"You almost sound hopeful."

She inwardly cringed. She didn't mean to be rude. "I didn't mean it to sound that way." She squinted at him for a moment, suspicion rifling through her. "You came over here just to ask me to go flying? You could've texted."

"I could've, but I was out for a ride anyway." He leaned against the doorframe in a careless but utterly sexy pose. "Plus, I had a radical thought. I wondered if you and I—" Aubrey held her breath as he paused. She and him what? "I wondered if we could be friends."

Friends? Was this some sort of National Friendship Day or something? How had tonight turned into friend conversations with two different guys? Belatedly, she realized it would be polite to invite Liam in. However, she still wasn't sure she should. *Friends, really?*

Why not? Maybe putting that out there, setting a boundary was exactly what she needed to get over the hump of putting Liam behind her for good. Plus, as his friend, she could offer friendly advice. Such as pulling back on the extreme sports before his mother had a heart attack or something. "Sure. I'd like to be friends." She added a smile for good measure.

"Does this mean you want to go flying?"

She had to admit that Liam flying her in a plane sounded pretty amazing. "When?"

He shrugged. "Let me check my buddy's schedule for the next couple weekends. It's his plane. I'm still saving up to buy one."

He was? She wondered if that would freak his mom out. It shouldn't. Responsible flying was one thing—he was a trained pilot, after all. Crazy-ass sports that endangered his life with heightened risk were something else entirely.

"I'm not sure about this weekend," she said. "I need to work on the brief."

"Next weekend, then. Provided I can get a plane." He flashed her his sexy smile, and she braced herself against the onslaught of attraction. It was still there, of course, but if she worked hard, perhaps over time she'd beat it into submission. Yes, she could do that. She *would* do that.

"Do you want to come in? I have wine." *Careful, Aubrey, keep him firmly in the damn Friend Zone.*

Showing a better flair for judgment than Aubrey, Liam shook his head. "I better not. I'm sure you have to be up early for work, and I have a seven a.m. conference call."

Aubrey exhaled—softly—with relief. "Yep, I do. Thanks for stopping by. I guess I'll see you...soonish?"

He pushed away from the doorframe. "I'll let you know about when we can fly. And keep me posted on the brief—you're going to send it over when you have a draft, right?"

"That's the plan. I have a few other things going on right now, too—hearings, a deposition next Tuesday."

His brow furrowed. "Are you sure you have time to get it done?"

She smiled placidly, trying not to let his doubt needle her. It was a legitimate question posed by a client. "Plenty. It was already partially done before the clock started ticking when Sutherlin filed his brief, and I have twenty-one days to file my response."

He held up a hand. "I didn't mean to imply you wouldn't get it done. My bad. I'm sure it's coming along great. See you later." He strolled off her porch and picked up his helmet from the seat of his bike.

She closed and locked the door without watching him ride away. His question had unsettled her. She was nervous about this brief, and she shouldn't be. She was a competent lawyer with good land-use experience. Yes, Sutherlin had been trying cases nearly as long as she'd been alive, but that didn't mean he would automatically out-lawyer her.

Though it sure as hell made her anxious. And Liam's uncertainty didn't help.

She blew out a breath and went to the kitchen to pour that second glass of wine. She was just tired. And stretched a bit thin, what with all the friend talk tonight. Two perfectly great guys had crossed her threshold tonight, and not one of them was boyfriend material.

That sucked.

LIAM WORE A frown as he took off from Aubrey's house. He'd seen Stuart the Accountant pulling away. Had they just finished a date? Aubrey had looked great—very date-like in white jeans and a sapphire blue sweater with a V-neck that showed the perfect amount of cleavage. Just enough to make you appreciate the view as well as tempt you to want more.

And he wanted more.

Only she'd been crystal clear on not continuing a physical relationship with him, and he couldn't offer more. He wasn't interested in being a boyfriend anytime soon. Hell, he wasn't sure he ever would be—there were just too many other things in life to do, and if he knew one thing for certain, it was that life was unpredictable and too, too short.

What he *could* offer was friendship. He was actually looking forward to being friends. He liked spending time with her even when it wasn't physical, which is more than he could say for his past flings. Yikes, he sounded like a total manwhore.

Anyway, even as friends, her romantic life was none of his business. So what if she'd had a date with Stuart the Accountant? He'd left before ten o'clock, so it couldn't have been that great.

Knock it off, Archer. None of your business, remember?

He rode to The Arch and Vine, which was only a couple of blocks from her house, and parked out front. At half past nine on Tuesday night, Ribbon Ridge was pretty quiet.

As he stepped off his bike, his phone buzzed in his pocket. He pulled it out and was disappointed to see that it wasn't Aubrey, but Whitney. She texted him every couple days and asked if he wanted to hang out. He always ignored her, and tonight was no different. This text said she was bored and invited him to come over. Her hot tub was a hundred and two degrees, and swimsuits were optional.

He gritted his teeth and made a mental note to block Whitney's number.

Suddenly eager for a beer, he went into the pub and was greeted by George, who'd been tending bar at The Arch and Vine since Dad had opened it over a decade ago. He'd been a close friend even longer than that, and the whole family saw him as just another Archer.

"Liam," George called. "Come sit next to Derek and talk to him so he'll leave me alone."

Derek, perched on one of the stools, turned. "Hey, Liam."

Liam nodded and sat on the stool next to him. "Derek. What's up?"

"I'm here to pick up Chloe when her shift is over."

Liam thought Chloe had stopped waiting tables here to focus on the art she was doing at The Alex. "I didn't think she worked here anymore."

"She helps out in a pinch. She just came in for a few hours because someone had an emergency. She's off at ten."

Liam set his helmet on the empty stool to his right. "You're early."

"I wanted a beer. Sue me."

Liam grinned as he clapped him on the back. "Me, too."

"Longbow?" George knew Liam's preferred beer.

"Yes, please."

Derek inclined his head toward Liam's helmet. "Out for a ride?"

Liam nodded as George set his pint on the bar in front of him. "It's a nice night."

"If I thought Chloe would put up with me riding a motorcycle, I'd join you. But I think she'd probably divorce me."

"This is why I'm not married. I can only imagine what she'd do if you came along with me windsurfing or skydiving."

Derek cocked his head to the side. "Actually, I've always wanted to skydive."

Liam picked up his glass. "I had no idea. You know I could make that happen."

"You should. I know Kyle wants to go. Maybe Dylan or Sean, too?"

Liam had actually talked to Dylan about skydiving. "Dylan's been there, done that in the army. I'm not sure he'd be into it again. Sean might, though."

"Sounds like a plan," Derek said.

"You're serious? Like, I can set it up this weekend." Liam's pulse picked up at the idea of taking his family on a jump. "The forecast looks perfect."

"I'm in." Derek picked his phone up from the bar and typed into it. "We'll see what Kyle says."

Liam nudged his elbow into Derek's arm. "You sure Chloe won't divorce you over this?"

Derek grinned. "No, but I can be convincing when I have to." He glanced down at his phone. "Kyle's in, too."

"Sweet. I'll check with Sean later," Liam said. "This is going to be fun. I'm surprised we haven't put this together before."

Derek laughed. "I'm not. You're hardly here! Kind of hard to plan something like this when you aren't around."

They could've gone without him, Liam reasoned, but that wasn't the point. What *was* the point? "Are you giving me shit like my sisters do for not coming to Ribbon Ridge more often?"

Derek raised his hands in surrender. "Absolutely not. You do what you gotta do, bro. That said, it is good to have you here, even if it's just temporary." He gave Liam a long look before taking a drink of beer.

That look seemed full of unasked questions. "What?"

Derek shrugged. "Nothing. It *is* good to have you here. Wish it wasn't temporary. But then, you haven't really said." He turned to face Liam. "What *are* your plans?"

Liam took a pull off his beer. "I haven't really decided for sure. I mean, I'll go back to Denver. That's where I live.

For now, I'm glad to be here for the zoning stuff. Not that I'm doing a whole lot."

"I think just your being here is plenty. Alex would be happy."

Liam took another drink of beer so that he didn't snap out an obnoxious response. He didn't make decisions based on what would make his dead brother happy. He was dead, after all, and nothing any of them did would change that.

Derek exhaled. "That was the wrong thing to say. You're still pretty pissed at him, aren't you?"

In the weeks following Alex's death, he'd been viciously angry, and the thought of coming home, of living here where Alex had lived—and died—made him physically uncomfortable. Over the past year, Liam's ire had diminished, but it was still there. "I think he made a bad choice and put the family through unnecessary tragedy."

"He was sick. In ways we didn't realize."

He was talking about Alex's bipolar disorder. But Liam had known about that. Liam had been the one to push him to get help and take medication, which he'd done for a while. Maybe if Liam had stayed in Ribbon Ridge instead of moving to Denver, he would've seen Alex stumble, could've helped him get back to the treatment he needed.

Oh, fuck that. He wasn't going to feel guilty about *that*, too. Alex had been seeing a therapist—Kyle's fiancée—for crying out loud, and even *she* hadn't picked up on just how far off the rails he'd gone.

"You're right," Liam said. "But I refuse to pity him. He made his own choices. Normally you'd tell someone they have to live with their shitty decisions, but in this case we're the ones dealing with the fallout, not him. Selfish bastard." He took another drink of beer.

"So yeah, still pissed." Derek shook his head. "I might not get it, but then the twin thing you had isn't something any of us can really understand. I respect your right to be pissed." He held up his glass and gave Liam a toast before taking a drink.

The twin thing they'd *had*. Liam had always identified as an identical twin, but now that he was alone, it felt like something was missing. No, he wouldn't go down that path. That way led to darkness and despair, and he'd avoided it since the day he'd heard Alex had died.

"So what do you think I should do? Move back to Ribbon Ridge and settle down like the rest of you?"

Derek let out a sharp laugh. "Right. No offense, but I can't see you doing that. Never could. And it's not that you're a player—though you are." He smirked, and Liam rolled his eyes. "It's that you're always moving. Settling down just isn't something you do. Honestly, you sitting in one place to watch *Game of Thrones* is about the most docile I've ever seen you."

Liam arched his brows in mock affront. "*Docile?*"

Derek chuckled. "Serene?"

"Damn, you make me sound like a whirling dervish or something."

"*You* said it…" Derek grinned before finishing his beer.

Time to change the subject to something a little safer than Liam's future. "I asked Dad about bottling last week, and he didn't say no—Tori heard him, too. You know anything about that?"

Derek nodded as he finished swallowing. "Just that he's thinking about it. I've been trying to wear him down for years—since Bex proposed bottling back when she interned with him." Bex was Hayden's ex. She was a brewer and had interned with Dad after college. "Things are kind of in flux right now, though. Kyle's transitioning out so he can focus on being a chef, and I don't think Hayden's coming back."

"To Archer or to Ribbon Ridge?"

"Definitely not to Archer, in my opinion, and I honestly don't know if he'll come home at all. Last time I talked to him, he seemed pretty smitten with Gabrielle."

The French girlfriend. "Is that right? I'm surprised. I always figured he and Bex would get back together. They seemed destined to be, if you believe in that shit."

Derek chuckled again. "As a matter of fact, as a happily married man, I do believe in that shit. And I hear you. Unfortunately, I think that ship has sailed. I guess we'll find out when he decides whether to stay on at the winery in France."

"Have they offered him a permanent job?" Liam had to admit he'd support Hayden staying in France. Then Liam wouldn't be the only one who'd left and stayed away. There was safety—and comfort—in numbers.

"Not yet, but I imagine they will. Either way, he said he'll be home in July for Sara's wedding." Derek peered at Liam. "You'll be home for that, too, right?"

"Of course. I haven't missed anyone else's. Except Tori's, and that was her own damn fault for sneaking off to Vegas."

"Totally. I could see you doing that if marriage ever did finally bite you in the ass."

"Ha! No thanks. To all of it."

"It's too bad. Rob would be thrilled if you came back and took over the real-estate division. I'm going to be really busy if he decides to pursue bottling. I could see building a facility just outside Ribbon Ridge—between here and McMinnville."

Liam liked that idea, and the real-estate developer in him wanted to participate. "That would be a lot of jobs for the area."

Derek nodded. "I know. But without a COO, things are going to get sketchy."

"Are you trying to hint that I should move back and be COO?"

"Not really, but that would be great!" He slapped Liam on the shoulder. "You've got your own thing in Denver— I get it. But like I said, Rob would be beside himself. He'd probably semi-retire if you came back."

Great. Dad would take it easy if Liam just moved home. No pressure.

"Dude, I am not trying to give you the hard sell," Derek said.

"Could've fooled me."

Chloe came up to the bar then, thankfully saving Liam from further guilt-tripping. "Hey, Liam, how's it going?"

"Good, except your husband is trying to make me feel bad about not living here."

Chloe scowled at Derek, but her eyes were warm with affection. "Leave him alone."

Derek stood. "Dude, I never meant to do that. My bad. We're just happy to have you here, even if it's just for a little while."

Liam lifted his glass to finish his beer. "Sure."

"No, seriously. I hope you know that."

Chloe touched Derek's arm. "He does. You guys just aren't good at expressing your feelings."

Derek smiled at her before dropping a kiss on her lips. Their casual romantic camaraderie was strangely annoying to Liam. "True," Derek said. He turned to look at Liam. "You'll let me know about this weekend?"

"Absolutely, but plan on it." Liam was a bit surprised he'd so readily agreed to take them all skydiving. He typically kept his sports life separate from his family. With the exception of Alex, who'd been with him—in the spiritual sense—every step of the way.

"What's happening this weekend?" Chloe asked.

Liam exchanged a look with Derek before smiling at Chloe. "Top-secret boys' day out."

Her gaze turned immediately suspicious. "Why do I think I'd disapprove?"

Derek pulled her against him and kissed her temple. "I'll tell you all about it on the way home. See you, Liam."

"See you." Liam waved at them as they left. When he turned to pick up his beer, he realized it was gone. Stay and have another, or head home alone?

He thought back over the evening. He'd agreed to take his siblings skydiving, turned down hot sex, and established a friendship with a woman. Shit, what else out of character was he going to do? If he wasn't careful, maybe he would find himself living back in Ribbon Ridge.

No, he'd worked too hard to build his empire away from here. Which he'd done to put distance between himself and Alex, for whom Liam was a constant reminder of what he'd never have. Alex was gone now, so what was keeping Liam away?

That was something he didn't want to contemplate, because he was pretty sure he wouldn't like what he found.

He stood and dropped some cash on the bar. "See you, George."

He picked up his helmet and stalked out into the night.

Chapter Eight

AUBREY WALKED INTO The Arch and Vine out of the light drizzle on Thursday evening. She pulled off her raincoat and nodded at George behind the bar.

"Hi, George!"

"How are you doing, Aubrey? The rest of the gang is here, I believe. They're back behind the screen so you can have a private get-together." He winked at her. "Don't get too crazy."

She laughed. "Hardly."

She made her way toward the back corner, where a screen was set up to block off a few tables for a private event. She came around the partition and was immediately greeted with hugs and chatter.

"I'm so glad you could come," Sara said. "Come and sit. You can hang your coat over there." She pointed at a rack of hooks on the wall, where everyone else had already deposited theirs.

Everyone else included Tori, Chloe, and Maggie, who were seated along the back of the table, as well as Sara, who sat opposite them and gestured for Aubrey to take the empty seat beside her.

"How's the brief looking?" Tori asked. Of the group here, she was the most invested in the zoning issue, since she was the architect. Actually, that wasn't a very good assessment. Everyone had a stake in The Alex getting up and running. Sara couldn't even do her job as an event planner until the zoning was finalized, and all of the work Maggie was doing on the garden and Chloe was doing on the art would be for naught if they didn't open.

But they *would* open—Aubrey wouldn't consider the alternative. It was just a question of when.

"It's good," Aubrey said. "I'm pretty stoked to have a night off where I don't have to think about it."

Tori winced. "Oops, my bad. I didn't mean to bring you down."

Aubrey hadn't meant to imply that. "No worries, I'm good."

Maggie lifted her pint glass. "I hereby declare work off-limits."

The others lifted their glasses as well, but Chloe frowned. "You don't have a beer, Aubrey."

There was an empty pint glass in the middle of the table. Aubrey snatched it up and looked between the two pitchers. "What are my choices?"

"Maid Marion hard cider for Sara mostly and Longbow," Maggie said.

Aubrey rolled her eyes. "You guys are wimps. I thought we'd be doing shots or something."

Chloe stood up abruptly. "Now we're talking! Be right back." She took off to fetch who-knew-what.

Maggie crossed her arms and shook her head. "I told you guys we should've lined up shots when we got here."

Chloe came back and slipped into her chair. "George is making us a pitcher of his signature margaritas. And Anna is bringing shots of Patrón."

Tori rubbed her hands together. "Sweet. Now we have a party."

Maggie leaned forward, her dark eyes sparkling. "No work talk and tequila shots. Sounds like we need a drinking game."

"Seriously?" Aubrey asked. "I haven't played a drinking game since college."

Maggie narrowed her eyes and looked between Sara and Tori. "Are you Archers going to play fair? I know how you people operate. You're cutthroat. Absolutely brutal."

Tori and Sara high-fived each other over the table.

"We'll take that as a compliment," Sara said.

Aubrey glanced around at everyone. "So what should we play? Quarters and beer pong seem messy. There's Thumper, Questions—"

Tori shook her head. "Has to be 'I Never,' right?"

Chloe nodded. "Totally. And what's shared at The Arch and Vine stays here."

The mood grew serious for just a moment as they all exchanged looks and nodded in agreement.

"Do we need to pinky swear?" Sara giggled.

Anna showed up with the shots and the pitcher with margarita glasses. "You want food to go with all of this, right?"

"Nachos, hummus, and maybe the grilled chicken salad all around?" Chloe suggested.

Everyone gave Anna their dressing preferences, and the server left again.

Tori handed out the limes while Chloe made sure everyone got a shot.

Maggie sprinkled salt on the back of her hand between her thumb and forefinger and held up her tequila. "To a night without testosterone."

Everyone else applied salt as well, except Aubrey. "I prefer my Patrón unimpeded."

Tori grinned. "Like Liam."

Yes, like Liam. Aubrey had forgotten that and was actually surprised she had. They'd done several shots last Labor Day weekend. But maybe the quantity was why she'd forgotten.

"What's that little smile, Aubrey?" Maggie asked shrewdly.

Aubrey blinked. "Nothing."

Chloe laughed as she tucked her blonde hair behind her ear. "Oooh, this game is going to be fun as hell."

They all held up their glasses and tapped them together before downing the contents in concert.

Aubrey swallowed the tequila down her throat and closed her eyes briefly to savor the sharp heat as it wound toward her belly. Yep, that reminded her of Liam. Maybe this hadn't been such a good idea after all. She'd done a pretty good job of blocking him out the past couple of days since his strange visit. Being super busy at work was a good thing in this case.

And his visit *had* been strange. He'd dropped by just to ask her to be friends? And to go flying, apparently. She hadn't heard back from him, so she wondered if it was really going to happen.

"Who's going first?" Sara asked before sipping her margarita.

"You may want to save your drinks for the game," Chloe advised. "Otherwise you're going to be plowed, and I'm pretty sure you're the lightest weight among us."

"You're undoubtedly right, but I also expect I'll be drinking far less than all of you." Sara gave them all a superior, saucy look, then dissolved into laughter, which spread around the table.

"I'll go," Maggie said. "Just to review, I say, 'I've never gone skinny-dipping' and anyone who *has* gone skinny-dipping has to drink."

Tori gathered her hair and dropped it down her back. "That's it."

Chloe looked at Tori and Sara. "Any rules for what we say? Meaning, can I say 'I never' about something I've done, or does it have to be things I *haven't* done?"

"Why are you asking us?" Sara exchanged a look with her sister. "We aren't the rule makers."

Maggie snorted. "You're Archers. You're rule makers, breakers, and just all around hard-core gamesters."

"Then I'll make the rules," Aubrey said, enjoying the banter. "Yes, you can say 'I never' about something you've done. Are you sticking with skinny-dipping, Maggie, or was that just an example?"

"I'll stick with it." Maggie took a drink, which was followed by laughter and everyone else drinking.

"Seriously, *everyone*?" Maggie asked, incredulous. "Damn, I'm going to have to up my game."

Tori sat between Maggie and Chloe. "Me next, I guess. Let's see…I've never gone streaking."

Chloe narrowed her eyes, then her face cracked into a smile. "I'm sensing a naked theme here."

Aubrey laughed. "Same." She took a drink. Maggie was the only other person who joined her.

Maggie set her glass down. "Streaking and skinny-dipping were almost a requirement with my parents. They loved to take us to a nude beach." She stuck her tongue out and shook her head vigorously. "I refused to go anymore when I turned twelve. There are just some things an adolescent girl doesn't need to see."

Tori touched her shoulder. "Yikes, do you need some brain bleach?"

This was met with loud guffaws. Aubrey knew Maggie's folks were total hippies with an open marriage. She'd heard some of Maggie's stories, and while Aubrey didn't enjoy spending time with her own parents, she couldn't imagine the things Maggie had endured.

Maggie looked at Aubrey. "What's your streaking story?"

"Nothing terribly exciting. Just a drunken jog around campus with the Pre-Law Society when I was a freshman."

"Is it just me, or does streaking at Stanford seem like a whole different level of streaking than a nude beach?" Chloe asked.

Everyone laughed. "Completely different!" Maggie said. "Your turn, Chloe."

Chloe blew out a breath and tapped her finger against her lip. "Let me see…" Her eyes lit, and she suppressed a grin. "I never got drunk underage."

Tori gaped at her. "Are you kidding? That's a total gimme. You're just trying to make us all drink."

Chloe lifted her glass. "Guilty as charged. What can I say, George's margaritas are delicious."

Everyone agreed as they drank.

"Okay, Aubrey, don't let us down," Tori said. "Give us something juicy."

Juicy. She racked her brain for something good. "Not sure if this is juicy enough for you, but it could be interesting. I've never shoplifted."

No one drank for a minute. They just looked around the table at each other.

"Sara?" Tori asked, staring at her sister.

Sara exhaled and picked up her glass. "Fine." She took a drink. "When I was five, I took a stuffed animal from a garage sale."

This cracked everyone up. Aubrey patted Sara on the shoulder. "I don't think that counts."

"It shouldn't, because my mom drove me back there and made me pay for it from my allowance."

Aubrey could totally see Emily Archer doing just that.

Anna returned with the nachos and hummus plate, and the game went on hiatus as everyone dove in. By the time the salads came out, they were on their second round of margaritas and had already done their second tequila shots. They jumped back into the game midway through their salads and had to order a third round of drinks so they wouldn't run out.

As Anna brought the next batch of shots and margaritas, she looked around the table. "Is someone driving you all home?"

"Derek's planning to pick me up," Chloe said. "I'm sure he can give you all a ride."

Aubrey swallowed the last bite of her salad. "And I'm walking distance, so you're all welcome to stagger back to my place for a sleepover." The alcohol had hit her, but she was pleasantly tipsy, hopefully nowhere near staggering.

Maggie prepped her hand with salt for the next shot. "Oooh, a sleepover! That sounds fun." She looked around the table. "Everybody ready?"

They all scrambled to pick up their shot glasses then drank.

Sara shuddered. "Oh, you guys, I should slow down."

Tori looked at her sister and gave her an encouraging nod. "You're fine. I've always got your back, remember?"

Sara nodded. "I wish Alaina was here. Can you imagine the stuff we could find out?"

Chloe pushed her empty shot glass to the edge of the table so Anna could grab it when she came back. "No kidding! Think of the fun we could have—'I've never made out with Ryan Gosling.'"

"Which she totally did in that one movie," Maggie said. "I wonder if she's ever met Sam Heughan or Gerard Butler."

Tori looked at Aubrey. "In case you didn't know, Maggie has a thing for kilts and brogues."

"Who doesn't?" Aubrey asked. "Oooh, I have one. Who's dated a Brit?"

Tori immediately drank and then smirked at everyone. "Married one!" Everyone took their turn high-fiving her.

"When you say dated," Maggie asked, "does that include a minor hook-up at a party?"

Aubrey squinted at her. Was the room starting to get brighter? Or worse, was it maybe moving a tad? "What's a 'minor hook-up'?"

Maggie had one hand on her margarita glass. "Make-out session, maybe a little groping."

"Counts for me!" Sara said. "Drink! Anyone else?"

Chloe looked around the table. "Does an Aussie count?"

Aubrey laughed. "I really figured Carnegie Mellon's geography department was better than that. Australia and Britain aren't even in the same hemisphere."

Chloe rolled her eyes and crossed her arms. "Fine."

Tori turned to look at Chloe. "I think you should have to drink twice for that nonsense."

Everyone verbalized their agreement, and Chloe giggled before taking two very long drinks.

"I've got one!" Maggie said. Her lips curled into a devilish smile. "I've never had a tattoo or a piercing that isn't in my ear."

Sara frowned at her. All of their facial expressions seemed to have become exaggerated, or maybe Aubrey was just seeing them that way. She made a mental note—for what good that was at this point—to skip any future rounds of shots. And maybe make this her last margarita.

"Isn't that technically two 'I nevers'?" Sara asked.

Maggie waved her hand. "Who cares? Or are you going to go full Archer on me and make up some penalty?"

Chloe leaned around Tori to look at Maggie. "Hey, we outnumber them. We're not letting them gaslight us."

"Okay, so who's drinking?" Maggie looked around eagerly.

Tori, Chloe, and Aubrey drank. Maggie clapped her hands. "Spill. Which is it Tori? And give details."

Tori set down her glass and wiped her lips with the back of her hand. "Tattoo. Dolphin. Hip."

"Why a dolphin?" Aubrey asked, thinking her voice sounded a bit too loud and incapable of making it softer.

"We all have animals associated with us—it started with Christmas ornaments or in some cases a nickname or something. Like Sara's is a kitten because Dad called her Kitten."

"Dad did not call Tori 'Dolphin,' " Sara informed the table with a bit of a slur.

"I just liked dolphins," Tori said. "Still do. What about you, Aubrey—piercing or tattoo?"

"Tattoo. Boring. It's a four-leaf clover with the number three inside of it. I've never been a very lucky person— I've had to work my ass off for stuff. I was hoping the clover would help." She smiled and appreciated the nods of encouragement from the other women.

"Very cool," Tori said. "And the three?"

Aubrey looked down at the table. She usually told everyone it was her law-school rank when she graduated. But whether it was due to the alcohol or the fact that she really liked these women, she told them the truth. She lifted her head and looked at no one in particular. "It represents my family—my parents and me. We aren't very close, but I guess I hoped that one day we might be."

Sara put her hand on Aubrey's shoulder. "That's so sweet. Why aren't you close?"

Aubrey rolled her eyes. "Ugh. They're self-involved control freaks."

"Yikes, sounds like my parents, or at least my mom," Chloe said.

"Joining my uncle's law firm in Ribbon Ridge was a major disappointment to them, as was my choosing Lewis and Clark over Stanford Law." She mimicked her mother's high-pitched whine, " 'Why would you do that?' Because I wanted to be farther away from them!"

"Yet you still hope to be a family," Chloe said softly. "Things are better with my folks now that I'm married. I think they just worried I wouldn't settle down after I broke up with my fiancé. Maybe your parents worry about the same thing."

"Since I moved to Ribbon Ridge, they worry I'll marry some farmer. And no, I don't think I hope to be a family anymore. I got that tattoo a long time ago." Before she'd even graduated from law school, in fact. "Besides, I have a family of three now with my aunt and uncle. They're the parents I never had, the people I look to for advice and support."

"Aw, that's so great," Maggie said, smiling. She turned her head toward Chloe. "That leaves Chloe, and I think we all know her answer—and no, it's not a piercing, unless there's something I don't know."

"Not a piercing, though I did consider having my nose done when I was in college," Chloe said. "My mother sent me to Paris for spring break as a bribe not to do it."

"My mom would've done the same thing," Aubrey said. "Maybe even locked me in my room!"

Maggie snorted. "Classic. Actually, I don't know about Chloe's tattoo. I just figured she had one instead of a piercing. What is it?"

Chloe shook her head. "Stupid tramp stamp. I say stupid because I created this really cool vine with flowers and I can't ever see it because it's on my lower back. Derek appreciates it, though." She arched a brow as her lips tilted into a seductive smile that prompted everyone to snicker and giggle.

Oh, they were so drunk.

And Aubrey had to work tomorrow. She ought to go. Really. It's just that her legs didn't want to move. The chair was super comfy. She didn't want to leave the crazy fun girls' clubhouse they'd created in this back corner.

Chloe scooted forward in her chair. "Let's see, Maggie hasn't had a drink in a couple turns, and that doesn't seem fair. This will get her: I've never had sex with an

Archer. Ha! Derek doesn't count," Chloe said smugly, sitting back.

Aubrey, feeling completely amused and more than a little blissed out on tequila, laughed as she took a drink.

Shit.

She realized just how drunk she was. Had she really admitted she'd slept with an Archer?

"Wait, what?" Tori sat up straight and blinked. "Did you just drink, Aubrey?"

Aubrey scrambled. "I was thirsty."

Four pairs of eyes were glued to her.

"Who have you slept with?" Chloe asked, sounding a bit slurry. Was that her voice or Aubrey's listening skills? Probably a bit of both.

Panicking, Aubrey fought to come up with something intelligent to say. "I thought you said you'd *had* sex with an Archer." She knew as soon as she said it that her attempt was a total fail.

The space between Chloe's blonde brows pleated into a little fan. "That doesn't make sense. I joked about Derek *not* being an Archer." Yep, massive, epic fail.

Sara put her arm around Aubrey. "I think it's safe to say we're all tanked. Aubrey could've heard that you'd never had sex with some guy named Archibald."

"Good point," Tori said.

Aubrey breathed out a sigh of relief and decided it was time to pull her butt off the chair and get the hell out of there before she was in completely over her head.

Just then a male head peeked around the screen. "Surprise!" said Derek. His gaze scanned the table, and he blew out a low whistle. "You all looked pretty blotto. Good thing I brought reinforcements."

Derek moved into the space and was followed by Dylan, Kyle, Sean, and…Liam.

Oh no, had any of them overheard what Aubrey had said? No, a few minutes had transpired, right? Surely long enough that they hadn't been within hearing distance.

Chloe smiled up at her husband. "You came to rescue us."

Derek grinned down at her in return. "Of course. And not a moment too soon, it looks like."

Everyone chuckled.

Tori grabbed her purse from the back of her chair. "We need to pay the bill."

"I took care of it," Liam said. He was standing a bit to the side. Why was he here anyway? He wasn't anyone's significant other.

"Why are you here?" Sara asked, echoing Aubrey's thoughts.

Liam's gaze connected with Aubrey's, and her insides heated instantaneously, like a gas stove turned up to high. "I thought I could help Aubrey get home."

"We were at the house playing pool," Kyle said. "He just didn't want to miss this. Come on, all of you drunk together? Who knows what we might learn?" He winked at Maggie, who rolled her eyes at him but ended up giggling.

Aubrey began to panic again. Was Kyle saying they *had* heard what Aubrey had said? She stood abruptly and wobbled on her feet. "I can get home by myself, thanks. It's just a few blocks."

Liam stepped forward and reached for her, grabbing her forearm gently to steady her. "It's no problem."

She snatched her hand away before she decided to move closer. Just that little touch had sparked an overwhelming lust she did not want to indulge. Okay, *want* wasn't the right word. She *wanted* to take Liam home and jump him, but that wasn't going to happen. She couldn't *let* that happen.

She grabbed her purse from the back of her chair and fished her wallet from the depths. "Here, let me pay you for my part of the bill."

Liam's hand closed over hers as he pushed the wallet back into her purse. "It's fine. Come on, let's go."

This time she couldn't seem to shake his hand away. She didn't even try. She let his warmth, his masculinity seep into her and feed the fire burning in her core.

When they stepped outside, the cool, damp night air rushed over her, giving her much-needed clarity. She took a deep breath and moved away from Liam, taking her hand from his grasp and slinging her purse over her shoulder. Then she started to walk down the street. Away from him.

But he only fell into step beside her.

"You're cute when you're drunk. Reminds me of Labor Day weekend."

She threw him a glare. "Do *not* talk about that."

It was chilly, so she wrapped her arms around herself. She realized it was also misting, like it had been earlier, and in her haste, she'd left her raincoat back at The Arch and Vine.

She turned a smile on Liam. "Any chance you want to run back and get my coat?" Then she could get rid of him.

He chuckled. "You really don't want me walking you home, do you? I'll grab it later. After I make sure you're tucked into bed."

She turned the corner onto her street. "Oh no you don't. You aren't coming anywhere near my bed."

"I promise to keep my hands to myself."

"I just realized your name is almost spelled the same as liar." She arched a brow at him. "Coincidence? I think not."

He laughed again. "You are too funny tonight."

It started raining harder. He pulled his jacket off and wrapped it around her. "Come on, let's pick up the pace." He grabbed her hand and pulled her along at a steady clip.

The cooler temperature had given her a much-needed jolt of sobriety, but the speed walking was making her feel off-kilter again. "Not so fast," she said, trying to tug her hand from his.

"Yes, fast. Or should I carry you?" His blue-gray gaze raked over her, and she realized it was possible to feel a shiver and a blast of heat at the same time. Or maybe she was just super extra drunk.

No, because if she was, she wouldn't be thinking that, right? She'd be blithely unaware and probably gleefully clutching more than Liam's hand.

They reached her house, and he ushered her up the driveway and onto her porch. He let go of her hand and held out his palm. "Key?"

Standing beneath the porch light, she rummaged around in her purse. Why did a woman's purse always get more cavernous when she was looking for something?

Liam took it from her and stuck his hand inside. He immediately came up with her keys.

She put her hands on her hips. "How'd you do that?"

He flashed her a heart-stopping smile. "I think I told you once that I had magic fingers."

Even if he hadn't, she remembered. For a brief moment, she gave herself over to the memory of his hands on her body, the way he stroked her inner thigh, the manner in which he cupped her breast.

He opened the door and pulled her inside. "You're wet." He tugged his leather jacket from her shoulders and let it drop to the floor.

Bummer because it smelled deliciously like him—cedar and citrus. God, she loved that scent.

"Did you drink any water?" he asked.

She blinked at him. "What?"

"Water. You need water, or you're going to be miserable come morning."

Right. Water. No, she didn't think they'd been drinking much water. Just tequila.

He took her hand again and led her straight back to the kitchen. He moved away from her, then came back and sat her down on one of the barstools. She half expected him to pat her on the head or something.

"You don't have to take care of me like a lost puppy," she said.

He laughed. "Is that what I'm doing?" He pulled a glass from her cabinet—he knew exactly where they were, which was remarkable since he'd only been inside her house a few times. She thought of the first time—that night last summer. Not cold and rainy like tonight, but hot and humid. Wet and sexy in a completely different way.

Holy hell she was horny.

He set the water on the counter in front of her. "Drink."

She saluted him before picking up the glass and downing it.

He swept it up and went for a refill. In the meantime, she realized she *was* wet. Her sweater was damp from the mist and the rain before he'd covered her with his coat. She glanced at his back and realized he was wet, too. Wetter than she was. His shirt was plastered to his skin, delineating every spectacular muscle.

She swallowed and splayed her hands on top of the granite to stop herself from leaping up and grabbing him. Would that be so wrong? How terrible would one more night with Liam be? She was a grown-up. She knew not to expect more from him. She could do that, right? Trade her common sense for a night of unparalleled, mind-blowing, soul-satisfying sex?

Aubrey whisked her wet sweater over her head and tossed it on the stool beside her. Common sense was extremely overrated.

Chapter Nine

LIAM FINISHED FILLING the glass from the spigot on the fridge door and turned. He nearly dropped the damn glass.

Aubrey was still sitting at the island, but instead of the caramel-colored sweater, she wore a green, lacy bra that cupped her breasts into the most inviting cleavage he'd ever seen.

Normally, he'd be completely on board with this plan. He'd sweep her into his arms, carry her upstairs, and take them both on a joyride. Except she was drunk. Or at least kind of drunk.

He was having a hard time discerning which. She didn't seem as lit as she'd been last Labor Day, but she also wasn't completely sober.

The gentleman his mother had raised said even a little drunk was too drunk, especially when Aubrey had told him that she didn't want to hook up with him anymore. But what if she'd changed her mind? It wasn't as if they didn't have a past history of exactly this kind of behavior. Minus him picking her up from a girls' night at which she'd clearly had a few drinks.

He took her the glass of water and tried to ignore her fabulous breasts. "How much have you had to drink?"

She shrugged. "A few shots."

That wasn't too much.

She drank half the water and set the glass back on the counter. "And two—no maybe three—margaritas."

Yowza. He fought to keep his gaze from dipping to her half-dressed state. Did she have any idea how badly she was tempting him? "Finish the water, then it's time for bed."

"Goody." She stared at him, her lids lowering so that her gaze went from warmly interested to provocatively seductive. Then she polished off the water and handed him the glass. "I'm ready for bed."

He stifled a groan as he took the glass from her fingers. She slid her hand over his and stroked his wrist. He pulled away from her and put the glass in the sink. When he turned back, she was already walking out of the kitchen, her hips swaying in her perfectly fitted jeans. She paused near the front door and kicked off her ankle boots. Then she turned and stood with one foot on the first stair, her hand on the rail.

"You coming?" she asked.

Oh hell.

"I really shouldn't."

She didn't appear to have heard him, because she made no response. She went up the stairs as if she expected him to follow.

Swallowing and trying to will his hard-on into non-existence, he walked to the front door and picked up his coat from the floor. "I'm going to take off. You'll be fine."

"Actually, can I have some help? My hair is caught in my necklace."

He looked at the ceiling and exhaled. He really ought to go. But her hair was caught...

In the end, he was just a guy, and the woman he desired most in the world was beckoning him to her bedroom.

He hung his coat on the newel post and jogged up the stairs. He remembered precisely where her room was located—at the back of the second story. They'd stripped each other the entire way up the stairs last summer. That had been an incredible night.

He looked down at his boot-clad feet and belatedly realized he should take them off before he tracked something on her carpet. The first floor and stairs were hardwood, but up here, his feet sank into the plush wall-to-wall. He quickly shucked his boots and set them on the top step before continuing to her room.

Her eyes found his as he stepped over the threshold. She'd turned on the lamp next to her bed, which only served to cast the entire room in a muted, sexy light that spilled shadows on her body in all the right places.

He licked his lips. "You need help?"

She presented her back to him and held her hair partially up. "My hair's caught, see?"

He did, in fact, see her red hair snagged in the fastening of her necklace, a short, almost choker-length gold chain with an A dangling from the front.

For Aubrey.

Or Archer.

What the hell?

He shook his head and studied the tangle. It was hopeless. He was going to touch her bare skin. He could already smell her clove and orange scent. It would be a very short leap to taste her.

If she invited him to stay, he might not be able to say no.

"Can't you just sleep in this necklace?" he asked, sounding a bit hoarse due to his pent-up sexual frustration.

She turned to look at him over her shoulder. "Are you being a wuss?"

"Oh, fuck it," he muttered. He gently tugged the hair from the chain, but a few strands were really wound in there. "Move toward the light." He guided her to back up so the lamp could aid him. "Tilt your head."

She did as he asked, and he got a fresh waft of her scent. Pure, unadulterated Aubrey. Delicious. He worked the remaining strands of hair free of the clasp and closed his eyes. He let his fingertips rest against her warm skin.

The silk of her hair fell against his hands, and he jerked his eyes open just as she turned.

"Your shirt is soaking wet." She freed the top button, then the second one.

Liam dropped his hands to his sides and thought about telling her to stop. He really did. He thought the word so loudly he was certain she must've heard it. But she didn't. Her fingers kept going until his shirt was open and she was pushing it off his shoulders.

As it fell to the floor, she braced her palms against his T-shirt-clad chest. And frowned.

"This shirt's a bit damp, too."

Again, he summoned the word *stop* to his brain, and again the word didn't find its way past his lips.

She tugged it up his chest and pulled it over his head. "Now this—" she said, running her hands over his shoulders and down his pecs, "—is warm."

Okay, he had to put a stop to this, because they were just about naked chest to naked chest, and that might be too near the point of no return. Who was he kidding? Liam could see that point as clearly as he could see the bed behind her, and both were far too close.

"Aubrey, I need to go. You're drunk."

She gave her head a single shake, sending her scent cascading over him once more. "Not that drunk."

He put his finger under her chin and tipped her head up. "I can't tell, but it sounds like you drank a lot from what you said downstairs." He looked into her hazel eyes and had to admit it was still hard to tell. Her pupils were a bit dilated, but that could be from arousal. He knew *he* was aroused.

"Do you want me to walk in a straight line? Maybe recite the alphabet backward?"

He smiled at her playful flirting but felt a sense of annoyance that he didn't know her a little bit better. He wanted to. And damn it, he should.

He traced his finger along her jaw. "Aubrey, you have me so confused."

"You've seen me far more intoxicated. Or don't you remember having sex at the amphitheater during the concert?"

He couldn't unremember that if he lived to be a hundred. They'd snuck off toward the bed and breakfast where some of the band members stayed. Figuring out how to have sex amid desert shrubs and towering birch trees on the other side of a wire fence had proved difficult, but in the end, he'd laid his shirt down on the dirt and she'd gotten on her knees. He could still hear the thrum of the music, smell the fragrant late-summer air, and feel her slick heat gripping him as he drove into her from behind. Yeah, they'd both been drunk. Deliciously, fiendishly devoid of inhibitions.

But there had been something else, too—a level of trust they'd shared in that moment. And if she was less intoxicated now and he wasn't the least bit drunk... What was happening? Maybe every time they'd been together, things between them had grown and built. Maybe something had developed, and he hadn't been paying close-enough attention.

What did it matter now? She'd cut him loose and had reiterated that decision countless times. Tonight was an aberration, and he didn't want her to regret it.

"I should still go," he said, despite his feet staying rooted to the floor.

"Or not." She tipped her head forward and drew his finger between her lips, sucking the tip.

Oh God. Her lips and mouth ought to have been illegal or at least have come with a warning. He closed his eyes for a moment and reveled in her tongue and the way it caressed his flesh. His cock, already hard as granite, lengthened and strained against his jeans, which had become far too tight for comfort.

She let go of his finger, and her hands splayed over his lower back, pulling him against her. The heat of her nearly bare chest scalded his feverish body. It was torture. He wanted more.

He opened his eyes and saw that hers were slitted. Sexy. Seductive. "How can I prove to you that I'm not too drunk to want you to stay?"

Holy hell, he was so screwed. "Just kiss me."

He cupped the sides of her head and pulled her mouth to his. Her lips were soft and supple. She tasted of lime and tequila and fucking fabulous Aubrey, a treat he could never get enough of. He held her while he slid his tongue into her mouth. She met him, licking at him eagerly as her fingernails carved crescent-shaped grooves into his back. She rotated her hips against his. The contact set off fireworks behind his tightly closed eyes. He didn't stop the moan that came from his throat, nor did he ease off the kiss.

Instead, he angled his head and speared deeply into her, immersing them both in the sensations of heat and wet and total abandon. Again her pelvis thrust into his. He slid a hand down her spine and splayed it across her ass, holding her hard against him in an attempt to ease the ache in his cock.

Still it wasn't enough.

He brought his hand back up to her bra and flicked the fastener open. She pulled her chest from his and shimmied out of the lingerie, letting it fall between them. He grabbed at one of the straps and flung it away.

She pushed up against him again, this time wiggling so that her breasts teased his chest. She drew her head back and nipped at his lip before kissing him again.

He held her lower back and brought his other hand from her head down to her collarbone. His fingers grazed the necklace that had prompted this insanity, but he moved right on by until he found the upper curve of her breast. He opened an eye long enough to gauge the distance to the bed—not far.

He guided her backward and broke the kiss as he pushed her to the mattress. He bent and cupped her breast, then put his mouth on the nipple, licking and sucking her flesh. She gasped and moaned and clasped his head, pulling at his hair. His cock raged as he feasted on her.

She curled her legs around the back of his knees and pulled him closer so that his groin pressed against hers. He moved to her other breast, licking and nipping her heated skin. He drew on the nipple with his teeth, gently tugging, then tongued her as he held her captive to his mouth.

She arched her hips off the bed and pressed up against his erection. Two pairs of jeans were far too thick to enjoy a moment like this.

He trailed his mouth down her ribcage, and his fingers found the waistband of her jeans.

She moaned as she twisted her fingers in his hair. "I think I like being friends."

Friends? What the hell was she talking about?

Friends.

He'd come over the other night and proposed they be friends. This hadn't been what he'd had in mind, not that he was complaining. But it had seemed the right thing to say, since he'd seen Stuart leaving.

Stuart.

Fuck. She was dating another guy! The hell she wasn't drunk. He was *such* an ass.

He jumped back from her, panting lightly as he wiped his hand over his mouth and fought to gain control of his raging lust. "Uh, I have to go."

She bolted up and instantly closed her eyes. "Uh-oh."

Yep. She was a lot drunker than she realized. And he was a first-class prick for letting himself be fooled.

"Could you get the room to stop spinning please?" She kept her eyes closed and fisted the comforter with both hands.

He ought to leave right now. Or he could be a real gentleman and take care of her like he'd intended to do when he'd brought her inside and made her drink water. Then she'd taken off her sweater, and he'd completely lost his mind.

First things first: She needed a shirt of some kind. "Where are your pajamas?"

She pointed an unsteady finger at the dresser against the wall. "Middle drawer." She still didn't open her eyes.

He went and opened the drawer and grabbed the first thing he found—a Stanford T-shirt. By the time he got back to the bad, she was lying down against the pillows.

"Hold on." He put his hand behind her back and held her up. "Can you sit for just a second so I can put a shirt on you?"

She nodded and then moaned, but not in the sexual way she'd done just a few minutes ago. This was the sound of a person whose alcohol consumption had just caught up with her.

He pulled the shirt over her head and somehow got her arms into the sleeves. Then he eased her back against the pillows.

He contemplated her jeans. *Just take them off. Pretend she's your sister. God no, don't do that! Pretend she's your friend and nothing more. Because she is.*

Moving as quickly and smoothly as possible, he stripped her jeans away. He ought to have put her in a pair of pajama pants or something, but fuck it. She was practically asleep as it was. He tugged the bedding down and managed to tuck her between the sheets.

She exhaled as she snuggled onto her side and laid her cheek against the pillow. Her red hair cascaded over the white linen. He couldn't resist stroking his fingertips against the silky softness.

He forced himself to turn from the bed, then bent to pick up his T-shirt, which he donned immediately. He plucked up his button-down, but she'd been right—it was pretty wet. Clutching it in his hand, he took one final look at Sleeping Beauty.

Then he turned out the lamp and tiptoed from the bedroom. Being friends, it turned out, was a lot harder than it looked.

AUBREY FINISHED HER third cup of coffee and massaged her forehead as she stared at her computer monitor. What the hell had she been thinking drinking like that when she was this busy at work? And especially when this zoning brief was so important.

The drinking and mild hangover were really the least of her worries, however, when compared to her behavior *after* the drinking. She'd almost slept with Liam. Would have, if not for him being a gentleman.

She groaned as she pushed her chair back from the desk and spun it around—slowly, so her head didn't splinter—to look out the window. It was a gray, soggy day. Perfect for crawling under a rock in abject humiliation. Or regret.

She'd practically thrown herself at him last night. Nope, there was no *practically* about it. From the minute she'd tossed her sweater off, she'd made her objective crystal clear. And he'd tried to politely decline, damn him. It would be easy—and vindicating—to tell herself that she'd been too drunk to realize what she was doing. However, the fact that she remembered everything in such horrifying detail told her she hadn't been nearly that drunk. Not until the tequila had finally caught up with her. She supposed she had to be thankful for that third and final margarita.

Her phone pinged on her desk. She picked it up and saw Chloe's name. She was the last to chime in on the group text that Tori had started that morning to check in on how everyone was.

Chloe: *OMG you guys, what a night! Pounding headache this morning but so fun! Next time we'll drink water and pace ourselves a little better, LOL.*

Everyone had reported a similar hangover-ish morning, minus Sara, who'd only said that she'd had a great time and was glad they'd all gotten home safely.

Aubrey couldn't help but fixate on what she'd said last night just before the guys had arrived. A dull, queasy feeling spread in her stomach—the kind of sensation that came when you had to have a difficult conversation or had been caught in a lie or, in her case, had been caught in a damning truth.

Why had she drunk after that stupid question? It's not like any of them would've known she'd been lying if she'd *hadn't* taken a drink. No one knew about her and Liam, for crying out loud.

She only hoped they'd all been too drunk to remember. She didn't think she'd be that lucky, however.

She had to believe in what they'd said at the outset—that whatever happened at the pub stayed at the pub last night. She didn't want to think about the alternative. She also didn't want to think about how awkward it would be next time she saw all of them, regardless of a dumb rule.

Her phone rang in her hand, startling her. She looked down and saw that it was Sara. Apparently there was no time like the present for awkward.

She could ignore the call, but why? She had to face them eventually. She *was* their attorney.

She slid her finger across the screen and forced a smile into her voice. "Hi, Sara!"

"Hi, Aubrey, how are you this morning?"

"Pretty good. Remind me to schedule future girls' nights on a Friday or a Saturday or at least when I'm not working the next day."

Sara laughed. "Good call. I'm so sorry. I hope we didn't mess up your day."

"It's fine. I'm a big girl, anyway, so it's definitely not your fault."

There was a pause in the conversation, just a slight beat, but it was enough to raise Aubrey's guard.

"So, I wanted to talk to you about what happened at the end there last night and let you know that no one's going to ask who you slept with."

Leave it to Sara to be as blunt as possible. With her sensory-processing disorder, she didn't always have the best filter. It was actually one of the things Aubrey liked most about her. She was incredibly real and as a result, delightful. She was also apparently the designated spokesperson for everyone else.

"Um, okay. Thanks." *I think.*

"I mean, it's clearly Hayden or Liam," she said. "It can't be Evan, obviously, or Kyle, and like Chloe said, Derek's not an Archer. I'm not even sure you'd met Derek before he got together with Chloe, right?"

Sara was talking pretty fast, and Aubrey wasn't sure she wanted to keep up. "Uh, no."

"Anyway, it seems like it's maybe Liam, since he walked you home last night, although it could've been

Hayden before he left. Except Hayden isn't generally the hook-up type, and Liam definitely is. Oh geez, listen to me. I'm doing exactly what Tori said *not* to do."

Definitely spokesperson.

Aubrey dredged up another fake smile so she wouldn't sound as annoyed as she felt—not at Sara, but at herself for being such an idiot. "It's okay."

"Well, I just want to say that it would be cool if it *was* Liam, because he could use a girlfriend like you. We'd love that actually." She said the last part with such a soft sweetness that Aubrey almost wished she could tell her she'd love it, too.

But they were talking about Liam, and Liam didn't have girlfriends. He had rotating arm candy.

"Uh, that's really nice of you to say," Aubrey said. She massaged her forehead and decided it was time for another dose of extra-strength Tylenol. "I should get back to work. This zoning brief isn't going to write itself."

"Oh! I'm sorry. I'll stop rambling. You sure you're good?"

"Yep, I'm good."

"I'm glad. I had such a great time. I'm glad we're friends. Even when the zoning and The Alex is done, we'll still be friends—just so you know."

Aubrey smiled, and this time it was genuine and heartfelt. "Thanks, Sara. Bye."

She disconnected the call and set the phone on her desk. She picked up her coffee mug and realized it was empty. That meant hauling her sorry ass out of this chair for a refill.

Ugh, girlfriend? She could barely be Liam's friend. In fact, she'd pretty much failed at that entirely. The very next time she'd seen him, she'd tried to jump his bones.

But they'd stopped themselves. Correction: *He'd* stopped them.

It seemed like he was maybe better at this friend thing than she was. And wasn't that surprising as hell?

She stood from the chair and resolved to stop thinking about last night, about what she'd admitted by drinking in that asinine game, about Liam. She needed to focus on work and get through this zoning business. Then Liam would leave, and she could work on flushing him from her system for good.

Chapter Ten

LIAM CHECKED THE gear that bound him to his brother Kyle as they neared the jumping altitude of thirteen thousand feet. He was certified to jump tandem, and Kyle had drawn the short straw and was flying with Liam. Derek was hooked up to Rylan, and Sean was going with Nate, another of Rylan's employees.

"You ready?" Liam asked.

"You going to drop me?" Kyle retorted.

Liam grinned. "On your head."

Kyle touched the cap that was sort of a light helmet. "This doesn't seem too sturdy. And why aren't you wearing one?"

"Because I've done this a hundred times. Pull your goggles down. We're nearly there."

Kyle nodded and tugged his goggles into place. "We're going first?"

"Of course. Would you want it any other way?"

Kyle laughed. "Touché."

They edged toward the door, which the copilot would open momentarily. He came up from the cockpit and stood in front of the three pairs. "About a minute of free fall. You'll be going over a hundred miles an hour. Then five or so minutes of gentle gliding to earth after your partner springs the parachute." He smirked at Liam. "Remember to pull the drogue—don't wait too long, or you'll lose your tandem license."

Liam saluted. "Yes, sir." He knew the rules. And he wouldn't try any crazy shit with his brother on board.

"You all ready?" the copilot asked. "Give me a thumbs-up."

Everyone flicked up their thumbs, and Liam patted Kyle's bicep. "Let's do this."

The door opened, and the whoosh of air and noise overcame him for a second. He loved this feeling—that buzz of adrenaline just before he leapt into the air. Kyle moved forward, and Liam trailed behind him.

Kyle hesitated at the edge, and Liam pushed him out with the force of his body behind him.

"Dick!" Kyle shouted but finished on a laugh. "Holy shit!"

Liam wished he could see Kyle's face, but it was enough to feel the vibration of his joyous laughter.

They sped through the air faster than a car on the freeway. Faster than most roller coasters. But it felt different, at least to Liam. He enjoyed going fast on the ground, but up here it was just your body and gravity. There was something natural, something pure, something he never felt anywhere else. And that was why his first extreme sport was still his favorite. Why he wanted to push that feeling even further and try BASE jumping.

It was time to pull the drogue, but damn he loved this. He saw Derek and Rylan, who'd gone second, to his left. Rylan activated his chute, and Liam knew he was out of time—there was a timer to automatically release the chute if they fell too fast or if they didn't pull by a certain altitude. He tugged the drogue, and they immediately slowed, gently, not jerkily.

"Damn, that was fun!" Kyle roared and pumped his fist. "Again!"

Liam laughed. "Sure. Anytime."

Kyle looked around, his head angling left, then right, then left again. "It's so beautiful up here."

Gorgeous. The rain they'd had the last few days had transitioned out last night, and today had dawned bright and beautiful. They'd completely lucked out. Clouds meandered overhead, but there was plenty of blue sky and miles and miles of breathtaking vista below.

"I can see why you're addicted to this," Kyle shouted.

Addicted. Is that how they saw him? Isn't that how they *should* see him? Scarcely a weekend went by that he didn't do something that would make most people cringe, even if it was just riding one of his motorcycles.

He steered them into the drop zone, and a couple of minutes later, they stepped onto the ground.

"Wow!" Kyle gave a loud whoop and looked around for the others. Rylan and Derek had just landed, and Sean and Nate weren't far behind.

Liam released the clips holding them together. Kyle took a few steps and pulled his goggles and cap off. "Damn, that was awesome!"

Derek strode over. "Dude!" He high-fived Kyle, and they both grinned from ear to ear. "I had no idea the landing would be that easy. It's like we just walked from the plane onto the ground. More or less."

Liam chuckled. He remembered his first time. He'd practically bounced back up into the air after landing, and he really hadn't come down out of the clouds for weeks. Maybe he never really had.

They turned and walked toward Sean, who was pulling off his goggles and cap.

"What'd you think?" Liam asked.

Sean's face split into a grin. "Brilliant. Next time Tori has to come. She tried to convince me to bring her today, but I told her it was guys' day, just like they had their girls' night."

Liam, Nate, and Rylan gathered up the chutes, and they headed out of the drop zone back toward the hangar.

Liam wasn't surprised Tori had wanted to come. She'd mentioned going with him a few times in the past, but they hadn't ever found a convenient time, since they'd both been busy growing their careers away from Ribbon Ridge. Then Alex's death had thrown them all into turmoil—her more than anyone, it seemed. But now things were maybe back to normal. Or at least not as turbulent.

His mind turned to the rest of what Sean had said—girls' night. He'd spent the last day and a half reliving everything about Thursday night. Every seductive look

Aubrey had given him, every stroke of her fingertips, every body-melting kiss.

He needed to stop thinking about that before he sported wood.

"That was quite a girls' night," Derek said. "I don't think Chloe ate a thing yesterday until midafternoon."

Sean chuckled. "Tori wasn't much better."

"What happened?' Rylan asked.

Kyle glanced over at him. "Our significant others went out for a girls' night at The Arch and Vine and got wasted. We had to go and rescue them."

Rylan stopped short just outside the hangar. "Wait, Liam has an SO? How'd I miss that? That's major news."

Kyle and Derek exchanged looks, then busted up laughing. "Yeah. No," Derek said. "Kyle misspoke. We—" he gestured to himself, Kyle, and Sean, "—have wives and fiancées. Liam has…his hand?"

This was met with guffaws by everyone, including the jump crew.

"Very funny." Liam was willing to bet he'd gotten more action that night than the rest of them. Their SOs had probably passed out on the way home or shortly thereafter. He said none of that, of course.

Liam strode into the building, and the rest followed. Liam, Nate, and Rylan dropped the chutes and packs. Normally Liam would help them repack the chutes, but Rylan had told him that he and Nate would handle it.

"Liam wasn't empty-handed though," Sean said.

Rylan's mouth curled into a smile, and he shook his head. "He never is."

This was met with agreement and more low laughter. Liam was glad they were all having fun at his expense. Normally he'd join right in with them. Why wasn't he?

Because maybe you're tired of that MO.

He shushed the violently annoying voice in his head.

"He picked up a girl?" Nate asked. Nate was younger than the rest of them and relatively new to Rylan's operation. Liam didn't know him very well.

"One of the women who went out was a friend of ours. She doesn't have an SO, so Liam took her home." Derek narrowed his eyes at Liam as they walked into the locker room. "How'd that go?"

The unspoken question—did you hook up?—didn't even need to be asked. Liam understood that's what everyone wanted to know. "She actually *does* have an SO. Or at least she's seeing some accountant."

Everyone stripped off their tandem rigging, and Nate went around picking it up. Then he disappeared with it.

"Why let that stop you?" Kyle asked. "I seem to recall you stealing at least one girl away from another guy. Remember Tracy in high school?"

Liam stowed his goggles in his locker, where he kept his personal chute. "Kyle, I was a teenager. I don't make a habit of poaching women. Get a life." He grabbed his wallet and slipped his shades on, then strode from the locker room, having tolerated all he could of their teasing.

Liam stalked outside to where Kyle had parked his car. Rather, Hayden's car. He was driving Hayden's car, living in Hayden's house, and for at least a little while longer, doing Hayden's job. Classic Kyle—riding on someone else's coattails instead of doing something for himself.

Liam blew out a breath. That was incredibly unfair. He was just pissed off. Not at Kyle, but at himself. At whatever the hell had him obsessed with Aubrey Tallinger twenty-four-seven.

He turned and saw Kyle coming toward him. He wore sunglasses, too, but Liam read the scowl on his face even from this far away.

"What gives, asshole?" Kyle stopped in front of him and crossed his arms over his chest.

Liam shrugged. "I was just tired of the needling."

"Seriously? You're the chief needler. You can dish it out, but you can't take it?"

Liam put his hands on his hips. "You know that isn't true."

"Not usually." Kyle dropped his arms. "Look, we give each other shit. That's what we do—you and I more than the rest of them. And giving you shit about your romantic life is about the only thing we *can* do. You're Mr. Perfect everywhere else."

Liam arched a brow as his anger faded. "You used to think I was Mr. Perfect in that department, too."

Kyle laughed. "Then we all fell head over ass in love. Now you're the aberration. Sorry, man."

He was right. Maybe that was his problem. He was just feeling left out. Or something. Whatever. He was tired of analyzing his stupid obsession with Aubrey. "I'm glad you came out today. It's about time you all did this with me."

"It was a blast. Maybe we can try windsurfing next. Since you're home for a while. Just think, if you moved back, we could have a regular thrill-seeking crew."

Liam doubted they'd want to keep up with him. It was one thing to skydive once in a while, but Liam was always on the hunt for the next rush. Plus, he wasn't moving back home. "I'm just here temporarily."

Kyle nodded and stuck his hands on his hips, tucking his fingers into the pockets of his jeans. "I get it. What's your next conquest?"

Had he been reading Liam's mind? He didn't want to tell Kyle about his plans to try BASE jumping. He might think it was cool, and hell, he might even support him, but if Kyle let it slip to Mom…Liam didn't want to deal with her worrying.

"Just the usual. I'm looking at buying a plane." Rylan was helping him out.

Kyle angled his head. "Really? That's cool. What kind?"

"Haven't decided yet. Looking at Cessnas and some others."

"New or used?"

Liam laughed. "Aren't you full of questions?"

"As much as you're full of secrets." Kyle took a step toward him. "Why do you do this? The skydiving, the rock climbing, the cliff diving, all of it?"

"Because it's fun. You just jumped out of a plane, and it was awesome, right?"

"Completely, but it doesn't make me want to go climb Mt. Everest."

That was actually one of the few things Liam didn't want to do. At least not yet. Who knew if he might change his mind? "I'm not doing that."

"Okay, not that, but you get me. You're always upping the ante, always going big. But maybe it's time you go home."

Liam laughed. "I see what you did there. Go big, or go home. You're a riot."

Kyle took off his glasses. "I'm being serious for once. And feel free to crack all the jokes that statement requires."

"I'll contain myself." But damn it was hard.

"Why do you do this?" Kyle asked. "Is it really just about the adrenaline?"

"Yep."

"But you're so...driven about it."

Liam tipped his head down and looked at Kyle over the top of his shades. "I'm driven about everything."

"True. But this is different. It's one thing to have professional ambition. These hobbies of yours actually carry a decent amount of risk."

"So does driving to work every day or eating a sandwich."

Kyle rolled his eyes and put his glasses back on. "You're being a dick again."

"I don't know how to be anything else around you." Again, that was their brotherly thing, but Liam didn't want to be a dick. Neither did he want to explain the reasons for his extreme sports. Those reasons were too wrapped up in Alex, in *their* brotherly—twin—thing.

Liam stepped toward Kyle and clapped him on the bicep. "I hear what you're saying. I've tried to…lay off a bit, especially while I'm home. Don't want Mom having a breakdown or something."

"I would laugh at that, except she nearly did have one last year after Alex died."

Liam knew that as well as any of them, even if he hadn't been home dealing with it. He'd talked to Mom on the phone plenty, and that entire mess was one of the reasons he couldn't forgive Alex for what he'd done.

"I know, and I don't want to add to her stress, especially when she's doing better." Liam dropped his hand from Kyle's arm. "She and Dad seem great now."

Kyle nodded. "Totally. They've been looking at beach property."

More and more it sounded like Dad was prepping for at least semi-retirement. "Really? I'll have to talk to him about that. I'd love to invest in some stuff on the coast."

Kyle grinned. "I bet you would."

Liam looked toward the hangar. "Here they come finally. What took them so long?"

"I might've asked them to give us a few minutes."

Liam grunted but was actually glad Kyle had done that.

"So tomorrow I'm making a special dinner to welcome Evan and Alaina back home."

"Right, they're due back late tonight."

Kyle shook his head. "Dude, we're going to be uncles. That's crazy."

"I really can't believe Evan is going to be a dad." Just the thought nearly gave Liam hives. To have someone that dependent on him...He inwardly cringed.

"I know, right? He's the last Archer I would've expected." Kyle gave him a taunting grin. "After you, of course."

Liam smiled back as they fell back into their brotherly teasing. This he could handle. "Natch."

Derek and Sean strolled up.

"Ready?" Kyle asked.

"Let's go," Sean said. "Tori and I told Evan and Alaina we'd stock their fridge with some staples before they got home. Can't leave a pregnant woman without pickles or ice cream or whatever."

Kyle laughed as he remotely unlocked the car. "Tori's being too nice. Aren't we supposed to short-sheet their bed or fill their bathtub with cornflakes?"

Derek snorted. "What is this, nineteen sixty?"

"Hey, that would be hilarious," Sean said. "But I doubt they'd appreciate us messing with their new place."

They'd scored a gated nine-acre property with a sprawling six-thousand-square-foot house just south of Ribbon Ridge and had moved in only a week before they'd gotten married.

"You've been watching the house while they've been gone, right?" Liam asked as they all climbed into the car. "Are those asshole paparazzi gone?"

"Finally," Sean said. "The last ones cleared out at the beginning of the week. They threatened to come back as soon as they heard Alaina was back in town, but I made it clear that everyone in Ribbon Ridge would make their lives difficult. Good luck finding a place to stay in town."

"Not gonna happen," Kyle said as he started the car.

"Or eating or getting gas," Sean continued.

Derek turned from the front passenger seat and threw a grin back at Liam and Sean. "I love this town."

Kyle pulled out of the parking lot and got on the highway toward Ribbon Ridge. "Is Aubrey coming tomorrow night?"

The earlier irritation Liam had battled resurfaced. Kyle wasn't going to give him shit again, was he? "No, why?"

Kyle shrugged. "She came last week to watch *Game of Thrones*, and it seems like she's pretty friendly with the girls. I just thought she might come. I'll talk to Maggie, see if she knows."

Liam didn't want to see Aubrey tomorrow night. He'd spend the entire time fantasizing about her and ending up picturing her with Stuart the Accountant. It was probably—no it *absolutely* was—selfish of him, but he couldn't do it. "I think she's too busy with the appeal." And that wasn't a lie. She had to finish it this week.

"Good point," Derek said. "I'll be so glad when that's over."

Kyle scoffed. "No kidding. Total pain in my ass. My restaurant should've been open months ago."

Though Liam wasn't personally involved in The Alex, he still wanted this resolved for his family. He was pissed that the Parkers had caused this nightmare in the first place. But it would be over soon, and then he could get back to Denver. Back to his life.

Away from Aubrey Tallinger.

Chapter Eleven

AUBREY CAUTIOUSLY LET herself into the back door of the Archers' house for dinner on Sunday night. She'd thought about declining Chloe's invitation, but why? She couldn't resist *Game of Thrones* on their theater screen with their theater sound system. Plus, they were her friends—including Liam.

Yeah, right.

She hadn't seen or talked to him since Thursday night. Would he be here? She assumed so. Would they pretend it had never happened? Would the air crackle between them like a late-summer storm?

Not if she didn't let it.

Determined to be as chill as the beer she was about to drink, she moved into the kitchen and smiled. "Hi!"

Tori immediately turned from the counter. "Hey, Aubrey, I'm so glad you came!" She moved closer and lowered her voice. "Feeling much better than Friday, I hope?"

"Yes, you?"

Tori nodded. "I'm going with I was out of practice. I haven't had a girls' night in forever."

Aubrey laughed. "I'll go with that, too. Perfect."

"What's perfect?"

Aubrey turned at the sound of Liam's voice. He'd come down the back stairs, apparently. His hair was damp as if he'd just showered, and he smelled like it, too—fresh, clean, way too sexy. He wore a heather-blue T-shirt and a pair of jeans with a snag on the thigh. Perfect, indeed.

Chill, Aubrey, remember?

"Oh, nothing," Tori said, thankfully saving Aubrey from her momentary lack of speech and reason.

Liam looked past them at the counter. "What's for dinner?"

"Taco bar," Tori said. "There's chicken and carnitas, corn and flour tortillas, shells, even salad makings if you'd rather have taco salad."

Aubrey's stomach growled. She could so get used to these Sunday dinners.

"I'm going to grab a beer." Liam cast his steel-blue gaze toward Aubrey. "You want one?"

"Sure."

He headed toward the tap, and she followed, thinking she ought to say *something* about the other night. Apologize, at least.

He grabbed a couple of pint glasses and set to filling them.

Aubrey stood on the opposite side of the bar from him. It was far safer to have solid granite and wood cabinetry between them. "I'm sorry about the other night. I was, uh, pretty toasted."

"I'll say." He chuckled as he handed her the beer.

So they were going to laugh it off? Sounded good to her. "I hope we're still friends."

"Yep." He lowered his voice and glanced around. "Did you know you're actually my first woman friend?"

Now it was her turn to laugh. "Why does this not surprise me?"

He shrugged. "Because you know me pretty well."

She ignored the little jolt of pleasure that shot through her. "I wanted to ask if you could recommend where to go rafting in southern Oregon. I'm planning a trip this summer with my aunt and uncle."

His eyes instantly lit, and she realized in that moment that an excited Liam made everything around him exciting. She suddenly felt more engaged, more *alive*. "There are so many awesome places. And I know a guy who does really fantastic trips on the Upper Klamath. I'll e-mail you a list tomorrow." He took a drink of beer. "I haven't been down there in years. Sounds like a great time."

Was he angling for an invitation? Even if he were, she wasn't going to offer one. Instead, maybe she could get him to talk about whatever he was planning for the summer. "Do you raft much anymore?"

"At least a couple times a summer, but usually in Colorado. I haven't done something up here in a long time. Might be overdue."

She perched on one of the barstools. "What else do you do in the summer?"

He swallowed another drink of beer. "Rock climbing, hiking, flying, lots of skydiving."

"Is that still your favorite thing?"

"Yep." He narrowed his eyes slightly. "Why all the questions?"

"Just curious, making small talk, like *friends* do." She sipped her beer. "Plus, you offered to take me flying, remember. Or was that riding on your bike? Assuming you got a helmet."

He winced. "Not yet. And yes, I remember the flying. We talked about next weekend, right?"

"Depends on whether I have to work—I've got a busy week ahead, and I still have to finish the zoning brief."

"What's taking so long?" He dropped his head briefly, then looked back up with a half-smile. "I didn't mean it to sound like that. I just thought you were going to send me a draft, and you're two weeks in."

Honestly, she thought she would've sent him a draft by now, too, but things had been really hectic. "I've had a couple of things blow up at work, and one of the other attorneys had a crisis last week that we all pitched in to help with." They did that for each other all the time. It was one of the reasons she loved working for such a small, intimate firm.

"No worries. I'm sure it's coming along great."

For the most part. For whatever reason, Aubrey was second-guessing almost everything she wrote. But then, she was more personally involved in this case than perhaps anything she'd ever done. She'd come to know this family so well. Plus, she'd been privy to the origination of the idea of the entire project—she was the first person Alex had shared it with, *and* he'd entrusted her to ensure it came to fruition. If Parker won his appeal, she sometimes thought that no one would feel the loss more keenly than her.

Aubrey only nodded. "I'll send it over as soon as it's done." She had a fleeting urge to bail on dinner and the show, but her stomach growled again, and she decided that was a bad idea.

Liam braced his palms on the counter. "Back to the flying. How about we go after you file the brief? It'll be a sort of celebration."

She squinted at him. "I'm not sure I want to celebrate before a decision is made. I don't want to jinx anything."

"I didn't realize you were superstitious. That's silly. We're celebrating you finishing the brief, not defeating the Parkers—but don't worry, we'll celebrate that, too." He said this with such certainty and his eyes were so clear with conviction that she couldn't help but believe it. At least right now, looking at him. He did wonders for her confidence, she realized. Maybe because *he* was so confident.

"Dinner!" Kyle called out. Archers filtered into the kitchen from who-knew-where, and everyone made a big deal of allowing Alaina to eat first. "We're having tacos tonight because that's what the expectant mother requested. I sense several taco bars in our future."

"For at least the next seven months," Alaina said, laughing. "Thank you. Fair warning, I might eat everything that's not touched, so dish up!"

The line formed for the taco bar, which was situated on both sides of the main kitchen island, and it moved pretty quickly. Liam and Aubrey were last, and by the time Aubrey had her plate ready, she realized there weren't any chairs left at the table.

Emily looked up from her seat. "I'm so sorry! I have two more chairs on order—they're being delivered Wednesday. For now, you'll have to sit at the counter. Or in the dining room. Sit wherever you like." She started to stand. "Or Rob and I can move."

Liam waved her back down. "Don't be silly. Aubrey and I will find a spot." He looked over at her. "Like Mom said, there's the island or the beer bar, or the dining room, but that's pretty formal, or we can head downstairs to the game area. The card table has a hard top on it. Or there's the bar down there, too."

The Archers' house was immense, but then, to fit a family of nine, it had needed to be. They were also a family of wealth, so they had things like game areas, theaters, wine cellars, gyms, and outdoor inground pools.

Going anywhere outside the kitchen meant being alone with Liam. "Here's fine." She took her plate back over to the beer tap and sat on the stool she'd used earlier.

Liam joined her, taking the stool to her right. He pulled his phone from his back pocket and set it on the counter.

They were close enough that Aubrey could feel his warmth and smell his shower gel. It would be so easy to edge toward him, to nudge her thigh against his. But friends didn't do that.

"You know, I should be the one apologizing for the other night." His voice was low, his attention on the soft taco he'd rolled in his hand. "I was the sober one, and I shouldn't have...Anyway, I shouldn't have."

Wow, this was a sweet side to him. Seemed like she was seeing all sorts of different sides of Liam—aspects she'd seen glimpses of during their various hook-ups. He was turning out to maybe be the man she'd hoped he was. The man she'd started to fall for. She liked this Liam. "It's not your fault at all. You were just trying to be a gentleman and make sure I didn't pass out in my own vomit or something. I'm the one who took advantage."

He laughed. "That's quite a picture. I'd argue there wasn't any advantage to take. I'm always game for a night of fun with you." He flicked her a glance, and its heat was enough to scald every part of her. In the most delicious way possible. "But I get that you're with Stuart."

He hadn't called him Stuart the Accountant. And she wasn't actually *with* Stuart anymore. If she ever had been. She didn't tell Liam that, however. If she could hide behind a faux relationship with Stuart, why not make things a little bit easier for herself? If Liam thought she was off-limits, he wouldn't flirt with her or touch her. She could handle a toned-down Liam far more than a Liam who was on the hunt.

But oh how she loved being his prey.

She forced herself to focus on her dinner. Wasn't she supposed to be starving?

His phone vibrated, and she glanced at the screen. There was a text that read: *Date confirmed! Let me know when you want to practice.* This was followed by a thumbs-up icon.

Liam picked it up and clicked the screen off. "That's my friend Rylan."

"What are you going to practice?"

"Just some acrobatics." There was something in his tone that didn't quite ring true.

Aubrey looked over at him. "Skydiving?"

He nodded. "Yep."

The fact that he wasn't regaling her with details seemed a bit suspicious, but she didn't say so.

She managed to make it through the rest of dinner and the show afterward without thinking of Liam naked. And by the time she was getting ready to leave, she was almost convinced that they *could* be friends. Still, she was glad for the opportunity to walk out with Sean and Tori before Liam could offer to escort her to her car. Not that he would've, but it was a bullet she'd just as soon dodge.

"I'll look forward to reading the brief," Liam said to her as she turned to go.

"Thanks, I'll send it soon."

She walked out with Tori and Sean and hoped the brief would be good enough. For more reasons than she cared to count.

LIAM HAD RETREATED to his room to catch up on some e-mail before heading to bed. His mind kept returning to Aubrey. He'd had a good time with her tonight, and they hadn't tried to paw each other. Or even flirt, really. Okay, maybe a little. He couldn't seem to *not* flirt with her. How could he avoid trying to make her smile or coax that sparkle into her eye? He quite simply couldn't. Around her, he became a boy with an infatuation.

His phone vibrated on the desk, and his pulse quickened, as he hoped it was her. But it was Whitney calling. He still hadn't remembered to block her number.

Annoyed with himself as much as her, he answered. "You have to stop calling me."

"Hello to you, too," she said, all sarcasm and spite. "I'm surprised you picked up. You seem to be treating me like the plague."

"I'd actually rather have the plague. It's easier to get rid of than you. But I suppose until they come up with an antibiotic that cures Whitney Stalking, I'm screwed."

Her loud laughter made him pull the phone away from his ear. "You are so funny. I'd say you're being mean, but I actually think you're flirting with me."

"I've never flirted with you." Not even when he'd slept with her. Not at all like he did with Aubrey. They weren't remotely in the same league, as far as he was concerned. "Whitney, I don't know how to be any more plain—I don't want to see you. I don't want to talk to you. I'd be happy pretending we'd never met." He gripped the phone tightly and practically growled into it. "*Really.*"

"Too bad because we *have* met. And I know you as intimately as anyone possibly could."

He regretted everything they'd done together. "You don't know shit."

"I know you've got this oval freckle on your inner thigh and that if I stroke your balls a certain way, you'll come twice as hard."

"And this conversation is over. I'm blocking you now." He pulled the phone away again but heard her yell.

"Wait! Don't hang up." She lowered her voice an octave. Thank goodness, because he was pretty sure all the dogs in the area were on high alert due to her pitch. "I have a proposition for you. About the zoning appeal."

He closed his eyes and exhaled. "Are you still going to pretend you have nothing to do with it?"

"My dad is completely responsible for hiring Sutherlin and filing the appeal, not me."

He believed that much. "But I can't imagine you mind. Or that you're an innocent bystander. Last time we saw each other, you said you'd talk to your dad if I slept with you."

"I don't remember saying that."

He rolled his eyes. "Not exactly, but I'm pretty sure that's what you meant."

"Well," she said pertly, "it doesn't matter. I'd like to propose a formal arrangement. You make your-self...*available* to me at least once a quarter, and I'll convince my dad to drop the appeal."

Once a quarter? What, did she want him to sign a contract or something? He might've behaved like a man-whore at various times in his life, but he wasn't *actually* one. "Let's be direct. Please? Do you want me to have tea with you every three months, or are you asking for some-thing else?"

"You'll have to spend the night with me. And have sex. At least twice."

Oh for fuck's sake. She was insane. "Good-bye, Whitney. I'm blocking you now." He disconnected the call and Googled how to block her number, then did just that.

As he set the phone down, he heard a footfall in the hallway and looked toward the half-open door.

Evan pushed inside. "Hey."

Liam turned, the stiff seat of his old chair creaking as he tried to maneuver it. In the end, he had to push on the edge of the desk to rotate properly. "Hey, Evan."

Evan's gaze was on the chair instead of Liam. "You need some new furniture."

Liam laughed. "A chair, maybe, but I don't spend enough time here to make it worthwhile."

Evan walked into his room. "Are you sure? I was pretty surprised to get back from my honeymoon and find that you were still here. What gives?" He went to the double bed, which felt cramped after Liam's king back in Denver, and sat down.

"I'm hanging out for the zoning appeal."

"Why? From what I understand, Aubrey's still working on her response, and then it could be a few weeks until the oral argument. Seems like you could do everything you're doing from Denver."

That was more than true. "I've, uh, been checking out The Alex, doing some skydiving, and working from here, of course." He gestured to his open laptop on the desk.

Evan vaguely nodded, his gaze landing on Liam periodically during the conversation. "I'm surprised. It's strange enough that *I* came home, but your being here defies logic."

Liam didn't understand what he meant. Logically, they all should have come home, at least temporarily or intermittently to help with the project Alex had laid out. But life wasn't logical. Evan, however, was sometimes ruled by logic.

Liam rested his elbows on the arms of the chair he'd gotten when he'd started high school. "Why is that, exactly?"

"Because you've worked harder than anyone to establish a life outside of Ribbon Ridge that would be difficult to leave. Kyle had no strings in Florida, and Sara wasn't that far away to begin with." She'd been living about forty-five minutes outside Ribbon Ridge and running a successful event-planning business when Alex had died.

"Sara still had a business."

"Which she sold, like I sold mine." Evan had been a tech consultant with his own one-man firm. "Are you really going to sell your business?"

Right. Sell off millions of dollars' worth of commercial real estate and the revenue that generated. "Hell no."

"My point exactly. You're never coming back here, and you set it up that way."

Liam still wasn't sure where Evan was going, but that wasn't necessarily surprising. He sometimes rambled or just outright talked in circles. It was part of his autism. It was also what made him the brother Liam loved. "So your point is that I moved away with the intention of never coming back."

"Yes."

"Didn't you do that, too?" Liam asked. Evan had moved a couple of hours north into southwest Washington.

"Yes, and do you know why? I mean, do you *really* know why?"

"To exercise your independence?"

Evan quirked a smile. "You could say that, too, but that's a lame explanation, and you know it. I left because of the noise. Everyone was always hovering over me. They did the same thing to Sara. That's why she left, too."

Liam didn't want to, but he couldn't help but think of Alex. No one had endured more hovering than him. But he hadn't been able to leave. Well, Liam supposed he could've, but who would've taken care of him when he was ill?

"You didn't really *have* to go, though. You had a built-in job and everything." Evan was referring to Archer Enterprises' real-estate division.

"I wanted to build something on my own. You know that."

Evan lifted a shoulder. "You could've taken Archer Real Estate to the next level, but you didn't."

"I'm really confused now. It defies logic that I came back, and yet you're saying I never should've left."

"No, I'm not making any kind of judgment what-soever. It defies logic that you came back, because you worked so hard to leave, to escape this situation."

Liam's chest twisted. This conversation was edging very close to something he'd never discussed with any of them. "And what situation was that?"

He leaned forward, his gaze landing on Liam for a long, solid moment. "Alex. You hated being here. Seeing him. And that's okay, because he hated seeing you, too."

Holy shit. Evan had laid it out perfectly. The things that he and Alex never said to each other but were tacit understandings. *I'll do my thing over here, you do yours over there. We keep in touch, we do the sports, we don't have to live together.*

Liam's pulse slammed in his throat. "Why are you bringing this up now?"

"Because I'm wondering if you're ready to come home now that he's gone. You can be here without feeling guilty, without worrying how much he resents you."

Of course Evan, who had practically zero filter, would state things so truthfully and also so accurately.

"You haven't talked about this to anyone else, have you?" Liam hesitated to ask him that. He didn't want it to seem like Evan shouldn't say anything. He was terrible at secrets.

"No, and I won't. I think some of them get it anyway, even if they don't really think about it. I mean, why *would* you think about it? It's kind of depressing and fucked up, isn't it?"

So. Much.

"Anyway," Evan continued, "I'm actually really good at secrets now. When I got the job at Archer last fall, no one knew it was me for a few months."

Liam stared at his brother. Like the rest of them, he'd changed. He'd…evolved or something. And now he was going to be a father. "You're going to be a great dad, you know."

Evan barked out a laugh. "I don't know that at all, but thanks for saying so. Alaina's going to be the world's best mother, so I figure I have a little wiggle room."

"You like being back here? Working at Archer?"

Again, Evan looked him in the eye. "I love it. I honestly can't believe how much. The job is…fantastic. And Alaina and the baby…" He swiped his hand through his hair. "I was pretty overwhelmed at first—still am sometimes—but I've never felt like this before. I never imagined I could feel like this. I mean, I've always been happy enough. I love the family. Things are good. But this transcends all that." He laughed. "Listen to me being all poetic and shit."

Liam was still trying to process everything Evan had said. What he was describing almost felt like the way Liam felt when his adrenaline rush took over, that indescribable high that, yeah, pretty much transcended everything. "I think I get it."

Evan shook his head. "You only think you do. Until you fall in love, until you find that person who just makes everything *right*, you don't really know. Sorry, bro."

Irritation scratched at Liam's brain. He didn't like it when people told him he didn't know something. But maybe Evan was right. Liam had never been in love. He had no idea what that felt like and probably never would. He'd actually have to let someone close enough, and that wasn't happening.

And why was that exactly?

Because letting someone into his heart meant exposing himself, being vulnerable. It meant letting them see the ugly truths Evan had just revealed out loud. It also meant tying himself to something permanently. Like to an oxygen tank.

Liam jerked in physical response. He sat up straight and pulled his arms from the chair, resting his hands in his lap.

If Evan saw him twitch, he didn't say so. He stood up from the bed. "I just stopped by to say hi. I had to pick up a few things that were still in my room. Can't be officially moved into my new house until my stuff's on display." He had to be referring to his myriad of sci-fi collectibles.

"If that was you saying hi, I'd hate to see what a heart-to-heart looks like," Liam joked.

Evan wiped a hand over his face. "Yeah, I hadn't planned on coming in here and getting all sentimental and crap. Sorry. I'm just glad you're here, for however long. See you later."

Liam watched Evan go, but the sense of unease his words had generated lasted long after he'd gone. Liam was just glad Evan hadn't pursued wanting to know whether he was staying in Ribbon Ridge permanently. Because right now the answer was still a fat no. It was becoming evident that those who came back settled down, and he'd just established that he couldn't do that. There was no way his future was in Ribbon Ridge.

Chapter Twelve

WAS THERE ANYTHING better than a smooth pinot gliding down your throat after a long day in court? Aubrey sat back on her couch and put her feet up on the ottoman.

Okay, maybe buttery soft yoga pants, fuzzy socks, and a favorite sweatshirt were a close second. She reached for the remote and turned on the TV, intent on checking out her DVR to see what treasures she'd missed the past few weeks while she'd been furiously working on perfecting the zoning brief along with all of her other matters. The only thing she'd kept up on was *Game of Thrones*, and that was only because the Archers had invited her over.

She had a great time at those Sunday dinners and would be disappointed when they stopped. When would that be? When the zoning was finalized? But she would still be overseeing Alex's trust until The Alex was finished. That would be in a couple of months or so. Maybe then she'd part ways with the Archers.

But she didn't see that happening. She'd become good friends with so many of them, and she had privileged access to their mudroom door. Plus, Ribbon Ridge was a small town, and she wouldn't be able to avoid the Archers even if she wanted to.

Okay, so they were friends forever. Or something. That didn't mean she had to continue going to Sunday dinner over there, especially when she found Mr. Right and started her own family. *Game of Thrones* only lasted a few more weeks, damn the short seasons anyway, so by the end of that, she could politely excuse herself from the routine.

Bummer.

She sensed it would be far easier than parting ways with Liam, although they'd made good progress on Sunday. They'd spent the entire evening in each other's orbit without touching, and she'd kept her mind out of the gutter. Mostly.

After finally finding satisfaction with the brief, she'd forwarded it to him last night. He hadn't responded. No *Thanks for sending* or *I'll get back to you soon*. Nothing. She might have fired it off into a black hole. If he could keep ignoring her like that, her job of ditching him would get a whole lot easier.

Sinking farther into the couch, she pulled up the DVR menu and scanned the shows she'd recorded. Ugh, why was she still recording some of these? There were shows she hadn't watched in over a year. As she set about cleaning things up, a knock on the door startled her.

She set the remote on the couch and stood up to look through the windows in the door. Liam again?

He knocked, and she went to the door, opening it wide. It was a good thing, because he walked right in without waiting for her to invite him.

"Hi, Liam. Come in." She shut the door with a loud click.

He walked into the front room and set his helmet on the window seat. "I read the brief."

She stepped toward him but kept her distance. Given the firm downturn of his mouth and the pitch of his brows, she gathered he hadn't liked what she'd written. "What's wrong with it?"

His expression didn't alter. "It's fine."

"Then why are you looking at me as if I've just fed you bad fish?"

At that, his features loosened, but only for a moment. The grooves in his forehead came back almost immediately. "Because it's not good enough to beat Sutherlin."

How dare he? She'd worked her ass off on that brief. Pure anger scalded her insides and burned away any trace of shame she'd felt at being in his presence again. "How would you know?"

"Because I've been a party to a dozen of these cases. Maybe more. How many have you done?"

One. *This* one. She bristled but refused to let him see her vulnerability. "Why does that matter?"

"Because Sutherlin has probably done *hundreds*."

She crossed her arms, and her shoulders tensed up. "Tell me specifically what's wrong."

"I e-mailed you a detailed list about a half hour ago."

A detailed list? "As you can see, I'm done working for the day. I'll read it tomorrow." She dropped her arms and turned toward the front door. "Sorry you rode all the way over here just to tell me something you'd already put in an e-mail. I thought you were a little more technologically savvy than that."

He advanced on her, his gaze softening, turning almost condescending—or so it seemed in her agitated state. "I wanted to talk to you in person. Like a friend would."

"A friend who tells you that you're a terrible lawyer? Thanks, but I think I'm actually good on the friend front." Unlike her vulnerability, she didn't bother trying to hide her smirk or her annoyance. "You know, if you had such a problem with me handling this case, you should've said so from the start."

He stared at her. "I did. I also never said I had a problem with you handling it. I just have a problem with the brief. Read my notes, and fix it. You'll see I'm right."

"Or maybe you should find a new attorney, and *they* can fix it." She turned and walked toward the door, intent on throwing it open and shoving him outside.

He followed her. "Hey, why are you so mad?"

She put her hand on the doorknob and was about to turn it when he put his palm flat against the edge, holding it closed.

"Tell me why you're so mad."

She didn't release the doorknob but turned her head to glare at him. "You just came here to tell me my hard work is subpar, and you have the gall to ask why I'm mad?"

He lifted his hand from the door and brushed it through his hair. "Hey, I'm trying not to be a dick. Sometimes with work stuff I can be a little too intense. Sorry. Was I a dick about it?"

Maybe not, but that didn't change things. Change what exactly? That he was here in her house again, and all she wanted to do was drag him upstairs and toss him on her bed?

She turned the knob and pulled the door open, but he slammed it shut with his palm.

"What the hell?" Her eyes widened, and she stared at him.

"I think you're picking a fight with me on purpose," he said. "This feels strangely like the first time we met. When I picked a fight with you. I accused you of taking advantage of Alex, of billing him for hours and hours of work when you knew he was going to kill himself. I did everything except come out and accuse you of helping him to commit suicide."

"Actually, I think you might've done that, too." She'd been horrified by his anger, but even more than that, she'd been anguished by his grief—because she'd felt it, too. She'd felt incredibly used and duped by Alex, a man she'd come to like, respect, and trust.

Liam had been so angry that tears had actually leaked from his eyes. Not many, maybe two or three, and she wasn't sure to this day if he'd even been aware of them. But from the moment she'd seen them, she hadn't been able to sustain her anger with him. Desperate to help him, she'd reached out and touched his face.

And that was all it had taken.

The contact had been like electricity—sharp and sudden, transformative. She hadn't known then but in hindsight recognized she would never be the same.

He ignited something within her. A power and drive, a connection to another person that seemed to eclipse any other relationship she'd had.

All of their grief, their desperation, their need had flowed between them. A moment later, when their lips met, it had honestly felt like some Grand Destiny, the kind of epic love story moment that made most people roll their eyes.

It was remarkable considering he'd stormed into her office like a giant...dick. Not like tonight. He might've been dick*ish*, but he hadn't been as awful as that night.

"I'd rather not think about that," she said at last, too aware of his hand on the door and its proximity to her hand on the knob.

"I can't seem to think of anything else right now. Something happened that night..."

Oh God, if he said anything close to what she'd felt, she would melt into a giant puddle, and there would be absolutely no hope for her where he was concerned. She was trying so hard to get over him, and he was making it impossible.

"Please don't talk about it." She sounded croaky as a frog.

He moved his hand down the door. She saw it happen, could've moved her hand away. But she didn't. When he touched her, it was that night in her office all over again. Except this time she knew. She knew how it could end.

His fingers grazed over her thumb and stroked up to her wrist. "It's too bad you're seeing Stuart, because if you weren't, I would put that night to shame."

Desire, already pooling thick and hot in her belly, ignited into a firestorm of lust. Unable to look in his eyes, she kept her focus on the door. "As a matter of fact, I'm not seeing Stuart, so I guess you'll have to rely on your 'friends' excuse."

He twined his fingers through hers and lifted her arm, pinning it against the door as he pivoted into her. She had no choice but to turn with him until her back was against the wood. His blue-gray eyes bore into hers, stoking the need rioting through her. "I'd rather be your lover than your friend. Will you let me? Please?"

She shouldn't. He wasn't her future. He didn't know how to plan past next weekend's thrill ride. But he was right now. Here. And she'd never wanted anything or anyone so badly in her life. One more time. One more night to carry her through all the other nights to come.

With her free hand, she grabbed the front of his shirt and pulled him forward. "*Yes*. For tonight. Just like the song." She knew he would understand the Dave Matthews Band song she meant.

He slipped his hand along her neck and cupped the back of it as his lips found hers. As familiar as his kiss had become, it was always as thrilling as the first time. Even when she'd been drunk the other night, she'd reveled in the rush of excitement and her insatiable need for him.

He pushed his tongue into her mouth as his hips came against hers, grinding.

Apparently his need was just as insatiable.

She pushed his jacket off and tossed it toward the window seat, but missed. Uncaring, she clutched at his back with her free hand, then moved it down to his ass. She widened her stance and pulled him harder into her body. She wanted to feel him against her core. She wanted him to ease the ache she'd been living with for far too damn long.

He licked and sucked at her mouth, reminding her of why he was the most skilled lover she'd ever had. He'd used that word—*lover*—and she'd been lost. She'd had boyfriends, but she didn't think she'd ever had a *lover*. She worried she wouldn't have one ever again.

She closed her mind to that thought. To everything but the heat of his tongue, the pulse of his chest against hers, the rigidity of his cock pressing between her legs.

He released her hand and brought his hand to her side, massaging her through the bulk of her sweatshirt. The cozy garment had been a great idea for relaxing on the couch. Not so much for sexy times with the hottest guy she'd ever known. She let him go in order to tug at the hem and pull it over her head.

Realizing her intent, he helped. And was much more efficient as he stripped it from her with one fluid movement. He had to break the kiss, and he'd apparently opened his eyes—as she had.

"You aren't wearing a bra," he rasped.

"I thought I was done for the day. You know, snuggled up on the couch with a glass of wine. Who needs a bra for that?"

The way he stared at her breasts made her heart pound. He made her feel so sexy and desirable. Like he could never get enough of her. But then, that's what *insatiable* meant, wasn't it?

"You don't need a bra ever again, as far as I'm concerned." He brought both hands up and cupped her, weighing her flesh, driving shocks of need deep into her core. Her legs quivered with desire. He ran his thumbs over the nipples, then rolled them between his fingertips before pulling just enough to make her gasp. He repeated the series—cup, thumb, roll, pull. Once, twice, by the third time she'd cast her head back against the door and closed her eyes, letting sensation overtake everything else.

Then his mouth replaced his touch, and she nearly crumpled to the floor. She clutched at his head, threading her fingers into his thick hair, and held onto him as if he could hold her upright. He braced a hand on her hips, squeezing her, and that helped her stay on her feet as dizzying waves of pleasure washed over her. He sucked and licked, making a feast of her flesh, before moving to the other one, where he repeated the delicious torture.

She widened her legs, and he seemed to understand her unspoken need as his palm covered her and pressed against her clit. But then, he always knew what she wanted before she did. He knew things she wanted that she'd never even imagined. Things that were now firmly entrenched in her dreams.

But this wasn't a dream. This was real. This was happening. And it flew in the face of every bit of common sense she possessed. He pressed harder against her. A flash of light ignited behind her closed eyes as ecstasy warned her that an orgasm wasn't far off.

Screw common sense.

He pulled his mouth from her breast and came back up. His lips and tongue teased her ear as his hand moved over her yoga pants. "Where? Here? Someplace else?"

They'd had sex in some interesting places and in probably every position imaginable—at least that she could think of. She wouldn't put it past Liam to have something up his sleeve.

She wanted him now. "Couch to your left in the TV room or dining-room table to your right."

His tongue traced the shell of her ear before he whispered, "There's the window seat if you want to give the neighbors a little show."

She wasn't really interested in exhibitionism, but damn if he didn't make it sound sexy as hell. "You're a bad influence, you know that?"

He chuckled low and deep, and she felt the vibration in her chest. "You like it."

She did. She loved it.

"But I think I choose dining-room table for now," he said. "The blinds in there are closed, I see. Later, I'm taking you up to your bed. If memory serves, it's particularly comfortable, and I think you have a vibrator in your bedside table—"

She pulled his head to hers and kissed him, her mouth open and wet and absolutely desperate. After plundering his mouth, she nipped his lip and looked into his eyes.

They'd darkened to the color of blue spruce. "You're so naughty."

He arched a brow. "You're the one with a sex toy at the ready."

If they didn't escalate this situation fast, she was going to abandon him for said sex toy. "Table. Now."

He slid his hands between her ass and the door and cupped her, squeezing her flesh. Then he lifted her up against the door and thrust, bringing him flush against her core and forcing a delighted gasp from her throat. "Put your legs around me."

She encircled his hips with her legs and locked her feet together behind his ass. He was nice and snug against her now. She wrapped her arms around his neck.

He kissed her hard and fast as he pivoted from the door. "You are so hot—in every sense of the word." With a few short strides he carried her to the dining-room table. "You sure this is going to hold?"

"It's well made. Thick. Hard." She laughed deep in her throat. "Listen to me. You are a *bad* influence."

He walked to the head of the table and moved the chair there before setting her ass on the edge. "I love it when you talk dirty. You might persuade me into a long-distance relationship after all, especially if you promise Skype sex."

His words should've dragged her out of the moment, brought her back to reality—the one where they had no future. But she'd become very adept at ignoring the voice of reason shouting in the recesses of her mind. He was just being flirty and sexy. A big tease.

She could dish it out as good as she could take it. "You don't want a long-distance relationship. You want a convenient screw, and right now that's what I want, too."

He stood between her legs and clasped her hips, frowning. Frowning? "You are much more than that."

"Am I?" Her pulse seemed to stop for a second, but it resumed its frenetic beat almost immediately.

He pushed her hair back from her face and pulled it down her back. "I care about you. A lot. You know that, right?"

She didn't want this conversation. Not right now. Maybe not ever. "You're killing my sex buzz right now, *you* know that, right?"

His mouth spread into a smile, and again her pulse reacted, this time speeding up. He was so unbelievably attractive, especially when he smiled. And when that smile was directed at you…She didn't think there was anything better.

"My bad," he said, looping his thumbs into the back of her yoga pants. "I think these are in the way."

"Along with everything you're wearing."

He pulled at her pants and her underwear, and she lifted her ass from the table so he could strip them over her hips and off her legs. He wasted no time in moving back to stand between her thighs.

She pushed his shirt up and exposed his abs. He was impossibly fit and toned, as if he'd walked out of a *Men's Fitness* spread. The worst part was that she didn't think it took a lot of effort. Granted, he was very active and he did go to the gym, but she'd never seen him worry about what he ate or drinking too much beer.

She pressed her lips to his pec, tracing them over the muscle until she found his nipple. "Your body is so unfair." She licked at him, then sucked hard. He loved that.

He sucked in a breath. "Are you complaining?"

"Only that you're moving too slow." She trailed her mouth across his chest.

He grasped her hips again, kneading her flesh. "My bad again. Is it my fault I enjoy our sexy banter?"

"We didn't always have sexy banter," she said. "I seem to remember our first couple of hook-ups being pretty much conversation-free."

He brought one hand between her thighs and stroked along her cleft. She trembled with need. Suddenly she didn't want any conversation at all. She gripped his bicep. "Liam."

"Mmm." His mouth captured hers in a bruising, delicious kiss while his fingers teased her flesh.

She brought her hips up, seeking more than he was giving her. He was still moving too damn slow.

He broke the kiss and laid his palm flat against her chest. Then he pushed her back—gently but firmly—onto the table. The wood was cool on her bare, heated back. But the exquisite shivers dancing through her body had nothing to do with the temperature and everything to do with Liam. He thumbed her clit, circling her flesh, pressing down, driving her wild with an urgent craving.

She closed her eyes as he thrust a finger into her sheath, answering her need. But it wasn't enough. She wanted more of him. She wanted all of him. Now.

When she felt his tongue against her flesh, her eyes flew open. She tugged on his hair. "No. I don't want to wait."

He licked along her folds and suckled her clit. "I've been thinking of this for days. Weeks. *Months*."

His words excited her more than anything he'd done to her physically. He'd wanted her as badly as she'd wanted him. But that wasn't the obstacle between them. It was, if anything, part of the problem. To want someone so much yet remain unable to forge a future...The direction of her thoughts threatened to devastate what was left of her rational mind.

"Later," she managed, barely clinging to sanity amid his touch, his words, his simple proximity.

He hovered over her, his breath tickling her cleft. "Promise?"

She dug her fingers into his scalp. "*Yes*. Now fuck me. *Please*."

He kissed her one last time, his mouth drawing on her flesh just before he stood. He pulled his wallet from his back pocket and withdrew a condom.

"I see you're prepared, as usual. You're such a cocky bastard."

He arched a brow at her as he unbuttoned his jeans. "I'll show you cocky."

She stared up at his hard chest, at the plane of his stomach, and lower as he revealed himself to her. He pushed his jeans and underwear down over his hips, and she snagged her lower lip with her teeth.

He rolled a condom over his length. "Damn it, Aubrey, this is going to be the shortest sex of my life if you don't stop looking at me like that."

His admission brought a self-satisfied grin to her lips. She came up off the table, intent on touching his cock, but he pushed her back down and shook his head. "Nope. You said you wanted this *right now*. And I'm not in the mood to wait anymore either." He pressed his palms against her inner thighs, opening her legs wider and positioning her at the very edge of the table.

The tips of his thumbs parted her folds, and the head of his cock inched in, stretching her. "God, you feel amazing. Better than I remember, and I remember you feeling pretty fucking fantastic." His voice sounded tight, unbearably aroused.

She couldn't answer him, could barely process his words. He slid in farther, stretching her, filling her, giving her *almost* everything she needed. She reached out and curled her hands around each side of the table, then wrapped her legs around his hips, drawing him fully into her.

"Aubrey, I can't…go slow." He grabbed her hips and surged into her before whipping back out and thrusting forward again. She cast her head back against the table and gave herself over to the rhythm. Her orgasm was close, a promise she could almost taste. But for now she wanted this moment to last. This connection where they couldn't get enough of each other, where yesterday and tomorrow didn't exist.

He moved even faster, pummeling into her with a delicious friction. She squeezed her feet against his ass and wished she could hold him, but there was something so primal about being laid out before him naked while he was still partially clothed, his pants around his ankles, his boots still on his feet. That image made her moan. Or maybe it was the wet heat of his mouth on her breast as he suckled her deep and hard.

She cried out as she started to come. His mouth was abruptly gone, and she worried her orgasm might fly away, too. But then he touched her clit, and her orgasm slammed into her like a meteor crashing to earth.

There was blackness followed by a bright, blinding light, then darkness again as she fell over the cliff. His strokes grew faster, and he yelled. He pumped into her several more times before pitching forward. He caught himself, bracing his hands and then his elbows on either side of her. His rapid breaths came hard against her shoulder, and she nuzzled her cheek against him. He kissed her collarbone, then brushed her hair away from her ear so he could kiss her there, too.

"That was amazing. And I'm holding you to your promise of later," he whispered.

Had she really promised that? Now that they were finished, reality was intruding on her mind, that voice of reason growing louder.

She'd said she would give herself tonight. She was already too far gone to save herself from heartbreak.

She would take tonight for all the other nights that she'd be without him. And she wouldn't allow herself to regret it.

Chapter Thirteen

LIAM POPPED A grape into his mouth while Aubrey refilled his wineglass. She'd graciously offered to share her pinot after their dining-room table adventure. She'd put her yoga pants back on but was now wearing his long-sleeved T-shirt while he was bare-chested. She didn't seem to mind, as he kept catching her staring at his abs.

He would've stared at her chest, too, if she hadn't been wearing his shirt. As it was, her nipples were clearly visible, and the swell of her flesh beneath the cotton only enticed him more. On second thought, he was staring at her chest anyway.

"What?" she asked, her brow furrowing for a brief moment before she took a sip of wine.

"Just appreciating the view."

She rolled her eyes. "I've looked better."

Actually, she'd never looked more beautiful. Her hair was slightly mussed, her cheeks were still pink from the sex, and he loved that he'd made her look like that. Pride and a savage sense of possession crested through him.

Possession? Where the hell had that come from? He inwardly shook himself. *Get your head on, Archer.*

He shoved another grape into his mouth before he said something stupid, like telling her that she was completely different from any other woman he'd been with. Would that be so bad?

It would be when the woman in question wanted a steady, long-term relationship headed for the altar. She'd been pretty clear about that when she'd told him she wanted Mr. Right instead of Mr. Right Now. He wasn't ready for that leap, and he might never be.

He'd built the life he wanted, and it wasn't even in the same state as her, let alone with the same goals. She wanted a husband. Stability. He wanted the next adrenaline rush. Which is what she was for him, he realized.

Fuck.

He took a long drink of wine.

"Listen, I can talk to my uncle. He's done a lot of land use. Honestly, he should've probably been helping me from the start—and he has been, in an advisory capacity. But I admit I didn't have him read the brief before I sent it to you. He's been really busy. He had a complicated trial to deal with."

Liam was relieved for the change of topic, even if it was a potentially touchy one. "I'm sorry I said the brief wasn't good enough. You did a great job, considering it's your first one."

She glanced at him as she plucked a cracker from the plate she'd set out. Once they'd pulled themselves together after the dining-room escapade, they'd come to the kitchen, where she'd assembled a snack plate of fruit, cheese, and crackers—and at his behest, salami. He was thankful because he hadn't eaten dinner.

"Don't feel like you have to pacify me," she said. "Do you want to hire a new attorney? Someone with more experience? Maybe you could get Martin Delacorte."

Delacorte was one of the few attorneys with even more land-use experience than Sutherlin. However, the brief was due in four days. "It's too late to hire someone else." He realized immediately that had been the wrong thing to say. "I don't *want* to hire someone else. You'll do fine."

She nodded, but he didn't think he'd made her feel any better. Damn it, he was an asshole. Wait, why was he overthinking this? This was business. She'd written a brief that needed more work. If she'd been anyone else, he wouldn't have thought twice about telling her that.

But she wasn't anyone else. She was the woman he was sleeping with. The woman he thought about more than he'd ever thought about another person outside of his family. That he was putting her in front of his family—this entire project meant everything to them, and by extension, to him—was disconcerting.

She lifted a shoulder. "If you say so."

He wished they hadn't had to talk about the brief. It had put a damper on his postcoital bliss.

It was also reality, and they couldn't hide from it. No, but they could live in the moment and forget about everything else. He wanted tonight with her. Needed it.

She rolled a piece of cheese and a piece of salami together and took a bite. Absurdly, the cylindrical shape of the food entering her mouth sent a jolt of lust straight to his cock. Shit, he was a man obsessed. Hard not to be when she was sitting across the table from him with her sultry, just-been-screwed gaze lingering on his pecs. Reality could go fuck itself.

He helped himself to the food for a few minutes, hoping to stave off his caveman instinct, which was screaming at him to throw her over his shoulder and cart her upstairs.

She sipped her wine. "So what's going on with taking me flying? I'm submitting the brief on Monday, and you promised me a trip in an airplane."

"I did. I'll see if we can go on Tuesday. If you can get away in the afternoon."

"As it happens, the deposition I had scheduled was canceled, so I am free."

Had they just made a date? No, this was part of their friends thing. Were they friends? Tonight they were definitely lovers, but like she'd said, it was only for tonight. And he'd take what he could get.

What did he really want?

Nope, not going there. That fell firmly in the reality category, and that was off-limits tonight.

As if she'd read his mind, she said. "This is not a date. Just to be clear. We go right back to the Friend Zone tomorrow morning."

He picked up a cracker and a piece of salami, then sat back in his chair. "Got it. Although, you missed out on some fun times when you decided to dump me."

She crossed her arms and also sat back. "Is that right? Why don't you enlighten me?"

And he'd walked right into that one, too. What would he have done? He would've seen her at Christmas if she'd been home. And New Year's if she'd bothered to answer his texts. And again in February after he'd dislocated his shoulder. Three perfectly good opportunities to spend time together and have a lot of sex. But that wasn't what she was asking. She wanted more. She deserved more. He wanted to give her more. Still, he didn't think he could ever give her what she wanted—a picket fence, a family, forever.

"I would've taken you up to our family cabin during the holidays. We would've skied, had a romantic dinner at Timberline Lodge, and made love in front of the fireplace."

She looked mildly surprised or maybe doubtful, her brow arching. "Really?"

Ouch, her opinion stung, but could he fault her? "Yeah, really." He'd had that exact plan in mind when he'd come home for Christmas.

"What else?"

"We would've spent New Year's together—either a swanky party in Portland or something quieter, maybe a cozy condo at the beach."

She picked up her wineglass and smiled. "Sounds great. I love the beach. I'm saving up to buy a place there."

His attention sharpened. "Are you?" He loved the Oregon coast. It was maybe the one thing that would eventually drive him out of Denver and back to Ribbon Ridge. Some day. "Where?"

"I like Pacific City a lot, but I love Cannon Beach. It's just so expensive. And not quite as accessible to Ribbon Ridge, since it's farther up the coast."

He'd looked at a few investment properties in Cannon Beach and around Lincoln City. "I love Cannon Beach, too. It's got a great, artsy vibe nowadays."

She nodded as she swallowed a drink of wine and put her glass back down. "I've been meaning to take a cooking class down there."

He knew what she was talking about—there was a culinary school that did interactive dinner and cooking shows. "Yeah, those sound fun."

"Maybe we'll go on our fictional beach trip."

And that right there told him all he needed to know about their future. She didn't see one. All of this talk was just that: talk. Meanwhile, he had tonight with her. He finished his wine and stood.

Without saying a word, he swept her from the chair into his arms and started toward the stairs.

She linked her hands behind his neck and held on. "What are you doing?"

"Surrendering to my inner caveman."

She laughed, and the sound banished the impending sense of loss that had lodged into his chest a moment ago. "Are you staying the night, then?"

He started up the stairs. "I'll stay as long as you let me."

She didn't answer him until he laid her on the bed. "Just tonight," she said softly.

Her room was almost dark, with only the light from downstairs filtering up and faintly illuminating her face. He drank in the sight of her, from her red hair to his gray shirt clinging to her breasts to the black yoga pants hugging her hips and thighs to her bare feet, with adorable aqua-polished toes. He admired women, of course, appreciated them. But looking at Aubrey this was something more than that. That feeling from earlier stole over him. Possession. She was his. If only for tonight.

"What are you waiting for?" she asked, looking up at him.

"Nothing. Just…never mind." He put his knee on the bed and leaned down to kiss her. She tasted of wine and desire. He pulled back. "I should go put the food away and turn off the lights."

She curled her hands around his neck and tugged him down on top of her. "Later. You made me a promise earlier, and my patience just ran out."

"Is that so?" He fitted his body over hers, marveling at how well they fit together. If he kept making these connections, he was going to be in way over his head.

She kissed along his jaw and nibbled his earlobe. "First one undressed gets to choose top or bottom for the preshow."

He drew back and looked at her. She smiled seductively, and he knew what she meant. That was among his favorite things to do with her. He jumped up and shucked his jeans and underwear. "I choose bottom." He loved the feel of her hair over his thighs.

"No fair! You have way less clothes on than me."

He watched her scramble to strip. "I didn't make the rules, babe."

"I'm surprised you're following them. You Archers are notorious for walking outside the lines."

He laughed. "You're onto us."

Nude, she kneeled on the bed and crooked her finger at him. "I'm onto *you*. Now get over here so I can literally get on you."

He'd never moved so fast in his life.

WHEN LIAM WOKE, the gray dawn was just creeping through the blinds of Aubrey's bedroom. She slept closest to the window, her hair fanned against the pillow. She lay curled on her side away from him. Even in sleep, he'd maintained a possessive hold on her hip, his hand splayed over her naked flesh.

There was that word again: *possession*.

But the night was over. Their fantasy had yielded to reality along with the darkness succumbing to the sunrise. Reluctantly, he let go of her hip, but not before he rolled close and brushed his lips along her collarbone.

She stirred, sighing, but didn't wake.

He slipped from the bed and went in search of his clothes. He glanced at the clock on her bedside table. His parents were early risers. If he didn't hurry, he might run into them as he snuck into the house, like some high schooler who'd stayed out all night. As it was, he might end up running into at least Dad, who loved bike rides at dawn.

He tiptoed downstairs and grabbed his jacket from the floor and helmet from the window seat. As he made his way to the door, he stopped in the entryway. Images of her plastered between him and the wood filled his memory. He looked toward the dining room and was immediately assaulted by the feel of her silky flesh as she held him tight between her legs while he thrust into her. He turned toward the stairs, recalling the final act—the delicious stroke of her tongue on his cock while he licked her slick folds, followed by her riding him with slow and devastating precision before he'd flipped her over and pounded into her until they'd both shouted their release.

Damn if he wasn't ready to go again right now. He set his coat and helmet on the bottom stairs and made his way up, not to initiate round three, but to tell her he was leaving. He didn't want to skulk off into the dawn like some one-night stand. They'd never been that, had they? He didn't think so.

He went back into her room and stopped short at seeing her sitting up in bed.

"You're leaving?"

"I was about to. I came up to say good-bye." He inwardly cringed at that word. It made the entire night seem like a prelude to the end. When all he wanted was a *to be continued*.

Her gaze dipped to his crotch. "Are you sure you came up just to say good-bye?"

He smiled. "I'd blame morning wood, but the truth is I was thinking of last night. I really did come up to say good-bye. And thank you. I had a great time."

She slid from beneath the covers and strode nude across the bedroom to her bathroom, where she opened the door and grabbed a robe from a hook on the back. His erection intensified and wasn't the least bit mollified by the garment now cloaking her spectacular body.

"I'll walk you down," she said, preceding him from the room.

He trailed her down the stairs. The house was quiet, the space between them equally so, but there was a peace and a comfort he'd never experienced. Maybe the magic of the night wasn't over, after all.

She opened the door as he shrugged into his coat. He tucked his helmet beneath his arm and went to kiss her, but she pulled back. "I'll let you know what my uncle says about the brief."

It was back to business, then. Back to being friends.

Maybe there hadn't really been any magic at all.

"Great. Talk to you later, then." The second he stepped over the threshold into the cool morning air, it was like waking from a dream. Suddenly he felt agitated and unnerved, as if he'd been sexually frustrated instead of deeply satisfied. The rush, he realized, had worn off.

Or been stripped away.

He climbed onto his bike and backed out of her driveway before speeding off toward home. He really hoped he didn't run into either of his parents. For maybe the first time ever, he worried they might ask questions about where he'd spent the night, and he didn't want to answer them.

How he wished he was going to his own condo back in Denver. He wanted his bed, his things, his world. Here, he was a visitor, a guest. Which was bullshit. Ribbon Ridge was his home. He ought to feel as comfortable returning here as the rest of his siblings had. Every single one of them had left and come back—save Hayden, who'd done the opposite.

They'd embraced the legacy that Alex had left them, working together and making lives in Ribbon Ridge, as Alex had hoped. A tiny voice in the back of his head said *you could do that, too.* Except he'd spent his entire adult life keeping everyone on the outside. Keeping all of the messy emotion out of his neatly ordered and carefully planned life.

Why was this bothering him now? Because he was spending too much time in Ribbon Ridge. And he liked it. He liked being around his family and helping with the zoning—it wasn't much, but it was something. Plus, it was what Alex wanted.

He gripped the handlebars and gritted his teeth. Alex shouldn't have the satisfaction. He'd already gotten what he wanted: death. While they'd been left to pick up the pieces. Watching his siblings and his parents, Liam would say they'd done a pretty damn good job, too. They laughed, they made memories, all without Alex being a part of it. It was almost like he'd never been.

A hole opened in his chest. It was black and sucking and threatened to pull him inward until there was nothing left. Alex was gone, and they'd all moved on. *How could they?*

He rode past the turnoff to the house and kept on going.

AUBREY'S WALK TO work later that morning felt like an arduous trek, thanks to the weight of her thoughts. After

Liam had left, she'd read through his comments and suggestions on the zoning brief. He was right about most of it. And she felt like an idiot for thinking it was ready. It wasn't bad, but it could be better.

She felt like an even bigger idiot for allowing him to spend the night. No, she'd promised herself that she wouldn't have regrets, that she'd accept and appreciate it for what it was—one last night with the man she'd worked so hard not to fall in love with.

She'd been infatuated with him for sure, but love? He was smart, funny, completely charming. And he was *nice*—all the little things he did when they were together made her feel special, like he really cared about *her*, that he wasn't just going through some motions. He was also incapable of commitment, so it didn't really matter what she labeled her feelings.

Once the zoning was decided, Liam would go back to Denver and she could go back to getting over him. But the zoning wasn't over yet, and the biggest hurdle—the oral argument—was yet to come. First she had to submit this brief, and right now she couldn't. Not without her uncle's help.

She walked up the steps to the remodeled house that was her uncle's law firm and made a beeline for her office, where she dumped her laptop. She came right back out again and stopped in the kitchen for a cup of coffee before heading up to her uncle's office.

His door was ajar, and she rapped on the wood before pushing it open. "Morning, Uncle Dave."

"Morning." He sneezed, then grabbed a tissue to blow his nose.

"Are you feeling okay?"

He tossed the tissue in the garbage and pulled his glasses off, setting them on his desk. "Just a bit of a cold." His eyes narrowed with concern. "What's going on? You have a look—like you're unsettled about something. Is it the zoning case?"

She exhaled, feeling relieved that he'd been the one to bring it up. She sat down in one of the chairs facing his desk. "How'd you know?"

He chuckled, which spurred a minor coughing fit. She scanned his desk and saw that he had a water bottle. She plucked it up and handed it to him as soon as he was done wheezing.

She didn't like the sound of that cough. "Yikes, that doesn't sound good."

He sipped the water several times. "Just a run-of-the-mill spring cold."

She'd had plenty of those. "If it isn't better by Monday, you should see a doctor."

"You sound like Aunt Cyndi." He gave her a warm smile. "I appreciate you both. Now, continue please. What's going on with the zoning? The brief's due Monday, right?"

She sipped her coffee, then set it on his desk. "Yes. I'm finished with the draft. I shared it with Liam Archer, since he's dealt with several zoning appeals in Denver. He found some places that ought to be strengthened." Or maybe completely rewritten, but she'd let Uncle Dave make that call.

Uncle Dave sat back in his chair and studied her. "I see. Why didn't you send it to me first? Liam Archer's not a lawyer."

"You've been really busy," she said lamely. "I should've sent it to you." She'd sent it to Liam because…because what? Because she'd hoped he would be impressed? Ugh, she was worse off than she thought. And she was tired of it.

"I'd love to take a look." He turned his chair and put his glasses on to look at his computer screen. "Did you send it to me?"

She shook her head. "Not yet, but I will as soon as I get downstairs. I hate to ask you to work on the weekend, especially with a cold, but it's due Monday."

He smiled at her as he turned back toward her. "It's okay. We'll get it handled. We're a good team."

They were. She loved working with him, and it went beyond family. He was an exceptional attorney with a loyal and satisfied client base. She couldn't have asked for a better professional path. She loved Ribbon Ridge and saw herself living here the rest of her life with her family. Her husband, whoever he turned out to be, and their children.

"Thanks, I really appreciate it." But there was more. She'd been thinking about it on the walk over this morning. "I was actually hoping you might do the oral argument, too."

His eyebrows arched briefly. "Really? I would've thought you'd be excited to do it."

She had been. She was particularly invested in this case because of Alex. He'd left this legacy for his family, and it was in jeopardy. "I thought I could watch you and learn. And I admit going up against a legend like Sutherlin intimidates me a bit."

Uncle Dave grabbed another tissue and blew his nose. "Don't let him. He's kind of a blowhard, actually, and I'd bet the land-use board knows it. I'll run through it with you—you'll do great. Unless it's more than that?"

It was. So much more. But she couldn't tell him that. Well, she could, but she didn't want to. "I might…I might need a break from this. It's so important that they win, that this appeal is denied. So much is wrapped up in the project—and not just financially."

"I know." His gaze was warm, sympathetic. He knew how upset she'd been when Alex died. He'd come to the funeral with her and held her hand while she'd cried. "It's important to me, too. If you really want me to do the argument, I will. But, Aubrey, this isn't about your dad, is it? His expectations of you were completely unfair." He was doing a good job of talking about her bouts of inadequacy without actually saying the words.

"I'm sure that's part of it. But it is really critical that this turns out in the Archers' favor."

His answering smile was deeply reassuring. "It will. Don't worry. Send me the brief, and I'll read through it. We'll work on it this weekend, okay?"

She realized how tight her muscles were as the tension seeped out of her. "Thanks."

She felt much better. Now if she could just feel better about the rest of her life. "That sounds great." She stood and picked up her coffee.

"Liam…Is he important to you somehow?" Uncle Dave asked, making her pause on the way to the door.

Was it obvious? How could that be? She'd barely talked about him, and Uncle Dave had never seen them together. "Not really." At least he shouldn't be.

The look he gave her said he maybe didn't buy her answer, but he didn't press the issue. And maybe that was why she spilled the beans. Or part of the beans, anyway.

"We see each other from time to time. Casually."

"I see. Are you sure it's just casual?"

She nodded.

"That's too bad. Those Archers are good people, and I know you're ready to settle down."

She felt heat rising in her cheeks. "*Uncle Dave.*"

He chuckled again and managed to keep from coughing. "Sorry, your aunt and I talk. We can't help it. Plus, I know you. You're bright, beautiful, and ready to put down roots. I know how much you love it here."

"I do. I can't thank you enough for opening your home to me and giving me a future."

"I didn't give you anything—you earned it. Cyndi and I are proud to be here for you, and we want to see you happy. If Liam Archer makes you happy, why not make it more than causal?"

Because he doesn't want what I want…the Ribbon Ridge life, the kids, the happily-ever-after. "I don't think that's in the cards. I'm not willing to compromise."

His dark eyes lit with pride. "Atta girl."

She nodded. "I'll go send that brief."

As she made her way back down to her office, she thought of calling Liam to tell him that Uncle Dave was on the case. But why? Just because she wanted to hear his voice?

Screw it. She was busy. Let him contact her. Or not, which was what he usually did after one of their hook-ups. Only this time was different, because he wasn't already on a plane back to Denver.

She walked into her office and shut the door.

So many things were different this time. First and foremost, the friend thing. They now had a defined relationship aside from their mutual attraction.

She flopped into her chair and cupped her coffee mug between her palms.

Even that—the sex—had felt different. She couldn't quite pinpoint why, just that it had felt richer, deeper, more intimate, if that were possible. That was probably only her wanting it to mean more than it did because of the feelings she was developing for him.

She didn't want those feelings. He was arrogant, self-involved, and his goals didn't remotely match hers. Still, she loved his family, his sense of humor, and his drive. She loved the way he put dishes in her dishwasher, like he'd done last night. And the way he set up her new television set. Most of all, she loved the way he held her, the way his lips caressed hers, the way he told her she was the sexiest woman he'd ever met.

She shivered and set her coffee on her desk. She didn't have any more time to waste on Liam Archer.

Pulling her laptop from her bag, she planned to work her butt off this weekend to win this case for the Archers. And to drive Liam from her mind.

Chapter Fourteen

LIAM PARKED HIS bike in the garage and strolled toward the back door of the house. His pulse was still thrumming from the excitement and craziness of the last few days.

After leaving Aubrey's the other morning, he found out that his latest deal in Denver had exploded with the results of the mold test. Then he'd spent Friday night and Saturday at the coast with his folks looking at the properties they'd planned to buy. Today he'd gone skydiving with Rylan, then mapped out the details of their trip to Idaho for the BASE jump training.

As he walked into the house, he instantly smelled whatever amazing meal Kyle had cooked up. He realized he'd started to look forward to these Sunday dinners. In fact, he'd made sure he would get home in time.

Home? Home was Denver and his sleek condo.

"Hey, Liam, dinner's just about up," Kyle said as he set out plates on the counter.

"Smells great. What'd you throw together?"

"Doing a little summer in the spring—roasted ribs, grilled corn, and Mom made her signature stacked salad."

"Excellent." Liam made his way to the beer tap and pulled himself a pint as people began to filter into the kitchen.

Mom walked in, followed by Dad. "You're back," Mom said, sounding relieved. She knew he'd gone sky-diving, and he knew she worried. When she'd found out that he'd taken the guys out, she'd told him he was a bad influence. Just like Aubrey had. Well, not *just* like Aubrey.

He'd texted her Friday to tell her he'd had a great time Thursday night. She'd responded that she had, too. And then nothing. What else was he supposed to say? He didn't think she'd let him come over again—she'd made a point of saying he could stay *that* night.

He was looking forward to seeing her here. He glanced around, realizing she hadn't arrived.

"I think Mom and I have finally settled on a beach property," Dad said. This drew everyone's attention. Even Kyle paused in plating the food. "Surprisingly, we went with Cannon Beach, even though it means the drive's a bit farther."

Aubrey would love that.

"Is it big enough for all of us?" Sara asked. She and Dylan had come up from downstairs.

Dad laughed. "Probably not at once. We're a pretty big crew now with all of you getting married."

Kyle cast a look at Liam. "Not *all* of us."

Mom went to Liam and slipped her arm around his waist to give him a squeeze. "Liam may surprise us yet. Look how long he's been home. It's a record."

He knew Mom didn't mean any judgment, but he also knew they were all scrutinizing his plans. Would he stay and for how long?

He put his arm around her shoulder and kissed her cheek. "It's still only temporary, Mom."

She withdrew her arm with a sigh. "I know. A mother can dream, can't she?"

Anyone could dream. The problem was when people's dreams didn't align. Like his and his mother's. Or his and Aubrey's.

Kyle pulled off his apron. "Grab your plate and eat!"

The extra chairs had been delivered, and so they all fit around the table tonight. Mom and Dad on each end, six on one side, and five on the other, leaving an empty chair.

"Where's Aubrey?" Chloe asked. "Did we forget to invite her?"

Mom set her napkin in her lap. "Doesn't she have a standing invitation at this point? She should."

"I invited her," Sara said. "But she's busy working. The zoning brief is due tomorrow."

Aubrey was now invited to Sunday dinners? Wait, hadn't he expected to see her? He was disappointed that she wasn't coming. Then again, she *was* really busy with the brief. And it wasn't like they were *together*. Shit, he needed to get his head straight.

Conversation turned to the zoning issue and how they were all looking forward to putting it behind them. "How long until it's fully resolved?" Alaina asked.

Dylan answered before Liam could finish swallowing. "Once Aubrey files the brief, the board will set a date for oral arguments. That should happen relatively quickly—within the next few weeks. Then it could take anywhere from zero time, meaning they'll make a decision immediately, to a few months. But nobody expects it to take that long. Aubrey will argue that we're already losing money by not being open."

Alaina's gaze turned shrewd. "Any chance you're going to go after Parker for that lost revenue?"

Liam grinned. "Evan, I like your wife immensely." He liked that idea, too. He'd love to stick it right back to Whitney and her dad, especially after her last outrageous proposition.

"I don't know that we should bother," Mom said, exchanging looks with Dad. "Let's just put this behind us and move on."

Liam took a drink of beer. "I don't know. Parker has cost us a lot—not just in money." The anguish and frustration they'd all endured seemed like it should be worth something.

Mom dabbed at her mouth with her napkin. "That's true, but I'd rather keep as much negativity out of our lives as possible. I'd prefer to focus on all the happy occasions coming down the pike." She glanced between Sara and Dylan, whose wedding was in July, Kyle and Maggie, whose wedding was in September, and Evan and Alaina, whose baby was due in November.

Right. Moving on. They'd all become quite adept at that. While Liam stuck to his same old, same old. It was an odd sensation—the comfort he enjoyed in being home and yet the distance he felt from everything going on around him. The coupledom. The blisteringly shiny happiness.

Liam dropped the topic, and conversation continued. When dinner was over, they rock-paper-scissored to see who would clean up. The losers were Sara, Tori, Derek, and Liam. Everyone else adjourned downstairs to prep for watching the show.

Tori worked the sink while Sara loaded the dishwasher, leaving Liam and Derek to clean the table, put leftovers— not that there were very many—away, and tidy the kitchen.

"I'm sorry Aubrey didn't come," Sara said, looking at Liam, who was wiping down the counter by the stove. "We thought maybe you were seeing each other."

Liam froze momentarily but kept wiping. "Why would you think that?"

He caught Tori elbowing Sara and narrowed his eyes. What was going on? What did they know? He hadn't gone out of his way to hide anything, but it wasn't like there was something to share.

Sara smiled. "No reason." She focused intently on lining up dishes in the side-by-side dishwashers.

He knew Sara well enough to realize she was lying. Her filter could sometimes be as faulty as Evan's, so it made sense that she might say something she shouldn't.

Liam stopped wiping and leaned his hip against the counter. "What gives? Are you all talking about me when I'm not around?"

Tori rolled her eyes at him. "Duh. We do that to everybody."

True. "But why about Aubrey specifically?"

Tori shrugged. "We're just playing matchmaker—wishful thinking. She's single, smart, funny, attractive, successful. You're single, smart, successful."

Despite being annoyed by the topic of conversation—for some reason he and Aubrey were off-limits—he couldn't help but be amused. Tori was good at deflecting and manipulating. It was what made her and him the alpha dogs of the family. He gave her a patronizing smile. "You left out funny and attractive."

She returned the bland expression. "You're funny *looking*. How's that?"

Derek laughed. "She's got you there."

Liam crossed his arms and pivoted his weight so he was leaning back against the counter. "Seriously, why the interrogation about Aubrey?"

"Dude, it wasn't an interrogation," Derek said. "Sara asked a simple question. You're the one making a federal case out of it."

Tori turned the sink off and dried her hands. "Yeah, because Liam's a douche. God forbid he has a *girlfriend* or something." The glare, which was a real glare and not a mock one, she tossed him said everything he suspected—they totally knew about him and Aubrey. Had she told them, or had they somehow figured it out? Hell, what did it matter? None of it was any of their business.

"I've had girlfriends." Defensive much?

Derek finished wiping down the table and tossed the towel on the counter. "Hot models and *Bachelor*-contestant wannabes who decorate your arm for a few months here and there don't count. A girlfriend is someone you'd consider spending your life with, someone you're committed to getting to know on the most intimate level possible."

Liam kept up his defense. "How would you know? Chloe was barely your girlfriend. Didn't you get engaged in record time?"

Derek grinned. "Yeah. What can I say? When you know, you know. Right, Tori?"

Tori, who'd also undergone a speedy courtship capped off by a secret Vegas wedding, leaned over the counter and high-fived Derek. "Absolutely."

Liam snorted. "Whatever. Just leave Aubrey out of the conversation, please."

"Why?" Sara asked, closing one of the dishwashers. "She's awesome. You could do a lot worse and not much better."

Liam uncrossed his arms and lifted them. "I'm not looking for a girlfriend! But if I were, I'd take your suggestion under advisement." Because he agreed—Aubrey *was* awesome. And so many other things.

Sara smiled. "Good." She closed the other dishwasher and programmed them both. "I'm done." She looked around at the others in question.

"Me, too," said Tori.

Derek nodded toward them. "You go on ahead. Liam and I will sweep up." He went to the pantry to fetch the broom and dustbin.

The girls left, and Derek started sweeping while Liam finished the counters.

"What's the real story with Aubrey?" Derek asked.

"Does it matter? Sounds like you've all drawn your own conclusions."

"No, we haven't. I have zero opinion other than I like Aubrey, and I obviously like you. Though sometimes I wonder why." Derek tossed him a sarcastic smirk.

Sometimes Liam wondered why, too. Aubrey was great, and she deserved to be someone's girlfriend in precisely the way Derek had said. Liam wasn't sure what he deserved. "I'm not to that point yet—for that intimate, potentially forever relationship you just described."

Derek paused in sweeping to look at him. "And she is?"

She'd said she was looking for Mr. Right, and she didn't want to be tied up with Mr. Right Now and maybe miss him.

Liam nodded.

"Then you should probably leave her alone." Derek held up a hand. "Not that you aren't, but if you aren't…just something to think about."

He'd been thinking of little else.

They finished cleaning up and headed downstairs. Liam lost himself in the show while it was on—thank goodness for fictional tragedies to take your brain offline—but as soon as it was over, the specter of Aubrey rose hard and fast in his mind.

Derek was right. He should leave her alone.

He looked around the theater at his family, at the couples, at the happiness and love filling the room. He didn't belong here. He'd moved to Denver to take himself out of the emotional equation, and after Alex had killed himself, it had been the perfect buffer to keep himself safe. The longer he was here, the more everything threatened to break through that wall. He'd have to do what everyone else was doing—move on, grow up.

He stood abruptly. He wasn't some kid who couldn't mature. He owned and ran a multimillion-dollar real-estate development company, for Christ's sake. And it was past time he got back to it.

THE IMMENSE SENSE of relief Aubrey felt at filing the zoning brief was tempered by the nudge of anxiety caused by how—or if—Liam would respond. She'd e-mailed all of the Archers as soon as she'd filed it and provided them with an electronic copy. She doubted most of them would read it but expected Liam to.

She and Uncle Dave had worked all weekend making it perfect, and she felt great about how it had turned out. It was out of her hands now, at least until the oral argument, which Uncle Dave had agreed to do.

Aubrey refreshed her e-mail again, but still nothing from Liam about the brief or the flying date he'd promised her. *It's not a date*, she told herself. Then she stood up from her desk to get another cup of coffee.

Tori appeared in her doorway. "Hey!"

Aubrey smiled in greeting, surprised to see her. "Hi, what are you doing here?"

"I wondered if I could take you for a celebratory cup of coffee. Since you filed the zoning brief."

Just like she'd told Liam, Aubrey was reluctant to celebrate anything yet, but she wasn't going to turn down an offer for coffee. "As a matter of fact, I was about to get a refill." She held up her empty mug.

"Put that down. We'll walk over to Books and Brew."

"Sure." Aubrey set her mug back on her desk and followed Tori to the door, telling the receptionist she'd be back in a bit.

The morning had started cloudy and cool, but the clouds were burning off to reveal a bright blue sky. Aubrey didn't bother grabbing her jacket. It was only a couple of blocks to Books and Brew anyway.

"It has to feel good to get the brief filed," Tori said.

Aubrey walked beside her along the sidewalk. It was still a little cool, so she wrapped her arms around herself as they made their way to the intersection. "It does. One step closer."

Tori nodded. "Have you talked to Liam?"

Aubrey cast her a sidelong glance, but Tori was looking straight ahead toward the main street that ran through town. It was an innocent question...maybe. Probably. "No."

Tori came to a stop at the crosswalk and turned to look at her. The breeze rustled her dark hair, and she tucked a wayward strand behind her ear. "He went back to Denver this morning."

Aubrey's gut clenched, and the slight chill she'd felt became a blast of ice that permeated every part of her body. He hadn't said a word. They'd exchanged impersonal texts on Friday, both of them saying they'd enjoyed themselves. It was the same thing they'd always done: hook up, bask in the afterglow, go their separate ways. Repeat.

Only she hadn't intended to repeat. She'd been so stupid to think she could allow herself just one more night without there being emotional consequences. Every time they were together, she became more vulnerable.

She should have shut him down. She'd tried, but the truth was she'd wanted one more night with him. She'd done it for herself, and she wasn't going to regret it.

They walked across the street and into Books and Brew, which was on the corner.

"Are you okay?" Tori asked as they made their way to the counter to order.

"Yeah, why wouldn't I be?" Aubrey stepped forward and ordered a latte.

Tori asked for a black coffee and paid for the drinks, then they found a table next to the wall.

"I thought you and Liam were maybe seeing each other," Tori said.

Of course she did. Sara had said as much the other day on the phone. "That would imply we were dating. You remember what I drank to that night, right? You weren't *that* drunk, if I remember correctly."

"So it was just sex." Tori pursed her lips. "Liam's such a jerk."

"Hey, I knew what it was. He never promised me anything, and I bailed as soon as I realized where things were going."

Tori raised her eyebrows. "Nowhere?"

Aubrey laughed softly to cover her inner sadness. "Exactly."

The barista called their names, and Tori jumped up. "I'll get the drinks."

Aubrey considered changing the topic when Tori returned, but why bother? It actually felt good to talk about this with someone who knew Liam, someone who understood his…issues. Or whatever.

Tori came back with the drinks and set them on the table before sliding back into her chair. "Can I ask how long you've been…what, hooking up?"

"Yep, hooking up is exactly right." Should she tell her the truth? That they'd jumped on each other in a fit of anger and grief? Opting for a less provocative description, she said, "Not too long after Alex died. When Liam would come to town, we'd get together. Not always intentionally, but we always seemed to end up—'in bed'—together. Then we actually planned to meet up at the Dave Matthews Band concert weekend last Labor Day."

Tori sipped her coffee. "Really? That's usually his dudes' weekend."

Just like it was usually Aubrey's girls' weekend. "That's when it became clear—to me, anyway—that I wanted more than he did."

"I take it you want a boyfriend?"

Aubrey sampled her latte. It was still pretty hot. "Yes. I'd actually like a husband. A family. I'm ready to settle down."

Tori stared at her. "Wow, that's so foreign to me."

Aubrey laughed. "But you're married!"

"No one was more shocked than I was." Now she laughed, too. "I wasn't ready to settle down at all. I had a rockin' job, a crazy bright future, things were movin' and shakin'." She snapped her fingers. "Then I met Sean, and they started moving and shaking in an entirely different way. He completely swept me off my feet. Still, I didn't think I'd change my trajectory. To be honest, we jumped headfirst without really mapping that part out." She looked down at the table for a moment. When her gaze came back up, it held the faint sheen of tears. She blinked several times. "Then Alex died, and everything came to a crashing halt. I didn't know you before that, so maybe you didn't realize that I was very different after he died."

Aubrey fought the urge to reach across the table and hug her. "I knew. I might not have known you personally, but Alex told me enough about each of you that I felt as if I sort of knew you."

"Is that because of the letters?" Tori's question was soft, tentative.

Alex had written each of them letters and entrusted them to Aubrey with explicit instructions on when they were to be delivered. "Not really. I didn't even know about those until he died. You understand that, right? I had *no* inkling he was going to kill himself." They'd all asked if she had. Liam had gone so far as to say she *had* to have known.

Tori nodded. "I do. When did you get them?"

Aubrey's gaze fixed on a poster on the far wall of a sunflower. It was a maybe twenty-year-old advertisement for the Ribbon Ridge Festival. The bright happiness of the sunflower was the absolute polar opposite of what she'd felt when she'd opened that package. "It was quite horrible, actually." She looked at Tori. "I'm sorry. You can't want to hear about this."

"I do." She circled her hands around her coffee cup. "If you want to tell me."

Aubrey hadn't recounted it to anyone except her aunt and uncle. She took a deep breath and decided she needed a fortifying drink of her latte first. "He sent me a package. It was waiting for me that morning. The morning after."

Tori nodded. "That was the morning after I got married."

Aubrey couldn't begin to imagine how Tori had rebounded from that, but then it had taken her the better part of a year. In hindsight, Aubrey was pretty pissed at Alex for instructing her to hold Tori's until the first anniversary of his death—which she hadn't done after Evan Archer had convinced her last fall that Tori *needed* her letter.

"Did you know he called me that night?" Tori blinked again, then cast her head back. "Ugh, some days these tears will stop, right?"

"Evan told me about the call when he came to demand your letter."

Tori dropped her head, eyes now dry, and her lips curved into a smile. "That sounds like him."

"He said you missed the call, that you felt unbearably guilty."

"It's true. I still do sometimes, but logically I know there was probably nothing I could've done. He'd planned everything out so thoroughly. He was going through with his plan regardless. I just wish I knew why he'd called."

Aubrey did, too. "His letter to you didn't say?"

Tori shook her head. "It read like he'd written them well before that night."

"That makes sense. The package he left for me was quite organized."

"He left it for you? Where?"

"On the front porch of my uncle's building." She'd gone into work early that morning, like any other Monday. So early that the building had been locked and dark. She'd walked up the steps and seen the package in front of the door addressed to her. "It was kind of scary, because it was this nondescript brown paper package with my name written in black Sharpie. I thought it was a bomb."

Tori smiled. "Because you were involved in some sort of dangerous case?" It wasn't a serious question, and it lightened the mood a little.

"No, it was just…weird. But then I saw there was writing in the bottom corner, so I squatted down to read it. It said, 'It's from Alex. It's not a bomb.'"

Tori laughed and brought her hand to her mouth. "Oh my God, that sounds just like him."

"Doesn't it? Anyway, I scooped it up and took it to my office." Where it had sat for maybe a half hour, during which she'd made coffee, watered the plants, and glanced through her e-mail. Then she'd turned her attention to the package, and everything had fallen promptly apart.

"What was inside?" Tori asked, sounding almost fearful.

"All of your letters, sealed into envelopes with your names on the outside. The one on top was addressed to me." She hadn't thought about that morning in a long time. It was one of those memories you didn't want to ponder unless you had a tissue handy and didn't plan on seeing anyone, because your face was going to be splotchy. She could still remember what he'd written, because she'd read it about a thousand times.

Dear Aubrey,

You likely haven't heard yet, but I died last night. You didn't realize it, but you were instrumental in helping me prepare everything so that I could leave this world on my terms.

At that point, she'd sunk into her chair and felt as if the world around her were crumbling into ruins. She'd drafted his will. She'd set up his trust. She'd laid out everything in the event of his untimely death. A death he'd been planning. She'd never felt more sick in her life.

In this box are letters to my parents and siblings as well as a detailed list of when they are to receive these from you. I trust you to distribute the letters as I've outlined, regardless of whether they might pester you about them. In addition, you'll communicate the specifics of my will and trust in person at a time mutually agreed upon by you and my parents. I thank you in advance for your professionalism and dependability.

Mostly, however, I want to apologize for lying to you for so long. I am sick. I've always been sick. But I'm not terminal. At least not in the way that people think. In my mind, I've been terminal since I was sixteen, when I decided that death wasn't something to be feared, but something to accept and even look forward to. In death, I wouldn't be sick anymore. I would be free.

It took me a long time to settle on my plans and bring them to fruition, and I never could have done it without you. I expect you will be horrified, maybe angry, but I earnestly beg your forgiveness—not for me, but for you. I don't want you to carry guilt or sadness. This is what I want. I have no fear and no regret.

Aubrey didn't recite the letter to Tori, settling instead for just the highlights.

Tears streamed down Tori's face unheeded. When Aubrey was finished, Tori blinked and wiped at her cheeks.

"I'm sorry," Tori said. "I don't know that he spoke about his illness—his mental illness—like that to anyone. He actually said that he would be free?"

Aubrey struggled to hold back her own tears. "Yes. I sort of like thinking of him that way."

Tori nodded, sniffing. "I do, too. Excuse me." She got up, grabbed a handful of napkins from the counter, and came back to the table, where she dumped them in a pile. "Help yourself."

Aubrey did, dabbing at her eyes.

"He really did a number on you," Tori said. "I would've been so pissed if he'd manipulated me like that."

"I was, but I was so shocked. The anger took a while. But mostly I was just really sad—especially for all of you."

"But to leave all of those letters to you to deal with. I mean, we're kind of obnoxious, us Archers. How many times did I bug you for my letter?"

Aubrey laughed. "Plenty."

"I'm sure Liam did the same. The only person in this family more Type A than me is him."

"Actually, he hasn't asked me once." Now that she thought about it, his disinterest seemed odd. Or maybe he was just really patient.

"So he hasn't gotten his letter yet?"

Aubrey shook her head. In her mind's eye, she saw the list Alex had left her. It had stipulated very specific instructions, right down to her driving Evan's letter to him in Longview, and had included mileage compensation in her ongoing fees as trustee. In the general instructions, he'd asked her to keep the list secret but noted that he trusted her to do what was right. That was why she'd given Tori her letter earlier than he'd stated, because it was the right thing to do. She'd be glad when she was done handing them out. That was yet another way she could untether herself from this family she'd come to care too much about. From Liam.

Aubrey took a drink of her latte and fiddled with the paper cup, running her finger along the edge of its top. "Is it odd that Liam hasn't asked about the letter?" It wasn't even a letter, as far as she knew. Instead of an envelope, Alex had left him a small box. She wondered if it held a trinket or some memento that was special to them. "I suppose it is, since you figured he had."

"I'm not sure," Tori said. "I would've thought he'd ask, but now that I think about their relationship, I don't know."

"What sort of relationship did they have?" While Alex had told her about his family, and from that she'd been able to tell how he felt about them, there'd always been an odd...*something* when it came to Liam. They were definitely close, but it was like there was a competition or some sort of strain between them.

Tori smiled. "They were peas in a pod, but I guess that's to be expected since they are—were—identical twins." She shook her head. "I still have a hard time with that sometimes. Everyone had a sort of buddy—Sara and Kyle, me and Evan, Liam and Alex."

Aubrey was curious about Hayden but didn't want to interrupt.

"Since Sara, Evan, and Alex all had challenges, the three of us sort of helped them."

"But you were the overall manager, I hear." Alex had told her that.

Tori laughed. "Yes. The little mother. Or something like that. Despite their physical differences, Liam and Alex were very much alike."

Aubrey thought she knew the answer to this but asked anyway. "Liam isn't bipolar, too, is he?"

"No, just super driven and ambitious. But I'm guessing you know that."

Yes, she did. "Was Alex like that, too?" It made sense, given how thoroughly he'd plotted his demise and the legacy he'd left behind for his family.

Tori nodded, then sipped her coffee. "I wonder what he would have been like if he'd been healthy. And I'm not the only one. I think that was a thing—a bit of a wedge—between Liam and Alex."

That had to be what Aubrey had sensed. "I'm sure that was difficult for both of them."

"Yes, but more so for Liam. We've never really discussed it, but I'm sure that's why he moved away. I think he thought it would be better for Alex if he wasn't there as a constant reminder of everything Alex couldn't do."

Aubrey knew how sick Alex had been—hospitalized on occasion with pneumonia, often oxygen dependent, exhausted and lethargic on a regular basis. She thought of Liam watching that his whole life, knowing that if not for a twist of Fate, it could've been him. "Why doesn't he move back now that Alex is gone?"

"I don't know. Maybe he's just really happy in Denver. Although I have to say, he's seemed pretty happy here the past few weeks. It's been great having him back." She slid a glance at Aubrey. "I was hoping it was because of you. It sucks that isn't the case."

Aubrey's chest tightened. She wished things were different, but they were exactly the same as they'd always been. They'd hooked up, and he'd left. If anything, he'd only hung around that long because it had taken that much time to wear her down into bed. She inwardly cringed. Is that what she really thought? She honestly didn't know. There was one thing she *did* know, however. "No, that ship has sailed. Whatever Liam and I had going is Donesville."

Tori clenched her hand around her coffee cup. "Ugh! I want to choke him for screwing up what could've been a great thing."

Aubrey appreciated the support. "Don't be mad at him. He never made me any promises." She wanted to think they'd just helped each other through a rough year. They'd comforted each other when they'd needed it most. That couldn't be a bad thing, could it?

"I should get back to the office," Aubrey said. "You ready?"

"Yeah."

They grabbed their drinks and left. When they got back to the law firm, Aubrey thanked Tori for the coffee and gave her a quick hug.

After they moved apart, Tori brushed her hair back over her shoulder. "Let's do this again soon. I hope we're still friends, despite my brother's douchiness."

Aubrey laughed. "Yes. We're still friends."

"Excellent. See you later."

Aubrey waved before turning and heading up the stairs to the front door. Their conversation hovered in her mind like a catchy pop song. And like a catchy pop song, Aubrey doubted she'd be able to shake it for quite some time. When she thought of Liam and his twin and everything the Archers had endured, the grief she'd conquered threatened to overcome her again.

But did you really ever conquer grief, or did you simply adapt and learn to live with it? She suspected that's what most of the Archers, like Tori, had done. For the first time, she wondered what, exactly, Liam had done with his.

Chapter Fifteen

BY FRIDAY LIAM was more than ready for the weekend. After being in Ribbon Ridge so long, he'd almost forgotten what it was like to manage his own company. That wasn't exactly true, but he'd missed the day-to-day. Or, as it actually happened, he hadn't missed it all that much.

He found himself thinking of Archer Enterprises and the changes going on there with developing the bottling operation, The Alex schedule, the zoning brief, and, of course, Aubrey. He hadn't heard from her since she'd sent the group e-mail about the filing on Monday. He'd read through the revised brief, and it was really damn good. He'd e-mailed her back and told her so, but she hadn't responded.

He also hadn't talked to any of his family. That wasn't really abnormal, but after spending so much time with them, he missed them. He was bummed he wouldn't be going to the Sunday dinner. All the more reason to accelerate his plane purchase. He could afford one. He just had to find the right deal. Liam picked up his cell phone to text Rylan, who was on the lookout for him.

"Liam?" Boyd, his right-hand guy, popped his head into the void between Liam's door, which stood ajar, and the frame. "I'm heading out. You good?"

Liam glanced at his open laptop. Shit, was it five fifteen already? He wiped a hand over his face. "Yeah. Wait, where are you going? It's past beer-thirty." Liam kept a keg of Archer beer tapped in the office kitchen. They typically gathered around for beer at least one night a week, and they hadn't yet.

Boyd pushed the door open and walked into the office. "I've got plans. Heading to dinner, then a party later. You should come."

Normally Liam would, but he was tired. And shockingly, he didn't really want to go. "Where are you going to dinner?" That he could do.

"I'm meeting up with Mark, Brett, and Dusty at Steuben's."

That was a heavy-hitting crowed. They'd be on the prowl. Again, Liam was surprised that he wanted to decline. "I don't know. Maybe. What time?"

"Seven." Boyd sat down on Liam's leather couch and stretched his legs out in front of him as he leaned back. "What gives, man? You haven't been out with us in ages."

"I've been gone."

"Nah, before that even. You haven't been to a party with us since…January?"

"I dislocated my shoulder, remember?"

Boyd shrugged. "Yeah, I guess." He raked his hand through his short blond hair. "Dusty says you've got a girl back in Ribbon Ridge. I'm beginning to think he might be right."

They were talking about him, too? Shit, he couldn't avoid people speculating about his damn love life. "Very funny."

Boyd chuckled. "I was kidding. I told Dusty he was high."

Liam snorted. "He probably was."

"True dat." Boyd sat forward and brought his legs up. "I figure it's more like you've got something up your sleeve. Something extreme." Boyd liked to do some of the same sports as Liam—he was big into skiing and rock climbing. He was a true Coloradoan.

"I just might. Listen, thanks again for holding things down while I was gone. I may spend a little more time back home than usual. My dad is transitioning some stuff and might need my help." Wait, was he actually considering splitting time between Denver and Ribbon Ridge? He *could* do that—temporarily. It didn't mean he was going home.

Boyd cocked his head to the side. " 'Home'? I thought this was your home." He looked genuinely surprised.

"You know, I'm from there and the rest of my family is there. It's home in a sense."

"Huh, never heard you call it that before." Boyd stood. "I hope you decide to come to dinner at least. Remember, seven at Steuben's."

Liam nodded. "Thanks."

Boyd left, and Liam realized he was still holding his cell phone. He pulled up Rylan in his text window and asked if he had any leads on planes.

With a plane, he could fly back and forth between Denver and Ribbon Ridge—at least until The Alex was open and Dad had sorted everything out at Archer.

He set his phone down and checked his calendar. He saw that tomorrow was a monthly hike one of his friends led. He was an outdoor guide, and once a month he took a group on an extreme excursion. They'd climb, there'd be water, and the mileage would be brutal. Sounded like just the high he needed to get his head back on straight.

That had to be what was wrong. He was bored. The injury had taken him offline for a while, and he'd eased back into things the past few weeks, but he needed more. The BASE jump training in a couple weeks would really reset his brain. He could hardly wait.

He thought of Alex, as he invariably did when he planned a new excursion. Alex had loved talking things through with him. He'd done a lot of the research into the things that Liam now enjoyed. The extreme-sport hobby was as much Alex's as it was Liam's, even if he hadn't actually done any of them.

Liam turned in his chair and stared out at the Denver skyline. He'd been thinking of Alex far too much lately. He blamed that on being home, too. It was hard not to dwell on him while spending so much time where they'd grown up and with the people who'd known them both.

Damn it, why had he gone and killed himself? He'd ruined everything.

For Alex it had already been ruined, hadn't it? He was the one who'd spent his life hooked to machines or oxygen, the one who'd told Liam on several occasions that he wished he'd died or, better yet, had never been born. Who needed six babies anyway?

The worst part was that Liam had actually considered that. Without Alex, he wouldn't have any of the guilt of being the one who'd dodged the bullet. And damn it if that didn't fill a person with self-loathing.

Liam closed his eyes. If anyone knew what went on in his head—what he really thought about—they'd be shocked. Or maybe they wouldn't be. Evan had figured it out.

Alex had known the truth, of course. He'd told Liam the night that he'd died. When he'd called Liam to tell him it was over, that he could come back to Ribbon Ridge.

Except in doing that, he'd all but ensured that Liam would never go home.

AUBREY PARKED IN the unpaved lot at The Alex. She hadn't been up here in a few weeks and was amazed at how great everything looked. They'd completely transformed this property over the past year.

The monks' quarters looked like a hotel instead of a derelict pile of wood and stone. The former chapel had been enlarged and reshaped into a gorgeous restaurant. She wondered how the underground pub was coming and hoped someone would give her a tour of everything after the meeting she was about to crash.

She'd called Tori that morning to tell her the oral argument was scheduled for next Tuesday. Tori was thrilled that they were finally going to have their day in court and had asked Aubrey to join them at their meeting this afternoon to share the good news.

Aubrey went to the restaurant, where Tori had said they were meeting. They'd grown too large for the office trailer at this point. Too many of them had come on board to support the project. Everyone, she realized, except Liam and Hayden. And Hayden had certainly done his part before taking his internship.

As she approached, she could see in through the windows flanking the front doors. Everyone was situated around a large table in the center of the room. She opened the door and couldn't help but smile at how beautiful the space was. They'd kept so many of the original features—the dark, rich wood had been polished to a gorgeous sheen, and the stained glass windows added a touch of history and whimsy. But they'd also introduced a trendy and elegant décor, including a handful of paintings by Chloe that matched the Archer brand.

"Hi, Aubrey!" Tori called from the other side of the table. "Come join us."

Aubrey scanned the group but didn't see Liam. She hadn't really expected to but apparently couldn't keep herself from looking. "You guys, this is stunning. I want to move in here."

This was met with laughter.

"Too bad, because I have dibs," Kyle said. He'd become a bit possessive about his restaurant, and rightfully so. He'd been filming its evolution with Sean for a television show that was set to air on the Travel Channel in the fall.

This place was going to hit the map in a huge way. And that didn't even take into consideration all the A-list celebrities and power people Alaina's presence would attract.

"You can stay in the hotel whenever you like," Sara said. "Definitely for the opening."

"Well, hopefully that will be relatively soon. Looks like you're almost ready." She looked around, and her gaze found Dylan. As general contractor, he'd be the one to say when it was done.

"Almost. We've got some exterior stuff to do still—lighting, paving, etcetera." He nodded toward Maggie, who'd designed all of that.

"Plus the underground pub isn't done, but we'd never planned for that to be up and running at the opening," Tori said.

Kyle nodded. "Right, but things have taken so long that it probably will be."

That was her cue. Aubrey moved toward the empty chair at the table but didn't sit. "We're close to the end," she said. "The oral argument is next Tuesday. We could have a decision as early as then."

Kyle pumped his fist. "Yes!"

Dylan cast his head back and closed his eyes. "Thank God."

Everyone was high-fiving and cheering. Aubrey loved their enthusiasm and just hoped it turned out the way they all wanted. "We haven't won yet."

"No, but we will," Derek said, smiling. "And you're going to be the hero of the day."

Gee, still no pressure. She was glad Uncle Dave was doing the arguing. "Correction—Uncle Dave will be the hero. I'll just be his assistant."

"Why?" Sara asked. "I thought you were presenting the case."

"I haven't done it before, and Uncle Dave has. Lots of times. You're in great hands. Anyway, that's all I came for."

"You want a tour?" Kyle stood.

"I don't want to interrupt your meeting."

Kyle grinned. "But you want a tour." He laughed. "We were pretty much done. Come on, I'll take you around."

Tori got up. "Hey, I'm coming, too."

"Me, too," Chloe said.

Soon everyone was traipsing about the property, sharing anecdotes about how something was chosen or some problem they'd encountered. She was amazed at how well everything had come together but not surprised in the slightest. "Dylan, you're incredible. Are we going to lose you to huge projects in Portland now?"

Dylan shook his head. "Not a chance. I've got a winery lined up after this—Tori designed it."

Sara put her arm around his waist. "*After* our honeymoon. I get two weeks of uninterrupted quality time with my husband."

He smiled and kissed her forehead.

After a while, people drifted off to attend to whatever work they had going on, and some left altogether. In the end, Tori and Chloe took Aubrey down to the underground pub.

It had a cool door straight out of the Shire in *Lord of the Rings*. Inside, the main room was larger than she'd imagined, with a bar along the right wall. On the left was a partially completed mural done in the style of a cave painting. It was incredibly intricate.

Aubrey went over to investigate it. "You did this, Chloe?"

Faint dots of pink colored her cheeks. "Guilty. It's in progress, so don't judge it too harshly."

"I couldn't possibly. It's fantastic. How'd you come up with this?"

"I did a lot of research." Chloe joined her, and Tori followed. "The idea itself was Alaina's."

"It's so cool. I love how you repeated motifs." Aubrey pointed toward the foxes that had crept up throughout the restaurant and hotel and several other designs that she'd seen.

"Thanks. I'm pleased with how it's all coming together."

"Alex would love it."

"He would," Tori agreed.

An awkward silence seemed to fall, and since things were already awkward, Aubrey figured it was a good time to bring up Liam. "Tori, would you mind letting Liam know about the oral argument?"

Tori turned toward her. "You haven't heard from him?"

"Not since I filed the brief." He'd sent a quick e-mail telling her she'd done a great job. She'd appreciated his praise but hadn't responded. What more could there be to say?

She could tell him that she'd fallen in love with him. She'd tried so hard to resist, to protect her heart, but in the end, she'd tumbled like a course of dominoes.

She nearly laughed out loud. What would be the point of that? He loved his family, and *they* weren't enough to bring him home. Even if he loved her in return, it wouldn't change anything.

"I'll let him know, no problem," Tori said.

"Thanks. I'd better get back to my office. Thanks for the tour." Aubrey smiled at both Tori and Chloe before heading to her car.

As she climbed into the driver's seat, she worked to banish the jagged feeling in her chest. Every time Liam went home after they'd hooked up, she'd thought of him and pondered the next time. Then Labor Day had been so great—right up until it hadn't. That time, she'd tried *not* to think of him. Instead, she'd focused her energies on moving on.

But every time he came home, he sucked her right back in. Maybe not into sleeping with him, since she'd successfully avoided him for several months, but the feelings she had, the longing for a future she couldn't have, were always there.

She simply had to find a way to get over him. For good.

Chapter Sixteen

A WEEK LATER, Liam grinned as he rode his bike into the lot at The Alex. They'd put down the asphalt and the curbs, but the spaces weren't painted yet. It gave the entire place an almost-finished quality that only added to the excitement thrumming in his veins. Because he'd just prepped all his new gear for his first jump course starting Saturday in Idaho. He could hardly wait.

But first, they had to get through tomorrow's oral argument. He'd come to the weekly meeting with the family to hear the plan for tomorrow.

As he stepped into the restaurant, Dylan was giving his overview of the week's work on The Alex. They were nearing completion, and Liam suffered a stab of envy. He should've been involved. They'd created an amazing property, and Liam was incredibly proud of them.

He made his way to an empty chair away from the main table and listened to the rest of the presentation, which included an overview from Maggie on the copious amount of landscape work that would be happening in the next several weeks.

When the meeting adjourned, Dad came over to greet him.

Liam gave him a quick hug. "I didn't realize you'd be here."

"Nor I you," Dad said. "When did you get in?"

"Early this morning." Rylan had picked him up at the airport and taken him back to McMinnville to prep their jump gear, but Liam wasn't going to tell Dad that. No one needed to know what he was doing. He'd tell them about it afterward, when it would be pointless for any of them to try to talk him out of it.

"I'm glad you're here in person. I wanted to tell you that I'm just about ready to pull the trigger on bottling my beer. I'm starting with Longbow, Crossbow, and Nock to see how it goes." He shook his head, a smile tugging at his lips. "I'm getting ahead of myself. We need to get a facility up and running first. We're going to lease some space near Portland until we get ours built out here. I've got Tori working on plans, and Dylan's going to build it."

Liam stared at him. "Wow, this is really happening."

Dad nodded, his gray eyes sharp with excitement. "I've decided to split up the company—Archer Brewing and Archer Enterprises. Derek's going to be president of Archer Brewing."

Liam was surprised. "Why not Archer Enterprises?"

"I gave him the choice." Dad grinned. "He prefers beer."

"Who's going to run AE?"

Dad lifted a shoulder. "Don't know yet. I'll contact some headhunters, put out feelers."

Liam noted that Dad didn't ask him. But then Liam had turned him down so many times, could he blame him?

"Hey, Liam." Tori joined them, her gaze narrowed at him with laser focus. Liam instantly knew something was up. "Did you come up for the oral argument?" Her tone was almost toxic.

He was curious why she seemed annoyed but wasn't going to let her rile him. "I e-mailed and said I was going to."

Dad seemed oblivious to Tori's nonverbal hints at agitation as he smiled at them both. "I need to head to the office. See you later." He turned and left, saying good-bye to everyone else on his way out.

Tori crossed her arms and let the full weight of whatever was pissing her off settle into a frosty glower.

Liam returned the ice with a glare of his own. "What gives? Why are you treating me like I just hid your favorite purple clogs?"

"Which you totally did when we were kids. We never did find them."

He exhaled. "I know, because I forgot where I put them."

"You'd think they would've turned up."

"You'd think," he muttered. "Anyway, why are you pissed at me *now*?"

She lightly socked him in the arm. "Because of Aubrey, you tool!"

Sara came up and joined them. "Are you reading him the riot act about Aubrey?"

Tori nodded, and Sara punched him in the other arm. Sara's punch made him flinch. "Ow."

"You deserve that and worse," Sara said.

"Why are you guys giving me grief?" He was afraid he knew the answer. And sorry he'd asked. He should've known better. In fact, he should've taken off as soon as Tori had given him the stink eye.

Tori dropped her hands to her sides. "Because Aubrey is fantastic, and you should be dating her."

How much did they know? What had Aubrey told them?

"We're not stupid," Tori said, accurately mind-reading his unspoken questions. "We figured it out."

They'd figured what out? That he and Aubrey had been hooking up?

"And don't be mad at Aubrey," Sara added.

"I wouldn't." But he'd sure as hell be asking how everyone knew. Not that it mattered. Unless Aubrey was pissed. What a mess. He'd never had to worry about one of his exes being championed by his sisters. And that's exactly what was happening.

Tori pulled her phone from her back pocket and answered it. "This is Tori."

She put her finger in her ear and said, "What? I can't hear you very well." She tipped her head down and listened. Her cheeks went pale, and when she looked up her eyes were wide. "Aubrey's uncle is in the ER in Newberg."

Liam turned and snatched his helmet from the table. "Tell her I'm on my way."

"We'll come, too," Tori said, but Liam didn't know if she was talking to him or if she was still on the phone with Aubrey. All he knew was that he was going to get there first.

As he fired up his bike and tore out of the lot, he wished that he had been the one she'd called.

AUBREY SAT IN the ER waiting room with Aunt Cyndi. "He's going to be fine," Aunt Cyndi said for probably the tenth time. "He's incredibly healthy."

"Yes," Aubrey agreed. He was going to be fine. And then she was going to smack him for not taking better care of himself. His cold had gotten worse, and even though he'd seen the doctor and been prescribed antibiotics for a sinus infection, the cough had intensified until this afternoon at work, when his breathing had become shallow and difficult. At least he'd had the cognizance to come to Aubrey's office and alert her to the situation. She'd driven him to the ER immediately and called Aunt Cyndi on the way to meet them there.

"He's never even been in the hospital, can you believe that?" Aunt Cyndi said. She adjusted her glasses and shifted in her chair. "And thank goodness for that, because this hospital furniture is really uncomfortable."

Aubrey smiled, glad for a bit of levity as they waited to hear the results of Uncle Dave's lung X-rays.

"I've had it." Aunt Cyndi stood, stretching as she got up from the chair. "I'm going for a little walk. Do you want to come?"

"No thanks," Aubrey said. "I'll just sit here on this hard chair."

Tori had said that Liam was on his way, which was both unnecessary and…surprising? Tori and Sara were going to come, too, but Aubrey had told them not to, that she would keep them posted. She'd texted Liam and also told him not to come, but he hadn't responded.

She pulled her phone out to see if she'd missed a text, but there was nothing except notes from the people back at work who were anxious to hear what was going on. Aubrey was pretty sure it was pneumonia. She'd known a couple of other people who'd come down with it—someone in her kickboxing class and one of the baristas at Books and Brew. It was always comforting to think that someone who'd been pouring your latte was that sick.

She glanced toward the door and immediately tensed at seeing Liam stride inside. He pulled off his Aviators and scanned the room, his gaze finding hers. He came toward her, his bike helmet tucked under one arm.

She stood to greet him, feeling far more nervous than she wanted to.

"How's your uncle?" he asked without preamble.

"They're doing X-rays and other tests. We're expecting the doctor soon."

Liam looked around. "Who's 'we'? Is your aunt here?"

"She went for a walk." Aubrey sat back down. "You didn't have to come. I texted you."

Liam sat down kitty-corner from her in the U-shaped seating area and set his helmet on the chair to his right. "I was riding, so I don't check my phone."

She glanced at his motorcycle boots, which were so sexy, and then up at his face, which was even sexier. "Probably a good idea."

He cracked a smile. "See, I'm not *that* dangerous."

Oh, he was plenty dangerous, and it had nothing to do with his hobbies. Once again, being in his presence tossed every reservation she had about him out the window. "Why *did* you come?"

He set his sunglasses down on the table between their chairs that formed one of the corners of the seating area. Then he pulled his black leather jacket off and laid it over his helmet. "I wanted to be here for you. We're friends, remember?"

Right, friends. She was foolish if she expected anything more. And this is what friends did. It was why she'd called Tori in the first place, because they were friends. She didn't, however, call Liam, although he'd apparently been with Tori. Did he care that she hadn't called him? They weren't that kind of friends. Yuck, she was so tired of trying to define this relationship. They liked each other, they enjoyed having sex with each other, they saw each other on a regular basis. If they were still having sex, she'd say they were indisputably dating.

The doctor came toward them then, and Aubrey jumped to her feet. Dressed in scrubs with her hair gathered into a bun, she was maybe thirty-five. She smiled warmly. "Are you David Tallinger's niece?"

"Yes, but wait. My aunt went for a walk. I need to find her."

Liam had stood up beside her. "I'll get her."

"You've never met her," Aubrey said.

"No, but I've seen her picture at your house. I'll know who she is." He kissed her cheek and took off, leaving her to stare after him in wonder. He'd gone into caretaker mode again, just like when she'd been drunk on girls' night or when she'd tripped on the steepest path at the amphitheater and skinned her knee over Labor Day.

Pulling her thoughts in line, Aubrey turned back to the doctor. "How's Uncle Dave?"

"He's resting comfortably. We can discharge him shortly—" She shook her head. "Sorry, I'll wait for your aunt."

Liam returned a moment later with Aunt Cyndi in tow. Her face was pale, her blue eyes wide behind her glasses. "How is he?" she asked the doctor.

"He's doing well. He has a pretty good case of pneumonia but nothing a stiff course of antibiotics won't take care of."

Aunt Cyndi instantly relaxed. She reached for Aubrey's hand and gave it a squeeze. "Thank you so much. Can he come home?"

The doctor nodded. "Yes. He was a bit dehydrated, so we're giving him some IV fluids right now. When that's finished, he can go. I'm having his prescription filled now. You'll need to keep him at home in bed for two to three days. Do you think you can do that?"

Aunt Cyndi exchanged a look with Aubrey. "I'll try, but he's hard to keep stationary."

Uncle Dave liked to walk and hike and work in his garden. He wasn't one to sit around.

"We'll get him some new books," Aubrey said, her mind already shifting to tomorrow's oral argument and how it couldn't be moved, meaning she'd have to do it. "He likes to read."

"Excellent. Well, go ahead and come on back." The doctor turned and started toward the double doors that led to the treatment rooms.

Liam touched Aubrey's arm. "I'll wait here until you're done."

"You don't have to." But she wanted him to.

His lips curved into a slight smile. "You're not getting rid of me today. I know you're already thinking that the oral argument is tomorrow and now Uncle Dave can't be there. We'll talk about it when you're done. We'll figure it out together, okay?"

She stared at him, impressed that he'd correctly gauged her thoughts and was behaving like her own personal knight in shining armor.

She followed her aunt and the doctor back to Uncle Dave's room. He looked at them sheepishly as they walked in. "Guess I should've listened to you and called the doctor this morning," he said to Aunt Cyndi.

"You should always listen to your wife," the nurse who was checking his IV bag admonished. "You'll be done here in about thirty minutes." She patted his hand and left.

The nurse went through his treatment plan and obtained assurances from everyone that he'd follow up with his primary-care doctor in three days. There was no way Aunt Cyndi would let him blow that off.

When the nurse left the three of them alone, Cyndi perched next to Uncle Dave on the bed. She brushed her hand along his face. "You nearly gave me a heart attack."

His eyes sparkled with love as he looked at her. "Impossible. You have the best blood pressure of anyone I know."

Aunt Cyndi laughed softly. "Fine. How about a nervous breakdown?"

He shook his head. "Not buying it. You're a rock. Why do you think I married you?"

Watching them, listening to them, Aubrey's heart swelled with love. This is what she wanted—this camaraderie, this care, this absolute devotion that was based in friendship and love and an emotion that was maybe even deeper than all of those things together. An emotion that couldn't be named. The emotion that came when you found your soul mate. And she knew that's what her aunt and uncle were. They shared a bond she'd never seen in her parents. A bond she'd seen repeated over and over when she spent time with the Archers. Maybe that was why she wanted it so badly. It was so close she could practically taste it.

Uncle Dave held his hand up on the other side of the bed from Aunt Cyndi. "Aubrey, I'm so sorry about tomorrow."

Aubrey took his hand and smiled down at him. "It's fine. You've prepped me very well."

He squeezed her fingers. "You're ready. Get your father's criticism out of your head."

Aubrey nodded, knowing that was the best advice she could hear. "I will."

"Don't feel like you have to hang around, dear," Aunt Cyndi told her. "I'm sure you want to get ready for tomorrow, and it looks like Liam's anxious to help you."

Uncle Dave's gaze snapped between them. "Liam Archer's here?"

Aunt Cyndi nodded. "I just met him. Charming young man, and so thoughtful to rush over to be with Aubrey." She looked at Aubrey, her blue eyes inquisitive. "Are you sure he's not boyfriend material? He seems caring, and he's gorgeous—if I do say so myself. Sorry, honey." She patted Uncle Dave's hand and grinned.

Clearly Uncle Dave had talked to her about Liam. Not that it was a secret.

"He doesn't even live here in Ribbon Ridge, so that should tell you about his boyfriend potential right there." Aubrey leaned down and kissed her uncle's cheek. "Feel better, okay? Will one of you text me when you get home?"

"We will," Aunt Cyndi said.

Aubrey gave her a quick hug and left. As she made her way back to the waiting room, her mind was already buzzing with thoughts of tomorrow. Damn, she wasn't mentally ready for this. She knew she *could* do it, but she hadn't planned on doing it. Which meant she had to get her head into the game fast.

She made her way back to Liam.

He stood. "Everything all right?"

"Yes, he's going home in a bit."

He smiled. "That's great. You ready to blow out of here? I'll follow you back to your house." He grabbed his coat and put it on.

What was it about that leather jacket that ramped his sex appeal from zero to sixty in nothing flat? No, that wasn't right. His sex appeal was *never* at zero.

"I don't remember inviting you." Her feeble attempt at protest sounded lame even to her ears.

He picked up his sunglasses from the table. "You don't want my help? Come on, Aubrey, I want to help. Why won't you let me?"

"Because...reasons."

"I promise to keep my hands to myself." His eyes narrowed. "But you have to do the same."

Point taken. She had no willpower where he was concerned. She really ought to tell him no, but she *did* need help. She needed to practice, and he was the best candidate to help her. "Okay."

"That's my girl." He slipped his shades on, and the sex appeal ratcheted even higher.

She scowled at him. "I am not your girl."

He lifted his hands. "My bad." He plucked up his helmet and escorted her from the waiting room. "I'll stop at the pub and pick up some dinner. You want a burger or something?"

"Cheeseburger, medium—no mayo."

"Got it." He walked her to her car, which was parked nearby since she'd brought Uncle Dave in. He edged his glasses down his nose and peered at her over the rims. "Any other special requests?"

She pressed the button on her key fob to unlock her car. "Just the one about the hands."

His brow arched. "The more you bring it up, the more I fixate on it."

She pressed her lips together and vowed to keep her mouth shut. "See you in a bit." She climbed into the car, and he closed the door.

As she pulled out of the parking lot, she saw him start up his bike and pull out of his spot. He looked so hot, so dangerous, so unattainable.

And he was coming to her house, where they couldn't seem to *not* end up having sex. She was so screwed.

THEY MADE IT through dinner and managed to keep their focus entirely on preparing for the hearing. That didn't mean that Liam wasn't appreciating the high ponytail she was wearing and the way it bared her sleek neck. Nor did it mean he wasn't eyeballing the jeans she'd changed into, which perfectly delineated her toned ass. And he was trying really hard not to look at the swell of her breasts beneath the striped, long-sleeved T-shirt. Horizontal stripes. Which only served to make her look even curvier than she already was.

After dinner, they took their wine to the formal dining room so she could practice. Liam sat at the end of the table closest to the front window and tried really hard not to picture her sprawled out naked over the other end while he stood between her thighs and brought them both to the peak of orgasm and beyond. As if he'd done that all on his own. No, she'd been every bit as instrumental in each one of their sexual encounters. She was, without question, the best lover he'd ever had.

"That was really fantastic," he said when she was finished, adding applause, which sparked her to bow. "You're a great orator, but that shouldn't surprise me. You're one of the smartest, most well-spoken people I know."

Her cheeks turned a pretty shade of pink. "You're sucking up. Knock it off."

He laughed. "I am not. Am I not allowed to give you a compliment? Hey, it didn't even involve how beautiful you are or how great you kiss."

"Aren't you breaking your own rules about being here?"

"I said hands to ourselves. I didn't say anything about words."

She rolled her eyes. "As if that's any better. For your information, words are every bit as much of a turn-on for women as anything you might do with your *hands*."

"They're a turn-on for men, too—at least they are for me. But I'll be honest. One look from you carries the weight of a thousand words."

She stood at the opposite end of the table, her arms crossed, her look decidedly guarded. "Stop that." Her voice was low, vulnerable. "Stop saying things that make me want you. I don't *want* to want you. We aren't doing this."

"Doing what?" he asked cautiously. He wanted to be very clear about what they were talking about.

"Hooking up. Having sex. Getting together."

He sat back in the chair and rested his elbows on the arms. "You don't want those things. I get it. Tell me what you do want."

Her eyes widened briefly with surprise. She stared at him for a moment, then pulled out the chair at the other end of the table—the end they'd used that night—and sat down. "You really want to know?"

He nodded. "I do."

"I want what my aunt and uncle have. At the hospital, they were talking in Uncle Dave's room." She looked at the table as she traced her finger over the wood. "They have this closeness that's just so real, so right. I want that. I want a partner, a lover—" she glanced at him but looked away before saying "—a husband. And I want that *here* in Ribbon Ridge." When her gaze found his, her hazel eyes were full of conviction. "Growing up, I never felt that sense of belonging. My parents were cold, self-involved. Nothing I ever did was good enough for them. My dad in particular had crazy, ridiculous expectations. Straight As weren't enough, not when I could've taken an extra class or joined another club. I got a B once, in English, when I was a junior in high school. That summer he made me read forty books chosen by him and write a reflection on each of them."

He wanted to put his arms around her. He also wanted to punch her dad in the gut. "Jesus, Aubrey."

"When I decided to move here and work with Uncle Dave, my parents were severely disappointed. They wanted me to take a prestigious job—I had offers—and marry a wealthy name. None of that matters to me, and they don't care."

He watched her talk, heard the disdain and the hurt in her tone, and finally understood her brand of crazy. "I had no idea your parents were such assholes."

She laughed sharply. "Yep."

"Do you see them at all?"

She laid one palm flat on the table and rested her chin on the palm of her other hand. "Rarely. They're super busy working on their golf game and picking up wine futures. They still live in Carmel, but they also have a place in Arizona. They come here for IPNC every year. Last year, I left town. This year, Uncle Dave, Aunt Cyndi, and I are going to the Shakespeare Festival."

"And rafting? You got my recommendations, right?" He'd e-mailed them not long after she'd asked.

She nodded, adjusting her position to sit back in her chair. "I think Aunt Cyndi made reservations for the Upper Klamath. I'll have to double-check."

He wished he could go with her. He'd love to see her face when she hit Satan's Gate and Hell's Corner. For the first time, he envisioned taking a woman along on one of his weekend jaunts. But then he'd already invited Aubrey flying—maybe he'd surprise her on Wednesday.

Wait, what was he doing? He'd heard what she'd just said: She wanted to settle down with a guy here in Ribbon Ridge. Probably start a family. But maybe not. Her family experience wasn't the best. Plus, she'd mentioned wanting what her aunt and uncle had, and they didn't have any children. "Do you want to have kids?"

She nodded immediately. "Definitely."

"But your family life sucked."

"Which is precisely why I want a do-over."

Liam tried to understand that. Personally, he chose to stay away from things he didn't like or that made him uncomfortable. Such as distancing himself from home because of the guilt he'd felt and because he and Alex had both preferred it that way. Families, in his experience, were messy. He loved them, truly—at arm's length.

Or so he'd thought. He honestly didn't know anymore.

"Despite having douche-bag parents, you turned out okay."

She rolled her eyes. "I guess. More wine? We should finish the bottle." She picked up her empty glass and went to the kitchen.

He snagged his glass and followed her. Standing at the island in the center of the kitchen, she refilled them both, pouring out the rest of the pinot.

"Thanks for picking up dinner and coming over," she said.

He tapped his glass against hers. "To wiping the floor with Sutherlin tomorrow."

"I hope so." She drank her wine and leaned her hip against the counter.

He heard the note of uncertainty in her voice. "Why am I more confident than you?"

"Because you're arrogant?" She flashed him a smile. "Kidding."

He took a drink and set his wine down. "No, you're not. Sometimes I am. You should be, too. You're a kick-ass attorney."

She looked down at her wine. "Thanks."

He stepped around the island toward her and took the glass from her hands, setting it on the counter. "Stop doing that. Don't doubt yourself."

He suspected her parents had everything to do with the expectations she put on herself as well as the flashes of self-doubt that he saw in her. Her parents were worse than assholes. And he hadn't helped matters when he'd come to talk to her about the brief. He could've handled that a lot better.

She looked up at him. Her eyes were so beautiful, with all the greens and browns that he loved in nature. "You sound like my uncle."

"Listen to your uncle—not the ghost of your dad." He cracked a smile. "I realize he isn't dead, but you get me. I hope."

She smiled back. "I do. You know, you don't suck at this friend thing."

"Don't sound so surprised. On second thought, *I'm* surprised." He backed away from her and picked up his wineglass before he did something that crossed over that friend line. "Speaking of surprises, I have one for you on Wednesday. To celebrate."

Her eyes widened with alarm. "Stop talking about celebrating before anything's decided!"

"There's nothing wrong with thinking positive. That's how most of my real-estate deals get done."

She finished her wine, and he finished his. With no more wine to drink and no more argument to practice, he figured it was time to go. But damn, he didn't want to.

"I should go."

She nodded, and they walked—slowly—toward the front door. He picked up his helmet from the window seat while she grabbed his coat from the back of one of her dining-room chairs. She held his helmet while he shrugged into the jacket.

He leaned forward to take the helmet, and she took a step back.

"No more kissing, like at the hospital," she said.

He opened his mouth to protest, then remembered that he *had* kissed her cheek. Huh, he hadn't even thought about it. In retrospect, it had just been a thing that he'd done, like breathing. Had he been about to do it again? Maybe. Probably.

He took the helmet. "It was a friendly kiss. Or can't we do that?"

She opened the door for him. "I'll see you tomorrow morning in Salem."

They were meeting at the courthouse. He would be caravanning down with his family, but she'd already declined the offer to travel with them. "See you then."

He turned and left. As he stepped off her porch, he realized she hadn't answered his question about not being able to exchange friendly kisses. But knowing what he knew—that their struggle to be friends instead of lovers was mutual—he already had his answer.

Chapter Seventeen

AUBREY ARRIVED A good forty-five minutes early for the hearing. She'd already had coffee at home and had stopped to get a latte on the way. Plus, she hadn't slept that great. Consequently, she was nervous and jittery and just ready for this damned thing to be over.

She'd already talked to Uncle Dave, who'd given her an amazing pep talk. She could do this. She was ready. And she had him to thank for that.

Well, him and Liam.

A lot of last night's sleeplessness was due to his visit. She could scarcely believe they'd had an hours-long interaction that hadn't involved flirting or kissing or sexual innuendo. Okay, it had, but she was certain it was unintentional on both of their parts. They were trying really hard to be friends.

Liam had gone above and beyond. He could be such a great boyfriend—or husband—if he wanted to.

Unfortunately, their attempt at friendship was maybe going to leave her even more heartbroken than before. And she didn't know what to do about that.

Was there any chance he'd changed? That maybe he wanted to try something more with her? She was afraid to ask. Anyway, he was Liam. He went after what he wanted. If he wanted her, he'd tell her.

She heard heels clicking on the marble floor of the hallway and looked up. A curly headed blonde in a black fitted dress with a matching sleek jacket—it looked like Armani—strolled to where Aubrey was sitting. Instantly on the defensive, Aubrey stood and was glad to see she towered over the petite woman, despite her heels.

This had to be Whitney Parker. She took stock of Aubrey, raking her from head to toe. Aubrey wanted to ask if she'd passed the test but wasn't going to give in to high school competitiveness. Instead, she smiled serenely and offered her hand. "You must be Miss Parker."

Whitney's nails were fake with a sparkly French manicure. Once again, Aubrey took pride in her real nails, even if they were just simply manicured with clear polish.

Whitney shook Aubrey's hand. "Yes, and you must be Miss Tallinger." She pronounced it wrong.

Aubrey let go of her hand.

"I'm surprised the Archers went with you," Whitney said. "You seem awfully young."

"We're probably the same age, right? Or are you a little older?" Aubrey asked sweetly.

Whitney laughed. "Ha! I see what you did there. You're a clever girl, aren't you, but then you did go to

Stanford, even if it wasn't for law school. Maybe you'll put up a good fight, after all."

Aubrey shrugged through her irritation. "I guess we'll find out." The longer she stood here talking to this viper, the more she wanted to pound them all into the dirt. Maybe this was a good thing.

Except she knew that Whitney used to be Liam's hook-up girl. Before Aubrey. The idea of Liam kissing Whitney, of him touching her…Aubrey brought her thoughts to a crashing halt before she considered pounding Liam into the dirt, instead of the opposing party.

"No Archers yet?" Whitney asked, looking around the mostly empty hallway. "I was hoping to grab a moment with Liam before the hearing."

"And why's that?" Aubrey wanted to take the question back as soon as she said it. What did it matter?

Whitney smiled at her, her heavily made up eyes slanting slightly. "We go way back. I was hoping there was a way for us to maybe settle this disagreement."

Wait, was there still a chance for a settlement? Or did she mean she was going to try to blackmail Liam again? Aubrey perversely wanted to hear what this woman had to say. "If there's any chance we can settle this before going in front of LUBA, we should do that."

The Archer contingent chose that convenient moment to arrive. They rounded the corner of the hallway en masse. If they'd been moving in slow motion, they would've looked like some superhero squadron coming to save the day. Rob Archer was flanked by his wife, who wore the frostiest bitch face Aubrey had ever seen, and

Liam, who'd never looked more devastatingly attractive in a navy pin-striped suit. All of the others—and it was pretty much everybody—appeared equally intimidating. They stalked toward Aubrey and Whitney like a well-rehearsed unit.

"Look who's here already," Kyle said, his lip curling as he glanced at Whitney.

Emily touched her son's arm, and he leaned down so she could whisper something to him. He nodded, then turned away with Maggie.

Whitney went right up to Liam. "Can I have a moment?"

Liam, to his credit, glared down at her. "Why?"

Aubrey stepped forward and halfway insinuated herself between them. "If this is about settlement, your attorney should be present."

Whitney tossed her a look of supreme annoyance that only served to make Aubrey stand taller. "Fine."

The three of them walked to a corner. Aubrey checked her watch. They still had about twenty minutes until the hearing started. She knew Sutherlin would show up with just a few minutes to spare. He and Parker were likely already in the building, just waiting to arrive with some sort of grand flourish. Their absence also told her that they were likely not privy to whatever Whitney was going to propose. Or maybe they were, and Aubrey didn't remotely understand the game they were playing.

Whitney angled herself in an apparent effort to exclude Aubrey or at least make it seem like the conversation between her and Liam was supposed to be intimate. Aubrey rolled her eyes.

"It's not too late," she said to him, her fake eyelashes batting provocatively. "Say the word, and I'll tell my dad to knock it off."

Yep, blackmail again. Aubrey sidled closer to Liam and narrowed her eyes at Whitney. "You've got to be kidding."

Whitney turned her head and gave her a condescending stare. "Liam and I have discussed an arrangement. If he agrees, my father will drop the appeal."

When he'd mentioned Whitney's involvement at that Sunday dinner, he'd made it sound like she'd hinted at something. But now it sounded like she'd made him an offer of some kind. Why hadn't he said anything?

Aubrey turned her full attention on Liam. "What arrangement?"

Liam flicked an irritated glance at Whitney before pivoting toward Aubrey so that now Whitney seemed like the intruder. "It's not important. I'm not agreeing to anything."

Whitney sucked in a breath. "I get it now. *This* is why you've been turning me down? So you could hook up with Ginger here? Priceless. Except you know I don't care if you screw other women." She inspected Aubrey again with her coffee-colored eyes, but this time there was a spark of something other than dislike. And it wasn't something Aubrey remotely appreciated. Whitney looked back to Liam. "In fact, if you want to do a three-way, I'm game."

Aubrey hadn't misread her look then. She tried to shake the distasteful suggestion from her mind. "Let me get this straight. You and your father are prepared to make this entire months-long nightmare go away if Liam sleeps with you?"

Whitney lifted her shoulder. "It has to be ongoing— not just a one-time thing. Like we used to do." She gave him a meaningful look followed by a wink.

Aubrey stared at Liam who, for maybe the first time in her experience, appeared speechless. "I keep waiting for you to say something, but I can see how you don't want to justify this with an answer."

He visibly relaxed and grazed his fingers against hers. The touch ignited heat in her belly—both on a sexual and professional level. "No, I don't. And thank you for understanding."

Whitney narrowed her eyes at both of them. "Fine. Sutherlin's going to cream Ginger here. Hope she's worth it."

"She's worth so much more."

Aubrey suddenly felt light. And powerful. And armed with the wrath of the righteous. She turned to Whitney with a satisfied smirk and looped her arm through Liam's. "Please excuse us. I hope you won't feel too sad after you lose. On second thought, feel sad, angry, just go to town with all the pity-party emotions you can find."

Head high, she walked toward where the rest of the Archers were watching them in open curiosity, and Liam strode beside her.

"You were magnificent," he whispered next to her ear. "If we weren't due in court in fifteen minutes, I would whisk you to the nearest closet."

"You can't talk to me like that. Not when I'm about to go into court." She threw him a desperate glance. "Not ever."

He exhaled. "It would be a lot easier if you weren't so damned attractive. In every way."

They'd reached the Archers. She murmured a last comment just for him: "How about I dye my hair blonde and get a perm?"

He burst out laughing, and Aubrey embraced the lightness that filled her. She was going to rock this hearing.

"What was that about?" Rob asked, his gaze darting suspiciously toward Whitney, who stood fuming in the corner.

"A failed attempt at negotiation," Liam said. "Trust me when I say you don't want to hear what she offered."

"I can only imagine." Kyle rolled his eyes. "Looks like Aubrey stuck it to her though."

Liam's gaze was appreciative and landed on her for far too long. "She absolutely did."

She needed to get her head in the game. "All right, Archers. The moment we've been waiting for is finally here. Let's do this."

LIAM WATCHED AUBREY park her car outside the hangar and appreciated the view of her stepping from the driver's seat. She wore sunglasses, and the breeze whipped her long red hair around her face. She came toward him, and he resisted the urge to greet her with a kiss. She'd said no kissing. Not even friendly kissing. Which he wasn't even sure he was capable of.

He'd tried. He'd really tried. But watching her in action yesterday had been a hell of a turn-on. They didn't have a result yet, but he'd bet his real-estate company they'd won. Aubrey had been flawless in her presentation—clear, sharp, persuasive. Sutherlin had been a good adversary, but yesterday Aubrey had quite simply out-lawyered him. Combine all of that with her air of confidence and her brutal takedown of Whitney Parker, and he was smitten. Never mind how unbelievably gorgeous she'd looked in a charcoal gray suit, pale blue blouse, and black patent-leather heels he wanted her to wear with absolutely nothing else.

"Hi," she said, coming to stand in front of him. But not too close. "Is it too late for me to change my mind about this?"

After the hearing yesterday, he'd invited her to meet him this morning for the airplane ride he'd promised her. "Yes."

Her brow pleated with worry—at least he guessed that's what it was, since he couldn't see her eyes.

He reached for her hand, then thought better of it, given their friend rules. "Come on. It'll be fun. If you really want to change your mind, you can."

"I don't. Let's go."

He led her into the hangar and over to the plane he was going to take her up in. "This is a Piper Archer."

She pushed her sunglasses up onto her head and looked at him. "Are you serious? You have a plane named after you? Or are you just being a smart-ass?"

He laughed. God, he loved her sense of humor. "Not guilty. To the last two questions. I'm quite serious. It's an awesome training plane—very easy to fly. And comfy."

She walked up to the plane and looked into the open door at the instrument panel. "Where are we going?"

"Just over wine country around here. I wasn't sure how long you wanted to be gone—I know you're taking part of the day off to do this."

She slid him a sidelong glance with a half-smile. "You're not going to try to sweep me off to New York or something?"

He laughed. "No. I couldn't even if I wanted to. The Archer only has a range of six hundred miles."

"You can't even fly this to Denver and back," she said.

"Nope." When he thought about planes he might buy, the Archer wasn't in the equation. Truthfully, he could've bought one of these a couple of years ago, but he'd been saving up for something bigger that *could* make the trip between Denver and Ribbon Ridge. "You ready?"

She took a deep breath and nodded.

He moved past her. "Pardon me for going first, but I'm going to fly the plane, so I have to sit over there." He gestured to the left side of the cockpit.

She stepped aside as he climbed in. After a moment of hesitation, she pulled herself into the passenger seat. She stared at the panel in front of her and gestured toward the control wheel, which was the part of a cockpit that made one think of driving, except it didn't really work like a steering wheel. She sent him a look of pure terror. "I'm not supposed to help you, am I?"

"No. You just sit back and enjoy the ride." He put on his headset. "Can you pull the door closed?"

She did as he asked, and he heard it latch. "That's it? I'm somehow certified to close an airplane?"

He loved her combination of nervousness and humor. "It's not a pressurized plane, so it's just like closing a car door really."

"Except if I fall out, I go hurtling ten thousand miles to the ground instead of tumbling headfirst into asphalt."

"You aren't going to hurtle out of anything, but put your seat belt on just in case."

He didn't have to tell her twice. She buckled up, then jumped as he started the engine. The cockpit space was tight enough that he could feel her movements beside him—and her heat. "Put that headset on so we can talk while we're in the air. It cuts out the airplane noise so we can hear each other."

She took her sunglasses from her head and set them in her lap. Then she slipped on the headset and adjusted it to fit. She jumped again as his voice came into her ears, asking if she was ready.

She turned her surprisingly excited gaze toward him. "Yes, I'm ready. You can stop asking me that."

He chuckled as he drove the plane out of the hangar. As soon as he was cleared for takeoff, he sped down the runway and lifted them into the air.

"Wow. That was really smooth," she said, putting on her sunglasses. "I usually hate takeoffs, though landings are worse."

"Not in this plane. It's so easy, you could do it."

She flashed him a smile. "Yeah, right."

"No, really, you could. After yesterday, I'm convinced you can do anything."

"Now you're just kissing my ass."

"You said no kissing." He smiled at her answering chuckle. "Really, you were fantastic yesterday."

"Thanks. It was fun."

He hadn't had a chance to talk to her about the Whitney encounter. "Does that include what happened with Whitney?"

She kept her head turned toward the window, away from him, as she looked at the ground below. "I could've done without that entirely, actually. I can't imagine what you saw in her."

"Honestly, I can't either." Looking at Whitney now, he was repulsed, and not just because of what she'd tried to do yesterday. It also wasn't because he'd grown tired of her. This was different. He was turned off by the whole idea of finding a hot, eager woman to screw on occasion.

Aubrey gasped. "Oooh, I can see Ribbon Ridge."

He'd purposely taken her east over the town. He glanced over at her, loving her sense of wonder and excitement. He was getting a rush just from *her* rush.

He flew her past the town. "I'm going to turn north now, show you The Alex from up here."

"Awesome."

He completed a gentle turn—he didn't know if she'd like acrobatics, and anyway this plane wasn't really built for that sort of flying. A minute later they were flying over

The Alex, which looked just as impressive from up here as it did from the ground.

"Look, there's the spire! And the hotel! It looks so great! I really hope they can open on time this summer."

After the hearing had gone so well, they'd jumped into making plans, assuming they were going to win. A few of them—Sara, Dylan, Maggie—had cautioned against getting ahead of themselves, but Liam had convinced them all that it was better to have a plan of attack than be caught with their pants down. So they'd gathered around the kitchen table and laid out a schedule for a soft opening in late July followed by a grand opening in August. In his mind, he was already planning to be here for both.

"We've got a plan," Liam said.

Aubrey nodded. "So I heard. Tori called me all excited this morning."

"You and Tori have become pretty good friends."

She turned her body toward him in the seat. "She told me that she yelled at you about me. I didn't ask her to do that."

"It's fine. I deserved everything she said." And probably then some.

"Is that right? Well, it's my fault for accidentally spilling that we'd slept together."

"Shit, is that what happened?" He laughed. "Sounds like a story I want to hear."

She grinned. "Remember the girls' night we had at The Arch and Vine?"

As long as he lived, he'd remember that night. "I'd be hard-pressed not to."

"There you go with your double entendres."

He was momentarily confused. *Hard-pressed.* He shook his head. "No entendre intended."

"Anyway, we were playing 'I Never' and somebody—I forget who—was trying to get Maggie to drink. So she threw out an 'I never' that would bait Maggie and no one else. She said, 'I've never slept with an Archer.' That's right, it was Chloe, because she giggled since Derek isn't officially an Archer."

Liam could practically hear their drunken laughter. "And you drank?"

"Without thinking. Then you showed up right after that, and I was horrified."

"Did you cop to it right then? I would've expected them to flip me shit that night."

She shook her head. "No. It happened right before you got there, then we left. Sara was somehow elected spokesperson and called me the next day to confirm that it was you and not Hayden."

"Confirm? They were all pretty sure?"

"Since it was sex they'd never heard about, yeah. Hayden doesn't have the reputation you do, apparently."

No, he didn't.

"Do you care that they know?" Aubrey's question sounded tentative.

"Not at all. So long as it doesn't bother you. If they're annoying you in any way, you have to tell me, and I'll make it stop."

She sighed. "My knight in shining armor."

He snorted in response. Damn, he loved spending time with her. This was the most fun he'd had flying in a long time. No, ever. And that included some pretty memorable flights with Alex.

"Did you know I used to take Alex flying sometimes?"

"Yes."

Liam was mildly surprised. "He told you?"

"He told me a lot about you."

Liam wished he hadn't brought Alex into the conversation. He'd been intruding on Liam's well-being more and more lately, and Liam was afraid to dredge up the feelings he absolutely needed to keep buried. Time to turn the topic to something else. Or better yet, land the plane. "We're coming back to the airfield. Time for your landing."

She sucked in a breath. "I thought you were kidding when you said I could do it!"

He couldn't resist laughing. "I was." He made sure they were clear to land and focused on getting them on the ground.

"How's that for a landing?" he asked as he steered toward the hangar.

"Perfect. Liam Archer, I'm beginning to think you don't know how to do anything badly."

He'd argue with her that he'd done *plenty* of things badly, and some of them with her, but he didn't want to ruin the moment. He was having way too much fun.

Once he had the plane reparked in the hangar, they pulled off their headsets and unbuckled their seat belts.

She took off her sunglasses, and her expression was beaming with joy. "That was incredible. When can we go again?"

He loved her excitement, her palpable buzz. It was even better than his own. Shit, what was happening to him?

"I guess I should get out!" She unlatched the door and opened it, then slowly stepped down.

He jumped out behind her and closed the door.

"Pardon me for a minute while I use the little girls' room?"

"Over there." He pointed toward the back corner near Rylan's office. "I'll walk with you. I need to let Rylan know I didn't crash his plane."

She looked over at him as they walked. "Uh, wouldn't he know that already?"

Liam chuckled. "Of course."

She disappeared into the bathroom, and he watched the door close, feeling stupidly disappointed that she was gone from his vision. What was *wrong* with him?

He had feelings for Aubrey Tallinger. That's what was wrong with him.

Hell and double hell.

What was he supposed to do about that? He lived in Denver, and his life was all about the next high. She lived in Ribbon Ridge and dreamed of a ring on her finger and a baby registry.

But damn, it was obvious they wanted each other, that they could barely keep their hands off each other. And they *liked* each other. This friend thing had only made the sexual part of their relationship even more pronounced. He desired her more fiercely now than ever before.

Maybe they could make something work. He was already planning to be here a lot this summer because of The Alex. They could spend that time together. Except she didn't want that. She'd quite clearly said she wanted a guy *in* Ribbon Ridge.

And he wasn't leaving Denver. His life was there. He was happy.

Had he been happy there last week? Not really—he'd missed his family, and he'd missed Aubrey. He decided to blame it on the funk of being home around all of his happy, lovey-dovey siblings and thinking of Alex. Yes, he'd blame Alex. Why not? He more than deserved blame for what he'd done.

"Liam, are you skulking outside my door?" Rylan called.

Liam moved into his friend's office. "Hey. We're back."

"I heard you pull in, obviously. Good ride?"

"Great."

Rylan leaned back in his chair, making it squeak loudly. "Sweet. We're all set for this weekend, right? You'll meet me here Friday at three so we can fly over."

"Yep. Can't wait."

"Can't wait for what?" Aubrey stepped into Rylan's office.

Rylan's gaze flicked to Liam, who gave his friend a look he hoped communicated that he should keep his mouth shut.

Rylan stood and offered his hand to Aubrey. "Just an excursion we've been planning. Hi, I'm Rylan."

She shook his hand. "Aubrey."

"Liam's told me all about you."

She slid a glance at Liam. "All?"

"Rylan wishes." He sent Rylan a grateful glance. "Thanks for the loaner today, Ry."

"You know you're welcome whenever. Aubrey, are you going to come back and skydive?"

She shuddered. "Definitely not. I'll leave that to Danger Boy over here."

Rylan chuckled. "Careful, that nickname might stick."

"I've been called worse," Liam said. He turned toward the door. "Come on, Aubrey, before Rylan decides to list off those names."

She waved at Rylan. "Bye, nice to meet you."

"Ditto."

Liam escorted her back into the hangar and walked her toward the opposite end, where her car was parked outside.

"What are you and Rylan planning?"

"Nothing, just a flight."

She stopped just before they reached the door of the hangar. "I'm calling bullshit. I heard him say that you were all set for this weekend, and I saw the calendar hanging in his office. There was a line Friday through Tuesday with the letters FJC. What's FJC?"

His pulse quickened, and a different kind of adrenaline started pouring through his veins. The kind he didn't like. "Flight gibberish."

She put her hands on her hips. "Still calling bullshit. You know what? As soon as I get to my car, I'm Googling FJC, so you might as well just tell me what it is."

He braced for her reaction. "First jump course. It's a training course for BASE jumping."

Her eyes widened, and she gaped at him. "How can you do that?"

"It's no different from the other stuff I do."

"The hell it isn't. If it wasn't, you wouldn't have tried to hide it from me. Who else are you hiding it from? Does any of your family know?"

He exhaled, but it did nothing to settle his roiling insides. "No."

"That's great. Go off and do your most dangerous stunt yet, but don't tell anyone first. Do you have an actual death wish, or are you just looking to give your mother a heart attack?"

He cocked his head to the side and stared at her. "Are you sure no one's talked to you about me?"

"Yes, they have. Your mom pulled me aside at Evan and Alaina's wedding breakfast to ask if I knew about your hobbies and if I could find out if you planned to scale back after your injury."

That was weeks ago. Back when they were former lovers, not friends, not anything really. He put his hands on his hips, his ire rising. "Why would my mom ask you?"

Aubrey threw her hands up and let them fall to her sides. "I don't know. She thought we were friends or something. Joke's on her." The look she flashed him next was full of hurt. "And me." She turned and stalked toward her car.

Wait, what had just happened? He followed her. "Why are you so mad at me?"

She spun around, her eyes spitting fire. "Because you're a selfish prick. You're going to kill yourself, but maybe that's what you want. You're not any better than Alex."

"Whoa." He gave in to his anger. "Do *not* compare me to him. I'm not actively trying to *die*."

"Well I don't see you actively trying to *live* either. You bury yourself in these sports. You're gone every weekend. You're reckless. You avoid your family and any other meaningful connection besides sex. And I know that holds about as much meaning for you as being honest."

Everything she said hit him like a bullet. "Sex with you was far more than sex."

"Then it's pretty sad that I'm just learning this now that we aren't having it anymore."

And another bullet—that went straight to his heart. "I don't want to be tied down to anything or anyone. Sue me, all right? I can't change who I am, what I want."

"No, you can't. And I can't change who I am or what I want." She took a deep breath and slid her sunglasses on, masking the disappointment and anger in her eyes. "Thanks for the joyride, Liam. It's been fun."

She turned and went to her car. He didn't stop her, just watched her drive away.

Chapter Eighteen

By the time Aubrey arrived back in her office a half hour later, her anger had simmered into a deep frustration. What had she expected? A caring, thoughtful Liam didn't necessarily mean he'd done a complete 180 as far as relationships went. In fact, it didn't mean he'd done a 180 about *anything*, including his hobbies. He was going to be as self-involved and reckless as he always was.

It was past time to give him the box from Alex. She unlocked the drawer in her file cabinet, where she kept the letters Alex had written. And this one box.

She picked it up and held it in her palm. It was small and square, and it rattled when she shook it, which she'd done when she'd first found it. Unless there was a letter folded up inside, she didn't think Alex had written anything for Liam. At first that had made her sad. Right now, however, she didn't think Liam deserved anything like that. For all she cared, the contents could be a rock.

She set it on her desk and sat down. Okay, she didn't want it to be a rock. She hoped it was something far more meaningful. Since Alex had instructed her to deliver it when Liam's hobbies became even more extreme, she hoped it was maybe something that would persuade him to back off. Liam's obsession with extreme sports was Alex's fault anyway.

Now she sounded like Liam.

She groaned and decided it was time to turn all this crap off and get some work done. She opened her e-mail and froze. The decision from LUBA was staring at her. It had come in an hour ago.

She opened the e-mail and scanned it, getting to the punch line as quickly as possible—they'd won. The Alex was officially rezoned commercial. The Parkers had lost their appeal.

She jumped up with a fist pump and a loud cry, prompting Stephanie, whose office was next door, to come running in.

Her face was crinkled with concern, but upon seeing Aubrey's face, she smiled. "I was going to ask what's wrong, but it looks like I need to ask what's right. Did you get the decision from yesterday's hearing?"

"Winner, winner, chicken dinner!" Aubrey grinned so wide, her face hurt.

"Yes!" Stephanie came over and gave her a high five. "We should celebrate. I'll pour champagne in the kitchen." They kept some on hand for occasions just like these.

"Definitely. Just let me give Uncle Dave a quick call." Aubrey sat back down and dialed her uncle's cell.

"This is Dave," he said.

"It's Aubrey, we won." She was too excited to say anything else, and anyway, he'd know exactly what she meant.

She had to hold the phone away as he whooped. This was followed by a minor coughing fit. "Hey, don't hurt yourself," she said, wincing.

"I'm fine. Don't I sound better? Your aunt says I sound much better."

"You do sound better," she said. "Better than last night even."

Aubrey had spent last evening at their house having dinner and giving Uncle Dave the play-by-play from the hearing. She'd left out the Whitney Parker confrontation, however. What would be the point in sharing that?

"I still wish I could've been there yesterday to see you in action. Next time," he said. "Because you're going to get a lot more work like this, I'd bet."

"Yeah, maybe." She wouldn't mind that. After what Alex had done to her, she'd removed wills and trusts from her book of business entirely, handing them all off to Stephanie. So Aubrey could actually use more land-use cases.

"Have you told the Archers yet?" he asked.

"Not yet. I wanted to tell you first."

"I appreciate that." A smile was evident in his voice. "But don't keep them waiting."

"I won't. I'll call Emily Archer and have her set a family meeting for tonight. Stephanie's pouring champagne to celebrate—wish you were here."

"We'll have another celebration soon."

"I'll hold you to that. Thanks again for everything, Uncle Dave. I couldn't have done it without you."

"You *could've*, but I was and always will be happy to help. Love you."

"Love you, too. Bye."

She hung up and smiled broadly. Every bit of anger from earlier with Liam had completely dissipated in the wake of this extreme joy. Damn, it felt good to win. She could hardly wait to tell the Archers.

She picked up the phone again and called Emily Archer, the one person she could trust to keep a secret. As the phone rang, she wondered if she should tell Emily about Liam's plans. Hadn't she agreed to do that when they'd spoken a few weeks ago? Didn't Emily deserve to know that he was taking an increased risk this weekend? *Someone* should know—what if something happened to him? He really was a selfish jerk.

Emily answered. "Hello?"

"Hi, Emily, it's Aubrey. Can you call a family meeting at say, six o'clock?"

There was a sharp intake of breath, but it wasn't quite a gasp. "Is it the decision?" Emily asked.

"It is."

"Should I chill champagne or not?"

"Can you keep it a secret?"

"Of course. I'll call it dinner, not a meeting, how's that? So champagne or not? You're killing me!" She laughed nervously.

Aubrey grinned, loving this part of her job. "Champagne."

Emily practically squealed into the phone. "Take that, Russ Parker! He always was an ass."

So was his daughter. "So, I'll come a little after six, sound good?"

"Yes. Thank you so much, Aubrey. They're all going to be over the moon. We owe you so much. I know it hasn't been easy, everything Alex asked you to do…but I deeply appreciate it."

Emotion clogged Aubrey's throat. How could she not tell this lovely woman what Liam was planning? "I'll see you later."

"Can't wait!"

Aubrey ended the call feeling slightly less exuberant than she had a moment ago. Her gaze fell on the box on her desk. She'd take that tonight and give it to Liam. Then she'd tell him he *had* to talk to his mother before he did this BASE jumping training. If he didn't, *she* would. Oh, that would go over like gangbusters.

"Aubrey, champagne's ready!" Stephanie called.

Aubrey picked up the box and slipped it into her purse. She'd deal with that later. Right now, she had a date with a glass of bubbly.

FROM THE GROUPING of cars parked between the garages at the Archer house, it looked like everyone was there. Aubrey slipped her purse over her shoulder and walked to the back door, where she let herself inside.

The moment she stepped into the kitchen, Kyle jumped out of his chair. "I knew it!" He looked at Emily, smiling. "I knew this wasn't just a dinner. Otherwise, you would've asked me to cook."

Emily narrowed her eyes at him but without heat. "I've been cooking for this family longer than you have, and I'm every bit as good. Okay, maybe not that, but I do get to cook sometimes. I'm your mother. Sit down."

Everyone laughed, and Kyle blew her a kiss before sitting back down.

Emily turned her head to look at Aubrey. "Good evening, Aubrey, would you care to join us?"

"Sure. But first I have some news." Every head had already pivoted to look at her, but now those whose backs were to her fully turned in their chairs. There was excitement, tension, worry. There was also no Liam. Where was he? "Not everyone's here," she said.

Emily pressed her lips together. "Liam isn't answering his phone."

Aubrey heard the edge of concern in her tone and vowed right then and there to tell Emily about his BASE jump weekend. Then maybe skewer him.

"Don't keep us hanging," Dylan practically growled. Of everyone, he had to be the most on edge. He'd spent the last year building a commercial property, and if it couldn't be a commercial property...Well, it went without saying that he'd be devastated.

Aubrey's pulse sped up. "I heard back from LUBA this afternoon. They declined the Parkers' appeal."

The shouts and exclamations of joy started as soon as she said "declined" and drowned out the rest of her sentence. They leapt out of their chairs and hugged each other, exchanged high fives, waved their excited hands in the air. Then they descended on Aubrey, practically mauling her in their jubilation.

She laughed and grinned until her face hurt. Emily and Rob appeared with four bottles of chilled champagne, and Rob popped the first one open. The sound of the bottle opening elicited more whoops and hollers, and the clink of champagne flutes lining up on the granite peppered the background.

Rob handed the first glass to Aubrey. "Thank you."

She nodded her head. "You're welcome."

Soon everyone had a glass, and they looked around at each other, probably to see who wanted to say something first. "Tori, you go," Sara urged.

Tori looked to Aubrey and smiled. There were tears in her eyes. "I can't thank you enough for all you've done to bring Alex's dream to fruition. It might've been his idea, and we were his minions, but you were the engineer behind the scenes ensuring that this could even happen. To Aubrey." She lifted her glass, and everyone followed suit.

Aubrey took a drink and managed to swallow past the lump in her throat.

Kyle raised his glass. "I want to thank Aubrey for showing the Parkers which end is up. You were a total firecracker in court. They might've had some fancy, legendary counsel, but we had the better lawyer. Cheers to you."

Everyone joined in saying cheers, and they all drank again.

Aubrey had already had two glasses of champagne at the office earlier. She needed to be careful she didn't end up like she had after girls' night at the pub. "If you all take turns, we'll need to pace ourselves."

"Agreed," Chloe said, chuckling. "We speak from experience."

While the girls laughed, Emily suggested they finish the dinner she'd made. Aubrey joined them, and they spent the first part of the meal reliving the high points of Tuesday's hearing before moving on to excited discussions about the soft opening.

"We need to get cracking on promo," Kyle said.

"It's a soft opening, remember?" Sara pointed out.

"We still need promo," Evan said. "I'm on it."

Aubrey listened to the joyous conversation and settled into a haze of contentment. Until she remembered that Liam was still missing. Where the hell was he? That reminded her of the box in her purse, which she'd left on the counter in the midst of her overwhelming arrival.

Seated between Emily and Chloe, she murmured, "Excuse me for a minute." She stood and grabbed her purse, then made her way up the back stairs. She'd had a tour of the house at one point last year and knew exactly which bedroom was Liam's. She went straight there and stepped inside.

It still bore the look of a teenager's room, but it was flawlessly neat and organized, with hints of his personality and lifestyle here and there. The closet door was ajar, revealing a wet suit as well as a pair of hiking boots. A compass and a hydration backpack hung from a board with hooks on one wall. A skateboard leaned against the corner. She hadn't realized he'd been a skateboarder in his youth. Maybe he'd been born an adrenaline junkie, and Alex's request had only encouraged him to embrace it.

She withdrew the box from her purse and looked around for a place to put it. His desk, which held his closed laptop and was clearly where he'd been working, given the stack of paperwork, seemed the most logical choice. She set the box next to his computer and stepped back. She ought to leave a note but didn't see any spare paper. Instead, she whipped out her phone and texted him.

I left you something on your desk.

She tried to think of what else to say, but there really wasn't anything. Except about talking to his mom. After a moment of consideration, she typed more.

You HAVE to talk to your mom about this weekend. She's already worried that she can't reach you tonight. You're going to do what you want anyway, what does it matter if you tell her first? So you have to listen to her counsel for a bit. There are worse things. I'd love a mother like yours.

Too much? No, it was just right. She hit send.

She stuffed her phone into her purse and left. When she got back to the kitchen, she saw that dinner had been cleared and champagne glasses were in the process of being refilled. She was ready to call it a night.

She cleared her throat. "Thank you, everybody, for this great celebration, but it's actually my second one of the day, so I think I'm done." She was glad things had turned out so well. "I appreciate all of your kind words so much.

I'm excited to get to the finish line on this project. You've all worked really hard, and you deserve massive success."

"It's all due to you," Maggie said, smiling.

"Thanks." Everyone took turns hugging her, including Rob and Emily. Aubrey inwardly vowed to follow up with her on Friday morning to make sure Liam had done what he was supposed to. If he hadn't, all bets were off.

As she drove off into the night, a thread of melancholy wound its way into her heart. The project now had an end in sight, as did her interactions with the Archers. Sure, she called them friends, but without the project to throw them together, would they maintain this level of closeness? She knew how friendships worked—they ebbed and flowed as lives changed and evolved.

One thing was certain, she didn't have to maintain anything with Liam. The acknowledgment pinched her chest but also gave her a sliver of relief. Maybe now she could really move on.

LIAM WOVE HIS bike through the cars parked between the garages. Clearly he was missing some sort of get-together. He wondered if they'd heard back on the zoning hearing, but he didn't see Aubrey's car.

Maybe not, then.

After stowing his bike and helmet in the garage, he walked into the house and immediately heard voices coming from downstairs. He poked his head into the kitchen, found it empty, and went to the lower level.

Everyone was gathered in the rec area—on couches, at the bar, standing here and there. Geez, they were a massive family now. And they were drinking champagne. He was definitely missing a celebration of some kind.

He pulled his phone from his pocket and saw three missed calls from his mom, as well as a text from her asking him to call as soon as possible. Then he read Aubrey's text. His stomach dropped into his feet. Of course she'd love a mother like his—who wouldn't? But it was more than that. She'd had a terrible mother, while he had the best and wasn't treating her very well by not being honest about his activities. At least that was the implication.

"Hey, there's the loser now," Kyle called out. "Can't find your phone? Oh wait, I see it right there in your hand. You missed out, bro. Come on over and grab a glass of champagne. We're celebrating."

Liam walked forward, feeling completely on edge. He'd gone for a long ride to try to clear his head after arguing with Aubrey earlier. From reading her text, she was clearly still irritated. So was he, although not necessarily at her.

"What are you drinking to?" He didn't head for the bar.

"The Parkers went down in flames," Derek said from the couch, where he sat with his arm around Chloe. "The Alex is now a fully commercial property, and we are full steam ahead to open in July."

Everyone with a champagne flute raised it and took a drink.

Liam knew Aubrey wasn't there, since he hadn't seen her car, but he looked around for her anyway. "Where's Aubrey?"

Tori set her glass on the bar where she was sitting. "She was here earlier but took off a bit ago. Sorry you missed her."

He was, too. He knew they'd win, but the confirmation was incredibly sweet. Except he wanted to share it with her. For so many reasons, not the least of which was that she'd made it happen and, hell, he was pretty sure he was falling in love with her.

Mom came up to him and gave him a hug. He held her close for a second, and when they parted, she smiled up at him. "I'm glad you're here. But I wish you would've answered your phone."

"Sorry—really. I was on a ride and out of cell service. Plus, I don't pick up when I'm riding. Too dangerous."

"Well, I appreciate you being safe." She patted his shoulder, and Liam felt like a dick for not telling her right then about the FJC that weekend. He should. He *would*. Just not here. Not now.

Dad cleared his throat loudly. "Now that Liam's here, I want to make another announcement. Seems like good timing, what with everyone clutching a champagne glass."

Sara nodded toward Liam. "Not everyone has a glass."

Kyle jumped up from one of the couches and grabbed a wineglass from the bar. "No flutes down here, sorry." He filled the glass and handed it to Liam.

"Thanks." Liam wasn't really in the mood for champagne but didn't say so.

Kyle sat back down. "What's the news, Dad?"

Dad exchanged a look with Derek before continuing. Liam tensed. "As some of you know, I've decided to officially launch Archer Brewing with Derek as president. And, this is the real news, I'm going to sell the real-estate division."

Everyone turned to stare at Dad. "Wait, what?" Tori asked. "You're going to sell the business that our great-great-whatever-grandfather started?"

Dad nodded. "It's time. It's never been my thing. I talked it over with Derek to see if he wanted to manage the division, but like me, he's ready to turn his complete focus to the brewpubs and bottling beer." He smiled at Derek, who lifted his glass in response.

Liam felt numb. This shouldn't have surprised him. He'd told Dad repeatedly that he didn't want the real-estate division, that he was too committed to, too wrapped up in, too happy with his own company. Only he wasn't happy anymore. About anything, it seemed.

"What about Liam?" Sara asked. She looked at Liam. "Why aren't you taking it over?"

"I'm, uh, busy. I'm good." Liam was so far from good it wasn't even funny. He was desperate to get back on his bike and try to find the high he hadn't been able to attain after arguing with Aubrey. Was that bliss-filled flight with her earlier the last adrenaline rush he'd ever know? Right now, it seemed completely beyond his reach. And because he didn't like the scrutiny currently being cast his way, he raised his glass in a toast. "Congrats, Dad."

Everyone joined in, and conversation resumed. Liam ended up downing his entire glass, then managed to extricate himself so he could go upstairs and see what in the hell Aubrey had left for him. His anxiety mounted as he climbed both sets of stairs to the top floor. Was it some sort of lawyerly fuck-you letter that laid out the various ways in which he'd been a total prick?

He went into his room and stalked to his desk, his gaze immediately landing on the brown-paper-encased box. Frowning, he pulled the wrapping off and saw that it was the original package of an old Christmas ornament—the lion he'd gotten when he was, what, twelve? All the kids had animals associated with them, and starting when they were eight or nine, Mom had bought them an ornament of that animal every year. Liam's was a lion.

He opened the box and stared at the contents. A flash drive. It had to be his letter from Alex. At last. Aubrey couldn't even print the letter off for him?

He pulled out the drive and tossed the box onto his desk. Then he opened his laptop and stabbed the drive into the USB port on the side. There was one file on it, and it wasn't a letter. It was a movie. Named *For Liam.*

A bead of sweat gathered on the back of his neck as he opened it. The still image that greeted him was not what he expected to see. It was Alex.

He slammed the laptop lid down and pushed back from the desk. The perspiration on his neck turned ice cold.

A knock on his door startled him.

"Liam?"

It was Dad. Liam wiped a hand over his face and willed his heart to stop racing. He turned the chair toward the door. "Come in."

Dad opened the door and stepped inside. "Hey, is everything all right?"

Liam knew Dad was asking in reference to his announcement, but Liam couldn't encapsulate his emotions to just that topic right now. In fact, he was having a hard time managing them at all.

He looked down at the floor, at his scuffed riding boots. "No." He raised his gaze to Dad's, feeling cold and shaky. "I've never been all right."

Dad's face paled with alarm. He moved slowly into the room. "What are you talking about, son?"

"My whole life I hated looking at Alex, seeing what could've been me. I pushed every limit to ensure I would never fall short, that I would never be pitied. But if I hadn't been such a successful prick...maybe Alex would still be here."

Dad shook his head. "That's asinine. Are you saying we pitied Alex?"

"Maybe not you personally, but most people did. He knew it. Don't tell me you didn't know it, too. Alex also knew that I was a total thorn in his side. That if I hadn't been such a rock star at every goddamned thing, his failings wouldn't have been so painful."

Dad sucked in a breath. "Don't say that."

"Why not? Alex did."

Dad shook his head, his face still pale. "I never heard him say anything like that."

Liam laughed, but there was no humor, just a chilling darkness that threatened to swallow him whole. "I did. Plenty of times. We talked all the time, or maybe you didn't realize. He called me up at odd hours in strange moods, often rambling."

"He was bipolar," Dad said.

"I know. He promised me he was getting help. Want to know the last time I heard him say that to me? That it was my fault he was so depressed all the time?"

Dad turned an odd shade of gray, as if he knew what was going to come next. Fleetingly, Liam realized he shouldn't tell him. He'd never meant to tell any of them. But the pain and the guilt were absolutely ripping him in two. "He called me that night. Unlike Tori, I picked up. He was borderline incoherent, drunk maybe. I wrote it off as another rambling phone call. He told me that it was over, that I could come home. I had no idea what he was talking about. Then he went quiet, and I figured he fell asleep or passed out. Turns out he died. And all I did was hang up the phone, roll over, and go back to sleep."

Dad stared at him in abject horror. "You did nothing?"

Liam shrugged exaggeratedly, emotion pouring through him. "There was nothing to do. It wasn't an unusual conversation. There was nothing about it that made me go, 'Huh, maybe I should make sure he gets some help.' How fucked up is *that*?" Liam stood with such force that his chair creaked and rolled a foot behind him.

"Liam, I can't…I don't know what to say." Dad went to the bed and sat down, looking utterly crestfallen.

Liam felt like shit. Worse than shit. "Look what I've done to you," he said softly. "All this time you thought I was the golden child, but I'm the misfit, *I'm* the broken one. Downstairs everyone else is happy and healthy, while I can't stand the sight of it. I can't bear to be here anymore."

He turned and pulled the drive from his laptop, then shoved it into the pocket of his leather jacket, which he'd never taken off. His legs trembling, he started for the door.

Dad's words halted him at the threshold. "Don't run away. We'll work through this. Tell me you're okay, that I don't need to have you committed or something."

Liam turned and went back to the bed. He rested his hand on Dad's shoulder. Dad looked up at him, tears in his eyes.

"I'm not like Alex in that way. But I *am* a selfish ass, just like he was. I don't know how to fix this."

Dad put his hand over Liam's. "We'll do it together." A tear slid from his cheek, and it pushed Liam over the edge.

"I can't right now. I'm sorry." He bolted from the room and ran to his bike, then sped off into the darkness.

Chapter Nineteen

THE POUNDING ON Aubrey's front door left no question in her mind as to who was making the noise. She'd gone upstairs to change but had only gotten as far as stripping her shoes and socks from her feet. Now she ran down to the entry, arriving just as he'd stopped banging.

She threw the door open and sucked in a sharp breath. "Liam."

His face was anguished, his eyes a stormy blue-gray. In his fingers, he clutched a flash drive. "Please tell me I can come in. I don't have anywhere else to go."

"Come in." She opened the door wider, and he stepped inside. "Give me your helmet." She set it on the window seat in the front room, then went back to him. "Your coat."

He shrugged out of it, and she took care of hanging it in her closet. When she came back, he was still standing there, a forlorn look in his eyes. He was scaring the crap out of her.

What had happened? Hadn't he gone home? Hadn't he heard the good news? It didn't look like it.

Oh God. What if he *had* gone home? What if this was because of whatever Alex had left him?

Aubrey's gut clenched. She took his hand and tried to pull him into the front room, to sit down with her so she could figure out what had him so paralyzed.

But he wouldn't move. He just stood there and stared at her fingers clutching his. "Will you watch this video with me?" He held out his other hand, the flash drive in his palm.

Oh no. Was that from Alex? That was what had been in the box?

"I can't watch it alone." He looked up at her, his eyes so wounded she wanted to cry. "Unless you've already watched it."

She shook her head. "No." She coughed to clear the emotion from her throat. "I didn't know what was in the box. He left everyone letters. He left you that."

"Always something different for me." He smiled wryly, but there was so much pain behind it, and it was quickly replaced with a grimace.

She clasped his hand more tightly and took the flash drive from him. "Come and sit down. I'll get my computer."

She situated him on the couch in her TV room. He sat on the edge, his expression one of fear and anxiety. He looked as if he might run.

She touched his knee. "I'll be right back."

Grabbing her laptop from her bag in the kitchen, she hurried back to him. She sat beside him and put the computer on the coffee table, opening it. Then she slipped the flash drive into the USB port and opened the file. *For Liam.* Her heart twisted.

She wound her fingers through his and squeezed.

The video started.

Alex stood at the airfield where Liam had taken her for their flight that morning. It was a bright day but was obviously winter, judging from the bare limbs of the trees in the distance behind him. Alex wore Aviators and a baseball hat. God, he looked so much like Liam. It was sometimes hard to remember that they'd been identical twins.

He grinned at the camera. "Hey, Liam! Look where I am. And guess what it's my turn to do?"

The camera panned to a plane. Standing just outside the open door was the man Aubrey had met earlier that day—Rylan. He was rigged up for skydiving.

Liam's jaw dropped. "He's going to jump. His doctor said he shouldn't do that. He begged me a thousand times to take him, but I always said no. I took him flying—with an oxygen tank—but never diving."

His grip tightened on her hand as Alex came back on the screen. "That's right. I finally get to jump. See you up there!"

The image switched to the interior of the plane. Alex was hooked up to Rylan, his face half-covered in goggles but his grin completely visible. He gave a thumbs-up to the camera, and the cameraman dove from the plane.

Aubrey inhaled sharply. Watching it was almost as terrifying as actually doing it. Or so she imagined. The camera caught the sky and the wind for a brief second before turning and capturing Alex and Rylan as they jumped.

"God damn you, Rylan," Liam breathed.

The camera picked up Alex's exclamation as he hit the air and tracked him as he descended. The noise was too loud to hear anything that was being said, but Alex's expression communicated everything—excitement, exhilaration, sheer joy.

After about a minute, the parachute went up, slowing their speed until they were gently coasting in the air. Alex shouted toward the camera, "That was fucking amazing!" Then he coughed until his face turned red.

Liam's grip on her hand was almost unbearably tight. "Why the hell isn't he wearing oxygen?"

She rubbed her thumb along his hand and murmured, "Liam."

He loosened his hold, muttering, "Sorry."

They watched Alex glide to earth and step onto the ground. Aubrey was surprised at how effortless it looked, as if he'd just stepped off a bus.

Rylan unhitched them from each other, cutting Alex loose. Alex pushed his goggles up and raised his fist to the sky. "Hell yeah!" He laughed as he turned back to the camera, then coughed again. "I wish you would've let me do this with you." His expression sobered. "Just once. Don't be mad at Rylan. It took me years to convince him, and I signed all sorts of waivers and shit."

Liam looked at Aubrey. She shook her head. "I didn't know anything about this."

The video went black for a second. When it came back, it was just Alex sitting in front of a camera. It looked like his bedroom. His hair was a bit long, and the top was mussed, as if he'd been playing with it. He looked pale, almost gray really, but he also wasn't wearing his oxygen.

He picked up a beer bottle and took a drink. "Shhh. Don't tell Dad that I smuggle this beer into the house."

Liam's lips curled into an almost-smile. "That was Alex's beer of choice when we weren't at an Archer pub. It was his favorite, but we never told Dad that."

That was cute. Funny. See, this wasn't so bad.

Alex wiped his mouth and looked into the camera. "So here's the deal. One week from today, I'm pulling the plug. I figure I've done everything I planned to do. The rest is up to all of you. I could spend hours sitting here talking to you, but we talk enough. Although it isn't really about anything important, is it?" He sat back in his chair. "We talk about sports, whether you're screwing someone, whether I'm getting laid at all, blah, blah. But we never talk about the Big Issues." He raised his eyebrows as he said the last two words. Then he smiled. "You hate me, I hate you, you love me, I love you. It's a vicious cycle. I appreciate you staying away—that was a very cool and selfless thing you did there. I know how much you wanted to stay and take over Archer Real Estate. But now you can come home. You better get your ass home."

Alex took another drink of beer.

Aubrey glanced over at Liam. His gaze was glued to the computer screen.

"I've set up this trust with an attorney. She's a total babe, by the way, but not interested in me. She's not your type either, so leave her alone. She's a nice girl, smarter than both of us put together."

Aubrey stifled a smile.

"I bought that crappy old monastery on the hill, and you're all going to come home and fix it up into a hotel. Plus there'll be a restaurant for Kyle to run. I know you think he's a loser, but he's not. He just needs the right motivation. We all do, right?"

Alex ran his hand through his hair. That explained why it looked the way it did. "Now that I'm gone—by the time you see this, I will be—I hope you'll get your ass home. For good." He cocked his head to the side. "You know, I honestly have no idea when you'll even get this video. I'm telling Aubrey to give it to you when you go completely over the edge with some trick. But maybe she won't know. Maybe you'll keep hiding stuff from people." He exhaled and shook his head. "Whatever. Like I said, Aubrey's a smart girl. I completely trust her to figure this out and do it right.

"So why am I bothering to film this video? Mostly I wanted you to see me jump. It was so awesome, I actually considered doing that—jumping off a bridge or a building—instead of taking the pills I bought for next week." He picked up a bottle from his desk and waved it in front of the camera. "See? All ready.

"Anyway, I decided not to jump because there's too much of a chance of some a-hole seeing me and stopping me. Not chancing that. I've got it all worked out so that no one can interrupt me or find me until it's over."

He took two drinks of beer in quick succession, then looked down for a moment. When he looked back up, he looked apologetic, which was a first for this video. "This is going to really suck for everyone. I know that. I'm sorry. I'm really, really sorry. But I just can't anymore. I'm done. I'm ready. I'm not afraid. Please tell Mom I wasn't afraid. And tell her I love her. More than anyone on this earth, I love her. And Dad." He bowed his head again, and when he looked up, there were tears in his eyes. "I love you, too."

He blinked, then drank more beer. "I think we're just about done here. I don't know what the future holds for you, Liam, but I hope it's good. I hope you'll let it be good. You deserve it. You really do."

He smiled into the camera. "See you on the other side."

Then the screen faded to black.

Aubrey reached forward and closed the laptop. When she turned her head to look at Liam, she saw a tear streaking down his face. He just sat there, not moving, his gaze fixed on the far wall.

Aubrey turned toward him and laid her free hand on his knee. "Are you okay?"

"My dad asked me that earlier. I told him I'd never been okay." He wiped a hand over his eye. "You heard what he said. He hated me, I hated him. It wasn't okay."

Aubrey understood why Alex might've hated Liam, but she wasn't sure she got the other half of the equation. Was it the guilt? "Why did you hate him?"

Liam exhaled and sat back, leaning his head against the top edge of the couch. "Because I spent my whole life thinking, 'There but for the grace of God go I.' Why was I born this way and he was born that way? Maybe it wouldn't have been so bad if we hadn't looked so fucking identically alike. It was like looking in a mirror, a sick, twisted, alternate reality…or hell." He turned his head to look at her. "Does that make any sense at all?"

She nodded, clutching his hand and trying to give him strength, understanding, love. "I've wondered how you dealt with that. I can't imagine. And it seemed…Well, it seemed you hadn't really grieved his death. You were angry, then you were sort of flippant. And then sometimes you were angry again. I don't remember you being particularly sad."

"I didn't let myself think about it. I still don't. Being here in Ribbon Ridge forces me to think about it. He's not here. Things are different. Everyone's different. They're happy, they've moved on. It's like he was *never* here."

She could tell he didn't like that. And it said so much about why he stayed away. On one hand, it seemed like he could maybe come home now and jump right in, moving on and leaving Alex in the past. But she sensed he didn't really want to do that. "If you aren't here, you can pretend that he still is."

"Uh, yeah." He stared at her. "I can't believe you get that. I wasn't even sure I got that until a minute ago."

She smiled. "I think I know you pretty well by now, Liam Archer."

He sat up and turned on the couch, facing her. "What he said in the video about you is completely true. You're smarter than both of us and not my type—at least not in my league."

She laughed. "I don't know if that's true."

His brow creased. "The pressure Alex put on you, the expectation…It's really unfair. I'd like to punch him out."

"No more than I do." She inwardly cringed. "Sorry, I shouldn't say that."

"Why not? I did."

"Okay, he deserves a swift kick in the ass. He left a package on the doorstep of the law firm with a letter to me and all of your letters—and your video."

"He left you a letter?"

She nodded. "He thanked me for doing this, knew I'd be pissed that he'd fooled me for so long. But he said he was free, and I clung to that. If I could help him be free, then maybe it wasn't such a terrible job."

"He said that? That he was free?" Liam snorted. "That's nice for him while the rest of us struggle to keep from drowning in all the shit he left behind."

She straightened her spine as she thought of all the emotional upheaval Alex had caused. "You know what? I take that back. This has been the hardest thing I've ever done."

"I haven't made it any easier, have I?" he asked softly.

"No, you haven't. It's been tough enough, but it's even harder when you're falling in love with one of the parties and you're trying really hard not to." She hadn't meant to say it but realized there was no point hiding it anymore. She loved him. So much. If she hadn't before tonight, she would've been helplessly gone by now.

He touched her face, his fingertips gentle against her cheek. "You love me?"

She nodded, her heart catching in her throat.

The deep, torturous emotions that had been so evident before had eased away. He looked at her with wry humor. "Well, I certainly don't deserve *that*."

"No, you don't. You also don't deserve me inviting you to stay tonight, but I'm doing that anyway. I don't want you riding your motorcycle after that."

He continued stroking her cheek, lulling her into a blissful state. "Should I sleep on the couch?"

He should. They'd resolved nothing. Were they friends? Were they lovers? She didn't know, and right now she didn't care. She just knew that he needed her, and she wanted him.

She cupped her hands on either side of his face and kissed him. Softly. Gently. With all the love bursting from her heart. "I don't care where you choose, so long as you understand I'm going to be there with you."

FOR THE FIRST time in ages, maybe in forever, Liam let go of his emotions. He didn't try to hold himself in check or turn himself away from the light. He tasted her kiss, and he utterly surrendered.

He clutched her waist and held onto her as if she were the only thing keeping him on the ground in a hurricane. Her lips moved over his, playing, teasing at first. He was content to just hold her, to simply relish the moment.

But then she took command. She pivoted and pushed him back against the couch. He scooted backward as she straddled his thighs. Her mouth opened over his, and her tongue slipped past his lips. He was overcome with desire—it was both familiar and somehow different. It was far more than his body reacting to hers, it was his mind, his soul connecting with hers.

She gripped his shoulders and ground her hips down against him, her chest grazing his as the kiss deepened. He raked his hands up her back, gripping the soft cotton of her T-shirt. He arched up, his cock throbbing where it nestled between her legs.

He pulled at her shirt, tugging until she broke the kiss long enough for him to rip it over her head. He brought his hands around and cupped her breasts, groaning into her mouth while she rode him.

She returned the favor of removing his shirt, yanking it up his chest and tossing it over his head with a vicious flick of her wrist. She didn't renew the kiss. Instead she leaned back and ran her hands from the sides of his face to his collarbones, down over his pecs, then skimmed his abs. All the while, she stared at his naked chest, her teeth snagged on her lower lip. She looked utterly sexy, her red hair cascading over her shoulders and resting against the top of her pink, lacy bra.

She traced his abs with her fingertips. "I try not to think of the other women who've enjoyed this view." She didn't look up, just kept her focus on his abdomen. "I imagine I'm the only one who gets to see this. Touch this. Taste this." She pushed herself back off his lap and kneeled. She leaned forward to run her tongue over his nipples, then down, licking his flesh with delicate, maddening whorls.

He slipped his hand to the back of her neck and massaged the flesh there, losing himself to the exquisite pleasure of her mouth. He tried to find words. He didn't want anyone else doing what she was doing—none of it. No looking, no touching, no tasting. Just her eyes, her fingers, her lips, her tongue. "I'm yours," was all he could manage.

She looked up at him then, her gaze hot, her lips curved into a saucy little smile. "For how long?"

"For as long as you want me." It was as close to a promise as he could get. He *was* hers. He didn't want to be anyone else's.

She flicked open the button of his jeans and worked the zipper down. She slid her hands back along his hips, pushing his clothes down. He came up off the couch to help her, and soon she was tugging everything from his legs—shoes, socks, pants, boxers.

She came back between his thighs, her palms pressing down on him as she eyed his cock. He watched through slitted lids as she encircled the base of his shaft with her fingers. "See, this right here. I'd like to think it's been mine all this time. Ever since that first time in my office."

He stroked her jaw and looked into her gorgeous eyes. "It has. There's never been anyone but you. Not since then."

"Not even after I dumped you?"

He couldn't help smiling, knowing the pride she took in breaking up with him. He shook his head. "What can I say? You ruined me for other women."

Her mouth formed an O. "I'll be damned." Then she took that mouth and covered the tip of his cock.

He leaned his head back and closed his eyes as sensation overtook his brain and every other part of his body.

Her right hand held the base of his cock while her left cupped his balls. Her mouth worked absolute magic, licking and sucking, slowly at first. Then more quickly as her hand stroked him from base to tip.

Her nails raked his flesh, and he moaned. He fisted her hair, unable to stop himself from pumping into her mouth. She took him deep, making sounds in the back of her throat that only intensified his pleasure. His orgasm was building, and he was going to completely unload if she didn't stop.

"Aubrey," he rasped. "Stop. I'm going to come."

She only sucked him harder, her head bobbing with his thrusts. She squeezed his balls, and he was done. He shot into her mouth, his orgasm breaking over him. He cried out as he gave in to the darkness. But it was only dark for a moment. Then there was light. There was Aubrey.

When he finally opened his eyes, he was still trying to regain his breath. She sat on the edge of the coffee table wearing her bra and a very satisfied smirk.

"Well, that wasn't what I had in mind," he said, taking in her mostly clothed state while he was buck naked.

"It's absolutely what I envisioned. Don't think I was giving you a gift—I wanted to do that. For me."

He laughed, but he also didn't believe her. "Seeing everything you've done for Alex, for my family, you're the most giving person I know. I don't doubt you wanted to do that, but I also think you wanted to do it because you knew how much I'd love it." He sat up and palmed the back of her neck as he kissed her fiercely. "And I did love it," he whispered against her lips. "But now it's your turn. I'm taking you upstairs."

She arched a brow. "Are you? Surrendering to your inner caveman again?"

God, how he loved this. He'd never had so much fun with a woman. She'd turned sex into something completely different. Because it wasn't sex, he realized.

He stood, pulling her up with him. "Surrendering to my need to make love to you. I'm picking you up now." He swept her into his arms, and she twined her arms around his neck.

He carried her up to her bedroom and laid her gently on the bed. The room was near dark, but he had enough light from the stairwell to see her sprawled across the quilt. Though her feet were bare, the rest of her was far too covered. He climbed onto the bed and straddled her knees. He locked his gaze with hers as he stripped her jeans from her body. That left the pink lacy bra and the matching pink lacy underwear. He loved lingerie, especially on her—she had a body made for it—but he wasn't in the mood tonight. He wanted her nude and completely open to him in every way.

He moved up and slipped his hands underneath her back. She arched up so he could unfasten her bra. He whisked the garment away and stared down at her perfect breasts. Her nipples were pink and hard. He heard the hitch in her breath and smiled to himself.

He bent down and kissed her breast, starting at the top, then dragging his tongue down and around her nipple in aggravating circles. She clasped his head, and he pulled back.

He looked her in the eye. "Put your hands up on the headboard."

She hesitated but complied, curling her hands around the top of the bed frame.

"Don't let go until I tell you to." He went back to his task, torturing her breast with gentle licks and nips everywhere but where she wanted them. She gasped and huffed and begged him to stop.

"Oh, I don't think you want me to stop." He lightly licked the nipple, and she nearly rocketed off the bed. "I think you want something else entirely. Tell me what you want, Aubrey."

"Do what you normally do."

"Not specific enough. I normally do a lot of things."

"Suck me."

He closed his mouth over her nipple and sucked. Hard. He cupped the underside, gripping her flesh and squeezing. She brought her hand down to his head and tugged at his hair.

He stopped, coming up and shaking his head at her. "I told you to keep your hands up here." He took her hand and put it back on the headboard.

He ran his palm down her arm and then over the curve of her shoulder until he met her breast again. He didn't torment her this time. He cupped both of her mounds and pushed them together, bringing the nipples close enough so that he could suck and lick them both in quick succession. He moved between them, lavishing attention on each. She moaned and arched and spread her legs wider, her body telling him in every way possible that she wanted more.

But he wanted to hear her say it.

He let go of her breasts and skimmed his hands down her ribcage to her hips. He kissed her navel, then the flesh just above the small patch of fiery hair she kept so neatly trimmed.

He brought his hands to her thighs and pushed them even wider. "Tell me what you want, Aubrey."

"Kiss me. There."

He stripped off her panties. "Here?" He lightly touched her clit and grazed her wet folds with his fingertip.

"*Yes.*"

He did as she said, kissing her soft flesh but in a rather chaste fashion.

"You suck," she said. "No, actually you don't. Kiss me with your *tongue.*"

He smiled against her flesh, enjoying the heady mix of intensity and lust in her tone. He kissed her again, this time using his tongue in the same way he'd use it on her mouth. He licked into her, using his lips to suckle her sweet flesh.

"Can I let go of the bed?" The words came out strangled. Desperate.

"*No.* If you let go, I stop."

"You son of a bitch."

He speared his tongue into her and licked up to her clit, then he sucked hard on the nub of flesh. She cried out, her hips jerking. "Liam! More. Your finger. Fuck me with your finger. *Please.*"

That time he hadn't even had to ask her what she wanted. But then Aubrey had always been incredibly responsive. They'd answered each other's wants and needs with alarming clarity, right from the day he'd met her. Damn, he just realized the day he'd met her was the first time they'd made love.

Yes, love. He loved her. So goddamned much it scared him to death. He kept everyone else he'd ever loved at arm's length. And that's exactly what he'd been doing to her. He didn't want to anymore.

"Liam!"

He held her flesh with his thumb and thrust his finger into her. He twisted and found her G-spot, pressing before stroking into her again and again with increased precision. He pushed at her thighs and kissed her deeply, tonguing her until she fucked his mouth. He sucked her clit and used his finger again, adding a second to put her over the edge at last.

He felt her orgasm shudder through her. "Let go, Aubrey. Let everything go."

She released the headboard and tangled her hands in his hair as she bucked wildly. He worked her through the storm, easing her back to earth until she was still.

"Oh my God." Her breath was hard and fast, her legs quivering around him.

He came up over her and brushed her hair from her face. She looked up at him, her eyes smoky and satisfied. "I love you. And not because you're fucking fantastic at that. I love you because you know me. You've always known me. Even that first time, you took me somewhere I'd never been. You swept me away from a really shitty day."

He loved her, too, but he was afraid to say it. Afraid to make promises he wasn't sure he could keep. He still didn't know what he was doing tomorrow, let alone next week or next year. She wanted stability—she deserved that and so much more.

But the love he had for her was too great. It made him too happy in this moment, and for better or worse, he'd always lived in the moment. "I love you, too." He kissed her long and deep, a slow seduction of lips and tongue.

She put her arms around him and held him close. After a while she curled her legs around his waist and brought her hand between them. She grasped his cock, which hadn't needed much time to rebound after their interlude downstairs, and positioned him at her entrance.

"Wait, condom," he said.

"Damn, I almost forgot. You know I'm on birth control, right? And if you've been tested and haven't had any partners in well over a year, I'm good going without. But I'll understand if you don't want to."

He desperately wanted to feel her skin-to-skin. "I can promise you I'm totally clean, and I don't doubt for a second that you are, too."

"Yes." She lifted her hips to urge him inside.

His fingertips grazed hers as he guided himself into her wet sheath. He closed his eyes as he entered her, the friction exquisite. "I, uh, I've never done this before."

"You've always used a condom?"

He nodded, momentarily devoid of words as he seated himself fully inside of her. The sensation was mind-numbing, overwhelming, absolutely life-changing.

He never wanted to feel this with anyone else. This was Aubrey's claim on him, and he would happily give it to her.

He opened his eyes and looked down at her. She was watching him, her eyes full of wonder. "I can't believe I get a first with Liam Archer. I must be pretty special."

He kissed her softly, lingeringly. "You are far more special than you'll ever know." He began to move, his hips gently rotating and thrusting. She moved with him. Her feet locked behind his ass.

As he stroked deeper, she moaned. Her legs gripped him more tightly, and their rhythm increased. It was slow and long, this dance. He savored every moment as sweat slicked their bodies. Gradually their pace increased until he was driving into her, and she was meeting him thrust for thrust. They came nearly together. Sensation rushed over him, crushing all rational thought as he surrendered completely to the utter bliss.

Later, as he held her and listened to the even sounds of her breathing while she slept, he marveled at what had transpired. He'd made love to her so many times before, but this had been revelatory. Unlike any other experience he'd ever had, in every way.

Because he loved her. Because he loved loving her. Because he was never going to be the same. He thought of his place, of where he belonged, and wondered if he might have finally found it at last.

Chapter Twenty

Aubrey heard Liam coming down the stairs just as she was pouring the coffee. As he came into the kitchen, she smiled at him and offered him a cup. "Good morning."

"I think we covered that a bit ago, didn't we?" He flashed her a grin that she would gladly wake up to every single day. Then he kissed her, and she clutched his shoulder, grabbing his shirt as she kissed him back. Yes, she could definitely get used to this.

She pulled back and picked up her coffee cup. "Is there a limit to the ways in which we can express our pleasure in starting the day?"

He sipped his coffee, then set it back down before snatching her by the waist and pulling her against him.

"Careful!" She held her cup with both hands lest it slosh all over him. Not that she wouldn't appreciate a reason to strip his clothes off again.

"To answer your question, no. There is no limit. And if I wasn't clear upstairs with how *good* this morning is, please allow me to rectify that." He nibbled at her ear and kissed her neck.

Aubrey sighed, her mind traveling back to him rousing her from sleep with kisses along her throat followed by an absolutely X-rated wake-up call. "You were quite clear. I wish I didn't have to go to work. Unfortunately, I have a client meeting at nine."

He raised his head, his eyes darkening with concern for the first time since she'd kissed him last night on the couch. "And I need to get home to talk to my parents. I, uh, I didn't leave my dad in the best shape yesterday."

She winced. "Uh-oh, what happened?"

He stepped back from her and picked up his coffee, taking a sip. "It's just a mess. I looked at the flash drive, saw Alex's face, and I freaked out." His mouth tightened. "Man, that pisses me off."

She wasn't exactly sure what he meant. "What exactly?"

"The video, Alex. I just…never mind. I should really go."

She needed to jump in the shower anyway and understood why he was anxious to leave. "I'm sure everything will be all right with your dad. The rest…We'll figure it out, too."

He looked at her over the edge of his coffee mug. "Alex? Or are you talking about…us?"

"Both, I guess. I'll be here whenever you want to talk about our future." Just because last night had been the most amazing night of her life and he'd said that he loved her—she still couldn't quite process that—it didn't mean he was moving back to Ribbon Ridge. "I'm hoping there's a future."

"I want that, too." He put his cup back down on the counter and took hers and did the same. He placed his hands on her waist and drew her close. "Hey, I meant what I said last night. I'm in love with you. I don't know how that happened, but it makes me feel better than I have in a long time. Maybe in forever."

Her heart was so full of joy, she was afraid it might explode right out of her chest. She splayed her hands over the front of his soft shirt. "I love you, too. We'll figure things out."

He kissed her again, then let her go. "I hope so."

She frowned, wishing he sounded more confident about their future. "What does that mean?"

He moved around the corner of the island, giving her at least the visual sense that she was driving him away. "It means I don't know anything right now, and there's a lot to figure out. I know you love Ribbon Ridge, but I can't live here. At least not full-time."

He *can't* live here? She crossed her arms and leaned her hip against the island, trying not to get worked up by his seemingly nonnegotiable attitude. "I can't split my time between Denver and Ribbon Ridge," she said. "I have clients, responsibilities. My uncle wants me to take over his law firm when he retires. Not to mention, I'm not a member of the Colorado bar."

"I know. That's why we have to figure things out."

She put the brakes on her emotions before she panicked. They loved each other. They'd been so happy last night, this morning. *Chill, Aubrey.* "Why won't you move back to Ribbon Ridge?"

He took a drink of coffee, then went to the TV room, where he sat down to put on his boots. "Aside from the fact that I live in Denver and my business is there?" He shook his head. "Look, I don't mean to sound like a jerk, but my life is in Colorado."

She moved toward the couch and watched him. "I'd argue that your life could be here. Everyone you care about is in Ribbon Ridge. You wouldn't have to sell your business in Denver. You could fly back and forth when necessary. I'd miss you, but I'd deal." Their time apart would absolutely suck, but it would be better than no time at all.

He stood up. "It sounds like you'd want my home base to be here. I can't do that." His gaze was direct, unflinching. Frustrating as hell.

She didn't understand his reticence. "Why not?"

"Aubrey, I don't really want to get into this."

"I know you have to go. We can talk about it later." She tried not to be irritated and failed miserably. Happiness was so close. For both of them.

He looked at her and ran his hand over his face. Then he made a sound that was part grunt and part defeated groan.

He came to her and took her hand. "Look. I'm going to tell you something that I've never told anyone before, until last night. I started to talk about it to Dad, then I bailed. Once you hear it, you'll understand why I need to go, and I suspect you might just tell me to go to Denver and never come back."

She ran her thumb over the back of his hand. "I'd never do that." Even when she wanted to throttle him, as she had a moment ago.

He looked down at their hands. "You might. There's a reason I don't dwell on Alex, that I don't…grieve. It's my fault he's dead." His voice was cold, dispassionate. It was completely at odds with what he was saying—and it worried her.

She squeezed his hand. "No, it's not."

"Not my fault exactly, but I could've saved him. I should've saved him." He looked at her, and his eyes were more anguished than she'd ever seen them. They were dark and flat, tortured. She'd compare them to the way they were during that first explosive encounter in her office, but this was worse.

"I knew he was sick—bipolar. He told me back in college. It was one of many secrets we kept."

"Like the extreme sports."

His eyes flickered with surprise. "You knew all about that, then?"

She nodded. "He told me."

"He must have liked you. He certainly trusted you. What else did he tell you?"

"Nothing about his mental state. Remember, he lied to me about his actual health. He told me he probably wouldn't see thirty. Naively, I believed him." How she wished she could turn back the clock and ask for medical records. As if she really would've done that. It wasn't like he'd asked for help with legally assisted suicide.

"Don't beat yourself up about that. He was diabolical in his planning. You saw that video last night."

Yes, and she was angry with Alex all over again. His death seemed to be the gift that kept on giving. The most horrible gift in the history of gifts.

"Anyway, Alex and I had a pretty good relationship from afar," he continued. "We liked it that way because we didn't have to be constantly reminded of the other person. He came up with stunts and sports for me to try, and I videotaped it all so he could live it with me." He frowned. "Not that he actually lived it. I'd fooled myself into thinking that it was a mutually appreciated arrangement, but I was wrong. He wasn't happy. He was worse than miserable. He was plotting his own death."

He stepped away from her and walked over to the window seat. She waited patiently for him to continue. He turned but didn't look at her. He focused somewhere on the wall near the couch. "You know that he called Tori the night that he died, that she didn't get the call. He called me, too, but I answered."

Aubrey lifted her hand to her mouth, so afraid of what he might say next.

"He called me late sometimes. He'd be drunk or just manic. He'd ramble, I'd listen. End of call. That night was no different, except his ramblings were extra dark. He talked about our relationship. He thanked me for staying away but said I could come home now. That it was all over. I...I didn't think anything of it. It wasn't unusual. I had no idea..."

She crossed the room but stopped a few feet in front of him because he still wasn't looking at her.

"He said he was glad he had me. No, what he said exactly was, 'I'm glad you're with me now.' Then he went quiet, and I thought he fell asleep. I hung up." He looked at her then, and his eyes were surprisingly dry. "My dad interrupted my run the next morning when he called to tell me Alex was dead."

Aubrey felt tears stream from her eyes, their wet heat tracking down her cheeks unheeded.

"You see, if I'd listened to him, if I'd realized he was *that* sick and wasn't getting the help I thought he was, I would've handled that phone call completely differently. But I didn't. Instead, I just sat there half-asleep and listened to him die." His voice was raw, ragged, but there were no tears in his eyes, just a cold anguish that ate at her heart.

When she'd thought of the guilt he'd endured his whole life, she'd wondered how he'd managed. But this...this went so far beyond what she'd ever imagined. "Oh my God, Liam." She went to him and touched his face, cupping his cheeks. "You just pushed this out of your head for the past fifteen months?"

"What the hell else was I supposed to do with it?"

"I don't know. Talk about it? Get therapy? Let it out? No one's strong enough to deal with this alone."

He wiped her tears away, and she dropped her hands from his face. "I'm *not* dealing with it, that's the point."

"But you should."

"Why, so I can relive that horror over and over again as I talk through it with a therapist? No thanks. Like I said, I've never told anyone, because I block it out of my mind. Being here in Ribbon Ridge around my family only dredges it up." He took a deep breath. "Now you know why I can't come back."

"No, now I know why you need to deal with this, so you *can* come back."

He shook his head, his eyes now sparking with anger. "I don't want to. I don't need to. My life is great."

She took a step back from him. "You can't possibly believe that. You were a mess when you came over last night."

"Only because of that goddamned video. I'm never watching it again, and I don't plan to discuss it with anyone." He pivoted toward the door, then turned back, as if he'd forgotten something. "There's a reason I never asked you for my letter from Alex. I didn't want it. He said his good-bye that night, and I didn't need another one. Damn it, Aubrey, this is my life. Don't tell me what I need to do."

She loved him so much, but love alone wasn't enough. "I was hoping it might be *our* life, but I guess I was wrong."

"Don't say that. Look, I have to go. We can talk about this later. I wish you'd think about coming to Denver. You'd be happy there. With me."

"I'm happy *here*, Liam. This is my home." She'd already built her life here, just as he'd done in Denver. And it looked like neither one of them was going to compromise. "Go talk to your dad. I'll see you later." Or not.

He nodded, then left.

She couldn't imagine where they would go from here.

LIAM DIDN'T BOTHER parking his bike in the garage. He was too anxious to get inside to see Dad. He felt terrible about leaving him last night. He went into the kitchen, but it was empty. Considering the time, he figured Dad was likely in his office, where he liked to drink his coffee and read his e-mail before heading to Archer.

Liam made his way to the front of the house and paused when he saw Dad—and Mom—sitting at the table situated in the front bay window. They were reading their iPads and drinking coffee, or probably tea in Mom's case.

Mom saw him first, her eyes widening. "You're back."

Dad turned his head and took his glasses off. "Where have you been?" The question came out sharp, a bit angry.

Liam deserved that. He went into the office and dropped into the other chair at the table. He sprawled his legs out and draped his arms over the sides of the wood chair. "I spent the night at Aubrey's." He saw no reason to hide that. He'd shielded his emotions for so long, and he didn't want to do it anymore—at least not about her. He wanted to bury his feelings about Alex so deep that an excavation team couldn't find them.

"You're seeing her, then?" Mom asked. "I like her a lot."

"Actually, I'm in love with her. I've been seeing her—off and on—since Alex died." He let a wry smile lift his lips. "You could say he brought us together."

Mom folded her iPad closed. "Like Kyle and Maggie."

Yeah, that made sense. Maggie had been Alex's therapist, and Kyle had sought her out to find the person who'd sold Alex the drugs he'd used to commit his ghastly final act.

Dad leaned back in his chair and studied Liam. "As happy as I am for you, I have to interrupt that good news to talk about what you said last night."

Liam glanced at Mom. "I'd rather not repeat it." Ever.

"You don't have to. I already told your mother. We don't have any secrets. Not anymore." He reached over and put his hand over hers, which rested on the table.

Great, so now Mom knew how he'd completely failed Alex.

"We don't blame you, Liam." Mom sniffed, but a tear leaked from her eye anyway.

Dad got up and fetched a box of tissues from his desk, which he set on the table. "Good thing we bought stock in this tissue company last year."

Mom smiled as she dabbed at her eyes. When she was done, she looked at Liam. "Forgive me. We don't blame you at all. Just like we don't blame Alex. He was ill. What happened was a tragedy. Was it preventable? Perhaps, but we'll never know. The way it played out, it wasn't. He went when it was his time."

Liam looked between them. "Do you both really believe that?"

Dad stroked Mom's back. "We do." He withdrew his hand from her and leaned forward, resting his elbow on the table. "To do anything else is absurdity and results in nothing good. Just look at you."

Yeah, look at him. He was practically crawling out of his skin. Anything was preferable to this. He imagined jumping out of a plane, the air rushing over him, the thrill of taking flight. The perfect way to lose himself.

Which is why he did it.

He ran his thumbs along the wood of the chair's arms and looked down. "Mom, Dad. I do all these extreme sports for Alex. He asked me to jump out of an airplane back in college because he couldn't. He wanted to experience it, so he asked me to go and film it. I did, then I showed it to him. We were both hooked." He looked back up, and Mom was staring at him, her mouth open.

"Why didn't either of you say anything?" she asked.

Liam shrugged. "It was just our thing. Now it's just my thing." That admission carved a piece out of his heart. It was, maybe, the first step in accepting that Alex was really gone.

"You didn't do it just for him," Dad said. "Otherwise you would've stopped when he died."

"It's my lifestyle now, but I wouldn't have stopped anyway. It…gave me something to focus on."

"Instead of your grief." Dad reached over and touched Liam's hand. "I get it. I was there. I did everything I could not to think about him or the fact that he was gone. For months, I drove everyone insane with my dark cloud. Your sister did the same sort of thing last year. I imagine it's been ten times worse for you. And I'm sorry. I should've known."

"*We* should've known," Mom said, her voice cracking. "You were his twin. You shared a bond. I should've come to stay with you in Denver for a while."

Liam almost laughed. He could just imagine his mom hanging around his ultra-modern high-rise condo, maybe joining him on an extreme hike or waiting up for him when he went out to a party. "Mom, it's okay. I wouldn't have let you. I wanted to be alone." He'd been about to say, "I *still* want to be alone," but he realized that wasn't true.

He wanted to be with Aubrey. With his family. He'd said more about Alex in the past day than he'd said in the past year. And it hadn't broken him. At least not any more than he was already fractured. Maybe he *could* come home. The mere thought provoked a surge of anxiety. Where would he fit in this new Alex-free world? Would he ever be able to work through the guilt and the shame? Most of all, how would he deal with the grief? Because if he came back, he didn't think he could keep it at bay any longer.

Mom sniffed again and blew her nose. "I think I understand why you moved away. I know it was difficult for you and for Alex. But I always thought you'd come home eventually. Why haven't you come home, especially since you have Aubrey now?"

The argument they'd just had arose in his mind. He tried to articulate it for his parents. "I've kept myself separate for so long, I don't know that I belong. Everyone here is happy. They've moved on."

He took in his mother's splotchy face and realized he was wrong. Yes, they were happy, and yes, they'd moved on, but they'd hadn't forgotten about Alex. They'd found a way to grieve and to appreciate and celebrate his memory.

Could he do that, too? He hadn't thought it was possible. But maybe, with them and with Aubrey, he could.

"We've coped," Dad said. "You'd fit in anywhere you wanted, so don't use that as an excuse. You just have to want to try."

Emotion welled up in Liam's chest, but he didn't want to succumb to it now. "There isn't even a job for me here—you're selling Archer Real Estate."

"I wanted to give it to you plenty of times, but you always turned me down, so I stopped offering. I'm not offering it anymore. If you want it, you have to take it. You have to *try*, son."

Suddenly things clicked. It wouldn't be easy to confront the things he'd worked so hard to avoid—Alex and the guilt and grief associated with him and with the place he called home. But he did want to try. "I want it." Everything. The job. His family. His home. Aubrey. He could maybe stop subconsciously believing he didn't deserve those things. No, he *had* to stop believing that. "If you want me to buy it, I will."

Dad laughed, and it broke the tension in the room into such small pieces, Liam doubted anyone could find them if they tried. "Even you can't afford it. I'm happy to turn it over to you. If you really want it."

Liam sat up in the chair. "I do."

"What about Denver?" Mom asked. "Lion Properties?"

Liam's brain was already working. "I'll merge the two and put someone in charge down there."

Mom's face lit. "Does that mean you're coming home?"

He nodded, feeling as good as he had last night in Aubrey's arms. "If you'll have me." Hell, even if they wouldn't. He was retaking Ribbon Ridge by storm.

Mom jumped up and rushed to hug him, practically tackling him off his chair. "I'm so glad."

Liam laughed as he hugged her back. "Thanks."

They straightened, and Liam stood. Dad joined them, hugging Liam for himself. "Congratulations. You're the new owner of Archer Real Estate."

"And you can stay here as long as you like," Mom said, stroking his arm.

"Actually, I think I'll be staying somewhere else, if she'll have me. I know we have an awful lot going on this year with two weddings and a baby, but you might have to add another wedding in there."

Mom started to cry again, but these were happy tears. "I honestly didn't know if I'd ever see you get married. We couldn't ask for a better daughter-in-law than Aubrey. She's already part of the family."

Yes, she was. It was one of the many, many reasons he loved her.

Chapter Twenty-One

AUBREY MADE IT through her client meeting. Then she made it through a phone call with a judge. By lunchtime she was ready to pull her hair out, thanks to Liam Archer and his stubbornness.

She left the building to get lunch at Barley and Bran down the street. After treating herself to her favorite roasted turkey sandwich with goat cheese and fig jam, she was feeling a bit better as she walked back to her office.

She was trying really hard not to be angry. While Liam had said he couldn't come back to Ribbon Ridge, he'd also said they would talk about it. Maybe she could change his mind. Maybe there was the slightest chance he was open to compromise. She'd do her damnedest to convince him—hadn't he told her she was a great orator?

As she climbed the steps to her office, she worked to push Liam from her thoughts for the rest of the workday.

She had a trial memo to finish and a deposition to read. Oh joy.

She went inside and said hello to the receptionist on her way to her office. When she hit the threshold, she stopped short. Sitting on her desk was a vase of long-stemmed red roses. She counted them—not a dozen, but seventeen. What an odd number. Red roses could only be from one person, couldn't they?

She stepped into her office, and the door swung closed behind her. Liam stepped away from the wall.

"You brought me roses," she said. "Eighteen of them?"

He came toward her. "There's a reason for that."

She took off her jacket and hung it on the hook on the back of her door. Then she rounded her desk, eager to put something between her and him. His presence here reminded her dangerously of their first encounter. She couldn't help glancing down at her desk.

No, she couldn't go there with him. There were too many things that needed to be resolved. But he *had* brought her roses. Red roses.

"What's the reason?" she asked.

"I heard the number three on your tattoo isn't your law-school rank."

One of the girls had to have told him that. When? Why? What they'd shared that night was supposed to be inviolate. "You aren't supposed to know that."

"Blame Sara. I ran into her at the florist—she was doing wedding stuff. I was trying to decide how many roses to buy you, and she told me to buy eighteen because it would mean something to you."

Aubrey frowned. "It doesn't mean a thing."

"It should—it means family. There's you and your aunt and uncle—that's three. My parents—that's five. All of my siblings plus Derek—that's another six, plus their significant others—that's five more for a total of sixteen. And I had to include baby Archer to make seventeen."

"There's one missing." Her heart soared as the math finally made sense.

He came around the desk and took her hand. His fingers were warm, his gaze full of love. "Eighteen is me. You can't have your family without including me—sorry."

"But I don't understand. Earlier you said you can't live here, and I said I can't move. What happened?"

"I realized I *can* move home, I just didn't want to. More accurately, I didn't want to move on." He dropped to his knee, and she gasped, her hand rising to her mouth as tears stung her eyes. "It's time for me to move on. From Denver, from Alex—*to you*."

This couldn't be happening, could it? She'd just barely gotten her head around him loving her, was trying to process how they were going to make this work, and here he was down on one knee.

"This isn't just a proposal. This is a promise. I promise I'm going to get help with my grief and my anger about Alex—I've already asked Maggie for a referral. I promise I'm going to spend as much time here as possible—I'm taking over Archer Real Estate and folding Lion Properties into the company. I plan to put someone in charge in Denver, but I'll have to travel there from time to time. I promise to scale back my hobbies—I've already canceled the FJC this weekend." He kissed her hand and looked up into her eyes. "But most of all, I promise to love you for the rest of my life and beyond. I know this might seem fast, but as Derek said to me once, 'When you know, you know.' Aubrey, will you do me the honor of becoming my wife?"

She was quite literally speechless. Gibberish swirled in her brain, and her mouth opened and closed like she was some fish out of water.

He smiled at her, that sexy little grin that hinted he was maybe enjoying her utter shock. "I called your uncle while you were at lunch—he sounds great, by the way—and he gave his permission, provided you agree."

Why wouldn't she? Everything she wanted was right here. All she had to do was say yes. "Yes. I'll marry you. Tomorrow. Next month. Next year. Five minutes ago."

He stood up. "How about fifteen months ago, when we broke in this desk?" He nudged his thigh against the wood, and she was instantly overcome with desire for this man. *Her* man.

"I don't know if I was quite ready to marry you then. We started out wanting to choke each other."

He tucked a strand of hair behind her ear and gently tugged the lock between his fingers. "I don't know. The minute I saw you walk into our house, I thought you were the sexiest woman I'd ever seen. You had this air about you—confident and crisp, but warm, too. Approachable." He put his arm around her waist and pulled her against him. "Plus your legs. And this red hair. Also your incredible eyes."

"We can't do that here, now. Everyone would hear—the office was empty the first time." Still, she was pretty sure the rest of her workday was absolutely screwed.

"I can be quiet when I have to be. The question is, can you?" His lips curved up, and his eyes glinted with trademark Liam sex appeal.

She slipped her hands beneath his leather jacket and dug her nails into the shirt on his back. "I'm not as fun when I have to be quiet."

He chuckled low in his throat. "I doubt that, but I do love the noises you make, especially when you have my cock in your mouth."

She felt that cock against her, hard as a rock, ready to go.

He let go of her and stepped back. She pouted in disappointment. "Where are you going?"

"I almost forgot." He turned and went to the loveseat beneath the front window. He came back with a shiny emerald-green helmet tied with a bow. He'd been a busy boy today. "I didn't want to pick out a ring without you—seemed like something we should choose together. Plus, I didn't have time to get to a jewelry store. Ribbon Ridge needs a jewelry store."

"Yet you had time to get a helmet?"

"I ordered it two weeks ago, and it arrived yesterday afternoon." He'd ordered it before he'd gone back to Denver.

"I guess that means I have to go for a ride." She imagined sitting behind him, her thighs pressed against his ass. There were worse things.

"Just a short one—your house isn't very far."

She grinned. "No, it isn't." She pulled the bow off, then set the helmet on her head. "How do I look?"

"Gorgeous. Perfect. *Mine*."

He pulled her close and kissed her, his mouth warm and eager. She held him tightly, never wanting to let go. Luckily she didn't have to.

She tugged her lips from his. "Let's go. How fast does this bike go?"

"Hey, I'm moving out of the fast lane, remember? From now on, I'm getting my adrenaline rush from one source: you."

She cupped his cheek and kissed him. "I hope that's enough."

"Baby, when we kiss, it's all I ever need."

Epilogue

July
Ribbon Ridge, Oregon

IT WAS SUNDAY dinner, and as usual, everyone was here. Everyone but Hayden, who would be arriving next week in time for Sara and Dylan's wedding. Between wedding preparations and getting The Alex ready for its soft opening in a few weeks, everyone was overwhelmingly busy. Still, they gathered every Sunday, and Liam had to admit it had become his favorite time of the week.

Except for every moment he was with Aubrey.

He looked over at her sitting at the table next to Sara, their heads bent in conversation. He couldn't believe how drastically his life had changed, almost overnight. But he was glad. Humbled, even.

He'd started seeing a therapist a couple of weeks ago, and though he'd only had two sessions, he already felt a lightness he'd never known before. It was strange to feel that way at the time when he'd finally started to grieve, but he supposed it made sense. As he let the heaviness of his guilt and anger fall away, he emerged unburdened, free. Like when he floated through the air in free fall. Like he imagined Alex must be now.

Aubrey's eye caught his in silent question. He'd gotten up from the table to refill his beer and had become completely lost in his thoughts. He'd been doing that a lot lately as he worked through the emotions of moving back home and letting Alex go.

He sat down next to her and listened to the conversation he'd been missing.

"The limo's picking us up Friday at five, right?" Chloe asked Tori.

Tori swallowed a bite of food and nodded. "And Aubrey's got the dinner all set." They had to be talking about Sara's bachelorette party, which was the same night as Dylan's bachelor party.

Liam looked at Aubrey. "Where did you decide to go?"

Aubrey rested her palm on his thigh, sending a bolt of lust straight through him. "We're taking Sara to the Ridgeview."

That was the cottage event space at The Alex that Sara had designed. It seemed a fitting place for her to have her bachelorette party. It was also a short walk from where they were holding Dylan's bachelor party at their underground pub, Archetype.

"So you'll be close, then," he said.

Aubrey's auburn brows pitched down. "What do you mean?"

"Did no one tell you that the bachelor party is at Archetype?"

"Shut *up*," Chloe said.

Aubrey's eyes widened. "Oh. No. That's kind of a problem."

"Is it? I think it'll be okay." Liam looked over at Sean and Kyle. "I mean, we'll ask the strippers to keep it down, right guys?"

Kyle nodded. "Absolutely. And if they can't, well…" He made an overly apologetic face and shrugged. "Sorry."

"Not sorry." Derek coughed the words, but everyone heard what he said. The guys laughed, and Derek and Kyle high-fived each other.

Chloe swatted her husband on the shoulder. "Cut it out. You losers don't need strippers, not when we're right down the road."

Liam chuckled. "We didn't know that. I guess we'll cancel them." There were no strippers, of course.

Aubrey rolled her eyes at him. "Whatever."

Tori took a drink of beer and exhaled as she set her glass back down on the table. "I guess that means we have to cancel ours, too. Damn. I had them flown in from Australia special."

Liam laughed heartily. "The Thunder from Down Under?"

Tori's eyes gleamed with mirth. "Yep."

"And I was so looking forward to them."

Everyone turned to stare at his mother, who wore a rather gleeful expression. Then she blinked. "Really. That sounds like great fun."

Dad cleared his throat, but his eyes glinted with humor. "Yeah, fun." He stood up from the table and took his plate to the sink.

"Why do I think we're going to end up merging parties on Friday?" Sara asked.

Aubrey leaned against Liam. "I see how this is going to work. You guys are going to wait until we're all tanked, then you're going to swoop in and save us again."

Liam put his arm around Aubrey and stroked her shoulder. "Ha, doubtful. We might be more tanked than you."

"Then it's a good thing the hotel has beds and plumbing, so we can all crash there."

"Dibs on the garden penthouse!" Chloe said.

The hotel had three penthouses on the top floor. With six couples, they were going to have to duke it out. "We'll let Sara and Dylan have first choice."

"Good plan," Kyle said, standing. "Time for cocktails out back."

Everyone but Liam and Aubrey got up from the table. He held her close and nuzzled her cheek before kissing the corner of her mouth. "I don't care what room we have."

"I know," she said, her eyes sparkling. "Location has never been something you put a lot of thought into."

"Hey, all I need is you and a surface. Surface optional."

She laughed, low and husky, and the sultry sound rocketed straight to his groin, via his heart and soul. She scooted to the edge of her chair so their thighs were touching. "You ready to go soon?"

"What about the cocktails?"

She sighed and retreated to the center of her chair. "I suppose we should hang around for a bit."

He snaked his arm around her waist and pulled her back against him. "No, no. Let's discuss this. We can probably make a case for leaving, right counselor? I do have more interviews tomorrow—first one's at eight thirty."

Her hazel eyes sparked with heat. "And I should probably draft a motion that's due tomorrow."

"Well, we clearly have work to do. I guess you're right; we should go."

They both stood so quickly that they nearly knocked over their chairs. Their intimate laughter provoked groans from the others, who were bussing their plates and tidying up.

Kyle rolled his eyes. "You two are disgusting."

"It's cute," Tori said. "Even if it is Liam."

"Disgustingly cute," Aubrey said, kissing him quickly before they took their plates to the sink.

Liam looked at them apologetically. "Sorry guys, we need to head home and get some work done."

Sean didn't look the least bit convinced. "Uh-huh."

Liam grabbed Aubrey's hand and pulled her toward the mudroom.

She waved and smiled, her face lighting up in that way that made his heart turn over. "Bye!"

As soon as he got her outside, he turned and pinned her against the house for a hot, fierce, far-too-brief kiss. "I just had to do that," he murmured. "Couldn't wait another second."

She brushed her hand along his jaw. "I hope it's always like this."

He didn't doubt it. Their love was too absolute, their bond too strong. "It will be. You have my heart, my body, my soul. Forever."

The end

The youngest Archer brother is back from
his wine-making internship in France,
and he's still looking for love…

The perfect woman has been right
in front of him for years, but will he get
a second chance at first love?

Don't miss Hayden's story…

YOU'RE STILL THE ONE

Coming April 2016
Preorder it today!

Acknowledgments

A HUGE THANK you to my husband, Steve, for all the legal information. If I got any of it wrong, that's on me.

I want to give a special thank-you to my fabulous friend Cami Curtis. I was remiss in not thanking her at the end of *The Idea of You* for helping me with some...stuff. She knows what it is. I'm so, so glad you came into our lives. You are the very best. Keep it classy. (No *really*, you need to keep it classy. For the children.)

I couldn't help but have at least one of these Archers love the Dave Matthews Band as much as I do, and Liam got to be the lucky one. I also couldn't resist having Aubrey love them, too, so that they could share the joy that is DMB. I saw them for the I-don't-know-how-manyth-time over Labor Day (I'm a huge fan, but I don't count shows!) right after I finished this book, so that was a fantastic reward.

Thank you guys for creating a soundtrack that speaks right to my soul—how sweet you rock and sweet you roll.

I am so thankful for my terrific agent, Jim McCarthy. You are a delightful human being and a true professional. I'm also hugely grateful to my editor, Nicole Fischer, for being completely awesome and the entire Avon crew. Avon KissCon was an absolute blast, and I can't wait to do it again. I just love being an Avon author!

Finally, I didn't go skydiving or flying in a small plane for research. And I never will!

Thank You!

Thank you for reading *When We Kiss*! I have so much fun writing about the Archers. They feel like family to me, and I hope to you, too. I'm so excited about the next book, which is Hayden's story, *You're Still the One*. I hope to see you back in Ribbon Ridge when it releases in April 2016! And never fear, while that will be the last of the Archer siblings' books, I have plans for many more stories set in Ribbon Ridge about people you've already met. When you read *You're Still the One*, you'll be able to figure out where we go next. Cheers!

Ribbon Ridge is a fictional town based on several cities and towns dotting the Willamette Valley between Portland and the Oregon Coast. It's pinot noir wine country, very beautiful and picturesque—and a short drive from where I live. My brother actually dwells right in the heart of it in a tiny town with no gas station or grocery store (he recently informed me they now have a smallish grocery store/carniceria). There is, however, an amazing antique mall in a historic schoolhouse.

Reviews help readers find books that are right for them. I hope you'll consider leaving an honest one on your preferred social media or review site.

Be sure to visit my Facebook page for the latest information and to say "hi," follow me on Twitter (@darcyburke), check out images of the northern Willamette Valley and other things that inspired this series on Pinterest, and sign up for my newsletter so you'll know exactly when my next book is available.

Thank you again for reading and for your support!

About the Author

DARCY BURKE is the *USA Today* best-selling author of hot, action-packed historical and sexy, emotional, contemporary romance. Darcy wrote her first book at age eleven, a happily-ever-after about a swan addicted to magic and the female swan that loved him, with exceedingly poor illustrations.

A native Oregonian, Darcy lives on the edge of wine country with her guitar-strumming husband, their two hilarious kids who seem to have inherited the writing gene, and three Bengal cats. In her "spare" time, Darcy is a serial volunteer enrolled in a twelve-step program where one learns to say "no," but she keeps having to start over. She's also a fair-weather runner, and her happy places are Disneyland and Labor Day weekend at the Gorge.

Discover great authors, exclusive offers, and more at hc.com.

Give in to your Impulses . . .
Continue reading for excerpts from
our newest Avon Impulse books.
Available now wherever e-books are sold.

DIRTY DEEDS
A MECHANICS OF LOVE NOVEL
by Megan Erickson

MONTANA HEARTS: SWEET TALKIN' COWBOY
by Darlene Panzera

An Excerpt from

DIRTY DEEDS
A Mechanics of Love Novel

By Megan Erickson

After a devastating relationship left her reeling, mechanic Alex Dawn swore off all men. She's got a chip on her shoulder no man will ever knock off, so she's content to focus on her family and her job at Payton and Sons Automotive. But all the defenses she's worked to build are put to the test when British businessman L.M. Spencer rolls into her shop late one night, with a body like a model and a voice from her dirtiest dreams.

He followed her outside, the clack of his expensive shoes a contrast to the clomp of her boots. She was hyper-aware of his gaze on her back, like fingers down her spine. When they reached her truck, she reached out to open the door but the next second, a hand spun her around and a body pressed her up against the side of her truck.

She looked up, up into the face of one turned-on Brit. Her knees nearly buckled.

When they'd arrived at the bar, the sun was still setting, so she hadn't thought to worry about where she parked. Now she realized she'd chosen a spot that the dim lights outside the bar didn't reach. They were mostly in darkness, and she probably should have been afraid. Spencer was much taller than her, broader. His forearms were muscular and she could see the roundness of his biceps under his shirt.

But for some reason, she wasn't worried. The only part of him that touched her was his chest brushing along hers. She'd worn a push-up bra today and she cursed the padding that was separating her from rubbing her hardened nipples against him.

His hand was braced on the side of the truck, the other hanging at his side in a loose fist. His entire body was tense as he stared down into her eyes.

Slowly, very slowly, he lifted the hand at his side and settled it on her hip. Her tank top had ridden up so a strip of skin was bared between it and the top of her jeans. He ran his thumb along that strip of skin, watching her face. She got the impression he was waiting for her to say stop, or keep going, and she appreciated that.

Although what did she expect from a man named Leslie Michael Spencer?

She curled her tongue around her top teeth and lifted her chin. "You too posh to take what you want?" she whispered.

He barked out a laugh. "I have to make the first move, do I?"

She swallowed. "I'm pretty sure my invitation to stick your hand up my shirt was the first move." She was proud of her chest, always had been. Dawn girls were blessed in the boob department, that was for sure, despite their small statures.

His eyes dipped to her chest, then back up. "Hm, I guess you're right."

"Your move then, Posh."

"This *was* my move. Not letting you get in the car, pressing my body to yours, showing you that I want you." He emphasized that with a slight roll of his hips. "So, actually, it's now your move, Sprite."

There were a lot of things about a man's body Alex liked. Hands were one. Legs and ass were another. She'd seen glimpses of the muscles in his thighs flexing in his pants, the perfect shape of his ass, so now she decided she needed to feel too. She reached down with both hands, running her fingers up the back of his thighs, then cupped his ass. She pressed his hips to her, and he exhaled roughly. "Your move now," she whispered.

An Excerpt from

MONTANA HEARTS: SWEET TALKIN' COWBOY

By Darlene Panzera

If it wasn't for an injury to his leg, Luke Collins
would be riding rodeo broncos all day, every
day. Until he heals, he's determined to help
his family's guest ranch bring in money any
way he can. But when a cranky neighbor gets
in the way of his goal, Luke turns to the only
person he knows can help: the gorgeous,
rodeo-barrel-racing spitfire next door.

Sammy Jo froze as he met her gaze, and it seemed as if he could see right through her. But could he see the love she had for him swelling her heart? Sometimes when they stood this near she thought her chest would explode with the emotion she fought so hard to restrain. But if she gushed like a schoolgirl and told him how she really felt, he'd never believe her. Not that he did now. And she'd only shown him a quarter of the affection she'd been hiding.

"Okay," Luke relented, "you can help. But keep your eyes on the job."

"Where else would my eyes be?" she teased.

Luke shot her a look of amusement, but didn't reply and she didn't dare push the subject any farther. Determined to show him she could be of value, she shot out her arm to retrieve the bucket of paint he'd placed on an upper rung of the ladder.

Except Luke reached for it at the same time and the double movement made the bucket wobble, tip, and then . . . dump the five gallons of thick, clover green liquid right over both their heads.

Sammy Jo let out a screech, jumped back as the bucket hit the ground to avoid another splash, and brought her hands up to her face to keep the paint from streaming into her eyes. The chalky latex enamel substance smelled as bad as it tasted and she had to spit several times to get the wretched stuff off her lips and out of her mouth.

She glanced down at her white t-shirt and denim cut-offs coated in green, as were her arms, legs, and what used to be her blue, canvas shoes.

Then her hands flew to the top of her head where gobs of the green goo weighted down her long dark curls and left them hanging limp over her shoulders. She tried to separate the icky green strands with her fingers and let out another cry. Returning her hair to its natural color would be no easy task. No easy task at all! Maybe next time she'd think twice before offering to help for the sake of spending time with him.

She glanced at Luke, also covered in green, except she'd been right—his clothes hid the paint better. Holding her breath, she waited for his reaction. Would he be mad? Blame her for wasting the gallon of paint?

No . . . he grinned. As if this was funny. As if . . .

"Did you do that on purpose?" she demanded.

"Of course not," he said, inspecting the new color of his cane. "If I had, I would have stepped back so the paint didn't get *me*."

"Then why are you laughing?"

"I'm not." He broke into another grin. "Although you *do* look a lot like the wicked witch from *The Wizard of Oz*."

Sammy Jo sucked in her breath. "And you look like a cow has spewed all over you with a whole day's worth of green cud!"

This time Luke *did* laugh. He laughed for several long

seconds, harder than she'd ever heard him laugh since he'd been back home.

"You know that Emerald Isle shade becomes you," he teased. "Matches your eyes."

"Not funny," she shot back. "How am I going to get all this paint out of my hair?"

"You can't. You'll have to cut it all off."

The thought of styling a bald head didn't hold much appeal. She'd rather sport her clover green curls until the color grew out, although that image too, was almost enough to bring her to tears.

Then his amused expression made her realize he wasn't serious and she pointed her finger at him. "Now who's playing games?"

Luke shrugged. "It'll wash out with a good shampoo. You'll just have to scrub real good. For now, we can rinse off with the hose in the wash room."

She patted the front pocket on her denim shorts. "I hope the paint didn't go through to my cell phone. What if I lost all my contact numbers? Or my photos?"

"Would be a shame," he said with mock concern.

Luke did not appreciate the finer aspects of having multiple apps available at one's fingertips 24–7. A fault she could easily forgive him for if he'd only pick up the phone to call her for a date.

A real date. Not just hanging out at the barn, or attending a rodeo together with the rest of their friends, or even roasting marshmallows by the fire with his sisters. But one-on-one time with just the two of them.

Luke led her toward the open double doors of the stable

to the large cement wash room where they usually gave the horses a bath. When she envisioned a date, this setting had never come to mind either.

"Stand over the drain and I'll hose you down," he said, turning on the water.

She took her phone out of her pocket and set it on a shelf holding the horse shampoo, a sponge and squeegee. Then stood ready to embrace the oncoming shower.

"Tip your head back and close your eyes," Luke instructed.

"So you can kiss me?"

"No," he said, shaking his head. "So I can do *this*."

Join Avon Impulse and celebrate the holiday season with our three, brand new romances about love, laughter, and those cold December nights.

LORD DASHWOOD MISSED OUT

A SPINDLE COVE NOVELLA

By Tessa Dare

A snowstorm hath no fury like a spinster scorned

Miss Elinora Browning grew up yearning for the handsome, intelligent lord-next-door . . . but he left England without a word of farewell. One night, inspired by a bit too much sherry, Nora poured out her heartbreak on paper. *Lord Dashwood Missed Out* was a love letter to every young lady who'd been overlooked by gentlemen—and an instant bestseller. Now she's on her way to speak in Spindle Cove when snowy weather delays her coach. She's forced to wait out the storm with the worst possible companion: Lord Dashwood himself.

And he finally seems to have noticed her.

George Travers, Lord Dashwood, has traveled the globe as a cartographer. He returned to England with the goal of marrying and creating an heir—only to find his reputation shredded by an audacious, vexingly attractive bluestocking and her poison pen. *Lord Dashwood Missed Out*, his arse. Since Nora Browning seems to believe he overlooked the passion of a lifetime, Dash challenges her to prove it.

She has one night.

BURNING BRIGHT

FOUR CHANUKAH LOVE STORIES

By Megan Hart, Stacey Agdern, Jennifer Gracen, and KK Hendin

This December, take a break from dreidel spinning, gelt winning, and latke eating to experience the joy of Chanukah. When you fall in love during the Festival of Lights, the world burns a whole lot brighter.

It's definitely not love at first sight for Amanda and her cute but mysterious new neighbor, Ben. Can a Chanukah miracle show them that getting off on the wrong foot doesn't mean they can't walk the same road?

Lawyers in love, Shari Cohen and Evan Sonntag are happy together. But in a moment of doubt, he pushes her away— then soon realizes he made a huge mistake. To win her back, it might take something like a Chanukah miracle.

When impulsive interior designer Molly Baker-Stein barges into Jon Adelman's apartment and his life intent on planning the best Chanukah party their building has ever seen, neither expects that together, they just might discover a Home for Hannukah.

All Tamar Jacobs expected from her Israel vacation was time to hang out with one of her besties and to act like a tourist, cheesy t-shirt and all, in her two favorite cities. She definitely was not expecting to fall for Avi Levinson, a handsome soldier who's more than she ever dreamed.

ALL I WANT FOR CHRISTMAS IS A DUKE

*By Valerie Bowman, Tiffany Clare,
Vivienne Lorret, and Ashlyn Macnamara*

*The holidays are a time for dining, dancing, and of
course—dukes! Celebrate the Christmas season with
this enchanting collection of historical romances
featuring the most eligible bachelors of the ton . . .*

A childish prank may have reunited the Duke
of Hollingsworth with his estranged wife, but
only the magic of Christmas will show this
couple 'tis the season of second chances . . .

Sophie Kinsley planned to remain a wallflower at the
Duke of Hollyshire's ball. Yet when a dance with him
leads to a stolen kiss, will the duke be willing to let her
go? Or will Sophie's Christmas wish be granted at last?

To the Duke of Vale, science solves everything—even
marriage. When the impulsive Ivy Sutherland makes him
question all of his data, he realizes that he's overlooked a
vital component in his search for the perfect match: love.

Patience Markham never forgot the fateful dance she
had with the future Duke of Kingsbury. But when
a twist of fate brings them together for Christmas
Eve, will the stars finally align in their favor?